With best wishes for a
Merry Christmas to you,
Bob
"R. D."

Also by R. D. Lock:

Taking Charge of Your Career Direction (5 editions)
Job Search (5 editions)
Activities Manual for Taking Charge of Your Career Direction and Job Search

No Greater Love

A Story of the Spanish Civil War

R. D. Lock

iUniverse, Inc.
New York Bloomington

No Greater Love

Copyright © R. D. Lock 2009

All rights reserved. No part of this book may be used or reproduced by any means, graphic, electronic, or mechanical, including photocopying, recording, taping or by any information storage retrieval system without the written permission of the publisher except in the case of brief quotations embodied in critical articles and reviews.

Certain characters in this work are historical figures, and certain events portrayed did take place. However, this is a work of fiction. All of the other characters, names, and events as well as all places, incidents, organizations, and dialogue in this novel are either the products of the author's imagination or are used fictitiously.

iUniverse books may be ordered through booksellers or by contacting:

iUniverse
1663 Liberty Drive
Bloomington, IN 47403
www.iuniverse.com
1-800-Authors (1-800-288-4677)

Because of the dynamic nature of the Internet, any Web addresses or links contained in this book may have changed since publication and may no longer be valid. The views expressed in this work are solely those of the author and do not necessarily reflect the views of the publisher, and the publisher hereby disclaims any responsibility for them.

ISBN: 978-1-4401-4038-9 (pbk)
ISBN: 978-1-4401-4039-6 (ebk)

Printed in the United States of America

iUniverse rev. date: 5/15/2009

For Barbara, on whom I gambled ... and won

"Greater love has no one than this; that he lay down his life for his friends."

(John 15: 13, RSV)

"Do not think that I have come to bring peace on earth; I have not come to bring
peace, but a sword."

(Matthew 10: 34, RSV)

AUTHOR'S PREFACE to NO GREATER LOVE

The idea of writing this novel lay dormant in my mind for over forty years. During the summer of 1960, my wife and I traveled with friends to Spain and Portugal. In a plaza of one of the Spanish cities, a priest pointed out to me an upper balcony; there he had directed the firing of guns into a throng of Republican defenders during Spain's civil war of 1936-39. The enthusiasm with which he told of this incident to an American traveler struck me as rather peculiar for a man of the cloth. Did he think I would approve? Perhaps he had seen me kneel moments before as a Tabernacle passed in a religious procession and thought I was sympathetic to Franco's government and the Nationalists, which had been aligned with many in the Church.

Years later, while listening to Joaquin Rodrigo's *Concerto de Aranquez* and *Fantasia para un Gentilhomme*, the idea recurred and formed a mental picture of my injured protagonist crawling toward the great cathedral at Santiago de Compostela as the fading rays of the sun brightened its façade. Still, nothing was written, my excuse being the responsibilities involved as a husband and a father of three and working in a full-time teaching job. Nonetheless, the seeds of a story had been sown.

A trip to Spain and Portugal in 2001 turned out to be pivotal. While traveling in Portugal and in Spain's regions of Extremadura and Galicia, the tragic events of September 11 unfolded. I had plenty of time to form an outline of a novel; our flight home had been delayed and we were on our own for over two weeks in Galicia and parts of Asturias. My mind began to fill in the details of the story I finally wrote. More trips, including one on the Camino de Santiago, resulted in repeated rewrites. Love, war, politics, and religion: Is there anything more absorbing than these subjects?

Why did I, as a lifelong citizen of the United States, write a novel about Spain? The Spain of 1936 had all the elements for the story born in my imagination, and among these were ferocious cultural conflicts provoking an explosion that had been building for well over a hundred years. With all of the earnest devotion and bitter revulsion political ideologies and religious beliefs can bring, the civil war in Spain stands out as intense a struggle as any found in the history of human events. Writers usually consider religious and civil wars as the worst type of armed hostility, inspiring hatreds that take generations to heal. When war of this kind is combined with the energy that is made evident in the spirited nature of the Spanish character, the result is most likely to be appalling violence and terrifying bloodshed beyond anyone's original intention – and that tragedy occurred in Spain. The Spanish civil war has been viewed as a prelude to the war that engulfed the entire world shortly thereafter. It provides a cautionary tale for any nation which, quite naturally, desires to maintain peace and stability within its own borders.

This novel is intended for American readers as well as those here with a Spanish ancestry. As I wrote, I was struck by the number of times I found similarities reflected in the divisions in the Spanish society of the 1930s and the political clashes of our times in the United States. Of course there are differences between Spain and the USA over a period of 75 years, but you can notice in our time comparable words expressed on morality, poverty, faith, equality, social conditions, minorities, wealth, regional contrasts, women's rights, justice, military influence, and education – among other subjects. The Spanish civil war offers lessons in the way political and spiritual beliefs can be carried to dangerous extremes.

NOTE: A glossary of Spanish words and groups of people that may be helpful to readers appears at the back of the book; many of these terms are italicized throughout the course of the novel. Some italicized words are explained in the context of the narrative and are not included in the glossary.

This is a work of fiction. The time is August, 1936. The place is Spain. The story begins in the region of Extremadura. Any resemblance to persons, living or dead, other than certain well-known historical figures, is entirely coincidental. Times of events in the Spanish Civil War are accurate, save for one incident which is slightly altered for dramatic purposes.

Contents

Chapter 1
Captured. 1

Chapter 2
Felipe 7

Chapter 3
Punishment. 18

Chapter 4
Antonio 22

Chapter 5
Home 31

Chapter 6
Maria's Request 38

Chapter 7
Divided Family 44

Chapter 8
"Abduction" 56

Chapter 9
Mother Maria, the Storyteller . . 62

Chapter 10
Captain Barcena's Decision 69

CHAPTER 11
  RAMON 72

CHAPTER 12
  TEMPTATION 77

CHAPTER 13
  THE FUNERAL 85

CHAPTER 14
  ESCAPE 90

CHAPTER 15
  BETRAYAL 99

CHAPTER 16
  TOWARD PORTUGAL 103

CHAPTER 17
  AN UNINTENDED CLUE 112

CHAPTER 18
  THE HANDSHAKE 117

CHAPTER 19
  SUSPICION 121

CHAPTER 20
  BONITA, THE STORYTELLER 127

CHAPTER 21
  MARCELO AND ANDRE 140

CHAPTER 22
  CAUGHT IN A LIE 145

CHAPTER 23
- Ramon's Mission 150

CHAPTER 24
- Sanctuary 153

CHAPTER 25
- Manuel 159

CHAPTER 26
- Happiness 165

CHAPTER 27
- Sunday 174

CHAPTER 28
- A Complication 184

CHAPTER 29
- A Sainted Queen 190

CHAPTER 30
- The Manor House 194

CHAPTER 31
- Darkness 203

CHAPTER 32
- Compulsion 214

CHAPTER 33
- Eduardo 220

CHAPTER 34
- Braga 230

CHAPTER 35
  THE NEW MISSION 235

CHAPTER 36
  RETURN TO SPAIN 245

CHAPTER 37
  TWO NATIONALISTS 250

CHAPTER 38
  A DEATH REVEALED 257

CHAPTER 39
  PABLO SANCHEZ 265

CHAPTER 40
  TO 'THE END OF THE EARTH' 272

CHAPTER 41
  PILGRIMAGE 278

CHAPTER 42
  SANTIAGO DE COMPOSTELA 284

EPILOGUE 295

GLOSSARY 299

CHAPTER 1
CAPTURED

"You are the luckiest bastard to be alive."

Jose Maria Martinez Garcia heard those words scornfully pitched at him as he lurched forward, hands over his head. Behind him strode a soldier cradling a loaded rifle, spouting contempt. "Who are you, anyway? I'm ordered to take you to a barracks ahead, not to the *Plaza de Toros* beyond. All I know is you are one fortunate son-of-a-bitch."

Jose was in no position to make any objection to his fate as a prisoner or to argue against the aspersions cast upon the circumstances of his birth. Nor dare he wipe away the trickle of blood that matted his dark hair and ran down the side of his face, a bullet having grazed him ever so slightly as it whizzed by. Not seeing a stretch of rough ground, he staggered nearly falling to his knees. That brought a stinging smack from the soldier's rifle butt into Jose's lean and normally limber body.

"Don't do that again!" bellowed the command. The prisoner resumed his halting gait. The limp in his walk had come from a slithering piece of shrapnel that nicked the flesh in his left leg.

I guess I am lucky, thought Jose. *If that metal had struck inches closer, I'd be back there waiting for a bullet through my brains.*

His mind went through the disasters of the day. Inside the walls of the city, Jose and his compatriots watched a legion of trucks in the distance disgorging thousands of troops and weaponry of the invading rebel army. Government militia, workers, and peasants waited for the inevitable assault; it started with artillery raining a steady stream of shells upon the town. Loud speakers urged surrender which was answered by obscenities and gunfire. Heavier bombardment pounded sandbagged gates and fortified towers. With rifles and fixed bayonets, the attacking insurgents finally stormed the gates.

The first charge was repulsed with appalling loss of life on both sides. Fallen bodies lay rotting in the late afternoon sun. The wounded writhed in forlorn misery; a lull in the fighting made their groans audible. Despite those ghastly sounds, the stillness suggested siesta.

A second charge was launched using armored cars to create an opening. The invaders slashed their way through defenders at the gates. Other columns scaled walls. Combat carried into houses and the main plaza. The rebels ran into barricades, their voices crying, *"Viva la Muerte!"* – Long live Death! As Jose's militia fell back, his scarred memory recorded only the flash of knives glistening in the sun and the jarring rattle of machine guns spreading lethal destruction.

The overpowered defenders grudgingly retreated. As their ammunition began to run out, they became terrified. They discovered first-hand how the Army of Africa acquired its ominous reputation. Whether the workers and peasants surrendered or tried to escape, they were shot or stabbed on the spot. Shortly thereafter, their bodies fed a roaring fire. Only those captured in a militia uniform were spared for an unknown fate that lay ahead.

"Over there," shouted the soldier, snapping Jose out of his reverie. He stepped around a disfigured body besieged by flies and torn with gaping holes, the battered head lying in a sea of blood slowly flowing into a depressed hollow of the dusty road.

A nondescript building loomed before them. "Through that door," ordered the soldier. Inside, he told his prisoner once more, "You are luckier than you'll ever know. Only the son of a whore could have such luck."

Ordinarily that insult would have provoked a response, but again Jose was in no position to start a fight. He was transferred to a guard who shoved him into a small, stuffy room after climbing to the top floor.

"Don't step out of here," the guard warned. "If you do, it will be the last step you'll ever take." The door closed behind him with the click of a lock. Any hope of gaining freedom was gone.

Or was it? In the oncoming darkness, a window became visible across the cramped room. Jose stumbled over a cot in his haste to look out. He opened it, encountering iron bars from the outside. A burst of machine-gun fire sent him reeling instinctively to the floor. A minute passed by before he realized the shots were not aimed at him; they had ended inside the bullring his captor had mentioned. Within the enclosure, his eyes focused on a savagery more terrible than any he had ever witnessed in his life. As a group of battered men marched through the toreador's entrance and entered the bullring with their hands up, blasts of bullets shredded their bodies, unleashing a grisly sight of flailing arms and lacerated flesh. After that onslaught, any prisoner still alive was dispatched with a bullet driven to the head or a bayonet plunged into the chest.

A vision of Francisco Goya's *Third of May 1808* flashed across the eye of Jose's mind. There, the painter had depicted a group of Spanish defenders mowed down by the rifles of a faceless Napoleonic firing squad. Now, machine guns delivered death with greater efficiency to greater numbers.

In the dwindling light of day, the gruesome scenes of absolute horror continued as the conquering soldiers descended upon the slain. A group of rebels recruited from the African protectorate carved out the manhood of the newly dead, displaying their severed treasure as trophies of war. Lifeless bodies surrendered booty that would be sent to families back home, the plunder serving as inducement for others to join the insurgents. The rebellion against the Republic had started in Spanish Morocco and spread throughout the Spanish mainland. All soldiers, those from the home country as well as Moors, shared in the bounty. Usable clothing was stripped away as were watches, money, rings, or anything of value. Legionnaires pried open mouths of the dead, using rifles to knock out gold found in teeth. The ravaged bodies were then loaded onto trucks, driven to pits, burned beyond recognition, and covered over with mounds of dust and dirt.

After the vehicles rumbled off, new columns of prisoners were driven into the enclosure for slaughter. Anyone trying to escape was immediately shot. Soon, the roar of machine-gun fire rent the air as riddled bodies fell in waves. Anguished shrieks accompanied the blazing spurts of bullets. Again, the still-living were finished off with knives or a shot to the head. When valuables had been gathered from the vanquished, more trucks appeared, hauling away bodies to be doused with gasoline and consumed by flames.

Over and over in the lingering heat the repulsive pattern was repeated, persisting into the next day. When each killing episode stopped, the triumphant would emerge laden with clothes, shoes, helmets, jewelry, coins – anything considered worth taking. Palm-deep blood lay upon the soil. A sickening stench of decay pervaded the heavy atmosphere. Jose could only guess at the number of dead: hundreds certainly, and maybe into the thousands. He had never expected to see such unmitigated butchery, yet here it was in front of his very eyes.

Jose stood anchored to his vantage spot by the window, his attention riveted by the hideous scenes before him. Watching militiamen with whom he had fought browbeaten into the bullring and annihilated, he knew their fate could have easily been his own.

Why are they keeping me alive? he asked himself. *What kind of sport do they want to make of me?*

Jose cringed whenever he thought of the punishments that could be inflicted at any given moment. Surely his captors would not let him report the revolting spectacle he was witnessing.

Victorious soldiers swarmed over the grounds below Jose's window. He heard a legionnaire gave an excited rendition of the government militia's retreat west of the city.

"Those stupid fools ran toward Portugal – right into our guns waiting for them." Another voice shouted triumphantly, "When those half-wits in Madrid hear of this battle, they'll know better than to resist the Army of Africa!"

From his newspaper work, Jose was aware this dreaded army had spread terror throughout southwestern Spain during the first days of civil war. *Legionairos* and battalions of Moorish *Regulares* led by Nationalist officers made up much of this force, battle-tested in Morocco and transported to Spanish soil. The Army of Africa constituted the best-trained division in the Nationalist campaign against the Republican government, sweeping through most of Andalusia and moving into the region of *Extremadura*, taking *pueblo* after *pueblo*, town after town, meeting little opposition – until here, at Badajoz on the Portuguese border.

Unknown to Jose being held in a makeshift cell, reprisals fell heavily upon civilians in the conquered town over the next several days. A merciless retaliation was inflicted on the defeated as payment for real and imagined wrongs. Vigilante patrols tore open the shirts of ordinary citizens to see whose shoulder carried the bruises of a recoiled rifle; those so marked were sent to the bullring. Government officials, teachers, workers, peasants, liberals, socialists – anyone identified with the Republic – were ferreted out and put to death. Summary executions occurred in cemeteries or on deserted roads in the middle of the night, the unburied bodies serving as a warning to those thinking of resistance in the morning. A select few expired by means of the garrote, an excruciating strangulation from a slow tightening of an iron collar around the neck of the condemned. Victims in hundreds of hamlets and cities could have informed the dead-to-be: a terrifying vengeance would be the typical outcome accompanying their overthrow.

Jose was mindful of atrocities being committed by both sides. Inhumane treatment imposed on Nationalists was as cruel as that suffered by Republican partisans. Priests had been assassinated and churches destroyed. Seeds of the current political conflict had been sown for over a century. The division between a modernizing liberalism and a reactionary church had never healed, becoming more virulent as time went on. Venomous retribution gripped the minds and hearts of all too many people. Leaders of the liberal Republic aspired to the rational forms of democracy practiced elsewhere, but the violence of the current civil war cast aside hopes of peaceful resolution.

After several nights, Jose was taken to a completely enclosed room in another building quickly converted into a temporary detention camp. The base was guarded by a platoon of rearguard troops, as the Army of Africa had departed to continue their advance toward Madrid. Executions became fewer than in the first days of capture, but Jose's worry was as strong as ever.

Will I be sent before a military tribunal? Will I simply be tortured and shot? When will they come for me?

Hundreds of questions like these kept Jose in a constant state of fear. Sleep was nonexistent or fitful at best. Agonizing screams that pierced the stillness of night could not be ignored.

"The dead are the lucky ones," Jose said to the bare walls upon hearing the sounds of abuse. He prayed again and again.

Dear God, help me; spare me the misery bound to come. He asked himself over and over: *Whatever possessed me to get into such a mess?*

At first, his mind was too muddled to think clearly.

He slowly recalled the belief that had spurred him into action: loyalty to a government elected by the people, a Republic rather than a military dictatorship. When the Army of Africa was initially blocked from crossing the Straits of Gibraltar, Hitler's Germany provided the aircraft necessary to transport Nationalist troops from Tetuan in Morocco to Seville on the mainland. With the conflict spreading, Jose was convinced an all-out fight against a Fascist rebellion was required to keep the hopes of a liberal Republic alive. If the uprising succeeded, losses ranged from his freedom as a journalist to the hope of mending Spain's long-standing social inequalities. Jose enlisted with a group of *milicianos*, giving up a part-time reporter's job. After a few days of inadequate training, he was thrust into battle. His story exemplified actions taken by thousands of common people in major cities and countless villages, joining local militias to thwart the ambitions of a powerful military *junta* counting on a quick victory to gain control over an entire nation.

How will they question me? Jose wondered despondently. He had heard rumors about ordeals endured by those not killed but captured and kept alive – blows to the head, lashes to the back, broken noses, shattered teeth, punches to the stomach, kicks in the groin, toenails pulled off – anything that would cause pain. When the guards carried truncheons or long wooden paddles, you had to be ready to protect yourself. Every other blow would be aimed at the genitals. There would be lots of threats about losing your 'cojones.'

If that is true, reckoned Jose, *a lot of my countrymen no longer will father children. How could so-called humans enjoy watching other humans mercilessly tormented?*

"I can't take this waiting much longer," he cried aloud again to no one but the walls surrounding him. Having arrived in the morning of the day of the battle with resolute anticipation, Jose suffered the ignominious experience of being captured by the enemy almost immediately. Never had he imagined seeing the barren confines of a Nationalist jail so soon. The windowless room and sweltering heat created a languor greater than any he had ever known. No reading material, no exercise in the yard, and no conversation with anyone was permitted in these first days of captivity. Separated from the few prisoners who languished in the foul dungeon-like basements of the camp, his only companions were a bed and a chair. His only activities were the occasional visits to the latrine and eating crusts of tasteless bread or swallowing thin soup twice a day. Yet, each time the cell door opened was an occasion filled with anxiety.

He reflected with critical bitterness. *What a life I've chosen! I trade a position I love, a news writer, for one I detest, that of a soldier trained to kill. Now I'm a prisoner waiting to be tortured and shot.*

CHAPTER 2
FELIPE

Jose trembled when the door to his room opened and another prisoner was thrust into the room. The two young men eyed each other momentarily and then mumbled their first names to each other. Felipe made a few observations to Jose about the stifling heat and small size of the room.

"We'll take turns sharing the cot," each assured the other. Almost immediately, each turned to his new companion for information, opinions, and a recounting of his experiences.

"My first taste of battle was at the bridge over the Guadiana outside of Merida," related Felipe. "My militia gave the Nationalists a tough battle. We countered-attacked with reinforcements a day later, but they overwhelmed us with better weapons. I was one of the lucky ones to avoid capture. We had to decide where to go next. We finally made our way to Badajoz. If we lose in one place, survivors go to another town to help in its defense. That's been going on all over Extremadura, Jose. I learned from one of the guards here that the Nationalist army has just swept by Trujillo and is now headed toward Talavera."

Felipe's last words made Jose quiver with alarm. "I was afraid you would say something like that, Felipe. Trujillo is my hometown, although I haven't lived there for several years. I go back there every so often to see my mother and my sister and her family. I thought I might even be able to help in Trujillo's defense, that is, until I became a prisoner."

"How did you end up in Badajoz?" asked Felipe.

"I joined an anarchist militia about a week before the battle here. After Merida, the Army of Africa turned west toward Badajoz instead of driving on toward Madrid. As the Nationalists approached, a Civil Guard revolt weakened the Republican militia at Badajoz. Maybe that's why my unit was sent here. Our training was a joke. My rifle should have been sent to a museum."

"Your mention of obsolete equipment sounds very familiar, although there's no lack of men and women willing to fight the rebels," said Felipe. "I suspect the Nationalists never thought they would meet such resistance in so many places all over Spain."

"They shouldn't have been surprised," said Jose. "That's typically Spanish. It's happened before. Remember 1808. France invades, conquers, and occupies Spain. Our leadership isn't organized; the people take matters into their own hands, resorting to guerrilla warfare in hundreds of places."

"And, when the French met opposition," said Felipe, warming to Jose's comparison of the current invasion to the Peninsular War, "they outdid the guerrillas in their brutality and wondered why the Spanish didn't take to their enlightened ideas. How history repeats itself! Meanwhile, we've got our own situation right here." He paused.

"Your family, Jose, will they be safe in Trujillo?"

"I don't know, Felipe. I wonder if I'll ever see them again."

"What are their political allegiances? That is decisive these days."

"I'm sure my father would have fought for the Republic. He was an Asturian coal-miner. Politically, he was more of a socialist than anything else, although at times he supported the anarchists since they seemed to be the only ones that had the miner's interests at heart."

"I take it your father's no longer living?"

Jose nodded his head. "Our home was in Mieres; that's where I was born and lived as a child. Like everyone who worked in the coal mines, my father's life was hard, but the money was good. He spent much of the day in awkward positions in narrow, crooked seams below. He always said he worked in the mines to give his sons an education so we wouldn't have to follow him there. How many times I asked myself: Did I appreciate the sacrifices my father made for us? He died an early death; too much silica and coal dust filled his lungs."

"That's one of the last jobs I'd want for myself."

"My mother begged me and my two older brothers not to follow father's occupation, not that we needed any convincing."

"Those others in your family," Felipe asked, "would they agree with your father's political views today?"

"My two brothers sided with the Nationalist army," said Jose. "Don't ask me why. Maybe it's a way of renouncing their past. That's all I'll say about them. My sister, Marisa, is married to a small landholder, but Jorge sees no reason to support a Nationalist cause. They approved efforts to break up the huge estates, the *latifundia*. We're split like so many families are in civil wars. Mama is very religious, yet she always said the Church should stay away from politics."

"Too bad the Church didn't follow her advice," remarked Felipe. "You grew up in a family that talked about politics; mine never did. They wouldn't understand why I got involved in this war. If you have to fight, they'd say, wait 'til you know who's going to win, then join that side." Felipe threw up his hands in a hopeless gesture. He described his parents and siblings for a few minutes before turning the focus back to Jose's relations.

"So, your family moved south and ended up in Trujillo."

"Yes. Mama didn't remarry after my father died. He had treated her with love and respect, and she wanted to remember her marriage that way. My sister's husband is a farmer and part-time stonemason and carpenter from Extremadura. His name is Jorge Cardenas and he was very kind to us. He suggested to mother that she and her three sons live with them. He simply did it. Not a hint of that old saying: 'Parents and in-laws are like potatoes – never useful until they're underground.'"

Felipe grinned and said, "I don't know if I'd be that generous. I want to get married and raise a family some day, but it would be hard to welcome my in-laws or even my parents moving in with me. When times are tough, though, you must do the right thing."

"Marisa and Jorge have a weather-beaten house, barn, and granary on a road going out of Trujillo. When we came, they added more rooms at the back of the house. Life was hard with four more of us there. Somehow, enough food was grown to eke out a living. The land Jorge owns was inherited from his parents. He's better off than many people in the region, not having to pay rent to an absentee landlord living in Madrid most of the year. Farming didn't attract my brothers or me. The soil around Trujillo isn't very productive and none of us wanted to pay someone for the land. My brothers joined the military and after university I became a news writer. Considering the lifestyle of the *latifundia* owners, no sane person would want to farm for them, but *campesinos* are trapped in the system and have no way out of their poverty."

"Most of the great landowner's property isn't even cultivated," added Felipe. "They shoot partridges on their property twice a year and look after their accounts. Their *caciques* produce tax breaks for them and run elections for their benefit."

Jose shook his head in agreement. "I know all about it. Slavery is gone, but farm workers are still treated as the subjects of landlords. The *caciques* tell them who to vote for, and if they don't, they're evicted and face starvation. My sister's husband was offered a job as a *cacique*; Jorge turned it down saying he didn't want anything to do with politics. Conditions aren't any better in the towns. The father of a friend of mine lost his grocery store when he became a member of the Socialist party. His party leader was run out of town."

"That sounds familiar," remarked Felipe. "I lost my job after my boss found out I had become a Socialist. I went to Madrid and became involved in radio. A month before the start of the war, I began broadcasting on Radio Madrid. When the insurrection started, I was interviewing a *Union Republicana* editor who was chastising the government for not being aware of how serious the rebellion was and not taking enough precautions."

"We have two things and probably a lot more in common, Felipe. We're both Republican soldiers and we're in communications. I started writing for the student newspaper at university. I worked for a paper here in Badajoz and then for the Left Republican *Politica*. I had a part-time job for *El Sol* when war broke out. Three weeks later, I decided I'd better fight for my convictions and joined the militia. Sitting in this prison, I can't help but think going into the military was a big mistake. I suppose the government will start conscription if it hasn't already done so. I probably would have ended up in the Republican army anyway."

"I believe you did the right thing, Jose. You've got to fight for your beliefs. Now, the *really* big question is this: do you have a *senorita* waiting for you when we leave this rotten place? Where is she in all of this?"

Jose's mind pictured Bonita. She was a spirited, beautiful, black-haired girl he had met at university in Oviedo. He wondered if he would ever behold the enticing curves of her body or look into her deep brown eyes again.

"Her name is Bonita Sanchez, Felipe. Her home is in Corcubion, a village on the Atlantic. As far as I know, she is with her parents this summer. She taught school for this past year in Noia, not far from her parent's home. I don't worry about her political sympathies; if anything, Bonita is more liberal than I am."

"Do you think she's safe? The Nationalists control *Galicia* these days."

"I hope she has stayed with her parents. She doesn't know I've become a prisoner, and I think it is better that way. When she graduated a year ago, we talked about getting married. With all that's happened, maybe it's just as well we didn't. In the midst of the political upheaval that's gone on in the last few years, Bonita and I have been through some harrowing times in our lives – although not quite like the mess you and I face now."

"What do you think is going to happen to us, Jose?"

"I have no idea, Felipe." Even though his own thoughts had been wracked with worry, Jose sought to bring some peace of mind to his new friend. "If they were going to do something awful to us, I think they would have done it by now."

The two prisoners voiced their personal concerns amid the desperate circumstances they now found themselves in. Having been snared by the excitement of political life from the vantage point of journalism and radio broadcasting, both spoke more highly of the dull, ordinary times which they agreed never to take for granted again. As the conversation went on, Jose noticed Felipe becoming more relaxed and drowsy.

"You need sleep," said Jose. "I've had chances to rest. Why don't you take the first turn on the cot and I'll follow you when you waken." Felipe found that offer too irresistible to turn down and thanked Jose for letting him go first. He promised to sleep no more than four or five hours and promptly dozed off.

Jose sat in the room's only chair. For the thousandth time he began to reminisce about the tumultuous events his country had experienced over the past five years. The ending of the dictatorship and the beginning of the Second Republic had occurred when Jose started his university studies at Oviedo. Liberals gained a majority in parliament and raised issues that had been smothered for decades. The debates in the *Cortes* on limiting military authority, separating church and state, distributing property to landless peasants, expanding rights for women, shifting more power to regional governments, creating living wages for workers were only a few of the problems that had festered for decades. All of this activity was reflected on university campuses throughout Spain. The political air crackled with excitement. A new progressive country was being born.

Jose met Bonita at this time. She had enrolled at Oviedo a year after Jose began his studies, turning away from the more conservative atmosphere of the university at Santiago de Compostela closer to her Galician home. Jose was attracted to Bonita by her earnest political convictions which, she explained, were inherited from her liberal-thinking father as well as her interest in ethical and religious matters which, she went on to describe, were influenced by her mother.

"Senorita Sanchez," Jose said gravely one day shortly after they emerged from a literature class, "not only are you appealing to one's eyes, you have a mind a person like me must take seriously." Bonita basked in that praise, but she took her time in committing herself to Jose. The following year Jose won a scholarship at Salamanca; he was joined there by Bonita a year later.

Meanwhile, a right-wing alliance had gained control of parliament and repealed most of the progressive policies enacted by the leftist Republic. In Jose's last year at Salamanca, the miners rebelled in his old home region of *Asturias*, the most serious revolt against the new Republic until the current civil war.

The workers put aside their differences and came together with socialist, communist, and anarchist unions joining forces. When ardent right-wingers were added to the Prime Minister's Cabinet, the unions called a general strike in protest, believing the workers in Germany had allowed Hitler and the Nazis to take over the reins of government without a struggle. Jose told Bonita the student newspaper was sending him to Asturias. The manager of the paper loaned him a car knowing Jose was familiar with that territory. It had been the home region of his early years. Jose's job was to send back first-hand reports to be published.

Bonita had said to Jose: "Take me with you even if I have to miss classes." They went back to Oviedo and roomed with friends made at their former school. Bonita thought of it as a grand adventure, but it turned out to be much more. Jose wrote and dispatched stories about the worker's rebellion; one even found its way into the mainstream press. Jose's sympathy was with the workers, especially since his father had worked in the mines. The miners, armed with rifles and dynamite, forced the Civil Guard to give up control in a number of towns, including Oviedo, a city of eighty thousand people. The news shocked everyone, particularly the middle class bourgeoisie and the conservatives then dominating the Republic.

The union committees set up a model community. Jose and Bonita were impressed by the way all people were treated as equals, even noncombatants. The bourgeoisie and business owners were given the same rations as workers. People in professions received the same protection as union leaders. Doctors were instructed to care for all the injured on each side. The one blemish was the violent actions of some workers, thinking force was the only way they would be taken seriously. Jose tried to understand their position, but believed violence didn't help the miner's cause by alienating the general public in the other regions of Spain.

Jose came to advocate for union coalitions like the one in Asturias, which he believed were necessary to avoid the temptations of Fascism gaining popularity among the working class. He was one of several reporters writing about that strategy in a news commentary. The article was reprinted in a number of papers as an eyewitness analysis only to be largely ignored in the midst of sensational news reports of bloodshed. The middle class was frightened and later Jose learned his writing had set off a quarrel in his family. His mother worried he had gone too far out on a limb. His oldest brother was especially unhappy, stating that only powerful leadership, strongman rule, would save Spain from disaster.

"Salvation from the man on the white horse," responded Jose to Antonio when the family gathered at Christmas in Trujillo, "always the authoritarian answer for the restless freedom of democracy. I may be liberal in my opinions, but I tried to be impartial in the reports I sent back to the student paper, to be fair and honest concerning the miners and the government."

"Liberals seem to be that way, Jose," Bonita told Jose as he related an account of the verbal combat within the family. "Maybe they are too fair-minded for their own good and get denounced from both sides, radical and conservative."

This image of not knowing which way to dodge in the warfare of politics kept a languid Jose from falling asleep in the chair, and it was this conflicted picture that stood sharply in his memory. Resurrected from his subconscious was a church burning he had witnessed in the Asturian uprising where he reported news critical of both the miners and the government forces. Some anarchists bent on destruction got into the church, shot holes in stained glass windows, smashed altars and crucifixes, tore down the *retablo*, and took an ax to the organ. They splintered confessionals and benches to make firewood. An arsonist appeared yelling playfully that they loved Baroque churches – "There's so much more to burn!" Gasoline was spread to start the fire. Jose had tried to reason with the arsonists: their destruction could only help their enemies, and the articles of value in the church could be sold and the money used to help the poor. They looked at Jose, telling him he was out of his mind for claiming they were thieves.

A priest ran through the front entrance and tried to stop the destruction. A rifleman wounded him with a single shot. He dragged the fallen priest to the altar and bound him with ropes with these words: "Death to parasites who feast on the poor and suck up to the rich!"

The flames became a raging fire. Everyone ran. Jose couldn't leave a wounded man to be burned alive. Maybe this priest had helped the poor. Jose hurried to him, untied the ropes, and carried him outside over his shoulders, away from the blaze. *"Gracias, mucho gracias, amigo"* were the words said when Jose laid him down. The priest blessed his rescuer with the sign of the cross. Jose promised to find medical help, knowing a hospital was two blocks away. Before he turned a corner, he stopped and looked back. To his everlasting horror, the rifleman had returned and finished off the priest with his bayonet.

Spotting Jose, he took aim with his weapon. Running for his life, Jose recalled his anguish.

I lived to write this sad story in my report to the paper, knowing right-wing papers would use it as propaganda.

Jose returned to Bonita at the university, only to find several of the school's buildings ablaze. They wondered why the strikers went after university buildings when so many of its students were sympathetic toward them.

The miner's revolt was brutally crushed. The conservative-dominated Republic called upon two generals to suppress the rebellion, one was *Francisco Franco Bahamonde*. Franco knew the Asturians well; he had grown up in neighboring Galicia. The miners could be fierce in their strikes; they were skilled in dynamiting and ambushing their enemy. Franco correctly reasoned the young government conscripts couldn't handle the miners. He brought in troops from the Foreign Legion and Moorish *regulares*. Then, as now in the current civil war, they were the most ruthless fighters in the army. Franco knew these men would be coldly effective; they were complete strangers to the local population.

Thousands of those well-armed troops arrived, accompanied by aircraft. The union leaders asked for peace on condition the Legion and the Moors withdraw from the region. That agreement was made but not kept. Jose could never accurately determine how many workers were captured and shot on the spot or executed later; two thousand was one estimate. Guards competed with one another in forcing confessions from captives: pushing needles under fingernails, flogging prisoners hung from rafters until they passed out, squeezing testicles beyond a man's endurance – plus rape and mutilation. The *regulares* lived up to their reputation of castrating corpses of fallen victims. Reporters were kept away from scenes like these; nonetheless, those events became known.

The conservative-run government censored reports of the repression; they excused the harsh treatment as penalty for the destruction of the churches. The conservative press rationalized the brutal conduct of the troops, printing accounts of atrocities by the miners such as raping nuns and gouging out children's eyes, later proven false. The workers were outraged. The middle class bourgeoisie were relieved order had been restored. Jose went underground for a few months when he heard that one reporter had been thrown into jail and later murdered by officers of the Legion. He even stayed out of school, thinking he could be considered subversive by the government in the super-charged political atmosphere.

With these recollections, Jose wondered if the Nationalists were holding him because he had written about the same forces composing the Army of Africa at Badajoz: foreign legionnaires and Moroccan *regulares*.

If they've made the connection between now and then, I'm in for a rough time, that's for sure.

Not wanting to continue with these depressing thoughts, he shifted from his own troubles to the nation's sad plight.

What is it about us? How does our country become so convulsed in such bloodshed and blind hatred? Why can we be so cruel to one another and still turn around and be so brave and generous? What an ugly picture other nations have of us – inquisitors, feeble-minded monarchs, bullfights, and now another civil war. We stumble from one tragic mistake to another – all that goes into the Black Legend.

He stopped, upbraiding himself for indulging in this cascade of negative thoughts.

His mind went back to the beginning of the Second Republic five years ago. Its birth was greeted with hopeful enthusiasm by most liberals and ominous dismay by many conservatives. Jose considered himself fortunate to experience the nation's new success in democratic politics. A peaceful revolution had taken place. Intellectuals and the masses all worked together; educated people furnished progressive ideas and common people provided the strength for those ideas. Jose believed he could truly be proud of Spain and its new spirit. Modern Europe would no longer stop at the Pyrenees. The future held such great promise.

As an idealistic student, Jose had welcomed the Republic's constitution, yet even then he couldn't hold back the worry that many of its fine words promised more than could be delivered. For example, war was renounced as a course of action.

As much as I cherish that ideal, Jose now reasoned, *what would any country do in case of attack? Will people simply let invaders take over without a fight? Look at what I did; I joined the militia to fight Fascism.*

The Republic's liberal leaders reduced the size of the army, especially its top-heavy core of high-ranking brass. Military academies were scaled back and compulsory military service was ended. Believing the nation's military was being degraded, right-wing officers expressed great fear and threatened action. Citizens waited for another *pronunciamiento*, a declaration by military leaders resolved to overthrow the government.

Jose's inner monologue brought back other memories. Desperate workers and peasants made demands that couldn't possibly be immediately fulfilled by the Republic, however long overdue they were. Wages were to be instantly doubled. Property would be taken from great landowners and redistributed equally to landless peasants. A furious reaction from the big landowners was promised; it was their own great-grandfathers who bought the land from the sales of church property a century ago.

The progressives in the government of the 1830s had designed limits on the power of the Church by breaking up its large estates, but those plans backfired. Few people had the money to buy property. Land ownership became even more concentrated.

The Church lost wealth, but it still had the power to frighten a lot of people. Jose was once told in church that voting for a liberal would be a mortal sin. He knew of several bishops who prayed for a Nationalist victory and referred to the Republic's platform as work of the anti-Christ.

When the Church gets too involved in politics, it gets into trouble – like Mama said, Jose recalled. And, as for politics, no one disputed the reality that parliament in the newly-established Republic had dissolved into bitterly hostile factions. In his newspaper reporting, Jose challenged the constant charge that only liberals were to blame for the developing chaos in the country.

The violence like I saw in Asturias actually increased when right-wing parties gained control of the Cortes, despite their claim they bring law and order to society.

However, he was careful to take note of problems afflicting the Left.

I rejoiced when the last election in February brought victory once more to the Popular Front, but its coalition of left republicans, socialists, communists, and trade unionists risks becoming an uneasy alliance among antagonists.

Jose sat lost in his own thoughts of the recent past. Felipe stirred in his sleep. Jose looked at him and reflected on how much in common the two of them had. He considered himself lucky; here was a like-minded, knowledgeable person to talk with.

With a loud bang, the cell door swung open. Two guards stood at the entrance. One soldier came to the cot and shook Felipe awake. "You!" he shouted. "Come with us."

"Good luck, my friend," said Jose rushing to give his dazed companion an embrace. "I hope you'll be back soon."

Jose was brusquely shoved away. "Oh, he'll be back," said the guard, giving a malicious grin to the other soldier. Looking directly at Jose, he smirked, "Another day, you'll have your turn for interrogation. Those who don't listen to reason receive justice."

The threat unnerved Jose as the door slammed shut behind the departing guards and their prisoner. All the images of abuse he had forgotten while in the companionship of Felipe now came back to him. He knew there were people supporting the Republic that had perversely committed grievous wrongs despite the efforts of Popular Front leaders to stop them. However, those in charge of the Nationalist insurgency appeared to be following a different course. To Jose, Nationalist commanders at the very top had a deliberate strategy of allowing random brutality, torture, and humiliation – not only to advocates of a liberal Republic, but to entire social groups designated as traitorous enemies. Stories of these outrages circulated throughout Nationalist-held territory as a way of intimidating the general public into compliance with Nationalist rule.

They certainly know how to keep the pressure on, Jose thought, *anything to keep you from getting a good night's sleep. You never know what's going to come next.*

A suspicion suddenly occurred to him, one he wished hadn't crossed his mind. Felipe had been with him for so little time.

Can I trust my newfound friend? Is Felipe a Nationalist agent, planted to get information from politically-minded prisoners like myself? If that is true, which I doubt, he is smooth – no doubt about it.

Felipe hadn't said anything that would make Jose question his genuine nature. He had been easy to talk with, maybe too easy. In the short time the two had been together, they had become *simpatico,* in other words, they shared a warm, compassionate regard for one another. Jose couldn't think of anything he had said that would bring him harm, but then he considered that the conversation had been about beliefs, politics, names, and family. Could any of that have been threatening? In wartime, especially a bitter, ideologically-driven civil war, those subjects were the most dangerous.

Chapter 3
Punishment

Felipe returned to Jose's cell two days later, his body dragged into the room and left on the floor by the two guards. They said nothing, letting the sight of Felipe's battered frame speak for itself. The guards departed, leaving their prisoners sealed inside and locking the door behind them. At first, Jose wasn't sure he knew his former companion.

"My God, Felipe! What have they done to you? Felipe? Felipe!"

Jose carefully lifted his friend and gingerly placed him on the bed. Felipe's body convulsed and then coiled into a fetal position. He was barely recognizable. His mouth was smeared with blood. His face was disfigured from slashes that had ripped the flesh. His arms and legs were swollen from repeated beatings. Bruises and bloodstains appeared all over his body. Fluid oozed from wounds. His kneecaps were shattered from the torture. He couldn't talk. The only sound he made was a low, inarticulate moaning. His nose was broken and off-center. A blood-soaked bandage was carelessly placed over where an ear was missing.

"Oh, my God," Jose gasped as he looked at his disfigured friend. "They reenacted the *corrida*; they took your ear like you were the fallen bull."

At least Felipe had retained his eyes. He pointed to his mouth and opened it. Inside, several teeth were knocked out. The front part of his tongue had been sliced off.

"So that's it," Jose lamented frantically. "They knew you were a pro-Republic radio news reporter from Madrid and made sure you won't be doing that again."

Jose held his friend's head in his lap with his hands and cried over and over with tears streaming down his face, "Oh, Felipe, oh, Felipe."

Then he wondered: *What will they do to me, a writer? Chop off my hands?*

For the remainder of the day and well into the night, Jose tried to comfort Felipe.

Pain must be coming from every part of his body, thought Jose as he listened to his friend's unrelenting groans. He focused his eyes upon Felipe's torn clothes, again seeing the monstrous bruises beneath. Finally, sleep, blessed sleep, overcame the lacerated man's suffering, and Jose was released to let an exhausted slumber come to him as well.

The next day, Jose saw his companion for the last time. A few minutes after Felipe disappeared through the door roughly carried by the guards, Jose heard rifle shots in the distance. A feeling of utter discouragement surged over him even though, as a reporter and a soldier, he had seen enough of this war not to be surprised. Killing prisoners had become all too normal.

Jose was in solitary seclusion once more, shuttered with this foreboding thought: *The sight of Felipe's body and the sound of his execution is a preview of the treatment waiting for me.*

For the next five days, Jose shuddered every time the cell door burst open. If he was standing, the guard would push him into the chair or yank him up if he was sitting or lying down. No matter what position he was in, it would be wrong. He would automatically change position whenever a guard entered the cell, but then he would be told to go back to his original place. When the door closed, Jose would be alone again to ponder what the next visit would bring.

On most days he was allowed outside under close supervision to help clear rubble and debris from the battle that had decimated parts of the city. He was grateful to be outside in the fresh air. The third day out, he glimpsed a group of prisoners which he took to be a punishment squad. On their knees, they were cleaning the streets of horse manure, using their bare hands as shovels. Just before he was taken back to his cell, Jose noticed a platoon of new recruits for the Foreign Legion whose training included the crack of the whip or a blow from a rifle stock for any misstep during a drill.

No wonder the legionnaires have the reputation of being so fearless in battle, Jose reckoned. *They're more afraid of their own officers than they are of the enemy.*

He agonized over the way sadistic people could abuse other humans, as they had done to Felipe and as they would do to him. His mind dwelt upon the vicious hostility let loose by war throughout the country. Jose whispered a rush of words to no one in particular as if he were sketching an editorial for a newspaper.

"Hate and revenge are in the saddle. Traditionalists detest reformers.

Monarchists loathe republicans. Bourgeoisie despise workers. Catholics condemn freemasons. Anarchists castigate government officials. Campesinos disgust their overseers. Huge landowners scorn peasants. Socialists declare capitalists corrupt. The political left is sickened by the political right. The National Front says the Popular Front is an abomination. In each case, you can reverse the names of the groups and the words will be just as accurate.

"Smoldering furies burst into flame and become uncontrollable. Wholesale slaughter of the enemy by individuals on both sides is justified. Each party resents its opposition to such an extreme that compromise or any settlement becomes dishonorable in the minds of each antagonist.

"Not only do we have all these conflicts, unyielding pressure for regional independence is exerted by many sincere, single-minded people in parts of the country. Maybe the anarchists are right; government doesn't work here. There are now two alliances formed for the insanity called war, yet they will fall apart and attack each other whenever there is peace. . ."

Jose was jolted out of his reflections when the door was hurled open. Entering were the same two guards that had come for Felipe. One lifted him to his feet while the other placed a blindfold tightly over his eyes, a move he hadn't expected.

I am being led to a foul-smelling room where I will be plunged into a big tub of human excrement. That was the first image that came to Jose's mind. *'Now you can wallow in the filth that comes from your Republican friends,' my captors will say. 'The mierda here is no different than their liberal ideas.'*

"You will come with us," directed one guard, shoving Jose in the back. Tugging at the blindfold, he smacked into the end of the open door.

"Clumsy dope," one guard joked to the other. They snickered. Down the hall they marched, the guards prodding the prisoner with their rifles. They laughed as Jose bumped into walls. He banged into a closed door; as it was opened, he was told, "Careful, there are steps ahead."

Will they shove me ahead, Jose wondered, *making me fall headlong into space?* He hesitated. *I'd better feel ahead with my foot and see if there's any flight of stairs.*

"Hurry up," decreed a guard. "We haven't got all day."

Jose braced himself for unbearable torment.

I'm about to be beaten, he inwardly figured. *I can't see a thing. I'll crouch and cover myself.*

Visions of Felipe's battered body haunted him.

Maybe they'll be nice to me and want me to cooperate with them, he hoped desperately in frantic confusion. *How can I talk to these bullies? They took two days with Felipe. This kind of humiliation has never happened to me. I'm not ready for it. Oh, God, help me.*

"In here," commanded a guard as he opened a door to a bare room with a chair placed in the middle. Jose was quickly guided to the chair.

"Sit," ordered one guard as the other one slammed the door shut.

Jose tried to steady his nerves. A minute passed; it seemed like an hour. Two minutes passed; they seemed like a day. He prepared himself for the worst. Excruciating pain could start at any moment. The terror he felt came close to panic. His body shook when the door opened. Footsteps from boots sounded. The door quietly closed and sharp footsteps approached, adding to the ominous suspense. The guards snapped their heels at attention. A tall, trim officer walked past Jose and came to a position in front. The officer was dressed in a resplendent Nationalist uniform bearing the insignia of a lieutenant. Taking a moment to study some papers and standing with his back to the prisoner, the officer then turned around and motioned to the guards.

"Remove the blindfold," commanded the voice. It was a voice Jose had heard before, but in his fear and trembling, he couldn't place it.

Time and events stood still.

Finally, the blindfold was unwrapped . . . and Jose looked up into the face of his oldest brother.

Chapter 4
Antonio

"Antonio? What are you doing here?"

"Listen closely, little brother: *I am here to save you.* Maybe it will be only temporarily. But, I might ask the same question of you: What were you doing here? Not that I think you really know."

"One thing at a time, Antonio. What do you mean, save me?" Jose asked.

"You would have been executed two weeks ago had I not told the commandant you were my brother. He had a hard time believing me. God only knows why you got mixed up with communists, anarchists, atheists, and other scum that hide behind the label 'republican.' What were you thinking of? Were you out of your head? I'm not sure I *can* rescue you. I've only been able to win you a reprieve. At least you have some more time. That's better than what would have happened by now."

Jose coped with Antonio's barrage of words. "If you don't know whether you can save me, why did you come?"

Antonio struggled to explain. "I don't have time to go into that now; it's a long story. We are going for a ride this evening. You and a couple of guards are coming with me. We know you are more than a soldier in the Republican forces."

Jose stared at his brother. *Good God,* he thought, *they're going to shoot me in the head and leave me somewhere in a ditch.* To Antonio, he said, "You give me a much higher standing than I have earned."

Antonio ignored the comment and went on. "Let's just say you are very fortunate that I found you. You need to know, Jose, you've been purchased at a considerable price."

Jose could not imagine what Antonio meant by that. Confounded, he asked instead, "How did you find me?"

No Greater Love

Antonio towered over the slightly-built Jose who was still seated in the chair in which he had been ordered to sit. "Little brother, I was *here* for the battle. I've been with Colonel Yague and the Army of Africa since General Franco landed at Seville. I will say this: you and your *rojo* comrades put up quite a fight here at Badajoz, the hardest battle we've had so far."

"Your use of the word 'red' is misplaced, Antonio. I fight for Spain, not for Moscow. There were no so-called '*rojos*' in my company."

Antonio was oblivious to Jose's words. "Only through luck and the grace of God are both of us still alive, little brother. More fighting is coming, of that I am sure. The battle for Madrid will begin shortly, as soon as we take Talavera. When we take the capital, the Republic will fall."

Jose was astounded at Antonio's complete confidence in a Nationalist victory. "You may wonder why you were kept here," Antonio continued. "I was ordered to our home town, where our army went through Trujillo, and then on to Navalmoral de la Mata."

Desperate for news, Jose focused on Trujillo and his family. "Marisa, Jorge, the boys, our mother – are they safe? Is our home still standing?"

"Thank God our sister Marisa, her family, and *madre* were secure in their hacienda," responded Antonio. "There wasn't any real damage done to the town. Yes, the Plaza Mayor with its equestrian statue is intact; Pizarro still rides on his horse with his plumed hat. Before I left Badajoz, I informed the commandant that you were to be kept safely locked up until I got back. Sorry, I had no time to explain."

With that, the conversation ended. Antonio started to walk toward the door. He ordered Jose to change into civilian clothes.

"Get out of the rags you call that miserable Republican uniform," Antonio called back. "And, for heaven's sake, I'll arrange for you to bathe. You don't know how bad you smell."

Jose looked at his brother with a flare of indignation.

Anything to let me know you're in complete control, Antonio: these were the words that came to Jose's mind but were left unsaid.

Antonio opened the door and walked out. Jose followed the guards to the wash room. He gladly discarded his tattered, sweat-drenched uniform that was spotted with dried blood from Felipe's tormented body and his own superficial wounds. The water and clean clothes were wonderfully refreshing. He shaved off two week's growth of beard, returning the razor to an armed guard keeping careful watch over him. Having no material possessions to call his own, he was ready to leave.

The military vehicle Antonio had requisitioned drove into the night as darkness fell along the bumpy road leaving Badajoz, the frontier city close to the Portuguese border. Antonio and a firmly blindfolded Jose sat in the back seat while a guard and a driver rode in front. All was silent until Antonio told Jose he had chosen the losing side to support.

"Jose, you need to know the Republic is fragmented as usual, divided beyond hope. Like all liberal states, it doesn't believe in anything. The Nationalists have a cause to fight for: a strong national unity based on our religion demanding service, sacrifice, and a stern military way of life. We have the army and the church, the armaments and men, tradition and most important of all – leadership from great warriors like Franco, Mola, and Yague."

Antonio didn't live long in Extremadura, thought Jose, as he pulled at his blindfold, *but he certainly has absorbed its hard-bitten, cruel exterior*. Antonio had always admired the conquistadors from the region, especially their ruthless determination and undeniable bravery.

"Why are you so enamored with Franco?" Jose asked his Nationalist brother. "He doesn't look like a person who could command a following – potbelly, balding, pipsqueak voice, and all."

Antonio brushed aside Jose's insults. "He is a leader, worthy enough to become *caudillo*, our warrior-king. He's demonstrated his personal bravery, many times. He speaks with authority and gets things accomplished. Leadership is the key factor in any nation's destiny. Look at *Salazar* across the border. His enemies call him a dictator, and maybe that's what he is, but think of the great things he's done for Portugal. I'm proud to possess the same first name he has."

"Nothing wrong with your name, Antonio, but Salazar should have remained Finance Minister instead of becoming an all-powerful Prime Minister."

"He is a brilliant leader. The trouble with the Republic is its lack of leadership and its suffocating indecision. The liberal politicians have rendered it immobile. One group cancels out another. Nothing gets done. Republican ideas may sound nice, but they produce weak government at the time it needs to be forceful. What our country needs now is a strong-willed man, an 'iron surgeon,' one who can act without being cut off at the knees by self-serving politicians."

Jose recalled his ideas about strongman rule. With a hand on his chin, he struck a philosophic pose, as much as his blindfolded eyes would allow.

"Ah, the authoritarian, militarist mind," said Jose. "It demands crude force and absolute rule to solve political problems."

"Don't patronize me, little brother. The first job of any government is to protect its people, which the Republic did *not* do. The military has had to save governments, especially democratic ones, from its politicians on all too many occasions."

"Or, destroy them," Jose broke in. "Conservatives allied with the military were always a part of our Republic, even dominated it for a couple of years, but most never really believed in it in the first place. A day will come when we'll wish those despised politicians were still running the government. Now, with armed rebellion, Nationalists are undermining any chance we may have had for peace and democracy."

"Your Republic had its chance," objected Antonio. "It failed miserably. Why wouldn't people give up on it? All it gave us was a breakdown of law and order, illegal strikes, Communist claptrap, anarchist pipe-dreams, virulent crime, bloody insurrections, killed priests, raped nuns, burned-out churches, demolished public buildings. There you have the legacy of the Republic, not the high-toned debates in the Cortes. The people are not ready to participate in government; they don't have the interest or the mind for it. The best people can do now is to follow and obey men who must act to save Spain."

"That's a prescription for disaster in a constitutional government," Jose protested, but Antonio was just getting warmed up. Whether it was real or false propaganda, there were enough alleged brutalities committed by the Republican side to arouse his Nationalist blood.

"Let me inform you about some things, since you've not been in a position to know. Today, ABC reported a story about Republican soldiers forcing a crucifix down the throat of the mother of two Jesuits."

"That's terrible, but ABC is a monarchist paper," attested Jose. "Its reports are slanted, giving only one side of the news."

Antonio was determined to get his message through to his captive brother. "Another article concerned a Basque nationalist who was told to extend his arms in the form of a cross and cry 'Viva Christ the King' as his limbs were being sawed off. His wife was compelled to watch his torture. She went insane when your Republican friends stabbed him to death."

"I don't have friends like that," insisted Jose, tugging on the blindfold trying to overcome his sightless condition.

"You may have gone to university, little brother, but you need to know about the atrocities your side has committed. Do you know about the priests who were shut inside a corral with fighting bulls? The priests were gored until they passed out. Some in the crowd behaved like matadors at a bullfight; they sliced off an ear from each victim."

"That's very similar to the treatment your people gave my cellmate less than a week ago," Jose replied sharply. If he were to go down, he wouldn't hold back his sentiments.

Antonio was not distracted by Jose's outburst. "There's more. Not far from here, a man devoted to God had his eyes gouged out. Nationalist followers have been buried alive after being forced to dig their own graves. Men have been impaled on spikes dying a slow death and forced to watch their wives and daughters raped and burnt alive. A nun was shot when she refused to marry one of your militiamen. At Navalmoral de la Mata before we came, the parish priest held by the Republican militia gave word he was willing to suffer as Christ did. He was told that he could die just like Jesus did, but if he would blaspheme, the militia would forgive him. The priest refused. He was stripped, scourged, crowned with thorns, tied to a cross, given vinegar to drink. Nails were brought to crucify him, but they finally shot him instead. I could go on, but the question I have is: How can you have anything to do with criminals like these people?"

The floodgates have certainly opened, thought Jose. *In my situation, maybe I need to appear more reasonable. I'm totally under his control and I don't know where we are going.*

Aloud, he said, "Antonio, I could tell you stories like the ones you have told me only with the labels turned around. I don't approve for a moment of the outrages you describe, whichever side committed them. I *can* tell you of incidents where Republicans have rescued Falangists, priests, nuns, bishops, monarchists, and Nationalist sympathizers from a fate like you've recited."

Antonio wasn't impressed. "That's hard to believe. Too often, your leaders bring contempt upon Church officials or advocate inhumane measures toward those who prosper because they work hard."

"Haven't Nationalist leaders issued cruel, pitiless orders?" Jose responded. "On the very day the rising started, General *Mola* gave instructions to spread an atmosphere of terror. In towns taken by Nationalists, people who supported the Popular Front are hunted down like animals. It's no secret Republican prisoners are tortured before being killed. You think I didn't hear the screams in prison?"

Antonio merely waved his hand at that remark saying, "Every war has isolated incidents." He turned to the subject of religion. "Jose, what caused you to lose the spiritual faith your mother gave you? The Church gave you an education as a youth. It also united our divided provinces during our golden age of conquest and made Spain a great empire. The Church has been the link that held our nation together. It took Christianity to the remote places of the New World. The Church has schooled the children of Spain for hundreds of years. It was the bulwark against the Protestant heresy."

"Hold on, Antonio. First, I haven't lost my religious faith, but I believe if our Church in the modern era had existed at the time of Christ, Jesus would have been its first heretic. The Church is the keeper of the faith to be sure; however, consider the times it has acted opposite to the teachings of its founder. Think of innocent people imprisoned, tortured, and set on fire – all in the name of God. The Church collected too much wealth for itself, taken from the poor in our own country and the New World colonies. Only a few in the Church protested when there should have been a general outcry for justice. Too often, the Church has been irrelevant in the world. For example: the time our theologians debated over which language angels spoke."

As an officer, Antonio was not accustomed to being lectured by a lower-ranking soldier. A diatribe, especially one launched by a younger brother from the opposition, was not to be tolerated.

Nevertheless, all he said was: "Maybe, the language of the angels is more important than you realize." Knowing he held the upper hand, he let Jose press on.

"The Church may have taught us as children, but our teachers overlooked a few things. For centuries, church officials often allied themselves with the wealthy to save their privileges, separating their interests from those of common people. Even you should know that, considering our family's background. Clergy and nobility were exempt from paying taxes. Peasants and commoners were not only burdened with taxes, they had to pay tithes to the Church which poor people couldn't afford. No wonder they resented the favors given to the upper class and the Church. The Socialists have been right about one thing: too many in the Church have pandered to the wealthy landowners and rich capitalists and ignored the plight of the poor and the working class."

Antonio cut in at this point. "That's the usual, perverse communist *mierda*, Jose, and you know it," he sputtered hotly. "The Church doesn't deserve all the filthy slime you and your liberal friends pour over it. I reject those charges and your sacrilege."

"It's too bad you didn't live in the sixteenth century, Antonio. You would have made a wonderful candidate for the Holy Brotherhood. You could have rooted out evil in a great *auto-de-fe*. The act of faith: how clean, how inspiring to see the Church burning people alive."

Those remarks brought a bruised silence. Each brother dwelt in his own thoughts.

I suppose Antonio thinks of me as the Prodigal Son, Jose said to himself. *He sees me as having traveled into a far different country, choosing university, embracing liberalism, disparaging Church primates, and abandoning religion. What am I supposed to do? Confess my sins and beg him for forgiveness? Who was the Prodigal in the parable: the youngest son or the eldest? Everyone says the youngest, but wasn't the eldest son just as prodigal?*

After a few minutes, Antonio broke the quietness. "We're getting closer to our destination, Jose. We need go over a few ground rules for the place we are going to."

"Antonio, what are you talking about? I haven't the faintest idea where we are or what is about to happen."

"All right, Jose. I guess this is the best time to give you some information. You must know, though, there are certain conditions that must be observed. You will be guarded at all times and you will be returned to the detention camp one way or another."

Well, thought Jose, *here it comes. Better to know now than to be in a constant state of suspense. Let's get it over with.*

"I saved you from death," Antonio continued emphasizing each word, "because our mother is dying."

Jose recoiled from the impact of Antonio's accentuated message. "Oh, no! No! I had no idea of this, Antonio. When did this happen? I knew mother had health problems, but I didn't know she was near death."

"When I was in Trujillo only a short time ago, *madre* begged me to find you. She wants to see you one last time. She believes she doesn't have long to live. I can only guess why she wants to see you, but it is her request, which I will honor."

"Of course I want to see Mama, Antonio. You understand I haven't been in a position to visit her lately. How soon will we get there? This car doesn't seem to move very fast."

"You know the condition of roads in Extremadura, Jose. We're going as fast as we can. This isn't Madrid, you know, but we are getting close to Trujillo now. Even though it's dark, maybe you'll recognize some of the landscape when I take your blindfold off."

"If keeping me anxious was your plan, you can be satisfied. For all I knew, you were going to push me out of the car and put a bullet through my head saying I tried to escape."

"I had no such thought, little brother," Antonio replied, slowing removing the blindfold. "You are very fortunate I found you. You probably heard the machine-gun fire shortly after you were captured. You would have been in that bullring if I had not intervened. Before I left Badajoz, I made sure the commandant, Captain Barcena, knew you were my brother and that our dying mother had asked to see you. I know the cell you were in was not comfortable, but it was a lot better than any other place where prisoners were kept."

Jose didn't feel like thanking his brother for his survival after the mental ordeal Antonio had put him through, but he said the proper words to appear grateful. Then Antonio returned to the subject of rules for the visit.

"Mother and Marisa and her family need not know of your situation. The sole purpose of this visit is to see them for a few minutes, certainly no more than an hour. You can explain that you must get back to your newspaper duties by morning, and you are required to return because you have reports to file. Don't mention you are a prisoner. If you do, you'll force a showdown. I will call both guard and driver and you will be taken out immediately. My men will be stationed at both entrances to the house. Don't even think about escape. The soldiers have orders to shoot – and that means shoot to kill – if they see you trying to get away. And, don't make any sudden movements."

Jose stared blankly ahead. "If mother is extremely close to death, will we stay longer?" he asked. "You would want to be with her in her last moments, too."

"I can't promise anything. It's been several days since I've seen her. We'll find out what her condition is. If you cooperate with me, Jose, I will try to reduce the charges against you. Right now, you are under a sentence of death."

How many more shocks can I take? wondered an alarmed Jose. This new charge was a complete surprise to him.

"How can that be?" he asked. "What am I guilty of? I don't even know."

"You are guilty of killing innocent civilians because they supported the Nationalist cause before they were liberated."

"That's absurd; it's totally false."

"There are people in Badajoz who will testify you were part of a firing squad that executed up to a dozen Nationalist supporters only a couple days before the battle."

"They are mistaken. I wasn't even in Badajoz until *the day* of the battle. I was never a part of a firing squad. I was captured before I could fire a shot at anyone. My worn-out rifle probably wouldn't have hit a target more than ten meters away."

"It's your word against their word, Jose. Right now, the military court isn't inclined toward friendship with former Republican soldiers. In addition, you have a paper trail. Your news articles haven't been exactly designed to curry favor among Nationalists. Your situation is not a strong one at this moment."

"Well, for once, there is something we can agree on," declared Jose in a tone of woeful resignation.

CHAPTER 5
HOME

The military car carrying Jose, Antonio, the guard, and the driver hastened to its destination as the two brothers fell silent. Antonio turned his attention to the driver and gave him directions. The home inhabited by Marisa and her family – husband Jorge, their two boys, plus mother Maria – was located on the edge of town before the road wound its way through barren landscape. Jorge's property consisted of about twenty hectares of land, an inheritance from his parents who had lived out their last days in two back rooms. The house was a rambling one-story dwelling, lengthened with additional rooms constructed years ago when Maria, Antonio, Ramon, and Jose had come to live with Marisa and Jorge. As the youngest of Maria's four children at that time, Jose had looked upon Jorge as a kind of second father.

Jose noticed the *huerta* adjacent to the house, a garden which provided vegetables for the family.

How many hours I have labored there, he mused to himself. Jose was familiar with the sections of land beyond, cleared of granite rocks, given over to growing wheat and barley. Jorge had to rotate the use of this land; the poor soil and dry climate of the area did not allow cultivation every year. One growth cycle depleted the soil of nutrients, and that ground would lie fallow for the next several years.

During his years of living in the Trujillo home, Jose shared the tasks of tending the family's garden and animals with his older brothers until they joined the military. About half of Jorge's property was used for grazing. The limited amount of grain harvested and modest number of animals raised could not provide a decent living for the family, requiring Jorge to work as a stonemason and carpenter for a builder who employed him when he was not farming.

Jose recalled being impressed with Jorge's ideas about agriculture, many of which were considered advanced for the times. Jorge would explain why he used the scythe instead of the sickle for harvesting wheat. Older people preferred the sickle, claiming the scythe's swinging motion lost grain when it was scattered as the stalks fell to the ground and were picked up and gathered into sheaves. Jorge contended the scythe was more efficient; the harvester could cut more grain in a shorter amount of time. Also, he argued, waste was avoided when gleaners collected the fallen grain and the poor were grateful for the extra bounty.

But it was the political aspects of those ideas that most interested Jose. Jorge was thought to be too liberal if not revolutionary by other landholders. Large estates should be made smaller, he argued, and if those landowners resisted, they should be required by law to give up some of their land which could be cultivated cooperatively by the men currently working on it. With modern machinery, everyone could be fed and the hatred landless peasants held for large landowners would decrease. Jorge tried to interest other growers in irrigation projects and in setting up a system of water distribution arranged by the peasants themselves, as the Water Judges operated in Valencia. The indifference he encountered when voicing ideas like these led Jorge to discouragement and silence. That silence, however, served him well when Nationalist forces tore through Trujillo on their way toward Navalmoral de la Mata and Talavera de la Reina.

Pigs, sheep, and a few cows were lodged in a barn about thirty meters in back of the house. Now, Jose surmised, Jorge or one of his boys, or a hired herdsman, would take the animals out to pasture each day. The family performed the work of farming: plowing, sowing, weeding, reaping, threshing and collecting the grain, and carrying it into a storehouse next to the barn. Jorge was regarded as an exceptionally small landholder in contrast to the large landowners, particularly those to the south in the more fertile areas of Andalulsia. They left much of their vast estates untilled. Their soil was not plowed and planted; instead, it was kept out of cultivation to keep the wages of the *campesino* laborers low and to raise bulls or to provide hunting space for themselves and their rich friends.

Life was not easy for Marisa's family, but in no way could it be compared with the hardships endured by the *campesinos*, the landless peasants working in the fields when there was employment. Each day early in the morning, they crowded into the center of town, hoping to be hired by agents of the great landholders. With most of the land uncultivated, there would always be a surplus of laborers, further depressing the meager wages for the workers.

During sowing and harvesting seasons, Jorge employed two or three day laborers for the extra work that was required. He had no difficulty in securing the labor necessary to sustain a livelihood for himself and his family. The campesinos generally preferred to work close to town where their families lived rather than go several kilometers to work and live in bunkhouses for a number of days before returning home. Jorge paid his workers reasonably well, which wasn't much – four to five pesetas per day and twice that amount at harvest time, but this was better pay than they could get elsewhere. He took care of them if they were injured or fell ill. The men ate at eight, thirteen, and twenty hours in Marisa's kitchen, thankful for good food and to be out of the hot sun for three hours in the middle of the day and decently paid at the end of the day.

For centuries, the campesinos had lived in huts of sun-dried brick or clay, malnourished and constantly near starvation. For much of each year many went without shoes, their only protection being the thick calluses on their bare feet. Occasionally, they would lose patience over their living conditions, their anger boiling over into revolt. Strikes proved to be useless; too many other desperate peasants waited to be selected for work. The campesinos would simply occupy unused land and cultivate it. In time, local authorities came to tell them their actions were illegal; they were taking land that did not belong to them. The Civil Guard would then be summoned to chase the peasants off the land with rifle fire. Members of the Guard never served in their home provinces; as a result, they were always seen as part of a foreign army that upheld only the interests of the great landowners and those politicians and clergy that went along with them.

Jose knew Marisa and Jorge hated the unfair arrangements among the landowners, the local political bosses, and the Civil Guard. They disapproved of a system that protected the ongoing wealth of the great landowners and insured the suffering of the peasants. They were caught in the middle, often deferring out of necessity to the bidding of the powerful landlords while their social consciences made them privately sympathetic with the campesinos. Any surplus in their harvest was shared with peasant families, Marisa advising them to tell no one where the food came from.

An image of his father appeared next in Jose's recollections. While Jose was growing up in the Asturias region, Pablo Martinez regaled him with stories of working class struggles and how peasants and workers were driven into political parties and unions, trying to ease hardships they could not solve on their own.

"The 1917 *Bolshevik* revolution in Russia stirred a lot of interest among

Spanish workers," Pablo had informed his young son. "But when their labor leaders discovered the Soviets crushed all political opposition, the socialists split into two groups. Workers supporting the Bolsheviks formed the *PCE,* the *Partido Communista de Espana;* Socialists opposed to Soviet-style communism stayed with the *Partido Socialista Obrero de Espana,* the *PSOE*."

"Most campesinos, discouraged by so little help from the government, joined the *CNT,* the anarchist trade union, rather than the socialist's *UGT* and certainly not the left-wing republican parties of the middle classes. Mikhail Bakunin was their hero, not Karl Marx who didn't think much of rural life. But the CNT wasn't radical enough for some anarchists, so they formed their own organization, the *FAI* or *Federacion Anarquista Iberica*."

Pablo Martinez gave lurid accounts of FAI direct actions and stormy uprisings. "They would march into towns, take over civic offices, imprison civil guards, burn all property deeds, abolish money, and declare the land to be held in common – all in the name of 'libertarian communism.' They thought they could create an anarchist heaven on earth, but all it did was to provoke a merciless suppression by the Civil Guard."

Jose had studied and written about the politics of agrarian reform at university and during the beginning of his career as a journalist. When Spain became a republic for the second time in its history in 1931, the new government rejected outright expropriation as a method of land redistribution. Instead, it tried to buy small parcels of land on which to resettle peasant families. This program provided too little, too late, barely scratching the surface of the problem.

As Jose had observed during his university days, the right-wing did not remain idle, having learned from leftist parties. The Catholic right and the great landowners created a formidable confederation of the 'autonomous right,' the *Confederacion Espanola de Derechas Autonomas* or *CEDA*. Their leader was Jose-Maria Gil Robles whose goal was a Catholic corporate state modeled after one established in Austria. In the third year of the Republic, the CEDA alliance and other smaller conservative parties won a majority of seats in the Cortes and subsequently repealed much of the earlier liberal legislation. Labor laws creating more employment were struck down. Wages were cut, often in half. Those who protested these actions were called subversive and fired. The right-wing government began collecting files on union leaders and making plans for rounding up the unemployed into labor camps. Civil guards destroyed crops on soil bought for landless peasants under farm reform laws. While some conservatives recognized the plight of the rural masses, the CEDA's only response was to protect the property of the *latifundia* by strengthening the Civil Guard. Peasants caught gathering bits of food on a landowner's property were arrested as criminals. Hunger marches and worker organizations were broken up by civil guards or attacked by ruffians hired by landowners.

When conservative control of the Cortes ended in February of 1936, the campesinos in Extremadura and elsewhere again established collective farms on the unused land of the wealthy owners. They hoped the takeover would go unnoticed or that a liberal government would not intervene. Marisa and Jorge, being small landowners who cultivated their land, were not threatened by this desperate and drastic action. When Jose had visited his family four months ago, he found them sympathetic with the landless peasants but uneasy about outright expropriation without some kind of legal justification.

These memories swirled through Jose's mind as the car turned into the driveway. Now, however, he was not aware of the collapse of the cooperative farm movement as the Nationalist army advanced into the territory. Any resistance by the campesinos had been swiftly put down accompanied by an outburst of killing. Even Jorge and Marisa could not know of the extent of the ruthless repression that had occurred so close to them.

Light shone through the windows of several rooms. More activity appeared in the house than Antonio expected. "Spaniards stay up to all hours of the night, but farmers retire early," he remarked. "Why are people still up?"

The guard and driver posted themselves outside in the cool night air. Jose and Antonio moved inside the house, astounding the occupants with their unforeseen appearance at such a late hour. Marisa and Jorge quickly overcame their shock and welcomed them with hugs and kisses, their faces and arms reddened by the hot sun of southwestern Spain.

Another unexpected surprise was waiting for Jose; this one was far more pleasant than any recent experience. Bonita came forward. She had held back, then stepped into the front room, ran to Jose, and kissed and embraced him. Jose put his arms around Bonita, kissed her eager lips, and swept her off her feet, swaying her radiant long black hair behind her and kissing her again.

"I didn't expect to find you here, not in the middle of a civil war," his low voice confided softly to her. Antonio moved closer to them.

"Marisa wrote to me about your mother," Bonita explained. "The letter came after I finished my first year of teaching. I traveled by car and bus, also on foot, to be with Maria and help your sister, and" . . . she added, looking up shyly, "I also came in hopes of seeing you."

"How long have you been here?" asked Jose, annoyed Antonio could hear everything spoken. "I tried to send you a letter, but I guess it didn't get through."

"I arrived just a few days ago. You had written back in June if civil war came, you were thinking of enlisting in a government militia, and your clothes tell me you haven't. I simply wanted to be with you."

Looking past Jose, she spotted Antonio, who was recovering from his astonishment upon seeing Bonita in the family home.

"Hello Antonio," she said sprightly. "You look very dashing in your uniform."

"Thank you, Bonita. It's good to see you." Jose knew that was a lie. Antonio never anticipated a visit from her.

At that time, into the room ambled the other member of mother Maria's family: Ramon. He was in his pajamas. Unfortunately, this emphasized his slack, stocky frame and absence of military bearing.

"*Hola*, everyone! Can't a soldier get a decent night's sleep when he's home on leave," Ramon joked, rubbing his eyes and scratching his mustache. Then he was on to giving greetings all around, not caring whether anyone noticed his unkempt appearance and disheveled brownish hair. Looking at his trim and polished older brother, he said, "Antonio, maybe I'd better get into my uniform so I can give you a proper salute."

"Save it, Ramon. Go back to bed." Here was yet another complication Antonio hadn't counted upon.

"I'll join you, Ramon," said Jorge. "I should have been in bed two hours ago. Nice to see all of you, but the cows don't appreciate my sleeping in late." The two men climbed the steps upstairs.

"How is madre?" Jose asked his sister.

"Come," she said. "You too, Bonita."

"Wait one moment, Jose," Antonio cut in. "I need to talk with you. I'll be very brief. Let's go outside."

As the front door closed behind them, they moved into the darkness of the night. Antonio guided his youngest brother, taking him by the arm. The words Antonio spoke were delivered quietly but forcefully. He reiterated the warning given earlier.

"I'll be standing next to the door of Mama's room, so don't even think of telling her about your situation. The poor woman doesn't need to know, especially now. If she did, there is nothing she could do. You would only greatly upset her. Knowing you are a captured soldier and are facing a trial might be fatal in her condition. You are not to say anything about being a prisoner or going back to the internment camp – not to mother, your girl friend, our sister, or anyone. Leave that to me. That's an order, Jose."

Jose wanted to say: *I'm not in your army, Antonio.* Instead, he simply indicated he understood.

"Right now, all I want to do is see Mama." Then he went inside to join Bonita and Marisa with Antonio staying close behind him.

CHAPTER 6
MARIA'S REQUEST

Maria lay in her bed with her eyes wide open. She had heard people entering the house, but was too weak to walk without help. She knew Ramon and Bonita were in the house. Antonio had been with her, making sure the family was safe when the Army of Africa moved through the country around Trujillo. Now she was anxious to talk with Jose, and her eyes lit up when he entered her room.

"Jose, I knew you would come," she whispered. "It's wonderful to have you here."

"Mama . . . Mama," he said in a low, deep voice as he walked over to her bed. Jose knelt and kissed his mother on both cheeks and the brow of her head, stroked her graying hair, and wiped away a tear from her eye. The atmosphere of the room carried a clean, antiseptic, medicinal smell. Jose was relieved to find his mother so well cared for and turned his head up to smile at the two women behind him.

After acknowledging Bonita and Marisa, Maria turned to Jose, making an effort to be clear and appear strong. "Jose, I'll get right to the reason I asked to see you. I have a great favor to ask of you while I am still alive. It's something I've hoped to do for a long, long time and cannot do now."

"What is it, Mama?" he asked. "I will do anything I can for you."

"I know you will, Jose, and I understand how involved you are with your work." Jose was not certain his mother knew he was no longer a newspaper writer. Maria placed his right hand into her own two hands and drew him near to her. "You are my son of the good heart, and you will understand what I ask."

"Name it, Mama."

"As long as I can remember, I have felt God's call to go on a pilgrimage to the Cathedral on the *Plaza del Obradoiro* at Santiago de Compostela. Ever since your father died, I have wanted to thank God for granting my wish for a family, but I have not found the time to go there. You know about Santiago, don't you?"

"*Si*, Mama. It is one of the great pilgrimage sites of Christianity. We think of Santiago as being equal to Jerusalem and Rome."

"Jose, I should have done the pilgrimage when I was young and living in the same region. Even after I married your father and lived in Asturias, we were much closer to Santiago than we are here in Trujillo. But, you know how you can put off going to a nearby place you want to see. As time goes on, you never get around to it."

"That happens to us all, Mama."

"While I made a home for your father and raised you four children, there was no time or money. Everything went for the family. Then your father died, and the little money we had was stretched even thinner. I have all kinds of time now, but I don't have the physical energy for a pilgrimage."

Maria hesitated for a moment before going on. "Jose, I'm asking you to take that pilgrimage for me. I hope it's not too much of an imposition." She lowered her voice. "At first, I thought I would ask Antonio. He's the oldest of you three sons of mine, and he *is* very religious. Between you and me, I've been concerned about that pious nature of his; sometimes, it strikes me as having an almost belligerent quality. I don't know where or from whom he gets it. He seems so austere about religion. He is dedicated to the Church, I know. I've wondered if he should become a priest. Right now, he's busy being an officer in the army."

She paused briefly. Jose could only listen. Apparently, his mother did not know her sons belonged to opposite armies fighting each other. Antonio was right; to inform her they were enemies on the battlefield might be more than she could bear.

Maria spoke in a barely audible whisper. "I decided not to ask Antonio. And, Ramon is too immature. Even though he is older than you, he doesn't take spiritual things seriously. I decided to ask only you, Jose, because I believe you are the right person to make the pilgrimage for me. I can rest at peace, knowing my youngest son is doing a mission for me, one I now cannot do for myself. What happiness that will bring me."

"Mama, I would go to the ends of the earth to bring peace and comfort to you," Jose said as he tenderly kissed her forehead again. "I've been to Santiago de Compostela once in my life. I'll never forget it. I went for my own reasons. As soon as I can, I will go for you."

"You are my adored son," she murmured. "Promise me, Jose, you will go to the Portico de la Gloria of the Santiago cathedral. In Saint James' pillar, place your fingers for me into the five holes worn by the fingers of millions of pilgrims. Go to Mass in the cathedral and pray for me. Of course, pray for yourself and your brothers and pray for your sister and her family. Pray for Bonita, too. Then, come back and tell me about your experience."

Maria fell back exhausted on her pillow. Jose didn't know what to say. How could he refuse his dying mother, but how could he fulfill her wishes? He caught a glimpse of Antonio standing just outside the room.

When his mother stopped speaking, Jose placed his hands around her face and simply said, "Yes, Mama, I will do this for you even if I die trying. It may take a while, but do not give up on me. Somehow, I will find a way."

"Yes," she said, "it is The Way of Saint James."

Jose wondered if she was becoming delirious or going through some kind of spiritual ecstasy. Bonita and Marisa couldn't tell either. All they could think of was the heavy burden Maria had laid upon Jose who was too kind to say anything other than 'Yes, Mama . . . somehow I will find a way.'

When Jose, Marisa, and Bonita left the room, they said nothing to Antonio about Maria's charge to her son. Jose loved his mother. She experienced a hard life before her husband died, and life was harder after he had gone. Maria had wanted a large family. Six children would have been about right in her mind, but two miscarriages had reduced the number to four.

"Maybe the Lord knew what he was doing," she had said. "Taking care of four children on my own was difficult, but it was something that could be accomplished if carefully done. Six might have been impossible." Marisa, Antonio, and Ramon had been born in her middle to late twenties. The miscarriages had discouraged having more children for a while, but then Jose was born when she was thirty-five.

Jose was unique; he was her 'gift from God,' her 'son of the good heart.' Maria kept those feelings to herself; she loved all of her children and she did not want any rivalry between them that would tear them apart. Despite her efforts to treat each child equally, she couldn't let go of the feeling that somehow Jose was special.

Antonio planned to bid farewell immediately as soon as Jose emerged from Maria's room. He announced to Jose that it was time to go and started ushering him to the door. Bonita ran to Jose, blocking the way.

"So soon?" she protested, holding on to him. "We've barely had a moment with each other." Before Jose could respond, Marisa told Antonio she wouldn't hear of their leaving. She insisted they stay through the night, especially since their visit had been so short and the clock had just struck midnight.

"We can't," declared Antonio. "Too many people are already here in the house, and we have two other soldiers waiting for us in the car."

"That's no problem," countered Marisa. "There's room in the barn and lots of straw to sleep on. You and Jose can use our sleeping bags and your soldiers can take blankets for the cots we can move out there."

Antonio tried another maneuver. "Captain Barcena, my camp commandant, gave us orders to return even if the hour was late."

"Us?" responded Marisa, deflecting attention from a military command. "I know my youngest brother." Turning to Jose and slightly wrinkling her nose, she asked, "Surely, you're not in the Nationalist army?"

"Never in a million years," answered Jose, beginning to enjoy Antonio's discomfort.

Antonio was caught off guard. He had to dissemble.

Oh, Mama, he thought. *What I am going through carrying out your wish to see Jose!*

To Marisa and Bonita, he said, "Jose tells me he's writing newspaper accounts of the war in southern Spain. Quite by accident, we met a week after the battle at Badajoz."

Jose marveled at how quickly Antonio had concocted a plausible story.

"Last I knew he considered giving up journalism for a while and joining a Republican militia," said Bonita.

"Apparently, he never got around to it. And, not knowing you were here, Bonita, Jose has interviews scheduled for tomorrow morning."

Antonio exchanged words with himself again: *Mama, how many more lies must I tell in your service?*

"Those interviews have been cancelled," said Jose, contradicting Antonio's fiction with his own fantasy. He thought of stopping the whole charade at this point, but then he remembered the two soldiers outside. To challenge Antonio's deception now could provoke an ugly, violent confrontation he didn't want forced upon his family. He decided to wait for a better opportunity.

"About your orders, Antonio," said Marisa. "Why don't you telephone your captain? There's a bar with a telephone that's still open in the plaza. You can explain you were delayed and it's later than you had anticipated."

"I don't want to wake him, Marisa. The army goes to bed early and gets up early, just like farmers do."

"Well, then, leave Jose here. He doesn't have to go back with you."

"I think he must get back. He tells me his editor wants the last article by tomorrow."

"We'll drive him back in the morning. I'm sure he wants to be with Bonita, now that she's here. We haven't had much chance to talk with him. It's been months since he's been here."

"Are you sure that car of yours would make it to Badajoz?"

"I know it's old, but Jorge keeps it good condition. Besides, how long is Mama going to be with us? Keep in mind we don't know how long she has to live. Antonio, this may be the last time either you or Jose will see her alive. You've been here less than an hour."

Against his better judgment, Antonio threw up his hands in surrender.

"All right, Marisa, you win. We'll stay here tonight and leave in the morning. Actually, the commandant didn't give a firm order; it was more of a suggestion."

He was worn out by the war, stressed by his mother's request, drained by keeping his brother alive, and now exhausted by his resolute sister. Antonio did not want to further discuss when to leave nor did he want to create an unpleasant scene in front of everyone.

They gave their 'good-nights' to each other. With his oldest brother irritatingly close by, Jose took his time kissing Bonita fervently before she headed to a back bedroom. There was no getting away from Antonio, determined as he was to keep Jose near him at all times.

Marisa wanted to tell her oldest brother: *For heaven's sake, Antonio, let them have a few minutes together; it's been months since they've seen each other.* But she had argued enough with Antonio, the hour was late, and people needed to rise early in the morning. And, she saw no reason why Jose couldn't be with Bonita after Antonio and his two soldiers were on their way back to Badajoz.

With Bonita out of the room, Antonio spoke to Jose. "Follow me," he said. Together, they went outside to tell the driver and guard they would be spending the night with them in the barn.

"Don't you get any thoughts about running off," cautioned Antonio as the two brothers headed back toward the house to get blankets and sleeping bags. "One of my soldiers will be awake at any moment during the night. They will shoot to kill if you make a wrong move. None of us want that to happen. You and I are going to be close to each other all through the night – just like we were when you, Ramon, and I shared a room growing up in this home. There will be the same togetherness tomorrow morning. I don't like this any more than you do."

No Greater Love

Laying in the sleeping bag next his brother, Antonio wrestled for a long time with the complicated dilemma he hadn't anticipated.

How could I know Bonita and Ramon would be here? Obviously, Bonita will struggle to keep Jose with her. If she knew I was taking Jose to prison and possible execution, she would fight me like a wildcat. Marisa will object, too; it's likely her sympathies are with the Republic. Jorge stays out of political struggles, but he will take his wife's side. I'm not sure of Ramon, even though he is a Nationalist soldier. Supposedly, he's on my side, but Ramon is unpredictable – you never know what he will do.

The last thing I want is a show of force. If coercion becomes the only way out, it will cost me the respect of my closest relationships.

As Antonio lay trying to get some sleep, the dangers of the battlefield now seemed less hazardous than the politics of the family.

Chapter 7
Divided Family

When morning came, Antonio's driver and guard asked permission to go for food in Trujillo's main square, the Plaza Mayor. Tempted by the prospect of eating Marisa's home-cooked food, Antonio acquiesced, telling his men to return no later than forty-five minutes.

With Jorge and his two young sons, Miguel and Angel, busy outside at morning farm chores, Marisa and Bonita joined Antonio and Jose at the table for coffee, omelet, sausage, potatoes, and *churros*. Antonio was dressed in uniform, ready to leave as soon as his soldiers returned. Marisa deliberated opening a subject she had wanted to bring up with her oldest brother. Suspecting it might be a contentious matter, she decided to start with a positively worded question.

"Antonio," she began. "Jorge and I thought at first the military rising might actually help the Republic. What benefits do you think a Nationalist government would bring us?"

"Marisa, maybe this is a topic we should discuss at a later time," responded Antonio warily. "We could talk about it then."

"I suppose life will go on as before," his sister continued, as if she hadn't heard Antonio's words. "I had hoped the Republic could move faster in breaking up the huge landed estates. The landowners would have been compensated for any land they gave up. Most of it wasn't cultivated anyway. Giving more parcels of land to poor peasants could have started as promised. Jorge and I didn't think the Republic's land reform program would have changed much for us, but it would have been a great help to the *campesinos* without land."

Antonio started to say something, but Marisa held up her hand and went on. "If the government is delivered into the hands of the generals, the grandees living a life of luxury away from their land will choke the farm workers even more. Antonio, I don't see where the National Front has anything good to offer for peasants, or even to us as small landowners. All they talk about is how communism will take over when there are few communists in Spain. Church officials say how unbelieving we are, when most of Spain is Catholic."

Jose looked at her in admiration for her plainspoken views.

Antonio rose to the bait. When any conversation turned to politics, it was hard for him to remain wordless. "The Center-Right coalition, when they were in power, passed laws to set up individual family farms in this region. Large landowners were required to rent land they didn't cultivate."

"A lot of good that did," lamented Marisa. "Those same laws allowed those big landowners to choose whether to rent the land or cultivate it on their own. Guess what they chose to do. They told tenants to get off their land because they were going to work it themselves, which in most cases they never got around to doing. You know what happened, Jose; you reported it in *El Sol* yourself."

Jose nodded in agreement. "Renters could buy land, but that usually didn't mean the land they were living on. People went on paying rent, without knowing whether they would ever own the land they were working. Most of them are still renters, that is, if they're still alive."

"In other words," explained Marisa, "owners of large estates hung on to their land as most right-wing politicians knew they would. The landowners through their *caciques* undermined the government's intent. Most renters and *campesinos* are worse off than they were before."

"You see, Antonio," added Jose, "the Republic's program came from the idea that when peasants take ownership of land, their attitude becomes very different from those who work the fields belonging to others they never see. Every *latifundista* gets rich and fat off of peasant labor. The landless get resentful and some resort to thievery and rebellion. The best thing for the grandees to do is to sell or lease their land permanently and then retire to Madrid. They would have the money and help the community at the same time."

"Jose, you live in a dream world," Antonio responded dismissively to his youngest brother.

Turning to Marisa, he said, "I don't understand you and Jorge. You may not realize it, but you are fortunate to be in Nationalist-held territory. In Popular Front towns, property records are burned and the worker's collective seizes all land. You own land, yet you don't identify with great landowners for protection, and only they are in a position to make Spain a great nation again."

"We're small landholders, far apart from them. The people you speak of think only of themselves and their wealth and power; they never seem to think of the common good. Now, they're fearful of what could happen to them because of the occasional outbreaks of violence."

"Marisa, if the Reds win this struggle, you and Jorge won't have any land to call your own. You'll be told what to do by some local cooperative, or a Red bureaucrat in Madrid, or maybe some commissar in Moscow. And, apart from Communism, look at what happens when you break up the land. The farmers in Galicia divide the land into smaller plots with each passing generation. Now, nobody can make a decent living on one hectare."

"I can agree with you on your last comment," said Marisa. "A lot of farms are either too small or too large. We Spaniards always go to extremes. Like your professor *Unamuno* said, Jose, Spain has never known a middle class."

Thinking her agreement was a concession, Antonio pressed home another point to Marisa. "You and Jorge couldn't have liked the way the Socialists in the Republic increased the wages of your farm laborers. Can you afford to pay your workers more, even if you want to?"

"We hire only one or two campesinos, maybe one or two more at harvest time. We would like to offer them better wages, although they earn more from us than they can get anywhere else around here. In addition to their pay, I feed our workers and send them home with food for their families when we can, and because we do, some big landowners are unhappy with us. They enrich themselves at their worker's expense."

"And, where are your rich neighbors now?"

"Oh, I know what you are getting at, Antonio. One of them is dead, and the others resisted the takeover of their land, although they could have been paid for it by the worker cooperative or the government. Now that the Nationalists are running things around here, I suppose the grandees will return from wherever they are to get their land back."

"That's as it should be," broke in Antonio. "They owned the land in the first place. Peasants illegally seized thousands of farms in Extremadura alone."

"But, how would you have felt if you had been promised your own land, only to be kept off of it by the big landowners and the guns of their Civil Guard? The rage of the peasants is understakable when their only choice is to seize land or starve."

Antonio's voice now rang out like a rifle shot. "Don't tell me you're sympathetic with the anarchists and their FAI goon squads?"

"No, not with the violent ones in their ranks, but sometimes the anarchists seem to be the only people that pay any attention to the horrible condition of the peasants," exclaimed Marisa, her eyes flashing irritation. "Castilbanco is a poverty-stricken village not far from here. The peasants called a meeting in the town plaza. They decided to farm some uncultivated lands around them. The Civil Guard broke up the meeting. The peasants resisted. Four Guards were killed. Who did the killing? No one would tell, not even under torture. The Guard said the whole town was responsible, not any one person. So, people were chosen at random and shot. What kind of justice is that?"

"That's not the whole story," Antonio answered. "The dead Guards' bodies were desecrated. General *Sanjurjo* declared he had never seen corpses so horribly mutilated, even among the primitives of Morocco. Their heads were bashed in, eyes were gouged out. The women danced obscenely over the mangled bodies. The Civil Guard had come into town only to restore law and order; no wonder there was great public sympathy for them."

"And that sympathy was lost only a few days later when the Guard fired point-blank into a crowd of unarmed peasants shouting slogans during a strike," retorted Marisa. "Women and children were killed. People wanted Sanjurjo removed as head of the Civil Guard, which happened a month later. After that, there was Casas Viejas . . ."

"I know about Casas Viejas!" interrupted Antonio. "The anarchists there refused to obey a surrender order and then wondered why it became a tragedy. They thought every campesino in the country was in revolt and some communist heaven-on-earth would be born next day. Poor, deluded fools! Little did they know how alone they were. Even the liberal government of that time knew those anarchists had to be put down. That scoundrel *Azana* got what he deserved; he never did get rid of that stain."

"Nor did the guards. Fourteen people shot in cold blood, Antonio, after all resistance had ended. That man in charge – he was guilty, but he tried to pass blame on up to the president."

Ramon entered the room rubbing his eyes after a night's sleep. He sat in an empty chair, looked at his older brother and sister, and rolled his eyes. "Sounds like we have a mini-civil war right here," he pronounced to everyone.

Antonio sought to change the conversation ever so slightly with a comment he hammered home in every political debate. "Marisa, since we're talking about the brutality of peasant revolts, I shouldn't have to remind you of the terror from anarchist strikes, assassinations, burning churches, killing priests – all of which should have been dealt with by the Republic. No society can tolerate the lawlessness we've experienced."

Bonita interjected a question. "Do you think armed rebellion against a legitimate government will bring law and order?" she asked. "Nationalists talk about how they hate violence, but they create plenty of it with their revolt. And remember, the Popular Front won the most votes and a majority of seats in the *Cortes* back in last February's election."

Antonio brushed aside Bonita's statements. "All of you know that election was rigged by the Left. The Second Republic lost its right to authority some time ago. Do you know what really started this civil war?"

Before anyone could reply, he answered his own question. "The final crime was the murder of Calvo Soleto by the Republic's own police because he was the monarchist leader. How can you trust a government if it does that? Next, Miguel Primo de Rivera was butchered because he had been the head of King Alfonso's government. On top of all this was the killing of General Sanjurjo, burned to death when his airplane crashed, sabotaged by Republican assassins."

Jose couldn't keep out of the discussion any longer. "Whoops! Hold on, Antonio. Let's keep our facts straight here. Sanjurjo's plane was crammed with the heavy medals and fancy uniforms he packed; he expected to wear them when he became Nationalist head of state. His plane was so loaded it couldn't clear the trees at the end of the runway. And, Primo de Rivera wasn't murdered; he died peacefully in Paris. The shooting of Calvo Soleto was revenge for the killing of a Socialist officer by the *Falange*. I didn't approve of it and thought it was stupid."

"It wouldn't surprise me if Communists from Moscow were behind Calvo Soleto's assassination," Antonio fired back. "As for the Socialist officer, his killing was brought on by the murder of Jose Antonio's cousin."

"Who is this Jose Antonio?" questioned Ramon. "I know quite a few people named Jose and Antonio; two of them are sitting right here in front of me."

Antonio glanced at his brother with astonishment. "Where have you been, Ramon? Jose Antonio Primo de Rivera is the leader of the *Falange*, a very magnetic, courageous man. He is in a Republican prison awaiting trial at this moment and no doubt will be murdered when the so-called trial ends."

"The death of Calvo Soleto only served as an excuse for rebellion by generals opposed to the Republic," asserted Jose. "Franco and company were waiting for something like that to happen. Besides, the wholesale shooting of unarmed prisoners by the Nationalists fits any definition of murder."

Antonio directed a warning glance to Jose as if to say: *Don't get into your troubles here.* He stayed on the attack, drawing a newspaper article out of his pocket. "If you want to know why the generals took action, let me give you a few well-established facts the Cortes heard in its final session."

"Let me get a podium for you, professor," chirped Ramon in a light-hearted way. "A lecturer needs a platform."

Undeterred, Antonio continued. "In one month's time before hostilities began, ten churches were burned and destroyed. There were sixty-one violent deaths, 224 wounded, thirty estates ransacked, sixteen seizures of private property, ten political buildings demolished, fifteen general strikes, 132 bombs and grenades thrown at people and nineteen cases of arson. All of this occurred within twenty-seven days. The government itself did not do these things, but the Republic tolerated this violence by doing nothing – probably because the Reds were behind it. You wonder why the military acted; it had to act or watch the country go to ruin in total anarchy."

"How much of that violence was committed by people supporting the National Front?" asked Jose. "Were the grenades thrown only by anarchists? Were any strikes caused by inhumane conditions? Were any fires set by Nationalists? Were there no Republican deaths or wounded? Creating an outrage is a well-known tactic provoked by those who want an excuse to go to war."

As Antonio struggled to respond, Marisa quickly jumped in ahead of him. "One moment, Antonio," she declared. "It seems to me we should bring in a woman's point of view here, something seldom done in this country. The forces backing the National Front have always dictated that women must remain second-class citizens. It's a man's world where the double standard controls women."

Bonita concurred, nodding her head. "For example, it doesn't matter how abusive a man is to his wife, the marriage cannot be dissolved. If a woman has a baby out of wedlock, the father doesn't legally have to recognize his child. The woman will bear all of society's penalties."

"Oh, come now Bonita," Ramon teased, "did you bring your *duenna* with you? A sweet, young thing like you needs to be chaperoned, especially around people like Jose."

Bonita simply smiled at Ramon. Then, looking at Antonio, she said with all the irony she could gather in her voice, "Before that dreadful liberal Republic, a married woman had no legal status. She couldn't go to work, sign a contract, or claim an inheritance without her husband's permission. If the

Republic seemed weak at times, at least it was starting to recognize women's rights."

"Women's rights means being right at home with her children," said Antonio with conviction. "That's always been true because God and nature intended it to be that way."

"Of course, Antonio. A woman should stay at home, even if you have to break her legs to keep her there."

"Don't get married to Jose, Bonita," Ramon joked. "You'll be on crutches before you know it!"

"Ramon, let me answer her!" barked Antonio in an exasperated tone. "I'm not as old-fashioned as some of you think. I thought it was right to give women the vote. Actually, they voted quite wisely, that is, conservatively, in their first election three years ago. As for working, that's acceptable if those women aren't raising children. We need women as nurses and teachers."

Bonita chose her words carefully. "I went into education, Antonio, but women should be able to seek other occupations than teaching and nursing. The greatest gains the Republic made were in education; it reduced our terrible illiteracy rate and put more children in schools than ever before. If your Nationalists become the government, we'll be back where we were years ago."

"Where we were then wasn't as bad as you think," responded Antonio. "Better to be illiterate than be filled with the radical hogwash the Republic's teachers were pumping into the heads of innocent peasants and children."

"That's a strange defense of illiteracy," remarked Marisa. "I thought the effort made by the Republic's teaching missions to the campesinos here was quite noble and inspired. The number of books in our school library was greatly expanded. In smaller villages with no library, the *misioneros* created new ones. Their selection of books included literary classics."

"Too much of that literature heaped scorn on Spain and her Church, which was jammed into previously uncorrupted minds," complained Antonio. "I don't remember hearing of any selections that would inspire patriotism or the moral life. As for the classics, how would you expect an illiterate peasant to get anything out of them? I'd call that a mission dreamed up by young idealists who knew nothing of the real world."

"The misioneros were aware of those difficulties," explained Marisa. "One told me he saw the backwardness and injustice that trapped the campesinos in their existence here. The *misioneros* did all they could do. They knew much more had to be done for the well-being of the peasants."

"Those teaching missions represent to me a great difference between the liberals of the Republic and those backing the National Front," contended Jose. "Changes attempted by the Republic were done by education, economic reform, and rational persuasion. The Nationalist campaign has much more to do with force and violence."

"If you think Communists and anarchists who burn churches and murder priests are not about force and violence," countered Antonio sharply, "you're more naïve than I thought. You're still in that dream world, Jose."

Jose started to reply when Bonita burst in with this: "How Christian and moral can the Nationalists be when they appeal for and get plenty of help from brutal dictatorships run by thugs such as Hitler and Mussolini as well as our own home-grown gun-toting fascists? How can I go back to my students and talk about any morality of the Nationalist position in this war when they align themselves with criminals like that?"

Antonio was not about to back down to any challenge, preferring to stay on the attack. "I don't like to inform you, Bonita, your secular public schools face an impossible task trying to teach morality. I've heard you say you believe in Christianity, yet you've also said the school must be neutral when it comes to religion."

"Remember, Antonio, in my school there are several Jewish children and a Muslim child, and maybe even some who doubt or have no religion. They must be respected along with the majority who are Christian."

"That's namby-pamby liberalism for you! Trying to teach morality without the religion of our faith is like putting up a building without a foundation. Human nature is subject to evil, and belief in eternal rewards and punishments is necessary to put controls on human behavior. Without God's authority, people do not respect any authority – other than brute force. That's my answer to your objection about force and violence, Jose; unfortunately, it's needed now. And, Bonita, you're a teacher. As you educate your students, tell me: What do you say to your students about living a moral life?"

"I don't teach morality by saying do this or don't do that, Antonio; that approach doesn't work with children. I try to guide them toward a moral life by example. It's been my experience that actions speak louder than words. What you *are* is more important than what you *say*. God knows what is in my heart; I don't have to proclaim it from the housetops."

"I can accept that as far as it goes," said Antonio, trying to soften his tone of voice, "although I wish liberal educators would consider the outcomes of their freethinking. Merely instructing is not educating. Giving only knowledge to bright students is like putting a dagger into the hands of a lunatic. I read that the crime rate in France increases greatly among young people while it stays the same for adults. Why? Secular schools have much to do with it. The same thing is happening here as education is taken out of the hands of the Church."

Bonita wasn't buying into that argument, her Celtic blood fully aroused by the impassioned debate. "When schools were placed solely into the hands of the Church, education was smothered in our country. There weren't enough nuns to educate all the children. The Church didn't provide enough schools; many children simply never went to school. For those that did attend, half of the time was spent saying the rosary. I'm not against the rosary, but there wasn't enough emphasis on preparing students for life in the modern world."

Those words set Antonio off on a censorious tirade. "As the Pope has declared, life in the modern world has become all too worldly and immoral, and in this country, your adored Republic is responsible for much of it. Our bishops warned us about the constitution liberals imposed on us. Actually, it was a blatant move to jam a godless state down our throats. Church officials call secular government the plague of our times."

"Some bishops in Spain have a tendency to go beyond the intent of the messages the Vatican sends them," commented Jose.

Ignoring Jose's remark, Antonio went on. "Think of the consequences of that unholy constitution, stating Church and state must be separated. This absurd notion says authority comes *only* from the people, and that is nothing less than a proposal of official atheism." He punctuated the air with his finger for emphasis. "Those ideas inspire agnostic democracies around the world. Christianity is regarded as no different from false religions, and that error must be opposed."

"I don't believe Christianity and democracy necessarily conflict with each other," challenged Jose. "One is spiritual and the other is secular; nevertheless, I regard myself as a believer in both Christianity and democracy."

"You might as well call yourself a Catholic Socialist," muttered Antonio.

"There are some of those strange animals," said Jose. "Religious and secular people can agree on many things, among them, their democratic beliefs."

Antonio was having none of Jose's point of view. "I thank God the right-wing was able to repeal much of the liberal program started by the Republic. Liberties for the individual mind, the press, education, and religion were claimed as rights given only by nature, whatever that means. There was nothing about God. People now think they can be removed from God's authority. No man-made law can fully regulate human liberty. Liberty becomes license with that kind of thinking. Human freedom goes to extremes *without* God's law. I've seen it happen!"

Jose broke into Antonio's argument. "The Nationalist Army of Africa goes to brutal extremes particularly after victory in battle – and this is supposedly *within* God's law?"

Antonio was too completely wrapped up in his own convictions to give the slightest recognition to anything Jose said. "The Church warns us," he counseled, "have nothing to do with the enemies of God who lurk outside the faith. Run from them, as you would stay clear of a poisonous snake. The same goes for the heretical, blasphemous press that demolishes faith and order in this country."

"The press I've worked for is dedicated to publishing the truth," said Jose. "*Ortega y Gasset*, a major *El Sol* contributor, sought truth as honest philosophers try to do. Newspapers are not out to destroy faith and order. And, who decides who the enemies of God are?"

Antonio thought he had justified his position and wasn't about to respond to any more of Jose's diabolical questions or comments. However, he felt alone and besieged. He was outnumbered. He had given away his superior position as oldest brother and as a military officer when he was enticed into a political discussion by Marisa. Ramon, his lone Nationalist ally, appeared interested only in making humorous wisecracks.

A strained silence prevailed. Marisa's unexpressed thought was that perhaps Antonio had been right in saying that this discussion should have been deferred or maybe not held at all. The war of words within the family seemed as unstoppable as the deadly clash of arms raging around them.

Suddenly, Ramon broke the volatile tension by announcing he would give up sex if Spaniards would give up civil war.

"May I quote you on that," laughed Jose. "I can see the headlines: Franco sues for peace. Nationalist soldiers make ultimate sacrifice to stop civil war."

Uncomfortable in being the target of any humor, however negligible, Ramon scowled at Jose. "You can't quote me on anything. You'll have to find a new line of work if the Popular Front loses the war."

"Let it be, Ramon," cautioned Antonio. He didn't want his sister or Bonita prying into Jose's circumstances at this point. "Let's talk about something else. I didn't want to talk politics and religion anyway."

Ramon took the hint. He had a humorous story he had been waiting to tell.

"All this babble about religion reminds me of a joke a Jewish *amigo* told me last week," he announced. "A priest and a rabbi were always arguing about religion, trying to prove the other wrong, even though they were good friends. One day while riding in a car, they have a terrible accident. They crawl out from the wreckage, amazed to be alive. The priest crosses himself; then he notices the rabbi doing the same.

"The priest shouts, 'Glory to God! You've seen the Light!'

" 'What are you talking about?' asks the rabbi.

" 'You gave the sign of the cross,' says the priest. 'You've seen the truth!'

" 'Cross myself?' says the rabbi. 'Oh, no, no, no. I was only checking to see if everything was still there – spectacles, testicles, watch and wallet!' "

Ramon's hand made an awkward sign of the cross, touching each item on his body as it was mentioned.

Everyone laughed with the exception of Antonio. He smiled indulgently; then sat as stiff as a stone and stared into space. He preferred not to hear jokes about his religion, but he didn't want to make an issue of it.

He barely heard Ramon say, "Oh, come on, Antonio, you've heard worse than that in the barracks." The family had regained some sense of companionship, although Antonio wished his Nationalist brother had taken his side during the family debate instead of ending it with a funny story. But Ramon wasn't finished.

"A priest confided to another priest, 'I've lost 500 pesetas promised to the bishop. Maybe the money was stolen, but I'm not sure.'

"The other priest advised: 'Preach a sermon about the Commandments and when you come to Thou shall not steal, describe the torments in hell for the guilty. Say, however, if the money is returned, no questions will be asked.'

"The first priest did so. Afterwards, he was asked: 'What happened?'

"'I never got to Thou shall not steal.'

"The other priest looked bewildered and asked, 'Why?'

"The first priest, his eyes cast down, said, 'When I got to Thou shall not commit adultery, I suddenly remembered where I had spent the money.' "

More laughter came forth as Jorge and his two boys tramped into the room, finished with morning chores. They greeted everyone.

Jose thought: *They are probably thinking how well Marisa's brothers get along with each other despite their different views.*

Miguel and Angel ran up to Jose and said, "Uncle Jose, come out to the barn with us; we've got a new calf to show you."

Antonio got Jose's attention and shook his head, saying, "No."

"Everyone is way too serious these days," complained Miguel.

"I agree with you, Miguel," replied Jose.

Jorge turned to Antonio and said, "Antonio, when I went out to the barn earlier this morning, I found two soldiers on the cots. They were fine. I assumed they came with you last night?"

His question was interrupted by a cry from Maria's room. It sounded like she had exclaimed "Oh!" Then, the noise of something falling was heard.

"Sounds like she dropped her scrapbook again," said Marisa. "I'll check."

Antonio started to answer Jorge's question. "Yes, those two soldiers are riding with us. As you know, we arrived late and it was after midnight when Marisa persuaded us to stay for the night. She sent them out to the barn. They've gone into the plaza for food. They should return any . . ."

He never finished his explanation. Marisa suddenly reappeared, white-faced. "Come quickly," she pleaded. "I think our mother just died."

Chapter 8
"Abduction"

Maria had suffered a massive stroke which brought her an instant death. As battle-hardened as Antonio was, he lingered longingly in her room shattered by the sight of the now-still body lying there. Irrationally, he wanted someone to blame. Had Marisa forgotten a medication? Perhaps Jose's appearance had brought his mother too much excitement? Jose and Bonita stayed in Maria's room too, struck by the abrupt nature of death. They were shedding tears and holding each other. Jose was gripped with a sense of guilt; they had spent their mother's last minutes of life laughing at jokes and arguing about politics and war. Ramon was stunned; he had hoped that somehow Maria would recover and live forever. To him, his mother's departure from the living had not seemed to have actually happened. Miguel and Angel stayed outside the bedroom waiting for permission to enter the chamber of a dead person.

Only Marisa had prepared herself emotionally for life without mother. Watching Maria become weaker over the past year, she had made plans in advance for Maria's funeral with her priest, Father Augustin. The three brothers and Jorge and his two sons would carry Maria's coffin to the altar. The Funeral Mass would be held three days after Maria's death. The church, *Iglesia de Santa Maria*, had been the family place of worship and Maria's church since she had arrived in Trujillo. Situated about halfway up a hill between the Plaza Mayor and the *castillo* where Our Lady of Victory kept her vigil over the town, this thirteenth century Gothic church possessed great historic value. Inside, by a wide rose window, rested two stone seats on which Ferdinand and Isabella, the Catholic monarchs, had sat during Mass when they once came to Trujillo. A wall outside the church held a grim-faced bust of Francisco de Orellana, participant in the conquest of Mexico with Hernan Cortes and in the subjugation of Peru with Francisco Pizarro.

Antonio asked Marisa to bring the family Missal to him after she brought in her two sons to say a tearful good-bye to their grandmother. When Marisa placed the book in Antonio's hands, he turned the pages and immediately began to read the litany at the time of death. "God the Father, Son, and Holy Spirit: Have mercy on your servant . . . May her soul and the souls of all the departed, through the mercy of God, rest in peace."

Laying down the book, Antonio asked Marisa to go over the preparations for his mother's funeral with him, Ramon, and Jose. As the oldest son, Antonio believed he had to take charge of the details concerning the Funeral Mass. On the other hand, there was a war being fought and he was an officer in the Nationalist army. He had promised to bring Jose back to the prison camp at Badajoz, and now, with Maria's death, those plans were thrown in disarray.

Thoroughly shaken by the suddenness of his mother's death, Jose nevertheless had the presence of mind to take advantage of Antonio's distractions. While Antonio was reading the litany, Jose discovered a small piece of blank paper caught between the pages and sticking out from Maria's fallen scrapbook. As Antonio completed his reading, Jose bent down in full view of everyone and picked up the scrapbook with his back turned to all in the room. Rising to place the book beside Maria's body, he simultaneously removed the paper and hid it in his hand, clearing his throat to conceal any noise he might have made. Turning again to face the group, he acted as if all he had done was retrieve the scrapbook. Going out of Maria's bedroom behind Antonio, he quietly slipped the paper under his shirt.

Marisa went over the funeral schedule with her brothers and Jorge at the kitchen table. When finished, she asked Antonio, "Would you go with Jorge to inform Father Augustin and the mortician of mother's death and select a casket?"

"I can't do that, Marisa, as much as I want to be helpful. We've got to leave as soon as my soldiers get back which should have been a half- hour ago. My captain is going to chastise me for being this late. I'm risking a reprimand as it is."

"Antonio, I've told you before there are telephones in town!" scolded Marisa. "Surely, your captain will understand why you're late."

"Marisa!" berated Antonio angrily. "There's a war on! If we're going to get back here for the funeral, I've got to go now to stay on the good side of the commander. Jorge is perfectly capable of telling the priest about our mother."

"All right, Antonio. You've got obligations I don't understand. Come with me to see the plans I've made with Father Augustin. I've anticipated this moment, although nothing quite prepares you for it. You're the oldest brother; you should be in charge, not me." She rose and left the room expecting Antonio to follow her.

With her appeal to his sense of importance mixed in a mild reproof, Antonio acquiesced.

Before he left the room, Antonio whispered in Ramon's ear, "Watch Jose, do not let him out of your sight. It's important! I'll explain why later."

Alone with Ramon, Jose reasoned this might be the only occasion he would have to compose a message about his desperate situation to Bonita or Marisa, despite his inward misgivings about exploiting his mother's death for his own purposes.

It's plain to see that Ramon is a rather disengaged Nationalist soldier. How closely will he follow Antonio's instructions to watch me? To all appearances, Ramon is not aware of the delicate game being played out here.

The gamble was worth a try. Seated at opposite ends of the table, Jose occupied Ramon in conversation about how much their mother meant to them. He took a pencil from a metal box on the table. Keeping his hand under the surface of the table, he removed the paper from under his shirt.

Jose pretended to draw pictures on the paper while scribbling a note explaining his situation: 'At battle – Badajoz. Captured – prisoner. Ant. kept me alive, talked CO into seeing Mama.' On the back of the paper, he wrote: 'On trial: killing Nat. people – no, did not. Don't confront Ant. – 3 days to figure out something.' Continuing his talk with Ramon, he brushed the pencil to the floor. Reaching down to pick up the pencil, he inserted the note at the bottom of his shoe. He would wait for an opportunity to slide the note into the hands of Bonita or Marisa.

Outside the house, the two soldiers returned, parking their car in front of the house near some bushes. Antonio and Marisa had finished the funeral plans and sent Jorge off on his errands to contact the mortician, arrange for a coffin, and to notify Father Augustin at the church. As Jorge drove out of the driveway, Antonio noticed that the military car and soldiers had reappeared.

Resolved to deal with the Jose problem decisively and immediately, Antonio motioned for the driver and guard to meet him at the door. They came, expecting a tongue-lashing for their lateness. Quietly, Antonio told them they could redeem themselves only by following his orders exactly. He directed the driver to start the engine again and to keep it running.

Antonio instructed the guard, a thickset youth with the frame of a wrestler, "Come to the front steps and stand on one side of the front door where you can't be easily seen. Take the prisoner to the car when he appears and be quick about it before there's trouble."

While Antonio was distracted, Jose retrieved the note from his shoe and pressed it quietly into Bonita's hand. She immediately disappeared with it and went into the barn where she could read it unseen.

Antonio called, "Jose, come outside for a minute."

When Jose opened the door, the burly guard quickly grabbed him by his arms and moved him briskly toward the car. The driver leaped out of the car to help subdue Jose as he struggled to shake loose.

Antonio called to those inside the house with a measured voice. "The soldiers are here to take Jose back to camp," he shouted. "He is in some difficulty there, which we haven't had time to explain. I will personally see that he gets back to Trujillo for the funeral."

That said, Antonio ran to help the guards push Jose into the back of the car. Any resistance by Jose was overcome. He was silenced when the guard picked up the cloth that had been used as a blindfold and wound it tightly around his head and into his mouth. Next, he pushed Jose's face against the back of the seat.

"Move out," Antonio commanded, getting in the front seat of the car on the passenger's side. The driver put the car in gear and began the short drive toward the road.

"Stop!" shouted Marisa as she ran after them. "Antonio, you owe us an explanation. You can't take your brother away like that! I don't care what he's done! His mother has just died!"

Bonita had nearly finished reading Jose's note when she heard the commotion. She ran from the barn and dashed up beside Marisa. Ramon stood immobilized inside the house, wondering what on earth Jose had done. Jorge had already departed in his car to notify Father Augustin about Maria's death. Miguel and Angel were too young and confused to comprehend the meaning of the turmoil about them.

"Stop the car," Antonio said to the driver, "but be ready to go at a moment's notice."

To the guard he ordered, "Secure the prisoner." The guard covered Jose's face and upper body with a blanket and then leaned against him in such a way that it would be difficult for those outside the car to see him.

"They're taking Jose to some camp," Marisa cried. Bonita was set to show her Jose's note at that moment; then she hesitated. She hadn't had time to digest the entire note, stopping before the last cryptic sentence.

Several questions paralyzed Bonita: *Is Antonio lying or telling the truth? Would she make Jose's plight worse by revealing the secret note to Marisa? What chance did two women have against three men? Hadn't Jose written not to challenge Antonio now? Would there be a better time when a strategy could be thought through?*

Antonio sought to calm them with reassuring words. "Don't worry. Jose will be here for the funeral. I'm required to carry out my orders. I must deliver him in person. Believe me; it will go far worse for him if he isn't returned."

"If you don't get Jose back here," Marisa shouted at Antonio, "I'll never forgive you!"

Bonita leveled a look at Antonio that could kill. "There'll be more than unforgiving if you don't return with him," she yelled with fierce determination.

Antonio tapped the driver on the shoulder. "Get going," he demanded. The car spun its wheels and roared out of the driveway and down the road. In less than a minute it was out of sight, covered by dust and dirt flying into the air.

"It isn't even noon yet, and already I've had enough trouble to last me for a lifetime," Marisa said to Bonita as she poured coffee to quiet their nerves. Jorge was still in town. Ramon was outside the house waiting for the arrival of the mortician, ready to help him take Maria's body in preparation for the funeral.

"We should have been more forceful," said Bonita with despair in her voice. "We could have jumped in front of the car and dared them to run over us."

"The driver probably would have done just that. Or, the guard would have manhandled us. I didn't like his looks. After all, what is death to them? They've seen plenty of it. Two more mangled bodies wouldn't have meant anything to them."

"This is a maddening quagmire, Marisa. I feel so helpless. That guard looked like he was smothering Jose, throwing what I think was a blanket over him."

"If Antonio doesn't get Jose back here, I'll never speak to him again. Why does my oldest brother have to be so obedient to authority? He didn't have to drag Jose all the way back to his camp. He could have gone into the Plaza Mayor and telephoned his commandant from there. He could have explained about mother's death over the telephone."

"Maybe we should have all jumped in Jorge's car and given them chase," said Bonita, still trying to figure out what could have been done.

"Jorge had already left in it to see Father Augustin," reminded Marisa. "Our beat-up old car probably wouldn't have kept up with them anyway. It's too rundown to be chasing military cars over dirt roads."

"Antonio's sudden move gave him the upper hand and we . . . I let him seize the moment to make his move. He showed a side of himself I haven't seen before. You're his sister, Marisa. What do you think he's up to?"

"He's very ambitious, Bonita. Antonio became a lieutenant about a year ago. Last time he was here to see Mama, he told me he's hoping to become a major or a colonel in the army whenever the war is over. I didn't say anything then. I didn't want to get into political affairs at that time. I'm sure I shocked him with my opinions this morning."

Bonita produced Jose's note. "Read this, Marisa. Jose slipped this message to me just before they took him away. I was in the barn starting to read his note when Antonio and the guards were hustling Jose into their car."

Marisa read the note, and then said, "I suspected something wasn't right when Jose and Antonio showed up together last night. They may be brothers, but a liberal Republican and a conservative Nationalist officer don't go off joyriding together at night, not while there's a war going on between them."

She handed the note back to Bonita. "This explains Jose's 'difficulty' as Antonio put it," Marisa continued. "It also explains Antonio's behavior. Maybe he believed he had to produce Jose or get a rebuke from his commanding officer, or worse, get a demotion. Too bad, I don't care. Antonio lied to us. I'm still mad at him."

"What do we do now?"

"What can we do but wait, Bonita. How far would any of us get if we went to Badajoz and demanded Jose's release? I hate to say this, but now he is in Antonio's hands, and we can do nothing except depend on him."

"Could Ramon do something – anything?" asked Bonita.

The two looked at Ramon outside in the yard, then at each other, and broke into a kind of laughter that conveyed pure desperation.

Chapter 9
Mother Maria, the Storyteller

Jose, Antonio, and the two soldiers were lost each in his own thoughts as their car headed into the Badajoz prison camp. The driver and the guard had expressed their sorrow to Antonio about his mother's death. Aware that Jose was Antonio's brother and also grieving, they said the same thing to him.

The noise of rifle shots ricocheted off the walls of the camp as they drove inside.

"Another execution," murmured the driver to Antonio. "Won't it ever stop?"

"Not as long as this war goes on," Antonio answered. "Both sides are using executions as a way of eliminating their enemy; it reduces the number of soldiers required to guard them. How do you like your duty at this camp? Wouldn't you rather be at the front?"

"Not if the front is always like it was here at Badajoz," responded the driver. "I was relieved when I was told I would stay here, but I suppose I'll be ready to push on after a few more weeks."

"I'd rather get to the front," said the guard in the back seat with Jose. "This duty is all right for a while, but I miss the action where the fighting is. I hope I'm sent to Talavera. By the time I get there, I bet we'll have taken the town. Can you imagine the look on some Republican bastard's face when he telephones Talavera from Madrid, and he's answered by a Moroccan?"

The three Nationalist soldiers laughed at that prospect. Jose grudgingly smiled.

The guard had removed the tightly-drawn cloth that stifled Jose's voice and relaxed the pressure he had put on his prisoner as they left Marisa's house.

Jose turned to the guard and said, "I appreciate your loosening the hold you had on me. I don't think you realize how much strength you have."

"Lieutenant, your brother is certainly very polite," said the guard.

"His mother taught him well," replied Antonio. "Just don't get into a political argument with him."

Not wanting to get into any political debate at this moment, Jose said to the guard, "I thought you were going to rip my arms off when you led me to the car and then suffocate me when you threw that blanket over me."

"Little brother," the guard replied, mimicking Antonio's disdainful name for Jose, "you got light treatment from me. You should see what I usually do to prisoners. Your brother here made it easier for you than you know."

Jose wanted to ask the guard: *Did my brother coach you to make that statement?* Instead, he left the question unasked. He could not determine when Antonio was being honest and when he was being deceptive with him.

The car stopped and all got out. Antonio turned to Jose and said, "The guard will take you back to your room. You should know the camp commandant, Captain Barcena, means business when it comes to running a detention camp. Your trial is scheduled to begin at any time. I need to learn exactly when it is. I don't know whether either of us will be permitted to attend mother's funeral. All I can say is: I'll try to get permission. When I find out, I'll come to your room as soon as I can. I want to talk with you some more about your situation here."

"Antonio, I was never part of a firing squad," asserted Jose as they parted.

The prisoner and the guard walked to Jose's cell. The guard looked at Jose's civilian garments and abruptly began snarling words in a menacing tone.

"Nationalists despise men in nonmilitary clothing. A man not in military uniform these days must be a sissy or queer."

"I had a uniform," Jose protested, "but a Nationalist officer ordered me to change into civilian clothes. Keep in mind I had a dying mother to see."

"All the more reason to wear a military uniform," informed the guard.

As Jose entered the cell, the guard sent his prisoner reeling to the floor with an unanticipated blow to the back. Jose lay there, spread-eagled and laboring for breath. Before he could get up, several vicious kicks were delivered to the ribs. The guard picked up Jose and shoved him against the wall, holding him with a tight grip.

"I won't break any bones this time," he grinned, breathing heavily into Jose's face. "Those were little love taps just to remember me by. Next time we do business with you, you'll thank God you're alive each morning. By the end of the day, you'll wish you were dead. One of these days, you'll have your wish."

Having made his point, the guard threw Jose to the floor again and left the room.

Jose lay on the floor of his cell for several minutes before attempting to move. The guard's sudden assault reminded him of the monstrous brutality Felipe had received. However, to Jose the relative discomfort from his tender ribs and sore back told him that he had merely gotten 'light treatment,' as his guard had called it. He pulled himself up to a cot where he rested his aching body.

So much had happened in so short a time. Dragged from a prison cell to endure expected torture only to learn he had been 'saved' by his oldest brother, the mysterious night ride to Trujillo, discovering his mother had not long to live, his unanticipated meeting with Bonita, the pilgrimage he promised to take for his mother, the contentious political debates, the shock of his mother's death and subsequent pangs of remorse, the forced return to prison, and now the brutish behavior of the guard – all this weighed heavily on Jose's mind.

Desperate to escape these thoughts, Jose reflected, *Maybe I should focus on my mother's pilgrimage journey, something I would like to do. It could take my mind off these pains. Was her request a plea or an order? Even if I wasn't in prison, how would I ever get to Santiago de Compostela? It's hundreds of kilometers away and a war is being fought all over Spain.*

Maria's death had occurred merely hours ago, yet that seemed to make her pilgrimage wish all the more powerful.

While he was growing up in as the youngest of four children, Jose remembered his mother Maria telling the story of Saint James and the religious journey carried on in his name. Whether it was myth or not, one undisputed fact was the belief that the Apostle James had been buried on the site which eventually became the cathedral at Santiago. James and his brother John, sons of Zebedee, were among the twelve men that Jesus had called to be his disciples.

"They were fishermen," Maria would say, "just like the Galicians who live in the region next to us, and Jesus called them to become 'fishers of men.' After his death on the cross, Jesus appeared to his apostles and sent them forth with the commission to go and make disciples of all nations."

Jose could picture his mother in his mind's eye now years later and hear her voice reciting the story. She would use a map to trace the route James sailed from Palestine at the eastern end of the Mediterranean Sea to the Iberian

Peninsula. According to tradition, he landed in southern Spain, carrying out his mission and using the scallop shell to hold water for the baptism of new converts.

"Saint James went to Galicia, and there he met resistance. He returned to the Holy Land. The Bible tells of King Herod persecuting Christians at this time. Herod had James arrested and 'put to death with the sword,' the first of Jesus' disciples to suffer martyrdom. His body and head were thrown outside the walls of the city to be devoured by ravenous animals."

At this point in his recollections, Jose thought of how all four Martinez children made ugly sounds to go along with that grotesque sight, requiring their mother to restrain them in order to go on with the story.

"The followers of James rescued his remains. Although he was dead, his head was somehow reattached to his body and placed on a ship bound for Spain."

Even the devout Maria found parts of the story hard to accept as true. As strong a believer as she was, she did not expect Jose and his siblings to take particular events strictly on faith.

"The essential meaning of the story was the important thing, not various details that could be argued one way or another," she would explain before continuing with the legend.

"Sailing the length of the Mediterranean Sea, the ship went around Gibraltar and went up the coast, ending at a Roman port near today's city of Padron. James' followers in Galicia took the body and requested permission to bury the dead saint from a pagan ruler, Queen Lupa." Maria had to make clear the word 'pagan' was a person who did not believe in God and then admonish them not to call others pagan because you couldn't know the true nature of their belief.

"After several miracles occurred, including the conversion of Queen Lupa, James' body was taken inland to a deserted cemetery and placed in an abandoned crypt. A chapel was built over the spot. Local Christians cared for the tomb for a while, but it gradually fell into ruin. Bushes and weeds covered the site and all traces of chapel and crypt disappeared.

"Nothing was heard of the burial place of Saint James for over seven hundred years. The Visigoths replaced the Romans on the Iberian Peninsula during the fourth and fifth centuries. The Visigoths had adopted the Christian religion, even though they were considered barbarians." Another warning came from storyteller Maria, this time not to call others barbarian.

"Christianity became the most important religion throughout the Iberian peninsula. However, when the Moors conquered vast stretches of Iberia, it became an Islamic stronghold. The Muslims allowed small groups of Christians to live in peace – but under the political rule of the Moors. The Spaniards won a victory at Covadonga to the east of us in east Asturias in 718, a battle that was to be the starting point of an eight hundred-year campaign to win back the country for Christianity – the Reconquest of Spain. In the year 813, a Christian hermit in Galicia heard angels singing from above. Their voices directed him to a star beaming a bright light from the sky to a spot on an overgrown field."

Jose was the child who would say in wonder to his mother, "The hermit must have thought the light was the same as the Christmas star."

Maria would smile and go on. "The hermit notified the local bishop at Padron who investigated and ordered the place cleared of bushes growing over it. Excavation began. The digging soon revealed the chapel and crypt. Inside the tomb, the bishop declared the bones belonged to the Apostle James.

"Stories of finding these bones quickly spread. Money poured in for the building of a church and monastery. A city began to grow around it. In those days, great importance was attached to the physical remains of a saint. Skulls were of the first order in the ranking of relics. Next in value came a hand or a finger, which would be used for blessings. The Muslims did the same thing; they used an arm of the Prophet Mohammed stored in a mosque in Cordoba. It's not surprising that the bones of Saint James took on tremendous significance. Christian soldiers had wearied of watching Muslims charge into battle with a relic of the Prophet Mohammed. Now, the Iberian Christians had a relic of their own."

Jose recalled thinking there were times his mother's story would grow fantastic. She related an account of a legendary battle between Christians and Moslems that took place at Clavijo in the valley of the Ebro River. "A king of Galicia put together an army to combat the Moors. On the first day of the battle, the Christian army was badly defeated and retreated in disarray. That night, the king had a dream in which Santiago promised him victory. James, himself, would ride into battle. The king told his men about his dream. With renewed courage, they hurled themselves into the fight. Being true to his word, Saint James charged out of the sky, leading the Christian army and wearing a scallop shell around his neck. Thousands of Muslim warriors were slain that day, many losing their heads as the Apostle James had lost his in Jerusalem. Cheered by the appearance of their saint ahead of them, the Christian soldiers finished the rout shouting 'Santiago!' From that point on, the same cry would be heard whenever the Spanish engaged the foe. James was now *Santiago Mata-moros*, Saint James, Moor-slayer."

No Greater Love

By now, Maria's children would be wide-eyed with amazement with Antonio proclaiming: "Someday I'm going to be like *Santiago Mata-moros*!"

"The word spread about the victory over the Moors," continued Maria. "Admiration of Saint James flourished. Spain had found its patron saint. The church at Santiago became a Cathedral. Slowly, pilgrims started to appear. Beginning like drips of water, the pilgrimage soon became a flood. From Spain and throughout Western Europe, thousands of pilgrims walked the *Camino de Santiago*. European ideas and culture came into the peninsula."

Maria spiced her story with accounts of disasters that would strike. "Bandits preyed upon defenseless pilgrims. Churches and monasteries received offerings, and those riches made them a target for the Moors coming north in search of plunder. The city of Santiago de Compostela itself was not spared. Al-Mansur, a Muslim general from Cordoba, announced a *jihad*, a holy war, against Christianity. He marched his troops into an empty city; the population of Santiago had fled to the mountains where the Muslims could not follow them. Al-Mansur spared the bones of Saint James or perhaps he could not find them, but the Moors looted and burned the city. He destroyed the church, keeping only the giant bells, carried all the way to Cordoba on the backs of captive Galicians. Two centuries later, Christian soldiers conquered Cordoba and forced Muslim prisoners to carry the bells back to Santiago."

"Served them right," Antonio had said, but Jose argued with his older brother that the Muslims of two hundred years later didn't have anything to do with taking the bells from Santiago.

Maria was not quite done with her story. "The number of pilgrims swelled to millions during the Middle Ages. Christians needed to be defended from Moors and from being robbed and mistreated by bandits. That's why the Military Order of Santiago was created.

"Hospices were set up along the pilgrimage route to provide shelter and food to the travelers. Businesses developed to furnish the pilgrims with religious symbols and other necessities of life. Merchants, artisans, innkeepers, and traders as well as priests lined the main pilgrimage routes to offer their services to the travelers that flowed by."

The story of the Saint James legend told to Jose as a child came under scrutiny in his adult life. Perhaps it was in the conflict with Islam where religion and the military became inexorably intertwined in the Spanish national character. Soldiers in military orders took religious vows. Priests, monks, and bishops joined armies and sometimes participated in fighting. Crusades brought them together. The image of Saint James, a sword in his right hand and the Cross in his other, expressed the highest conception of Spanish manhood.

This was the mental picture that attracted Antonio and bothered Jose the most. Jose wouldn't deny the allure the portrait presented of the virile but virtuous believer; however, here was a contradiction that didn't fit the message Jesus had actually taught. Jesus had not aspired to be the commander of a mighty military force ready to do battle with the Roman conquerors. When he could have summoned an army of angels, he told his followers that those who take up the sword would perish by the sword. Jesus submitted to savage scourging and the cruelty of crucifixion, dying as a common criminal before being raised from the dead. Jose was conflicted by the machismo nature of his culture: the notion that to be a man, he must exhibit a hard-bitten toughness prepared to wreak havoc or wage war on those who did not share his own religious and political convictions.

A sudden insight lifted Jose out of his memories of Maria's story of the pilgrimage to Santiago de Compostela. It was a revelation he could not deny.

I'm not going to be able to get my mother's pilgrimage idea out of my mind – until somehow, someday, I actually do it.

Chapter 10
Captain Barcena's Decision

Antonio sat before the camp commandant in the early evening, not knowing about Jose's rough treatment by his guard. The captain offered condolences to Antonio and began discussing the situation created by his mother's death and Jose's upcoming trial before a military tribunal.

"It looks like a clear-cut case, Lieutenant," explained Captain Barcena. "Three people in town will testify that the prisoner had participated in the execution of political group members supporting the Nationalist side. I'm sorry for you that he is your brother, but facts are facts. We've shot men for less."

"Sir, all I can do is to ask for your permission to postpone my brother's trial for three days and allow him to return for our mother's funeral. No one in the family knows he is a prisoner here – nor do they need to know. I am willing again to take responsibility for bringing him back here for trial and judgment. Trujillo is no more than three hours away. We're not talking about great distances."

"Lieutenant, your request is understandable, but highly unusual under the circumstances. We're fighting a war, and funerals often take second place out of necessity. Your brother got to see your mother before she died. He probably would have been dead two weeks ago if you hadn't intervened."

Antonio knew he was stretching his luck in asking permission for a second trip to Trujillo for Jose. His experience had been that once a military commander made a decision, convincing him to change his mind was about impossible. However, there was one last piece of strategy to try.

"Sir, would there be any difference if my brother could be persuaded to join our side, if not now, eventually? Others have done it. There is plenty of motivation for him to do it. Obviously, he is aware he is likely to be executed.

He values his life. He loves a woman who wants to marry him. I have reason to believe he has useful information he could give us at some time."

Captain Barcena gave a skeptical smile as if he almost expected an approach like this.

Antonio went on. "This may not be as far-fetched as it sounds. My brother could be wavering. I've talked with him over the past twenty-four hours on two occasions, when we were in the car on our way to Trujillo and at our sister's house. He was more agreeable with me in the car than with the family where he felt he had to put up a good front. He has told me several times how stupid certain Republican leaders have been and will likely be in the future. He was disgusted at the so-called training he received when he enlisted in the Republican militia. He told me the weapon he was given was antiquated and just about useless. I can't promise my brother would change sides immediately, but I would like to try. I think, given enough time, he could be persuaded he chose the wrong side."

"Lieutenant, you started down this line of reasoning yesterday when you were given permission to let him see his dying mother. I allowed it, not that I thought you could bring him around to join us, but because you so obviously wanted to please your mother. Now, she is dead; she can't be pleased any more. And, let's say you can prevail upon your brother to switch sides. I don't know who I despise more, the enemy or deserters willing to change their allegiance to save their own skins."

"I understand and fully agree with what you are saying, sir. I truly believe Jose is one of those misguided young men, but will be all right when he matures. Who was it that said if you're not socialist at twenty, you have no heart; but, if you're not a conservative at fifty, you have no head?"

"He must have been some politician from somewhere, no doubt some old conservative," the captain volunteered. "But, we can't wait for your brother to turn fifty."

"I don't know why my brother enlisted in the Republican militia, and I don't think he knows either. I don't see him as a fighter; he's a writer. I'm not saying he isn't brave. If he fought here at Badajoz, he was part of a force that gave fierce resistance. That brings up another point. He claims he wasn't here until the day of the battle and was captured almost as soon as he got here. If that's true, sir, he couldn't have been part of a firing squad executing Nationalist supporters."

"That's for the court to decide, Lieutenant. He will be given the opportunity to tell his side of the story. Your brother's trial will be one of the last cases to be tried here, possibly the very last one. We've got urgent business northeast of here. The camp is being turned over to local authorities. We can't wait for another trial three days from now."

"Is there any way for a Republican prisoner who was with him to verify his story?"

"I doubt you could find one. All of them are dead, at least the ones we know about, which is why we're preparing to move out in a few days. I can't think of anyone around here to testify for him. Even if they could, they'd be too busy trying to save themselves or doing what you are proposing for your brother, claiming they are ready to serve us. You'd be surprised how many have tried to strike a deal with us. It hasn't worked for them and I don't see how it will work for your brother."

"It's hopeless for him then," said Antonio, standing up. He came to attention and saluted his military superior. "Thank you for hearing me out, Captain. I would have been disgusted with myself if I hadn't tried to come to my brother's aid."

Lieutenant Antonio Francisco Martinez Garcia turned and started to leave the room.

"Just a moment, Lieutenant," he heard. "Permission granted."

Antonio turned around again. Captain Barcena rose from his desk. He came over to Antonio and put a hand on his shoulder.

"Antonio, war is a brutal affair, and you have to be rock hard almost all of the time. However, war doesn't mean a military man must be completely without feelings toward his own men or even the enemy. I am not unaware that you, yourself, want to attend your mother's funeral, but you didn't bring that up. You didn't ask for yourself. You asked only for your brother, knowing full well if he didn't go, you weren't likely to be going either. Despite your feelings about your mother's death, you elected to obey my orders. I don't always see that kind of discipline, even among men above your rank."

Antonio stood there at first doubtful that he had heard the captain's decision correctly and then concluding that he had been rewarded for his compliance with a superior officer's judgment.

Captain Barcena was not done in his praise of Antonio.

"I also appreciate the fact that you brought your brother back here to Badajoz, knowing it could mean his death. It would have been so easy to let him slip away and blame it on the guards. I will explain this whole matter to the court. I believe they will go along with my decision."

"I am very grateful to you, Captain," said Antonio. "I can't thank you enough."

"In the meantime, work on your brother, Antonio. Maybe, you *can* bring him around."

Chapter 11
Ramon

Needing sleep after a short night and an exhausting day, Marisa's family headed for bed in the back rooms of the house as night began to settle in. Bonita called to them from the front steps, saying she would join them as soon as she was done watching the last rays of a sunset. She was tormented with the fear she had seen Jose for the last time. His life was in the hands of his brother and if not Antonio's, then under the control of some camp commandant unknown to her.

Nationalist prison camps had a nasty reputation for summary executions. Would Antonio come back to them alone, faking or honestly feeling remorse because he hadn't been able to save Jose's life? Restful slumber for Bonita would not come easy tonight. She and Jose had been in danger before, but it was nothing like this. Antonio aspired to higher military rank, yet he seemed to care for the people in his family. She remembered feeling almost as bad for Antonio as she had for Jose when they discovered Maria had died. Antonio's grief was genuine. It was entirely possible Antonio had enough sensitivity for his family to do whatever he could to bring Jose back for the funeral. That appeared to be the only hope she had.

"I've had enough trauma for one day," said a voice in front of her. The voice belonged to Ramon who came up to the steps and sat next to Bonita. He had returned from an evening stroll. "The walk was relaxing, but I'm not quite ready to call it a day this early. By the way, how are your parents, Bonita?"

"They're fine," she said without thinking. Caught up in the swirl of Maria's last days and Jose's predicament, her own family hadn't been on her mind since she left them in the Galician town of Corcubion near Finisterre, or Land's End, reputed to be the westernmost place on the European continent.

"I've always wanted to visit Galicia," Ramon said, "especially in the summer when the sun is so strong here in Extremadura and the heat is so intense. The green fields and ocean breezes must be a wonderful cure for those of us who bake in this semi-desert."

"You'll have to visit us sometime, whenever this awful war gets over," said Bonita in an offhand manner. She had one thing on her mind: rescuing Jose. "Ramon," she asked, "is there anything that any of us can do to make sure Jose will be back here for the funeral?"

"Let Antonio handle it," Ramon responded. "If anyone can get him released, it's Antonio. He's got connections, power, finesse." His answer reflected the same conclusion she and Marisa had reached before.

Ramon changed the subject of their conversation.

"You know, Bonita," he began, "I've always admired you – from a distance. I have longed to be closer to you. You possess so many characteristics I find attractive in women. I can understand why Jose likes you so much. But, Jose isn't here. Don't misunderstand. I hope he beats whatever charge has been lodged against him. Right now, there is not much we can do but comfort each other. At this moment, there's only you and me."

Bonita felt uneasy. She didn't like the veiled implication of Ramon's words. He fancied himself as some kind of modern-day Don Juan. At one time, Jose had told her he believed the only real interest Ramon had in life was sex. Ramon's relationships with women seemed to focus on designing ways of getting them into bed. Sometimes, Ramon would expound on the subject to his brothers when they were alone together.

"When it comes to mastering women, Don Juan always succeeds. His sexual impulses are inexhaustible; they are powerful and cannot be denied. As for women, while they won't confess to this, they secretly want to be ravished against their wishes by a Don Juan. And I," he would sigh with false modesty, "a poor imitation, only wish to accommodate them."

Jose would only laugh at Ramon's showmanship, but Antonio would admonish him by trying to demolish the magnetism of Don Juan. "You know, Ramon," he would lecture, "Don Juan is incapable of love; he simply wants to possess women. And, by possessing them, he destroys them. In doing this, however, he eventually destroys himself."

"But, what fun, what pleasure, he has in his incredible pursuit," Ramon would say in his defense. Later, alone with Jose, he would judge Antonio to be incapable of human love, perhaps loving only an untouched ideal such as Our Lady of Victory.

Bonita remembered an appraisal Jose had made of Ramon. "He, along with Don Juan, is the type of Spaniard that flourishes in periods of lawlessness and anarchy," he reasoned. "Ramon talks of honor which he and all Spanish regard highly, but then he usually ignores it in practice."

Bonita had come up with a different interpretation. "I think the two – the real person and the mythological figure – are afraid."

"Afraid of what?"

"Afraid of being inadequate, sexually inept, maybe impotent."

"Ramon is not an old man," protested Jose.

"Fear can strike at any age," said Bonita. "Fear can paralyze, shut down any system. He may be like those men who only get their satisfactions from prostitutes they can dominate with money and contempt."

"That's pathetic, Bonita!"

"Please don't tell him, Jose, but I find Ramon rather pathetic in some respects, his extravagant interest in sex being the main one."

Ramon's voice brought Bonita out of her reverie. "Do you like flamenco, Bonita? It's an exciting dance. I think it's the most erotic dance in the world. There's the staccato beat of the feet. The man and the woman are as close as they can get to each other, but they never touch. If they did, the seductive tension would be broken and the dance would be spoiled. I'd love to dance flamenco with you, Bonita."

"You'll have to find another woman, Ramon. I haven't danced flamenco style. The best female dancers are older than I am. We don't do flamenco where I come from."

Ramon quickly followed with another question. "Are all the young women of Galicia as beautiful as you, Bonita? If that is true, I intend to go there as quickly as I can."

Bonita blushed and dismissed his words with a wave of her hand. Ramon wouldn't stop.

"I'll be completely direct and honest with you, Bonita. We need to get right to the point. Ever since I have known you, I've wanted to make love to you. Every time I see you, you're with Jose. I can't tell you how frustrated I've been. But, now, we are together without Jose. Such an opportunity may not come up again."

I hope it never does, she thought.

Then she said, "Please, Ramon, let's not get into this. It's been an exhausting day." He didn't seem at all affected by the death of his mother, as he was earlier. He appeared unconcerned about what could be considered the abduction of his younger brother. She wanted to tell him that he was thinking only of himself with no regard for the feelings of others.

Ramon moved closer to her. A Don Juan, after all, is not easily dissuaded.

He took her hands and looked into her eyes. "You are truly beautiful, Bonita. Just like your name. You have a wonderful name. Wasn't yours the name newspapers gave the Republic in its first days, *la nina bonita* – the pretty girl?"

She stood up. He continued to hold her hands.

"You have a beautiful body, too, Bonita. Did anyone ever tell you that? I'm telling you, because it's true." Then, he rose, took her by the waist, and pressed her to his chest.

She tried to back away from him. He tightened his grip on her. "Remember the flamenco dancers, Ramon," she gasped, trying to move away. "The best ones don't touch each other."

"Oh, how I love your quick sense of humor and your charm, Bonita. How you weave a spell over me! I love everything about you." He drew her closer again. "I love to feel the warmth of your body, touch the round curve of your shoulders, press against the softness of your breasts, take in the smell of your hair, look upon your flashing eyes."

"Ramon, please stop! You forget I'm pledged to Jose. He has pledged himself to me. We love each other. We would be married by now if it wasn't for this wretched war."

Marriage never stopped Don Juan, thought Ramon, *and she's not officially married to him.* He began to unbutton her blouse. He felt the passion and excitement rising within him, and he was more determined than ever to have her.

"This has got to stop!" Bonita exclaimed. She had wanted to let him down gently, but he was becoming uncontrollable. "Look, Ramon, we've always gotten along with each other. We're friends; let's leave it that way. Anything more will spoil a good relationship."

"Our relationship lacks something good, Bonita."

Seeing the glittering lust gleaming in his eyes, Bonita abruptly tore herself away from his grasp and gathered all the hateful scorn she could convey in her voice.

"No, Ramon, don't touch me," she burst forth savagely. "You make me sick, you ... you're ... pathetic!"

She bolted through the door and slammed it in his face, and hurried through the house to her bedroom. Ramon started to enter the house, but he was too late; sounds could too easily be heard in nearby rooms.

He cursed her, spitting out the words "Galician whore," and slumped down on the outside steps.

Bonita crawled into her bed. She pulled up a sheet and began to weep softly, muffling the sounds in her pillow. She was furious with Ramon, and she supposed he was furious with her. It took a long time for her to calm down. Finally, her thoughts turned to the young man she loved.

Jose, Jose – will I ever see you again? she cried to herself in despair. Too much had happened that day: the suddenness of Maria's death, the forcible seizing of Jose, the coarse sexuality of Ramon, and now the loneliness of the night.

How can Jose be so different from his brothers? Bonita wondered.

Ramon is a libertine, thinking only of his own selfish needs. All he wants is power over women, to use them, and then cast them away.

Antonio is harder to figure out. What makes him so driven in his strict, severe way? He, too, is consumed by power, only in a different way. He is willing to serve the powerful, but he wants it over others, too – typical fascist!

Jose is so compassionate and gentle, compared to those two.

Bonita worried occasionally that she and Jose were losing the hopeful optimism of their earlier days – who wouldn't in the corrupted, brutal world in which they lived? Somehow, though, she knew they would not lose all of their idealism and succumb to complete discouragement.

We love each other too much for that, she believed. *Jose has too much regard for me, as I have for him. There will come a time when we will be joined together in marriage, officially, and we will raise a family and live a complete life as God intended it to be. A good marriage is really what a Spanish woman wants from a man; that sounds terribly traditional, but it's something Ramon doesn't understand and Jose does.*

As she consoled herself with these thoughts, the horrendous events of the day slowly faded into sleep.

CHAPTER 12
TEMPTATION

The day after Antonio had received permission to attend mother Maria's funeral, he went to Jose's cell. As he walked in, he noticed Jose nursing some bruised ribs and a sore back.

"Your guard gave me a few of his little 'love taps' as he called them," Jose remarked. "Spare me his warm-hearted embrace. Does he enjoy beating prisoners when he can't shoot them?"

"Did you provoke him in any way?"

"No, I said nothing to cause a pounding like that. He struck me in the back with all his might. I didn't see it coming. I fell to the floor and got several swift kicks in the ribs. He told me he would really work me over before my execution."

Antonio hadn't come to commiserate with his youngest brother. He was irritated that the guard had acted brutally because he wanted to maneuver Jose into a different frame of mind.

"Jose," he said to his brother, "that guard overstepped his authority, and he will be disciplined for his actions."

"Let it go, Antonio. If you say anything to him, he'll seek some kind of retribution when you're not around. I know the type. I've run across a few avengers in my newspaper work. It's not a pleasant life, trying to avoid them."

"All right, Jose. We've got other things to do. First, here's good news. The commandant has given permission for both of us to attend mother's funeral. Again, you are my prisoner. The same rules apply as before. It wasn't easy to gain that approval. The captain trusts me and, while you may not have any warm feelings for a Nationalist officer, he actually had some concern for you. Of course, he expressed his sorrow for the loss of our mother, but he also understood the hard time you're going through."

"Your captain must be a rare humanitarian for a military man, especially one who serves Franco, Antonio."

"Wars are a ruthless business, Jose. Your mission is to kill the enemy, but that doesn't mean a military person must banish all human feeling, even toward men who are on the other side," replied Antonio, paraphrasing Captain Barcena. "There are fine men in the Nationalist army and many express ideals you may not have considered."

"How do you put together noble ideals with terror and fear? You've wondered why I've been loyal to the Republic and I wonder why the National Front attracts you. What ideals do you fight for, Antonio?"

Antonio hesitated answering, thinking a political discussion would not serve his interests at this time. It seemed to him that as Jose's situation became more dangerous, his brother was more determined to instigate contentious political arguments with his words growing less cautious.

Hearing nothing, Jose pressed his argument further. "I can't get around the opinion that Nationalist leaders strive for an authoritarian dictatorship that they can't get any other way, except through plain crude force and physical coercion."

Normally, Antonio would have strenuously denied this strong assertion by his younger brother. However, he was on a mission to turn Jose at least partially away from his partisan preferences as a means of his survival, and this purpose could not be accomplished by an emotional outburst. Antonio kept a calm voice.

"All right, Jose. There are ideas behind what you claim is only force and coercion. Keep in mind that ideas contain their own power – they have a quiet sort of compulsion. A good place to start is with the Falange's 'Twenty Seven Points.' Some of its guiding principles are the unity of our people, a strong military that secures our independence, a state serving the fatherland, and state guidance of all economic producers into corporate syndicates."

"Sounds like the start of Fascism to me," was Jose's reaction.

"That term can be endlessly debated," responded Antonio. "Our leaders don't use the word. We're not an imitation of Italian or German fascism."

"But, you do take inspiration from them," argued Jose. "I'd rather draw inspiration from democracies such as France, Britain, and the United States."

"We believe human liberty is eternal, but people are free only through being a part of a powerful, sovereign nation," said Antonio. "The Falange recognizes private property, the right to work, and access to higher education. Perhaps because of this, a number of former liberals and socialists have joined

- N -
FRANCE
Cercubion
Finisterre
Santiago de Compostela
Oviedo
Mieres
PICOS DE EUROPA
Bilbao
Roncesvalles
Vigo
ATLANTIC OCEAN
Braga
Porto
Salamanca
Madrid
Spain
Barcelona
Coimbra
Talavera de la Reina
Toledo
Nazaré
Cáceres
Trujillo
Valencia
Portugal
Lisbon
Merida
Badajoz
Córdoba
Seville
MEDITERRANEAN SEA
Gibraltar (UK)

our ranks. We advocate relief from the misery suffered by rural masses. We will nationalize banking and public services. We condemn the materialism of both capitalism and Communism. Our movement will restore a spiritual reconstruction of the country."

"I know, Antonio, you don't have to cover all twenty-seven points. I poured over them, like all students did in our political studies courses. Some students became members of the Falange as a result, but not me. Now, again I ask, what makes *you*, personally, support the National Front as avidly as you do?"

"To me, more than anything else, politically speaking, this is a fight between the forces of unity and anarchy. Nationalists seek to unify the country. They speak of one Spain, united as a nation. Republicans are wrong to encourage independence for Catalonia, Galicia, and the Basques – and they do it just to get their support. Spain must *not* become a land where every region achieves its goals without any regard for the consequences affecting the entire nation. Every great country must put the national interest first, and if they don't, they are no longer great."

"All right, Antonio. Unity certainly has its place in a world of nation-states. Nationalism can be positive; it can bring people together and not be an oppressive desire to rule over others. But, remember, Spaniards everywhere tend to be more kindly disposed toward their *patria chica* – their native town or province. The region comes first and then the nation. I have sympathized with Basque and Catalan separatists without fully supporting their extreme demands. I believe granting them a certain degree of regional autonomy is the best answer; it can even reinforce national unity. That's quite different from separatism. As long as the nation respects the rights of individuals and allows regional traditions based on their *fueros*, its foremost priority is the national interest."

"I'm pleased to hear your last words," noted Antonio, unable to resist a comment on Jose's final point. "A Nationalist couldn't have said it any better."

"Don't tell that to my friends," remarked Jose whimsically. "But, let's get away from philosophical principles and into pure politics. Where I have trouble with the National Front is this: Who gives voice to the national interest? Nationalist support comes from the wealthy landowners, big industrialists, a clerical elite, militarists, monarchists, even a few conservative intellectuals – all of whom have their own axe to grind. They talk of a national interest, but that disguises their own narrow interest."

Antonio could not accept Jose's evaluation of Nationalist support. "Every group in our cause accepts the idea of national supremacy," he protested. "That's why we are called Nationalist. Whenever liberals have dominated the Republic, they have not safeguarded foundations that should be conserved – namely, the religion of the Church, monarchy, and the military. These institutions serve the national interest and unite people as no others can. Leftists can't agree among themselves on what they want to build. How could they? They are too fractured to agree on much of anything. In the long run, they don't stand for anything."

"No, Antonio, they stand for quite a few ideals," Jose asserted. "They gather around such things as the freedoms of religious belief, political debate, peaceful assembly, and economic liberty plus freedom from hunger, terror, and oppression. Too often, groups backing the Nationalist cause have violated every one of those rights. Of course, freedom has its limits; I know it's not absolute. I believe our nation, given adequate time, can build a liberal democracy based upon toleration of those freedoms and not slide into lawlessness."

Antonio answered, "Toleration and freedom can be carried too far. When that happens, a nation falls into the lawlessness you hope to avoid. We've had that discussion, so let's turn to something else."

"All right, that's fine," concurred Jose, "What else?"

Antonio sought to take any harshness out of his voice, hoping to soften Jose's political biases. "Opposition to Soviet Communism. As Communists grow stronger in the Republic, you'll find their support of movements to obtain regional autonomy or actual separation is not really their goal, but rather a way to weaken us in preparation for a future takeover. The current leaders of the Republic will discover their Communist allies don't want independence for anyone. By accepting aid from Soviet Russia, the Republic is setting itself up for total domination by Joseph Stalin and the Bolsheviks."

"Most liberals have become wary of Stalin," countered Jose. "They think the Soviets want France and Britain in a war with Germany and Italy which would weaken all of those nations, so much so that it would leave Russia to pick up the pieces and be the strongest country in Europe."

"But, the leaders of the Republic welcome Soviet help," said Antonio, keeping his voice restrained. "They've made no secret of that."

"So far, Russia is the only country willing to help the Republic. The government's leadership wishes that were different, but Britain, France, and the United States remain neutral. Germany and Italy claim they are neutral, yet everyone knows they are sending aircraft, troops and weapons to the Nationalists. I'd rather the Republic not get aid from the Soviets, but the war would be lost if it didn't accept help from Russia."

"Jose, that help will ultimately undermine the Republic. If the Republican army wins, I firmly believe Spain will become a communist nation. Lenin predicted it and Stalin plots for it."

"But, Antonio, Spain becomes beholden to Hitler and Mussolini if the Nationalists win. Franco doesn't see that danger when he accepts aid from Germany and Italy. Already in Nazi Germany, we hear of a one-party system, political repression, brutal terror, concentration camps, persecution of Jews, and total control by a single leader. The Fascists in Italy pour castor oil down your throat if you don't agree with them."

"Franco isn't a Nazi or a Fascist, nor will he be either one in governing Spain. He will use Hitler and Mussolini, not be dominated by either one. He must get aid in order to win, which is the same reason the Republicans are trying to get help from Russia."

"We'll have to agree to disagree on this part of the argument," said Jose. "You say if Republicans win, Spain becomes Communist. I say if Nationalists win, Spain becomes Fascist. Neither of us believes our side will bring either state of affairs to our country, but we believe the other side will. Are there any more ideals in your platform?"

"Respect for our Church and its Christian religion, first and foremost," answered Antonio. "Most groups supporting the Republic are atheist or agnostic. Without belief in God, man's mind runs amuck. Communists say any method is all right as long as it advances their goal. The communist 'God,' if you will, is revolution. The Communist catechism says anything that hinders the revolution is criminal and anything that helps the revolution is ethical. Strange ethics, if you ask me. The Left gets nourishment from anti-Christian sentiments of groups like these."

"Well, Antonio, there are Christian liberals, believers in Christ as God who vote for candidates of the Left. The overwhelming majority of Leftists are not communist. As for communism, the Soviet Union is only the latest version. The idea isn't exactly new. The early Christians were communist, each one contributing and sharing in a common treasury. Some anarchists I've come into contact with, especially in rural areas, remind me of those Christians. They have few worldly possessions and adapt to a hard life. There is a quiet dignity about them that is visible in the peace and kindness shown to others."

Antonio fought to keep himself from getting overheated in partisan debate. To steady his nerves, he remained silent and confined himself to thoughts.

Doesn't Jose realize the danger he is in? He acts so innocent. Doesn't he care for his life? He's got a lot to live for. Bonita would be of no help; she's more of a zealot than he is. How do I find a way to break through the wall of misguided loyalties he's built up and reason with him?

Meanwhile, Jose was going on with his analytical recital. "I don't agree with the violence of some anarchists and their call for complete abolition of government; however I do believe there is a side of anarchism – call it a philosophical side – that is like a religion."

With that statement, Antonio nearly lost his composure. "The beliefs and practices of anarchists I've known are as far from religion as a person could get," he said with all the mildness he could bring into his voice.

"I didn't say anarchism is a religion, but it has characteristics similar to a religion. The anarchists believe they will inherit the earth in time and the rich bourgeoisie will ruin their own world before leaving their stage of history. They must have great faith in human perfectibility to believe we all can live in peace and harmony without a government."

"I haven't known any peaceful anarchists. All they do is throw bombs. Their words are just as explosive, too."

"Their verbal bombs make me think of the Old Testament prophets," said Jose. "Anarchists are scathing in their rejection of a corrupt political system and a deceitful Church. Yes, they give fiery speeches, but most anarchists I've known are more gentle and temperate than the average Spaniard."

"That might not be saying much," said Antonio, trying to bring an element of light-heartedness into the conversation. "You know the saying: 'three Spaniards, four arguments.'"

Jose smiled in recognition, but he wanted to finish his point. "The main difference between religion and anarchism is that one seeks the kingdom of heaven somewhere beyond and the other a kingdom of heaven here on earth. Skeptics say they're both crazy; maybe that's why they have something in common."

"Something to think about," agreed Antonio.

"Look, Antonio, there are up to two million anarchists in our country. Yes, they have an aggressive union. Where do they draw their support? It's the downtrodden and hunger-stricken that flock to the anarchists. How many meals are any of us away from doing something drastic we would later regret? Would you support the government when all it has ever done is take things away from you? No wonder they get violent at times."

"That violence is counter-productive to their interests. Any government is required to provide security for its people."

"Burning, pillaging, and killing is wrong such as in the Asturian miner's strike I wrote about, but the revolting punishment the government gave them as prisoners afterwards was inexcusable, despicable, carried well beyond the violence of the miners."

"I know, Jose," spoke the benign voice of Antonio, striving to sound as genuine as possible. "I read your newspaper article. I couldn't believe it at first; then I could, knowing some of the things father went through. The government denied it, then they justified the harsh treatment, and I knew the report you wrote was true even though most people didn't want to know."

Jose looked into his brother's eyes. "Thank you, Antonio" he said quietly. "You've never told me that before. I value those words."

Antonio sensed this moment might be the best time to bring up the subject for which he had tried to lay some groundwork. "Thanks from my brother is always welcome, Jose," he began. "I actually like talking about politics with you, but we need to put it aside for a while and discuss your problem here. I don't think you quite understand how close to execution you have been, or still are. No matter how innocent you actually are, the military court is apt to find you guilty."

"Do you believe I am innocent, Antonio?"

"Yes, I do. Somehow, I can't see you in a firing squad. You really don't belong in a Republican army, or *any* army. Were you coerced into joining the militia, Jose?"

"No, I can't honestly say that I was. I joined because I believed it was the right thing to do."

"Have you had any thoughts of regret since then?"

"Yes. Doesn't any soldier? You make a good case for national unity and independence from foreign control. Maybe someday, you'll convince me. That's the good thing about the freedom of a democracy; you have the right to speak out and think for yourself even if those ideas deviate from the ones of your family or friends – or the government."

"Well then, don't immediately respond to what I'm about to ask. Give it some thought." Antonio paused for emphasis. "Would you be willing to declare yourself a neutral, at least while the trial is going on? I'm not asking you to turn Nationalist just to save yourself or please me. I know you wouldn't do that. You've admitted you had misgivings about joining the Republican army. To show some wavering of your position might influence the court's decision – a reduced charge or sentence, possibly."

"As much as it might help me, Antonio, you and I know I'm not neutral in this civil war. I can't pose to be something I'm not."

"Not even to save your life? My brother, saving your life is what I'm trying to do. I said those very words when I first talked with you here."

"Yes, I remember." Jose was touched by his older brother's display of sincerity. Jose also remembered how Antonio had promised Bonita, Marisa, and Jorge to bring him back to Mama's funeral. Antonio had delivered on that promise; it would make him look good in the eyes of the family. Now, Antonio seemed to be moving on to something else.

Is he suggesting becoming neutral only to save my life? Jose couldn't shake the suspicion of some hidden motive in Antonio's behavior. Their political argument had been more reasoned and reserved than usual. It was so measured and so uncommon of debate they had engaged in before.

I'm in a prison cell, Jose reasoned to himself. *This is Antonio's territory. I'm not in an equal position with him. He's holding all the trump cards; I don't have any. I haven't heard him argue so calmly when he has such an obvious advantage. There must be something going on that I'm not aware of.*

Despite all the goodwill Antonio might show, Jose could not erase the notion that he was being manipulated.

The thought came to him: *Antonio will try to move me in stages to the other side. He's always wanted to control any situation he encounters in life, and he would want to control me along with it.*

A moment of silence had passed between them.

"Jose," Antonio said finally, with all the tenderness he could bring into the sound of his voice. "Think of Bonita and the wonderful life you could live with her. She is an exceptional person. I think the two of you are ideally suited to each other. I believe she would do anything for you. You are extremely fortunate to have found her."

Another trump card – both brothers were aware of that.

"Yes, I am," Jose replied with earnest feeling. "Bonita is a beautiful person, more than simply a pretty girl."

"Then think about what I said. Think about moving to a middle position, if only for a few days. It doesn't mean you are compromising your principles. I would not ask you to do that."

Jose wanted to think Antonio truly believed everything he was saying. There might have been a time when Jose would have taken Antonio's words at face value. Political turmoil and civil war had taken its toll. He had experienced too much from the conflicted world around him.

"Antonio, all I can say is I will carefully consider your idea. Don't think I'm not appreciative of the things you've done for me. I truly am. I can't go any further in my thinking at this time."

And that is where they left it. Antonio rose and walked to the door. "We'll talk some more, Jose" were the only words he spoke.

Chapter 13
The Funeral

Jose, Antonio, and the driver of the military car headed into the driveway of Marisa and Jorge's home after a late afternoon's trip from the Badajoz detention camp. Maria's funeral was one hour away. Antonio had left the roughneck guard out of consideration for Jose's feelings about him. Nothing further about Antonio's suggestion of neutrality had passed between the two brothers.

When walking to the car with Antonio, Jose had said, "Let me think some more about your idea. I'll make a decision when we get back to camp."

Antonio had hoped to take up the subject again, but decided not to press Jose any further. Antonio brought up the subject of the Olympic Games in Berlin. Jose countered with the People's Olympiad in Barcelona planned as a protest of the Nazi Olympics but cancelled upon the outbreak of the Nationalist uprising.

Bonita was the first to catch sight of the car as it rolled to a stop. She ran out of the house and hugged Jose ecstatically.

"Am I thrilled to see you!" she declared with heartfelt enthusiasm. "I prayed to God for this moment. I can't believe it. You're actually here!"

Jose held Bonita closely and kissed her warmly, ignoring the stiffness in his recovering muscles. "We owe a lot to Antonio" he said plainly. "If it hadn't been for him, I wouldn't be with you now."

Bonita went over to Antonio and gave him a hug and a light kiss on the cheek. "I don't care that you're wearing a Nationalist uniform, Antonio," she said. "We are all grateful to you. I can't thank you enough."

Not accustomed to demonstrations of affection, Antonio was somewhat flustered and merely replied, "You're welcome, Bonita. I would have felt terribly bad if Jose couldn't have come to mother's funeral. Actually, we owe our gratitude to Captain Barcena, the head of the company in Badajoz; he's the one who gave permission."

"Let's give a hurrah for Captain Barcena!" Bonita exclaimed. "It doesn't matter that he's a Nationalist officer. The important thing is that Jose is here. And, of course, Antonio, it's important that you are here, too."

Antonio smiled. He thought: *Maybe even a hot-headed fanatic like Bonita can be kind and considerate.*

Marisa came up and went through the same words and emotions Bonita had expressed. Jorge and his boys added their welcomes to the happy reception.

Ramon showed up, and said, "The three musketeers are back together again. How did you pull this one off, Antonio?"

Antonio modestly shrugged his shoulders. He directed the driver where to park the car and to stay with it. The family went into the house, Bonita remaining close to Jose – and Antonio staying close to both of them.

Marisa came up to Antonio. "At the funeral, would you say some things about mother's life?" she asked. "I've asked Father Augustin to include it in the service as a homily, and he agreed. Ramon and Jose will read lessons. For the homily, Father Augustin thought you should do it, being the oldest son in the family."

Antonio was pleased to be given this responsibility. "I'd be honored to make some remarks about *madre*," he said. "Thank you for suggesting it, Marisa."

Marisa had another question. "You knew mother's funeral would be in three days, but how did you learn the service was in the early evening?"

"I telephoned the town hall from our camp to get the time and they called the church to find out for me," Antonio replied. He had a question of his own. "Why was the funeral scheduled for early evening instead of during the day?"

"Father Augustin wasn't available in the morning; he buried a *miliciano* from Zorita in that town. Another funeral for a Trujillo boy killed near Talavera was scheduled ahead of us after siesta. So, we had to wait; otherwise, the funeral wouldn't have been on the third day. You see, Antonio, while there hasn't been much fighting here, the war is all around us. Father Augustin told me in the past month he's had more burials than baptisms, confirmations, and marriages combined."

"Yes, that is very sad, Marisa," he said.

As she talked, Antonio thought to himself: *Another night here? No, it was bad enough before. I'd better squelch that idea before Marisa suggests it again. All it does is give Jose an opportunity to communicate something about his situation to someone in the family. How do I keep the knowledge of Jose's trial from becoming known? This thing gets more tangled than ever.*

As if they had intercepted his thoughts, Bonita and Marisa bombarded him with a torrent of questions.

"Antonio, what is this 'difficulty' Jose is in? Why was he rushed back to your camp? Is he in a Nationalist prison because he enlisted in the Republican militia? What's going on? We need an explanation."

"Marisa, Bonita, stop. Please, stop. I can't go into the matter with you or anyone else here. It's between Jose and me. Right, Jose?"

Jose nodded his assent. *You're calling the shots, Antonio,* he murmured only to himself.

"If either of you get involved, you'll only make things worse for Jose. And, I'll tell you right now; we must leave soon after the funeral. I know you don't like that. I don't either, but believe me, it's the best way. Please, don't ask any more questions; they will upset the arrangements Jose and I have agreed to."

Having read Jose's note, Bonita and Marisa knew they weren't getting a complete story from Antonio; however, they said nothing more. Antonio had fulfilled his promise to bring Jose back. Now the time had come for the short trip to the church for the funeral.

The shadows of the day were beginning to lengthen as Jorge's battered old car carrying Marisa's family and Bonita motored into the Plaza Mayor, the central square of Trujillo. Following them was the military car transporting Antonio, Ramon, Jose, and the driver. Antonio told the other three to stay in the car for a moment while he hurriedly finished some remembrances about his mother on paper. Jose looked at the town's familiar sights, especially the stork nests resting on church spires and the bronze statue of Francisco Pizarro riding on his horse. Antonio's driver stayed with the cars as the family walked silently up the narrow streets to the front of the Church of Santa Maria where the closed coffin had been laid. Father Augustin was standing there. The church had opened and was nearly half full of people. The three brothers and Jorge and his two sons carried the coffin up several steps and set it at the door of the church. The priest began the litany for the reception of the body.

"With faith in Jesus Christ, we receive the body of our sister Maria for burial. . ." The group then proceeded through the open doors. Father Augustin went first. The six pallbearers carried the coffin down the nave of the church and placed it at the transept. Everyone in the family took their seats assigned to them by Marisa. Jose moved to Bonita's side at the end of the front row. After a few more people entered by the side door behind Jose and Bonita, Father Augustin began the funeral with an anthem.

"I am Resurrection and I am Life, says the Lord . . ." intoned the priest. When he finished and a hymn had been sung, Jose moved to the front lectern and read the Old Testament lesson from Job, Chapter 19: 'I know that my Redeemer lives . . .' Ramon read from the 15th chapter of First Corinthians about "the imperishable body." The 23rd Psalm was recited and Father Augustin read from the 5th chapter of the Gospel of John: ". . . whoever hears my word and believes him who sent me has everlasting life . . ." A soloist sang a devout *Ave Maria*. The Apostle's Creed was recited and prayers were said. Antonio's time came to deliver the homily concerning his mother. He had quickly composed a short message with cryptic notes on a sheet of paper. At first his voice shook, but soon he was able to speak with clear devotion and deep respect.

"Maria Isabel Garcia was born in Galicia, practically within the shadows of the cathedral at Mondonedo. She lived there during her youth. The cathedral enlisted young people to work as guides explaining the history of the church to visitors, and Maria was one of them. One Sunday morning, a young man from the Asturian town of Mieres worshipped at the cathedral. After Mass, Maria took him around the building and grounds. Together, they viewed the portal arches, the rose window, the frescoes and other works of art. Attracted by her knowledge and quiet demeanor, he asked if they could meet later that afternoon at a local restaurant. This was rather bold; a young woman was not supposed to meet a young man unattended. To his surprise, she said 'yes,' but he would have to invite her parents to come along with her, which he did. That chance meeting in the Mondonedo cathedral led to a relationship that was to last as long as both of them lived.

"Mother and Pablo Martinez were married in that cathedral three years later. Four children were born during their marriage; she gave birth to Marisa, myself, Ramon, and Jose, in that order. Maria never complained of her hard life, the wife of a coal-miner and the mother of four young children. She never complained of the constant cleaning she had to do, for her husband's clothes and those of her children always needed attention. Mother never complained about having to serve *desayuno, almuerzo,* and *cena* day after day to six hungry people. Her selflessness taught us, her children, a kind of self-discipline when she would ask us to meet the obligations of work around the house. Some might say she did what any good mother would do, but there was one thing more she gave us that is irreplaceable – her unconditional love. Our mother was always there for us. I cannot think of a better example of what a good,

No Greater Love

caring mother should be. She literally gave her life for us, never thinking of her own hardships.

"*No greater love could have been given by anyone.*

"Our father gave his life for us, too. He worked in the coal mines near Mieres. He would have preferred a different job. Miners were paid fairly well and father hoped someday to save enough money to own and operate a food and dry goods store. However, mining is exhausting, dangerous work and father did not survive it. His death left our mother with the complete responsibility of rearing a daughter and three sons, which she did, again without complaint. Shortly after father died, Marisa married a farmer from Trujillo, Jorge Cardenas, whom many of you know. Through their generosity, the family was able to move all the way from Mieres down to Trujillo here in Extremadura."

Sitting at the end of the front row on the side opposite the lectern where Antonio was speaking, Bonita nudged Jose. "Get ready to move," she whispered in his ear. Jose had been listening intently to his oldest brother's heartfelt expressions. He was startled upon hearing Bonita's words, but he made no sound.

"Our madre was a supremely religious person," Antonio continued, his misty eyes deep in his notes. "She believed in God, the Father, and in Jesus as her Savior, and in the Holy Spirit working in her life and in the lives of those around her. Her faith was simple and pure. She passed on that faith to her children, not so much in words, but more by the example she set before us. She prayed daily, asking God for the grace to do His will in all she did. At meal times, after father led us in the Lord's Prayer, she would give thanks for everything God had granted her – family and friends, a blessed marriage, the good earth around her, the food on the table. Of course, she continued these prayers after father died, except that one of us children would start the meals with the prayer our Lord taught us. *Madre* had compassion on those that suffered and grieved. How many times she journeyed to console a troubled friend, offer sympathy, and feed a hungry person. We thought of her as a living saint, a perfect mother, and a very great lady."

Antonio stayed with the religious theme for two or three more minutes. He closed his eyes for another moment of prayer, petitioning God to accept the soul of Maria. Lost in thoughts and memories, he ended his words as Father Augustin rose to begin the communion ritual.

Suddenly, Antonio noticed something was wrong. At the end of the front row, Jose and Bonita were *not* where they were supposed to be. His eyes searched frantically. They had simply vanished.

Chapter 14
Escape

With Antonio immersed in the notes of his eulogy, Bonita knew instinctively that this was the time for her to act. The only other time to make a move would be at the cemetery burial, but there it would be considerably more hazardous with fewer people around to conceal their motions. Taking Jose by the hand, they tip-toed silently to a nearby side door of the church. Bonita crouched low, clutched her throat, feigning illness. Quietly, they opened the door, went through and closed it without a sound. They ran down the steps to a military vehicle that was waiting with its headlights on and its engine running. Bonita gave a signal to a man seated in the car. The man got out of the car and held the door open.

"Get in on the driver's side, Jose," Bonita instructed as she ran to the passenger side. With both of them inside the car, she picked up a Nationalist cap from the floor and pressed it on Jose's head. Jose released the brake and moved the car down the steep, narrow pathways into the main square of Trujillo.

"How did you ever manage this?" Jose inquired of Bonita, incredulously.

"Don't ask now, Jose. I'll tell you later. Just get us out of town! I don't like taking you from your mother's funeral this way, but Antonio is bound to discover our absence at any moment."

"Where do we go?"

"Anywhere. I don't know. We haven't had time to figure it out. You know this territory better than I do."

Jose was familiar with the streets of Trujillo. The quickest way out of town would take them past Marisa's and Jorge's house. As the car moved past the edge of town and into the countryside, he lowered his shoulders below the windows and saluted a Nationalist guard.

Jose smiled and asked Bonita, "Did that Nationalist soldier return my salute?"

"No time for pointless questions, Jose. Just go faster."

Hundreds of localized civil wars were being fought within the context of the larger war. Any route chosen would have its dangers. Jose made an instant decision about the direction to take and prayed it would be a good choice. With a straighter country road, he increased the speed of the vehicle.

After they had traveled for several minutes, Bonita said, "Now, I'll ask you, Jose. Where are we going?"

"We'll be on a road that will connect with the Merida-Caceres road about fifty kilometers southwest of here," he responded. "Antonio took the route we're on to get here both times; however, we won't go to Merida because it's occupied by Nationalist soldiers. Instead, we'll turn west. Taking some back roads, we'll come out some place north of Badajoz . . ."

"Why there?" interrupted Bonita. "I thought that's where you were in jail."

"It was, but just like Merida, we're not going there. Any place near Badajoz is probably the last place Antonio would guess we're going. And," he added, "we've got to get you back to your school in Galicia where you teach."

"Jose, that's the last thing concerning me now! Don't worry about it."

"All right, we'll deal with that later. I hope we're headed in the best direction. North of Badajoz, the border bulges east and getting into Portugal will be a shorter distance for us."

"Marisa heard a rumor that Salazar's police are sending back any Republican soldiers they find."

"I've heard that, too, but I'm no longer in a militia uniform. It's a risk we'll have to take. A few minutes ago, I had to make a quick decision when I asked you where to go and you said 'anywhere.' I hope we're taking the best route. There was no time for me to plan anything."

"Maybe this way is best, Jose. Franco may have Madrid surrounded by now. Barcelona and Valencia are so far away. The Nationalists have almost everything north of us. At least, the southwest is not completely controlled by Franco. Going west on back roads into Portugal may be best. Seems that no matter which way we take, we'll be going through Nationalist-held territory."

"Bonita, are you sure you want to be so involved in this escape?" Jose asked earnestly. "I could go back to Trujillo and let you off near Marisa's house. If we're stopped, you could say I forced you to come with me."

"Don't be silly, Jose. Trujillo is several kilometers behind us. The

Nationalists could be alerted to us by now. Antonio will assume I arranged your getaway."

"Do you think Marisa and Jorge will be held responsible for it?"

"They'll be able to cover themselves; they've been doing that ever since the Nationalists took control of Trujillo. From now on, where you go, I will go."

"You make me think of Ruth in the Old Testament," was Jose's grateful response. He quickly squeezed her hand.

Just like Mama, too, he thought. *Do I deserve such selfless devotion? No greater love, as Antonio said in the homily.*

He inquired of Bonita: "Sounds like the war isn't going very well for the Republic? I'm asking because I've not been able to get much information except for Antonio's biased opinions. I'm starved for news from a different source."

"I wish I could tell you the Republic has won back the regions and cities that went over to the Nationalists, but I can't. However, I think the Nationalists were disappointed they didn't win over more territory in the first days of the rebellion. Here we are into the first of September and the National Front thought they'd have the whole country under their rule by now. Madrid is still governed by the Republic. Barcelona stopped the revolt. The Republic controls Catalonia, and the regions south of it. Most of Asturias and a couple of Basque provinces remain with the Republic. That's a quick rundown on the war over the past month."

"What about your home region of Galicia – still in Nationalist hands?"

"Yes, although I would guess they have had to overcome stiff resistance. Galicians voted liberal in February, but the Nationalists have overwhelming superiority in military weapons. I left before the rising, but I'm sure many people escaped to the mountains to fight back. Before the Nationalist rebellion, there were drive-by shootings – Falange youth firing out of car windows at, say, a known Liberal. They'd claim they were carrying out a cleansing operation to rid the town of vermin and scum. I will bet it is far worse now."

"Giving 14- or 15-year olds cars and pistols, filling their heads full of hate, and telling them they are saving the nation from evil communism – that's a lethal recipe for fanaticism and mindless violence."

"Marisa told me Nationalist prisons everywhere are loaded with captured people," reported Bonita. "It's been bad; at night several prisoners are selected at random and taken outside of town to a lonely place and shot. Their bodies are left along the road to serve as a warning not to oppose the rebellion. The dead, they'd say, were guerrilla terrorists, not eligible to be treated by rules governing war. Marisa also said even teachers have been one target, particularly those who came from universities suspected of dangerous, liberal thinking."

"Maybe that was a good reason for you to leave home."

"I didn't know about it at the time. Your mother's ill health and helping Marisa were the main reasons. And, of course, I wanted to be with you. I figured you would come home at some point. Now I *am* nervous about the possibility of a Nationalist purge of teachers. You never know when they'll come after you."

"How did your parents react to your leaving?"

"I left with their blessing, although I promised I'd be back for school if it would have me. I haven't been exactly reticent about my beliefs. Honestly, Jose, you can't tell whether a place is secure anymore or what might be the safest thing to do."

"How did you get to Trujillo? That was very brave of you, to travel in the midst of all this fighting."

"Actually, I started only a couple of days before the war began. You may remember my friend Remedios; she taught school with me. She bought a car with a payment from savings and was driving to Salamanca for a course in a summer session. She was happy to have me along as a passenger for company and to share expenses. When the war broke out, Salamanca declared for the Nationalists, and I had to stay hidden with several friends for two weeks until things quieted down there. All transportation stopped. The distance to Trujillo was shorter than going back to Galicia. Even so, it was almost a month's journey. That's a long story. I'll tell you about it when we're not running for our lives."

"I want to hear it. Thank God you're still in one piece. Did Marisa say anything about what's been happening near my home since the war started?"

"Yes, she did. The atmosphere probably seemed calm in Trujillo, but Marisa tells me it's been wild all around the region. Naturally, the big landlords support the Nationalists. The campesinos, figuring they had nothing to lose, fought any Civil Guards that went over to the Nationalist side. Where they won, it was because of their larger numbers. Much of the land owned by the aristocracy was confiscated and run by peasant committees and trade unions. The latifundia owners were typically absent when the rising began; now, they're probably lying low in Madrid or wherever they've gone, moaning the loss of their property."

"Are the peasants still in control?" Jose wanted to know.

"In some cases they are. The Nationalists don't control all of Extremadura – yet. They haven't established their authority everywhere in this region; the battle line is not continuous. Many campesinos wanted land redistributed to them individually. Their leaders wanted to manage the land through cooperatives, and that has been the usual result. There's no general agreement between peasants and leaders. Farm labor goes on as before. The only difference is that union committees pay the laborers instead of a landowner's agent."

"You're right when you say there's been a lot going on here."

"Eventually, I'm afraid everything is going to change back to the way it was," continued Bonita, voicing a similar worry Jose had heard from Felipe. "Despite resistance, the Nationalist army is advancing through Extremadura. I had to be extra careful to stay away from their front lines. Marisa told me people here are terror-stricken. Many peasants enlisted in their own town's militias. They're poorly equipped, not well trained, and are fighting a professional army. They usually flee when the Nationalists come toward them. They know there will be terrible reprisals when Franco's troops take over. Some rush to another town, join another militia, and retreat again when the Nationalists approach. There's been precious little military leadership on the Republican side."

"Yes, I know. Antonio made much of that point. Leadership is the key, as he put it. He's certain the final result of the war will be a Franco dictatorship. Antonio believes he can convince me to switch to the Nationalists and, by doing so, he could save my life."

"No, Jose! I couldn't stand it seeing you in a Nationalist uniform!"

"Well, why did you put this Nationalist hat on me?" Jose teased, throwing the cap into the back of the car. Immediately, he had another question.

"How did Jorge and Marisa handle things when the Nationalist Army of Africa went through Trujillo?"

"They're very cagey, Jose. They keep their real feelings well hidden. For example, Jorge urges renters to pay their landlords so both he and they can say to the Nationalists they are loyal to their side even though they secretly hate them."

"Tell me how you were able to get hold of this military car. You can imagine how surprised I was to see it waiting for us at the church."

"Thank Marisa and Jorge. After you were snatched away from us, I showed Marisa your note and she shared it with Jorge. He doesn't say much, Jose, but Jorge is bitter toward the big landowners because they treat the campesinos arrogantly and they often demean small farmers like himself. Marisa and Jorge were able to contact a Republican *guerrilla* fighter, probably a friend of theirs. He arranged for two men to attend the funeral. Marisa and I met them briefly to get our signals straight."

"How did you know this car would be available?"

"We didn't. If Antonio was able to get you back to your family in Trujillo, we simply assumed he would have a car. Of course, if you weren't at the funeral, nothing would have been done. One *guerrillero* came early and sat in the back of the church. The other waited for us in the Plaza Mayor to see where Antonio's driver parked this car; he walked behind us to the church. You didn't notice them leave when they were signaled by Jorge during the singing of the hymn?"

"No. Apparently, Antonio didn't see them either. All of us were facing the front of the church."

Bonita resumed her account of the *guerrilleros*. "They must have followed our two cars to the Plaza Mayor where we parked. If the driver stayed with the military car, and fortunately he did, the plan was to engage him in conversation and offer a drink to make things look normal in case other Nationalist soldiers were around. Actually, there probably weren't any. The Nationalists took the land around Trujillo rather easily. I don't think they need much of a force to keep the town under control."

"Whatever happened to the driver? His key must have been left in the ignition and he was kind enough to leave us with a half-tank full of gas."

"What they did with the driver is anybody's guess. I wasn't there." Bonita shrugged her shoulders and held out her hands in a helpless gesture. "The only thing I know about him is that you were wearing his Nationalist cap."

"I hope they didn't have to do anything rash," said Jose. "He seemed like a rather decent fellow."

"Don't go soft on me now, Martinez," Bonita replied, breaking her blunt words with a smile. "We've got a tough journey ahead."

"Don't worry. I'm breathing free air for the first time in over two weeks. It's wonderful. What's in the back of this car? I noticed some bags when I got in."

"Those are two rucksacks, Jose; one for you and the one I've used since leaving Corcubion. Marisa packed clothes and food in your bag; I did the same for mine. Jorge put them in the trunk of his car. I had visions of that car breaking down at any time; it's so old, I don't know how they keep it running. Jorge unlocked the trunk of his car so one of the *guerrilleros* could transfer the rucksacks."

Their car had passed by La Cumbre and Ruanes and was headed for Salvatierra and Alcuescar. The air turned cooler in the night breeze.

"We owe a lot to Marisa and Jorge," Jose said thinking about the risks they had taken for him, "and we can thank those *guerrilleros*. I should also say I owe a lot to you, Bonita. You haven't escaped from a Nationalist jail. I'll ask you a second time, are you sure you want to be involved with me?"

"And, I'll answer you for the second and *last* time. I'm involved with you for the rest of my life; you don't need to ask me that question again. My *caballero*, you're stuck with me forever."

Jose suddenly stopped the car in the middle of the road and kissed her passionately. "Those words I just heard from you," he said, "are worth the price of any escape no matter how dangerous."

Bonita waited for a second and then exclaimed, "That's wonderful, Jose, but get going! We don't know whether Antonio has another Nationalist car coming right behind us." As she spoke those words, Bonita looked over her shoulder at the darkness and the clouds of dust that swallowed up the road they had just traveled.

"You are my practical wife-to-be! Do you think they will marry us in Portugal?"

"You're crazy to be talking this way. Let's deal with that later."

"Okay, let's deal with this car right now. When we get by Alcuescar, we'll join the road from Caceres, go south toward Merida, then head west on a back road. We'll go through La Nava de Santiago and La Roca de la Sierra and over to Villar del Rey."

"Instead of going to all those places, maybe you'll want to ride up to Caceres and pay a visit to General Franco," said Bonita mischievously. "I understand he's established his headquarters there for the coming battle of Madrid. I'm sure he'll be glad to see you."

"Oh, sure," Jose responded. "I could return that Nationalist cap you gave me." He continued outlining his plan. "We'll drive south again until the Rio Zapaton separates from the Rio Gevora. After that, we'll take the first road or path west, hopefully cross the Gevora at some point, drive as far as we can go, ditch the car, and walk our way through fields and hills into Portugal. The Nationalists could be alerted by the time we get there, but they won't have guards stationed every ten feet along the border. We must enter Portugal . . ."

He suddenly stopped talking. Without warning, a car had turned on to the road ahead of them, requiring their full attention.

As the approaching car moved closer, Jose said, "If this car is carrying Nationalist soldiers, they'll block the road and force us to stop. I'll get out of the car with my hands up and try to distract them. You try to get away. It's dark; they may not see you."

"No, Jose. They'll be armed. We have no weapons. We're in this together."

The car came closer, slowed down, and moved on by them. Jose sighed with relief. "Thank God. I was afraid this journey had come to an end."

They drove on, barely moving at first with the dry earth swirling in front of them. Bonita murmured, "I'm scared, Jose. You don't know how scared I am."

"You're my brave girl, Bonita. I know how brave you are. It took courage for you to travel through Nationalist territory and get to Trujillo."

"I ran into endless delays. No trains or buses were running. A bus might occasionally go a few kilometers. Twice, I was able to get rides in a car with people staying in the same hostal. Once, I had to wait while five ill-fated people were executed; the driver wanted to watch that sad spectacle. I was anxious, being a young woman on lonely country roads. I waited days to walk with another woman between villages, pretending to be chaperoned. Going through one village in the midst of several soldiers, a woman called me a slut under her breath."

"You didn't deserve that," declared Jose. "People make stupid judgments about others, especially when they know nothing about their circumstances."

"Nothing awful happened to me, thank God. If I had known how difficult the journey would be, I'd still be trapped in Salamanca."

"Bonita, I'll be forever grateful you came all that way for me. I had no idea of what you were going through. At Marisa's, I knew if I could get that note to you, you'd find a way to do something."

"I had lots of help from Marisa and Jorge. Having them on our side made me much more confident."

"How about Ramon? Nothing has been said about him. How did you keep him from knowing what you were doing?"

"Marisa and I talked only when Ramon was outside or in town. I don't believe his heart is in this war. The only problem with Ramon . . . I'll tell you more, later."

"Tell me now."

"No, Jose. It will keep. We've got important things to do now. You need to concentrate on your driving. By the way, Marisa told me when she asked her priest to have Antonio give the eulogy for Maria and he agreed, she got the feeling he sensed there was more to her request than she was letting on."

"Father Augustin won't have to worry about his church being burned or even threatened by anarchist peasants or campesinos," said Jose. "He would never allow his church to be used as a fortress for Nationalist troops like some priests have done. He has always treated the poor the same as the rich, and the people respect him for that. He must be very careful, though. I'm not surprised he was helpful."

"I met Father Augustin when Marisa was planning the funeral with him. I was impressed with him. He seems to be a warm, caring priest, the kind of person who would understand the danger we're in."

"He's got to live with the Nationalists, at least while they control the town. Like Jorge and Marisa, our sympathetic priest must act as if he doesn't know anything, which he did magnificently tonight."

Chapter 15
Betrayal

In Trujillo, Antonio was a study in helplessness, rage, and self-pity at his unmerited betrayal. When he discovered Jose and Bonita gone, momentary bewilderment was replaced with utter frustration.

Walking down the steps from the altar, a wave of absolute futility swept over Antonio.

What have I done to deserve this? How will I ever explain it to my captain?

He spied Ramon and motioned him to meet outside. Once there, with the church door closed behind them, Antonio berated his brother with scornful words.

"Ramon, were you asleep in there? Maybe you still don't know what has happened! Didn't you see Jose and Bonita leave? Where were you?"

"I was in my assigned place on the other side of the room from them, Antonio. No, I didn't see them leave. I was listening to you. You know, Maria is my mother, too."

"I didn't think I had to tell you to keep an eye on Jose and Bonita," scolded Antonio. "Which side are you on in this war? This is terrible!" He paused for a moment. "Come with me to the Plaza Mayor. Maybe they can still be found."

When Antonio and Ramon reached the center of town, they both noticed Antonio's military car was missing. "They've stolen my car!" Antonio shouted. "Where in hell is that driver?"

"Disappeared into thin air," announced Ramon with a tinge of sarcasm in his voice. He was angry with Antonio for placing the blame on him for Jose and Bonita's getaway. "Maybe a Republican plane airlifted them out of town and now they're headed for Madrid."

"Do you think Jose is that important, Ramon?" asked Antonio earnestly, dropping his tone of accusation. "I've thought all along that Jose has been holding back on something important. Sometimes, I suspect he could be a ranking officer in the Republican army. Other times, I think he is a major propagandist for the Popular Front. I believe he is far more significant than he has let on. Has he ever said anything to you about his position with the liberal republicans, socialists, communists, anarchists, or any group?"

"Not to me. He doesn't discuss politics with me, Antonio. He knows I don't talk politics with anyone if I can help it."

Antonio took Ramon by the arm and led him toward a bar. "You're friends with the manager here, aren't you, Ramon? You drink quite a bit on occasion, I've noticed."

Ramon acknowledged he knew the bar owner.

"Ask him for the use of his telephone. Communication has been restored in Badajoz for some time now."

"What do you need a telephone for?" asked Ramon innocently.

Antonio looked at Ramon as if he had asked the dumbest question of all time.

"You can't just let them escape like that," thundered Antonio. "I've got to get word out that a Nationalist military car has been stolen with two Republican fugitives in it. Then we'll go back to the funeral and talk with the family."

Antonio made his telephone call. He and Ramon returned to the church. The Funeral Mass was over. Marisa and Jorge were on the front steps of the church with their boys. Antonio immediately asked Marisa if she had any knowledge of Jose and Bonita's disappearance.

"No," said Marisa. "Their flight was a complete mystery to us. We thought they were still in church. We couldn't figure out why you and Ramon left in such a hurry without taking communion."

"How could he, Marisa?" stormed Antonio. "How could Jose have betrayed me so? We were making progress. I could have saved him. How ungrateful can a person get? Jose has forfeited any trust I had in him."

Marisa tried to stay safely neutral. "Jose must have been in a desperate situation to leave mother's funeral that way. This means he won't be at the cemetery for the committal. What would provoke him to make such a reckless move as that?"

"He had no reason to just disappear," Antonio carried on. "What an insult to his mother! By running away, he's put both himself and Bonita at grave risk. I should have kept a closer eye on him. With the volatile atmosphere we live in today, I wouldn't be a bit surprised if we find them dead along some roadside."

"Good God, not that!" cried Marisa.

Antonio was ready to explode again. "I know we disagree politically, but this act tonight is really beyond all reason. He dishonors mother's memory. He desecrates her funeral, using it to make his escape. He scorns anything I tried to do for him. He puts Bonita's life in great danger. He thinks only of himself. If there was ever a mistake our parents made, it was spoiling him rotten. This proves it! The fires of hell burn brightly for him!"

"Oh, my God in heaven, Antonio, don't send him there," appealed Marisa. "Jose loved his mother. He wouldn't deliberately hurt her. He must have been frantically troubled to do what he did tonight." Artfully playing dumb, she added, "Maybe he will come back later."

"Don't count on it, Marisa. His kind never does the honorable thing."

"Is there anything we can do?" asked Jorge with pretended innocence as he was trying to move the group out for the ride to the cemetery. "We know Jose has put you in an awful spot."

"Thank you, Jorge. I can't think of anything, although Ramon and I will need a ride to the cemetery and back to the house since Jose has stolen my car."

"Yes, that is serious," agreed Jorge. "Certainly, you can ride back with us, if you and Ramon don't mind holding the boys on your knee. And, please, Antonio, don't bring up this business about Jose with Miguel and Angel; they think highly of him. While he's done a dreadful thing tonight, I don't want them upset still more. Keep in mind they just lost their grandmother."

They drove to the cemetery in silence. When they arrived, Antonio was still fuming.

"What do I tell my commanding officer?" he grumbled to Marisa with a low voice. "He'll think *I've* betrayed his trust! Yes, Jose was being held because of a charge made against him. Now, there'll be an extreme penalty of some kind. Captain Barcena will want to know what's happened to the car and the driver. And, there's the humiliation of appearing back to camp empty-handed. I don't want to think of the sniggering that will go on behind my back. You have no idea of the position this puts me in."

Marisa put her hand on Antonio's shoulder and said, "I can only guess what he's done to you and I am truly sorry for what has happened. Excuse me now. I've got to get some candles from the caretaker; we need some light at the burial. Try to put this out of your mind at this time. Think of our mother and all she meant to you."

Antonio was only slightly mollified. "I wish my youngest brother would have thought of her," he said curtly.

Then, with bitterness returning to his voice, he pursed his lips and vowed, "Jose will pay for his betrayal. Believe me – I speak from the bottom of my heart when I say this, Marisa: I'll never forgive him for what he has done tonight!"

Chapter 16
Toward Portugal

"Do you think we can get into Portugal by morning?" Bonita asked Jose. Coming off the road to Merida, their stolen car had swerved to the west on to the dirt road going toward La Nava de Santiago. They had encountered two cars, each time expecting the worst before the oncoming cars moved past them.

"We'll try," Jose answered with determination. "Antonio will get the news to some Nationalist official about our escape, and that will set off alarms in Nationalist-controlled areas throughout this region. We may have been luckier than we realize to go this far undetected. My guess is that we're into the heart of Nationalist-held country now."

"I'm glad you're driving, Jose. I'd be completely lost at this point. Do you know how we're going to get into Portugal?"

"I have in mind a road that goes south from Villar del Rey," Jose explained. "Then we head southwest for fifteen kilometers, and by that time, we'll be close to the border. When we find a path going off to the west, we'll take it. I think we'll be all right – if we don't meet any Nationalists before then. We don't dare go to the border on a main road; we would more than likely come face to face with their soldiers."

Another car headed toward them, the dust flying behind it. They braced themselves again. Once more, the car drove on by them and disappeared in the darkness.

"I don't know how much more of this I can take," said Bonita, looking back. "Even when they pass, I expect them to stop, turn around, and chase us."

"What time is it?"

Bonita looked at her wristwatch. "Almost midnight," she replied. "Why?"

R. D. Lock

"I thought there would be more traffic."

"Most people are staying inside at night these days, Jose. You don't want to be out after dark if you can help it."

The road was straight over the flat land. Jose pushed harder on the accelerator. A few clouds dotted the sky. A full moon shone brightly most of the time.

Reaching Villar del Rey, they turned south again. Jose let Bonita know what he was thinking. "We're moving toward Badajoz now and in about fifteen minutes we'll take off on the first pathway to the west. If we get to Valdebotoa, we'll have to turn west there. Any further will bring us too close to Badajoz, and I've had enough of that place. We may get wet crossing the Rio Gevora."

"How do you remember all these different roads, Jose? I think I'd end up going around in circles."

"Remember, part of my growing up was in Extremadura and I had a job for a few months in Badajoz, but I'm going strictly on memory."

"Can we hide the car wherever we leave it?"

"We can try. I don't know the territory that well, though."

On they sped through the blackness of night. The closer they moved toward Badajoz, the more nervous Jose got. Another car approached them in the distance. "I don't like the looks of that car coming at us," Jose revealed to Bonita. "I think it's slowing down!"

As they passed the approaching car, Jose looked in the rear view mirror and caught sight of the car as it turned around and headed down their road behind them.

"Oh, no," groaned Jose. "That car is following us." Bonita turned in her seat to get a better look at the car behind them.

Jose pressed further on the accelerator.

"I see his lights through the dust," yelled Bonita. "He seems to be stopping. He's turning into a driveway! Oh, thank God," she whispered, her last words murmured like a prayer. "He must have overshot his turn."

Jose breathed another sigh of relief. "I was worried," he told Bonita. "Yes, thank God I was wrong thinking the worst. I'm going to stay on this road for about five or six minutes, and then turn west on the first road after that. We'll go about another four or five minutes, and then we should be fairly close to the border."

They drove in silence again until Jose spotted a one-lane dirt road headed west. As they slowed down, a signpost came into view that read "Valdebotoa 3 km" and "Badajoz 15 km."

"We've gone as far south as we should," said Jose, pointing at the sign. "I would guess we're about five kilometers from Portugal where it bulges east. Keep your eye on the odometer, Bonita, and tell me when we've gone three kilometers."

The one-lane road went past a house and narrowed to a path.

"It's a good thing we're not in mountains," Jose announced. "I don't how much longer we can go. I just looked at the gas gage; it's on empty." A half-minute later, he stopped the car.

"What's wrong?" called Bonita. "We've gone less than a kilometer." Jose pointed his index finger forward. A stream flowed ahead.

"Oh no!" she cried. "How are we going to get through that water?"

Jose got out of the car and ran to the edge of the stream. When he came back, he said, "The water doesn't seem very deep. It must be the Gevora, or an offshoot of it. We are lucky we're near the end of summer, not the beginning of spring."

Jose drove slowly ahead. "Get the rucksacks," he directed. "Hold on to yours and put mine in my lap – just in case."

Bonita did as she was told. In the middle of the stream, the car stopped and a trickle of water started coming under the doors. The engine sputtered and died. Jose jammed the accelerator to the floor and tried the ignition. It failed to start.

"Never a dull moment," Jose shouted to Bonita. "We're at the end of the road for this car! Water could have gotten into the engine's cylinders or it's out of gas."

"I could use a dull moment, Jose. Here's your backpack. Let's get out while we can."

They pushed open their doors, emerged from the car, and threw their rucksacks on to their backs. Water swirled around their feet. They splashed their way to the other side of the river, using stones to step on wherever they could find them in the moonlight.

Reaching the other side of the river, Jose noticed the path had disappeared. He started looking for a place where they could dry themselves and gather a moment's rest. Beyond, he could see that there was some flat land to cross. Ahead, they could be climbing gradually uphill.

Taking Bonita by her elbow, Jose looked at the sky and searched for the North Star. "We're going in the right direction," he said.

"We've got to keep going, but I need to change this dress," said Bonita. "I'm still in my church clothes."

"We can dry ourselves under those trees over there," he said. Looking back and turning Bonita around, he continued, "Say good-bye to our marvelous chariot. It got us this far."

"Good-bye, sweet car," murmured Bonita. "I love you, even if you are Nationalist military."

They walked to the trees where they removed their wet shoes and socks. Bonita took off her funeral dress and shoved it into her backpack. She stood for a moment in her white undergarment pondering what to wear for walking. The shimmering glow of the moonlight caught her figure like an apparition.

"Seeing you in your slip like this makes me think I'm dreaming," remarked Jose appreciatively. "I'll have to ask you to clothe yourself in a nondescript dress or I'll have to fight off every young man in Portugal."

That comment brought a kiss from Bonita. She put on a dark blouse and skirt. She selected a pair of shoes more suitable for hiking.

"I'm throwing these wet shoes away," she said. "They're not much good for walking anyway."

"I don't have any choice," said Jose, wringing out his socks and eyeing his water-soaked shoes. "These wet shoes are the only ones I've got. They'll dry out better and won't shrink if I keep them on. They must be sturdy; they've been through a lot."

They grabbed their rucksacks and slung them over their backs. Hand-in-hand, they started their walk toward Portugal.

"I hope we don't meet any wild animals," said Bonita.

"I think the worst we'll run into is a flock of sheep." A pack of hungry dogs or a wild boar was the most disagreeable prospect he could think of, but he said nothing about that possibility to Bonita.

"We're fortunate to have a moonlit night, Jose, but everything looks so luminous. We'll be easy to spot by Nationalist soldiers if they're nearby."

"They're concentrating on Madrid or Toledo," said Jose, trying to reassure her. "Just look above occasionally and keep the north-star to your right."

"How can you be so calm and reasoned? I'm as jumpy as a cat."

"All we can do is move on as fast as we can. I'm not as calm as you think, but I'm glad we're doing something. Sitting in prison for a couple of weeks doing nothing is far worse." He told her about Felipe, how contemptible his jailers were, and the terrible things that had happened to him. He gave her an account of the massacre of the republican prisoners in the Badajoz bullring.

"How awful, Jose. What monstrous atrocities the Nationalists commit! I never imagined how inhumane those beasts could be."

"From a strictly military point of view, I suppose they are doing the logical thing. Like Antonio told me, in any war the mission of any soldier is to destroy the enemy. The more you kill, the fewer you have to guard which releases more men to fight. That's the thinking behind machine-gunning prisoners. The bigger the kill, the greater the success you have in wartime."

"*You* don't really believe that, do you?"

"No, I don't want anything to do with killing after the scenes I've witnessed, but that's the way our enemies operate in this war. I suppose some in our varied Republican forces are behaving the same way, thinking it's necessary to win."

"But, you don't have to torture people in the process."

"No, no, of course not. Killing is bad enough; torture and sadism are completely barbaric. There must be a special place in hell reserved for those who mutilate others for their own pleasure."

"What about international law? Doesn't it apply in this war?"

"It should, but who is going to check on it when the violations happen? And, if the Nationalists are victorious, who will hold them accountable? 'Might makes right' as that old saying goes."

"Jose, is that someone ahead of us? We're not exactly invisible. I feel like I'm almost glowing in this moonlight." The wind and full moon cast odd shapes in the distance ahead of them. Shadows danced in the foreground. Jose and Bonita stopped and knelt until they could identify the shapes as shadows from trees and bushes. Then they moved ahead until the scene was reenacted again.

Once, when the shadows brought them close together on their knees, Jose kissed Bonita as tenderly as he could. That glorious moment lasted for approximately three seconds.

Nearly in unison, they said to each other, "Better keep going."

For another hour, the two refugees walked until they began a slow ascent to higher elevations. The moon disappeared under a bank of clouds. Both of them imagined Nationalist soldiers suddenly coming out of the darkness and apprehending them at gunpoint, but they didn't say anything like that to each other. On and on they walked, stopping momentarily to catch their breath and then starting up again. They kept going until a path approached and Jose spotted the outline of a fence in the distance. The ground leveled and seemed to start downward beyond.

I wonder if we're coming to the border, suggested Jose to himself.

"Be extra quiet," he whispered to Bonita who was breathing harder with the exertion of a steady pace. "I can't see very well, but that could be Portugal ahead of us. We'll move about half way to our right."

They walked for several minutes, Jose reckoning northwest was their best direction. Meeting a barrier, they inched along it until a gate appeared in front of them. Jose came to a sudden standstill and took Bonita by her arm.

"Let's go back," he murmured in her ear. "There's a gate ahead, but using it may not be a good idea."

When they retraced their steps without a sound, Bonita asked softly, "Did you see something at the gate?"

Jose motioned for her to stay silent and follow him. After five minutes of quiet walking, he pointed right and they resumed their westerly direction.

Another five minutes elapsed before Jose said quietly, "I don't see a fence in this field and it looks like we go gradually downhill. I think we're in Portugal now. You'd think they'd have signs with the words *Adios Espana; ola Portugal*."

He made an elaborate gesture of welcome and Bonita stepped through an imaginary portal. Jose followed and pretended to shut the gate. "Let's move quickly," he said firmly. "I don't want to stay here. We're not out of danger yet."

The two walked down hills and across fields until they came to a path that appeared to be a trail. "Maybe this path will take us to a road," said Jose, as he looked above at the stars. "It's going in the right direction."

"You saw something back there near that first gate, not the make-believe one, didn't you," said Bonita flatly.

"It could have been my imagination, but I thought there was a car parked in some bushes just off a dirt road that came up out of nowhere. It looked like a military vehicle. I'll never know for sure, but I could have sworn I saw someone in that car. It was hard to see in the dark; the moon was under a cloud at that point. I read somewhere that airplane pilots claim Extremadura to be the darkest spot in Europe from the air."

He looked at Bonita's timepiece. "It's almost four o'clock; if there was a person there for several hours, it was long enough for him to get tired. He may have been sleeping. Suppose he was a Nationalist soldier – could he have been trying to desert? You don't know what a person's motives are these days."

"Oh, Jose, I'm so keyed up; I don't think I'll ever be able to sleep again."

"What else is there to say other than keep moving?"

The trail went downward and veered off in the wrong direction. A narrow stream had to be forded. The night air was drying Jose's socks and shoes. This time, stones allowed them to arrive at the other side without getting their feet wet. They crossed field after field. Dogs barked and growled in the distance, but fortunately none came near. No lights were turned on in the few houses

No Greater Love

they passed. Jose worried once more about mangy dogs having gone wild from hunger. Again, he said nothing to Bonita. Finally, they came to a road. On they walked until a glow in the sky signaled the coming of dawn. Bonita looked at her wristwatch; it read seven o'clock. They walked another kilometer until they came to a sign that read: Compo Major 5 km.

Jose gave a quiet sound of triumph. "Although we've not been going the exact right way for a short while, now I definitely know we're in Portugal. I thought we had reached Portugal when we came to level ground and that gate, but I wasn't absolutely certain of it," he confessed.

"What do we do now?" Bonita inquired. "We could use a rest to get off our feet." They moved away from the roadside so they could hide if an early morning car drove by.

"Let's see what's in our rucksacks," said Jose, swinging the bag from his back to the ground in front of him. Bonita did the same. Resting their feet gave them a good feeling.

Bonita opened her backpack. "I have most of the clothes I brought with me from home. Marisa washed and packed them for me," Looking further into the bag she said, "Here's a little food, a bottle of water, a hat, a few aspirin tablets, another pair of shoes – I hope they fit. Here's an umbrella and a little Spanish money. Marisa couldn't have guessed we were going into Portugal. I still have pesetas I brought from home. I started with half of my year's salary."

"I have some pesetas from Marisa in my bag, too. She put in a razor and some shaving cream for me – I hope she's left enough for Jorge. Ah, a cap, beaten up, but it fits and it's better than that ugly Nationalist cap we left behind. Here's a map! It includes Portugal. That's wonderful. How about this – a bar of soap and a wash cloth! Marisa has thought of everything. How can I ever thank her and Jorge? Someday, I hope I can."

"You will, Jose. Clothes? What about your clothes?"

"Oh, I have a couple of changes of clothing here. Good thing Jorge and I are about the same size. Good – here's a belt; Jorge is a little heavier than I am."

"Food?" asked Bonita.

"Some bread, crackers, cheese, and – what do you know – a small bottle of wine tucked in among the clothes. We're really living, Bonita!"

"We're going to make it, Martinez," she said, gaily. "Shall we walk to Campo Major? Maybe we can get *pequeno almoco*," using the Portuguese words for breakfast.

R. D. Lock

"What are we going to use for Portuguese money?" responded Jose. "We can rest in a few more minutes, but then . . ."

"Yes, I know, keep going – but, where to, Jose?"

"Maybe, some place where we can blend in with a lot of people."

"Lisbon?"

"No, too obvious. I have a friend in Coimbra. Manuel is a graduate student at university there. From Coimbra, we'll go on to Porto, a big city, lots of people, and we're close to your home region – Galicia."

"That's back in Spain. Wouldn't we be safer staying in Portugal?"

"I don't think it makes much difference, Bonita. We could be in as much danger in Portugal as in Spain. Dr. Salazar may be a low-keyed dictator, but he has his *Policia de Vigilancia e Defesa do Estado*, or PVDE. Salazar gives them free reign to do anything to keep order. 'I'm busy running the country,' he says in effect to them. 'You do what you have to do, only don't tell me about it.'

"The Police for Vigilance and Defense of the State may be as ruthless as any secret police organized by our Nationalists. Suspects are arrested without warrants and held for a long time without any charges brought against them. The police carry out secret operations within the labor movement, universities, and armed forces. I've heard disappearance and beatings are routine."

"We're out of the frying pan and into the fire, as the old saying goes."

"No, we're still in the frying pan; we haven't been caught yet. We've got to be careful, though. Salazar may be cooperating with the National Front, allowing foreign munitions and military equipment to go through his country. If we're caught, as you've said, his police could return us to Nationalist authorities."

"One of these years, I'll be able to relax," said Bonita. "Be sure to let me know when." They got up, brushed some dust from their clothes, and started to walk.

Jose stopped after a few steps and deliberated for a minute. "It's terribly unromantic for me to say this," he said to Bonita, "but, you should walk behind me."

"Jose! What are you talking about?"

"Camouflage, deception, disguise. Get out your umbrella. Cover your head with something. Your *bufanda*, my dear – I thought I saw a scarf in your backpack. We are going to look as old as we can. I'll put on Jorge's worn cap and I'll look for a walking stick. You need a cane, don't you? Be sure to limp a little whenever you see another person or a car."

Bonita looked at Jose like he had taken leave of his senses. "How many paces behind you, my lord and master?" she asked. "Will six paces be about right?"

"Not that far, Bonita," he pleaded. "It's only to conceal our identity as best we can. This will last only until we get further away from the border. I give you my word of honor!"

Chapter 17
An Unintended Clue

The rays of the morning sun filtered through the windows of the kitchen as Antonio, Ramon, and Marisa sat at the table with their cups of *café con leche*. Sleep had come to Antonio only two hours before dawn. His feelings of resentment at the way Jose had managed his escape had grown, not diminished. At the same time, he wanted to keep his emotions concealed in front of the others, lest they think he was losing the composure a proper military posture required.

Slumber had proven to be difficult for Marisa, too; she had lain awake for hours after Jorge had fallen asleep. On top of her mother's death and funeral, a civil war was being waged within the family as well as in the nation. Only Ramon was actually refreshed by a full night's rest. He faked tiredness thinking the others would assume he had spent the night too upset to find peace.

"Jorge and the boys are outside," Marisa explained to her two brothers. "They'll be in as soon as they're done with their work."

"There's one thing about farming," observed Ramon, in an effort to make pleasant conversation. "The routine of care for your animals and plants must go on despite any other important things that are happening."

"Mother's death is a time when the family should be together," said Antonio in a measured voice. Marisa looked at him. "I'm sorry," he apologized. "You'll probably get tired of me saying it, but Jose should be with us at a time like this. I moved heaven and earth to get him here."

"We know you did," Marisa offered, "and he knows it, too. I'm sure he appreciates your efforts, Antonio. However, for Jose to be in some 'difficulty' in what appears to be a Nationalist prison camp – well, you can't blame him for being confused and anxious at a time like this."

"I know I could have worked out some arrangement. I don't believe his problem was serious. We could have gotten him off with a light sentence. Now, if a Nationalist soldier catches him, he'll be shot, maybe Bonita will be, too. His rash act of running away ruins any chance of a successful outcome."

Marisa knew she wasn't getting the full truth of Jose's dangerous situation; his 'problem' was far more alarming than Antonio was letting on. She had already decided in her own mind she wasn't going to tell him everything she knew about Jose and Bonita. And certainly, nothing would be said about her own involvement in their escape.

Two of us can play the same game, Antonio, she thought. *You haven't been completely truthful with me, so why should I reveal everything to you?*

Ramon got up from the table, grumbling to himself: *If they are determined to keep talking about Jose, I want no part of it.* Aloud, he announced, "I'm going outside. Maybe Jorge and the boys could use some help."

"All right," said Antonio, "but don't go off without seeing me first. I need to talk with you."

After Ramon left the room, Antonio turned to Marisa. "How could Jose do this to me?" he began, bringing up the grievances he had expressed last night. "I just don't understand it. I never will. I don't know when I've felt so victimized. He's given me a wound that will never heal."

"Don't let it fester so much that it takes over your life," counseled Marisa. "I know that's easy for me to say at this moment, but you've got to let Jose live his life. You have your own to live."

"Where do you think he and Bonita went?" asked Antonio.

"I have no idea."

"Do you think they might still be in Trujillo?"

"Antonio, how would I know? I'm just as mystified as you are."

"They stole my car. If you escaped from here, where would you go?"

"I wouldn't know where to go. You're asking me questions I have no answers for."

"I'm sorry, Marisa. I can't get this out of my mind."

"Maybe it is better that Jose is out of your life right now. He's out of sight; now keep him out of your mind. You can get on with your life now that he's no longer involved in it."

Yes, it's easy for you to say these words, Marisa, thought Antonio. *But you don't have to live with the idea that your own brother made a fool out of you, betrayed you, and took advantage of you – all at our mother's funeral. The devil must have entered Jose's mind. What he did was evil.*

"I understand why you can't get it out of your mind," Marisa was saying as Antonio inwardly gave full reign to his bitter thoughts. "However, time does heal. One of these days, when this stupid war is over, you two will look back on all this and laugh and make jokes about it. I know it doesn't seem possible now, but it will happen. We wouldn't have any friends or family, if we didn't forgive and forget."

"I don't know if that can happen. It seems impossible. I think of last night as the worst night of my life. I lose my mother, and then I lose my brother."

Marisa was truly moved by Antonio's outpouring of emotion. She couldn't remember when she had seen him so distressed by an event. Antonio's next question caught her by surprise.

"Speaking of mother, why did she want so much to see Jose? I couldn't hear everything she said to him."

"She must have had some premonition of dying soon, Antonio. She simply wanted to be with Jose before death came between them. They hadn't been together for some time. She must have had some kind of insight that she wasn't going to see him unless you or someone could bring him to her."

"I got the feeling there was more to it than just bringing Jose to her. Her request to me was more like a command. I tell you, I've received and given a lot of orders in my military life, and mother's request was definitely a command."

Marisa thought for a moment on how to answer Antonio. She hoped to find some way that would help to heal the breach between her two brothers. A sudden idea entered her mind, convincing her Antonio may have handed her a way to do it.

"You know, Antonio, I just had a thought that could be an explanation for Jose's behavior last night. Mama gave Jose a mission the night you brought him to her. She asked him to go on a pilgrimage in her place because she could no longer physically do it. He said he would, however long it might take. Maybe that's why Jose felt such a compulsion to escape when the first opportunity arose."

"Why didn't she ask me? I would have done it for her willingly."

"I know you would. I don't know why she laid this charge upon Jose. We can't ask her now."

"Where did she ask Jose to go? Jerusalem's too far; no one here has enough money to pay for that trip. Rome? No, it wouldn't be Rome when we've got Santiago de Compostela right here in Spain. That's where it is, isn't it?"

"It could be the reason Jose made his escape, Antonio: to fulfill Mama's dying wish!"

Let her imagine he was thinking only of mother's wish, thought Antonio. *Jose is not that noble. He's too self-serving.*

To Marisa, he said, "You've come up with a reasonable assumption. I hope it's true. It says something better of Jose than anything I've been able to come up with."

"Oh, that's got to be it. I know it's true. Jose said he would do anything to bring peace and comfort to her, even if he were to die trying."

"If he isn't careful, that's exactly what will happen to him. I could have helped him succeed in the mission mother laid on him. I could have made it possible."

"How?"

"To get to Santiago, if that's where they are going, Jose and Bonita must travel through Nationalist territory. They cannot do that on their own. They're bound to slip and make mistakes, especially with the sympathies they have for the liberal Republic."

"Bonita was able to get here from Galicia on her own, much of it in Nationalist-held areas."

"She was lucky or more skillful than I would have thought possible," said Antonio. "Also, she wasn't traveling with an escaped prisoner at that time."

"They're both brave and resourceful. Neither of them will give up easily. Those are the characteristics that gave you so much trouble last night, Antonio. Ask yourself, what would you have done had the roles been reversed? Would you have meekly surrendered and done nothing?"

"It's a question of right and wrong. The escape they made was criminal. It was sneaky. They went about it dishonestly; it was the coward's way. There was a better way, Marisa, but they didn't choose it."

"So much was happening. They didn't have time to sit down and reason it out."

"Jose and Bonita are two of the same kind. They're both impulsive and thoughtless. Their instincts are the same thing as their reasoning.

Marisa saw no advantage pressing her argument any further. Her purpose had been to plant a seed of doubt in Antonio's mind and try to shake him from his absolute conviction his brother had an evil intent to betray him.

"Well, think about what I have said," she insisted. "Jose may have had better motives than you are willing to admit to yourself."

"Oh, I'll think about it," Antonio promised. "I'll probably think about it too much, like you warned me not to do. Right now, I need to talk Ramon into walking with me to the Plaza Mayor. We've got to arrange for a car to get us back to camp at Badajoz. Afterwards, both of us will move on to the front near Talavera."

"Ramon's going with you?"

"He might as well since both of our companies are there by now. Ramon must be on some kind of extended leave, probably to be with *madre* in her last days."

"That's what he told me," said Marisa.

"I promised Captain Barcena I'd return as soon as the funeral and burial were over. As I said last night, I must give an explanation . . ." Antonio stopped in mid-sentence. A car was entering the driveway. He went outside the house to ask if there was anything needed. Marisa followed him. She recognized the driver as a bank clerk in town.

"Lieutenant Martinez?" he called.

"Yes," answered Antonio.

"I have some bad news for you." Pointing to the back of the car, he continued with his message. "A body of a Nationalist soldier was dumped by the fountain of the Plaza Mayor about an hour ago. I have it in a black shroud in the rear seat of my car. Someone said they thought the dead body was that of the soldier who drove you and your brothers into town last evening for your mother's funeral."

Marisa nearly choked on her breath. "Oh, no," she gasped.

These words came to her mind: *Those guerrilleros; they went too far.*

CHAPTER 18
THE HANDSHAKE

Antonio and Ramon sat on the steps of the *Iglesia de San Martin* on Trujillo's Plaza Mayor. They had quickly packed and said their good-byes to Marisa and her family. Antonio had asked the bank clerk to take them into the main square of the town with the dead body. Once there, he telephoned the Badajoz detention camp and explained the situation, asking for a car to assist them.

"Why did you want me to pack my things?" Ramon inquired of his brother. "I'm due back with my company day after tomorrow. Because of Mama's condition, they gave me a week's leave."

"I'll see that you get there," Antonio responded. "After we deliver the body to Badajoz, we'll move out toward Talavera. Your unit is probably there, too. I'm going to ask your commanding officer to transfer you to my company. I've got a job for you, an important one. When I explain it to your superior, there shouldn't be any problem getting the transfer."

Ramon was not enthusiastic about returning to the front lines. The transfer idea just mentioned made him interested in the mysterious job Antonio was proposing. "What do you want me to do?" he asked.

"Before I get into what I have in mind, tell me, Ramon, while I was gone before the funeral, did you hear anyone – Bonita, Marisa, or Jorge – plotting to help Jose escape?"

"No, they had no such discussion when I was around."

"You know, Ramon, you haven't been very alert when you needed to be. I even suspect Bonita enlisted our sister or her husband or both of them to help with the escape, but I can't be sure of that since you saw nothing, heard nothing, and know nothing."

"If they did make some plans, they certainly would not have told me about them."

"Of course, they're not going to tell you," snapped Antonio in frustration. "But, there are quiet ways to find out what's going on. And then, to top it all off, you go to sleep at the funeral and do nothing to prevent Jose and Bonita from slipping away from us."

"Don't blame it all on me. I'm not the villain of this piece."

"I'm not blaming you for anything, Ramon. I only wish you could have been more awake. There was a lot going on under your nose. You just didn't want to be involved. How many brothels did you frequent while I was gone?"

"None," said Ramon, defiantly. "I certainly wasn't in the mood for that sort of thing after mother died."

Ramon was irritated by Antonio's domineering attitude. This wasn't the first time he had been chastised by his older brother. Resentment boiled up inside.

One of these days, Antonio, he thought, *I'm going to punch you in the nose if you don't quit harassing me. I'm not your little brother any more.*

Antonio kept going with his message of reproach. "Let me say one other thing as long as we're talking about things you could have done but didn't. You might stand up a little more firmly for your Nationalist cause. When we were discussing the politics of the war, I felt like I was carrying the whole load. You could have said something other than crack a few jokes."

"I'm only doing the same thing as your hero Franco does, Antonio. He always plays his cards close to his chest." Ramon brought up his hands in front of him. "He didn't tip his hand to be pro-nationalist, pro-fascist, pro-monarchist or pro-anything until late in the game. His closest allies were not certain Franco would actually join the rising until a few days before it began."

"He is cautious, to be sure, but he is involved. Ramon, you're not involved."

"I don't want to be involved. The 'ins and outs' of politics bores the hell out of me. I dislike it intensely; it usually leads to trouble and war."

"Well, my brother, you are involved, whether you like it or not. Jose's escape with Bonita now involves the murder of a Nationalist soldier, something that might have been avoided if you had been more alert. There's a dead body of a fellow Nationalist soldier in that bag, right there in front of you. If you're not man enough to avenge murder, you're not a man."

"You think Jose or Bonita killed your driver?"

"Of course I can't say they actually did it, but their escape definitely had something to do with it. Whether or not they killed our driver, they're responsible for it. He's been murdered; they should answer for it."

"Oh, I agree," said Ramon, relieved to be no longer the focus of attention. "They should be called to account."

"One other matter," said Antonio. "There are people in Badajoz who claim Jose was in a firing squad that executed dozens of civilians before the battle. He says he wasn't there until the battle actually took place. I tended to believe him at first. Then I remembered Jose was a reporter for a newspaper in Badajoz for a while, just long enough to know who would be in favor of an overthrow of the Republic. As I look upon the dead body of our driver, I'm more inclined to think our youngest brother is a person who has experienced the pleasures of killing."

"I never thought Jose had a murderous heart. It's hard for me to even conceive of him doing such a thing."

Antonio looked Ramon square in the eye. "It's time we considered our little brother for the person he is. Let's face it, Ramon. Jose was mother's favorite, the little boy who came to her later in life. She overindulged him, pampered brat that he was. Poor little dear, she'd say. We both got meager portions because of him. How many times did you get put down in favor of him? And, what happens as a spoiled child grows up?"

"He gets away with everything."

"Yes! What kind of person is he as an adult?"

"He becomes rotten, like a piece of spoiled fruit."

"Yes again, Ramon. That's perceptive of you. Now you're becoming more observant, wide-awake."

"You've had these thoughts, too?"

"Of course. I've had them for a long time. I didn't say anything for the sake of family harmony. But now, we've got something far more serious on our hands. Jose – and Bonita, too – they may not have done the killing, but their plans and thoughtless escape set off a series of actions that led to murder."

"Yes, I can see that," Ramon agreed. "Somehow, the right thing must be done."

"Exactly. I couldn't have said it better myself," said Antonio. "And to do the right thing – that's where you come in, Ramon."

"How?"

"I want you to do a job. Here's a chance for you to be noble. Find Jose and bring him to justice."

"I'd love to, but – how?"

"Track him down. Devote your whole self to it. I think I will be able to arrange a transfer for you. You could become a member of my company. I can explain it to my commanding officer at Talavera and perhaps he could request the transfer himself. You could get a start on finding Jose and Bonita. You might come back here; they could still be around Trujillo. There's got to be someone who saw something. I'll join you as soon as we occupy Madrid."

Ramon silently considered Antonio's idea. He would not look forward to being placed under Antonio's command where he could suffer more of his brother's verbal abuse. Yet, there was an advantage to the mission Antonio had suggested; it would take him away from the danger of combat on the front lines.

Not wanting to reveal any of these thoughts to Antonio, he asked, "Is there any possibility Jose is not responsible for this death?"

"I suppose it's possible. In this world, anything is possible. Maybe, Bonita is twice as guilty as he is."

"Yes, that's true." Ramon leaped at that idea. "We've focused on Jose, Antonio. If anything, Bonita has more of a temper than he has – or, she could have planted the idea in his head. Or, even this: Bonita, herself, killed the man."

Ramon felt bitter toward Bonita. The memory of her rejection of him was humiliating and infuriating, more than he let on. "She's capable of unreasonable fury," he said to Antonio. "I saw it once while you were gone."

Antonio did not probe for the details of Ramon's observation. Instead, he summed up: "All we can say right now is they're both guilty and they must be brought to justice. We agree on that."

"Definitely!"

"Are you willing to go after them, assuming I can secure your transfer?"

"Yes, I'm willing."

"Let's shake hands on this, *mano a mano*."

"*Si, senor*." They clasped hands. Then, they held each other, each patting the other on the back.

"I'm with you on this, Antonio."

"And, I am with you, Ramon, my brother."

Chapter 19
Suspicion

Antonio and Ramon were in sight of the Badajoz detention camp when Ramon said to their new driver, "You might want to be careful after you bring my brother to his destination in your car. The last driver he had is in the black bag we're carrying."

The driver nodded that he understood.

"Don't make a joke out of this," Antonio warned Ramon. "I must give a full accounting of our driver's murder to Captain Barcena. How innocent are we of that death and Jose's disappearance?"

"We have an explanation for Jose's escape," reasoned Ramon. "It's easier to understand because of the body we're bringing back."

"What bothers me is that our dead driver was entirely blameless in this whole affair," said Antonio. "So, let's have no more excuses or light-hearted comments, please."

"Sorry," Ramon replied. "I was just trying to make conversation."

"That's all right, Ramon. Just choose your comments more thoughtfully."

As the car pulled up to the commandant's office, Captain Barcena happened to be walking out of the door. Military salutes were exchanged and Antonio introduced his brother to the captain.

Before Antonio gave his report of the escape, Captain Barcena had news for them. "The camp is buzzing about a dispatch we received from Madrid," he said. "Rumors of a massacre of Republican soldiers here at Badajoz reached the capital city a week ago, despite censorship efforts. A mob led by Republican militiamen stormed the Model Prison where three thousand Nationalist political prisoners are being held. We hear that a hundred prisoners were trapped in the courtyard and shot in retaliation. Threats have been made to kill all three thousand of them. Hopefully, cooler heads will prevail."

"I suppose the mob was enflamed by the 'sweet' words of La Pasionaria," declared Antonio. "There's a woman who'd be knitting by the guillotine if she had lived in the days of the French Revolution."

"Actually, some Socialist Party leaders tried to urge moderation, but the crowd wouldn't listen. After the killing spree, Republican militiamen paraded the dead bodies in front of the prisoners to frighten them. I can imagine that's my fate if the Republicans win this war, but I swear to you, Lieutenant, the machine-gunning that went on in the Badajoz bullring was not my responsibility. At that time, I was not the highest officer in command here."

"I will be only too happy to vouch for you, Captain," Antonio volunteered. He knew his support would mean little in a Republican court; the passions of war would overwhelm reason and reconciliation. He sought to reassure the captain.

"I wouldn't lose any sleep over it. We're going to win this war, even if we have to fight for a decade."

Ramon broke in to say emphatically, "Yes, we are, even if it takes a century!"

There, he thought, *that should be enough support, Antonio!*

The captain cracked a quick smile at the idea of such a long war, but then turned serious again. "Speaking of killing prisoners, I understand you've brought the body of your driver back from Trujillo."

"Yes," replied Antonio. He went on to describe the events of the past twenty-four hours without mentioning Ramon. "I will write to the driver's family," Antonio offered. "It's the least I can do. He seemed to be a well-trained young man."

"I'll join you in that letter," said Captain Barcena. "Do you have any idea who did the actual killing?"

"None, although I have my suspicions."

"Let's hear them."

"I hate to say this, sir, but the greatest suspicion falls upon my escaped brother and his girl friend. They had to sneak out of church, run to the Plaza Mayor, surprise our driver, overpower and kill him at some point, dump his body, and take off with the car. This morning, a bank clerk from Trujillo found him dead at the fountain in the center of town."

"Have you examined the body?"

"No. I thought it might be better if that were done professionally."

"Well, we'll have a look. I'll ask one of the local citizens to get a doctor for a professional opinion."

Thirty minutes later, the captain, Antonio, Ramon, and the doctor were peering at the body of the dead soldier, laid out on a slab in the makeshift morgue of the camp. His face had been severely beaten and his throat slashed by a sharp knife. There were other wounds with encrusted clumps of blood where the knife had entered his body.

The doctor spoke first. "I'd say this was the work of at least two people, maybe more. Our man here put up a struggle. Look at his fingernails; there are pieces of skin under them. He's been hit on the head several times; that probably knocked him out. The knife hit plenty of veins, but the most likely cause of death was the blade cutting into the carotid artery and severing it, causing him to bleed to death. There are no bullet holes, so a knife was the weapon."

"Would the skin reveal the identity of his attackers?" questioned Captain Barcena.

"I don't have any way of analyzing bits of skin to prove identity," answered the doctor. "I could send samples to Madrid, no, maybe Seville. I'm not sure they have the equipment for this kind of analysis. Heaven knows they've got other things on their mind at this time. How would they ever match this skin with that of his assailants? The killers aren't about to volunteer their skin for examination."

"What about the knife and other weapons?" Ramon inquired of everyone. "If we find the car, we might find the weapons used in the killing of this man. They would have fingerprints on them."

"Find the car first," was the only response made by the doctor.

"Are there any pieces of clothing worn by his attackers on him?" asked Antonio. "I think I could remember the clothes worn by Jose and Bonita."

"None that I have noticed," the doctor replied. "Without more evidence I don't think we're going to be able to prove conclusively who did the killing."

"It could have been a random murder carried out by any Republican soldier, a militiaman, civilian sympathizer, guerrilla fighter – anyone," suggested Captain Barcena. "With all the hatreds loose now, we can't be sure who did it. You don't have to be so hard on your brother, Lieutenant."

"In my opinion, he's the most likely one, sir. He had the greatest motive – escape. The car offered the means of getting away. The only person blocking them was our driver who was in the car, waiting for us to take my brother back here. There's a line of logic to my suspicions."

"His girl friend, she was a real spitfire," Ramon chimed in, trying to support Antonio's contention. "I wouldn't put it past her to wield a knife. The driver wouldn't expect her to be armed with any weapon."

"You may have something there," admitted the captain.

Antonio judged this moment could be the most promising time to suggest sending Ramon after the two escapees. Perhaps Captain Barcena had contacts with higher ranking officers that could help.

"His mission, sir, would not necessarily be to apprehend them by himself. I would want him to discover where they have gone. My brother Jose could lead us to something important. I'm almost certain he was concealing his true identity in the Republican military. I believe he has an importance much greater than he let on to us. It's not out of the realm of possibility that he had plenty of help in making his escape. I think he's that vital to the Reds. He and his girl friend may not have done the actual killing, but their escape was important enough for any group in the Popular Front to use force in order to free him."

All Captain Barcena would say was, "Interesting speculation, and maybe it's true. I'm willing to call my commanding officer and inquire about how a transfer for your brother Ramon could be arranged."

"Thank you, sir, and I apologize to you for being misled by my brother," said Antonio, seeking exoneration for the driver's death. "I wouldn't have asked your permission for him to attend his mother's funeral had I realized he was capable of killing a man in this underhanded way, or having him killed in order to escape."

"War makes people do strange things," reflected the captain as the doctor wrapped the body in a new shroud.

A knock sounded on the door.

"Come in," called Captain Barcena.

A soldier appeared, saluted his commanding officer and said, "Sir, the lost military vehicle has been found. There's nothing wrong with it. After we put some gas in it, we were able to drive it back to camp. It's parked outside."

"Good work. Where did you find it?"

"Hard to believe, but it was in the middle of the Rio Gevora, north of here. The car may have gone past Alburquerque and turned west toward Portugal."

"Captain," said Antonio, holding a map he had carried with him, "this information puts my brother on the road from Merida. Then he turned before reaching Badajoz, went north to where Portugal juts out to the east. He took a side road going west and abandoned the car. He and his girl friend must have gone on foot the rest of the way into Portugal."

"Sounds plausible – let's take a look at the car," said the captain, motioning to Antonio and Ramon. They thanked the doctor and went outside.

The first thing Antonio spotted in the car was the driver's cap in the back seat. "That's the cap worn by our driver. Get the doctor before he leaves, Ramon. Maybe he can determine if there's any evidence – hair, blood, whatever – left on the cap or somewhere else in the car."

Ramon hurried after the doctor. He was glad to get away from the company of the two Nationalist officers, however brief the interval might be.

"Jose would have had just enough gas in the car to get this far," surmised Antonio. "We filled the tank before we left yesterday. I've got to hand it to him; he was clever to head this way. It didn't cross my mind he would head back toward Badajoz. I figured he would want to be as far away from his detention camp as possible. I told Ramon that Jose and Bonita could still be somewhere around Trujillo. I also guessed they might head for Madrid or even Talavera and join Republican forces there."

"He may not have wanted to expose his girl friend to that much danger, Lieutenant. Why do you think he came this way?"

"Portugal is a neutral country, sir."

"The Salazar regime is helping us in every way short of jumping right into the war themselves."

"Here's another idea, sir. His girl friend is a teacher living with her parents in Galicia. Her school year starts soon, and he may have thought of getting her home because of her job."

As Ramon was coming back with the doctor, Antonio added, "The discovery of this car narrows our search considerably. If and when you are able to arrange my brother's transfer, sir, could you inform me as soon as possible? I am duty-bound to report to my commanding officer at Talavera, but as soon as I am done there, I could join Ramon in tracking down my brother."

"I believe we can arrange the transfer you want, Lieutenant. I will report this incident as the murder of a Nationalist soldier whose death must be avenged. We don't allow such events to go unanswered."

Antonio was pleased to hear the captain's flat, adamant statement. "More than anyone else could," he said, "Ramon and I feel responsible to bring justice for an innocent man's willful murder – even if his killer is our brother."

"I understand," said Captain Barcena. "Now, if you'll excuse me, I have other matters I must attend to."

After the captain left, Antonio turned to the doctor and asked, "Can you look in the car for evidence that would give us the identity of the killers? Traces of blood, bits of clothing, weapons – anything that could help us?"

The doctor went into the car. "The knifing must have taken place outside the car," he reported. "There's no evidence of any killing inside. No weapons are here. All I find is the cap that must have been worn by the soldier. It's in good shape. Nothing is on it. I'm not an experienced detective in matters of murder, but I can't see anything here that would provide us with clues."

Antonio felt stymied. He wanted conclusive evidence that Jose and possibly Bonita were implicated in murder. He would have to be content with circumstantial evidence and speculation – until the doctor said, "Wait a minute, there's a trace of blood on the back of the driver's seat."

"Let me have a look," Antonio said with renewed hope. "The blood could be that of the driver. If it is, that would implicate my brother Jose. However, I remember Jose was struck in the back by a guard here. He complained about it to me before we left for our mother's funeral. It's possible a cut from a wound reopened and blood coming from Jose's back seeped through his shirt. Is there any way we could match the blood in the car with any blood on the dead soldier's body or clothes?"

The doctor responded in the negative. "I don't have any equipment to do that," he said. "However, I'll check to see if such an analysis could be made."

"I'd appreciate that," Antonio responded as the doctor departed.

Antonio looked at Ramon. "Seems to me it's very likely Jose and Bonita had plenty to do with our driver's murder. We must keep reminding ourselves they're guilty of a killing. They dishonored the memory of our madre, took advantage of the distractions of her funeral, violated our good-will, made an ugly escape, stole our car, and killed our driver or had him murdered. Murder is a strong word, but if they didn't do it themselves, it was done on their behalf. They benefited from it."

"Murder is murder," said Ramon. "It's not to be practiced – even in war. It's against the law, and it's a violation of one of the Ten Commandments."

"Absolutely, Ramon," declared Antonio, again looking at his brother straight in the eye. "I'm proud of the statement you just made. You're so right on all counts. It's so military – so lawful – so religious."

Chapter 20
Bonita, the Storyteller

Jose and Bonita trudged past whitewashed houses along the road toward Monforte, nearly forty kilometers west of Campo Major. During the mercifully cool day, they had been able to stop for interludes of rest among the olive groves and cork trees that mark the Alentejo province of Portugal.

Bracing their backs against the bark of a cork oak at one pause, Bonita asked Jose about life in his militia, commenting, "Somehow, I could never quite picture you as a soldier."

"That experience was unlike anything I'd ever imagined about military life," he replied. "Almost complete social equality existed between officers and men in my militia. Every one from the highest officers on down – all ate the same food, wore the same clothes, and received the same small amount of pay. Our militia was more of a democracy than I thought possible. I expected the usual military hierarchy. We all knew orders were to be obeyed, especially if they were from seasoned veterans. But it was understood these directions were from fellow comrades, not between superiors and inferiors. Rank didn't mean much; there was no saluting or heel-clicking. I was impressed with this version of a classless society, especially in a place where I least expected it."

Bonita weighed Jose's words for a moment and then said, "Maybe there is something to the Socialist dream of human equality. I've often thought it was too naïve, too idealistic, too contrary to human nature. So many of the people who have promoted it are anti-religious, I've usually dismissed it without any more thought."

"I admit at first I questioned how an army of this kind could ever hope to win a war. Our militia was a group of mostly workers and peasants – raw, untrained, and undisciplined. Most of us came voluntarily to the defense of the Republic. At Badajoz, we were facing a battle-tested, professional military:

Moorish *regulares* and the Foreign Legion. We, on the other hand, were fighting for our homeland. We lost the battle, not that we lacked spirit and courage, but because they had more experience and were furnished with better weapons. We gave the Army of Africa the hardest fight they had had up to that point of the war, and maybe it's why the retribution was so excessive. The most important point, though, is this: we were willing to sacrifice ourselves for our country. Call it an idea, an ideal of liberty and equality, a better future based on brotherhood, not the class-ridden social order we've been trying to get rid of."

"That's worth fighting for."

"Yes, and you're probably right when you say you couldn't see me as a typical soldier, whose training and discipline are based on fear and punishment. The sadism, abuse, and bullying that go on in an ordinary army wouldn't have been tolerated for a moment in my militia."

"I thought war was primarily hideous brutality. Jose, you make it sound actually inspiring."

"Well, war can inspire the best *and* the worst in people. There is bravery *and* there is behavior that would get you hanged if done in peacetime. I suppose the Nationalists are scornful about the way we ran our militia. I'm sure Antonio would say it would never work, and that's true of an army of mercenaries and conscripts. I saw their way while I was in prison; the Legion's training resorted to the whip and lash. Our way does work with free people in the long run. When orders are appeals in the name of reason or comradeship, discipline gets better as time goes on. I've seen it happen in a limited way. Officers in our militia told me they had no trouble getting men to obey or volunteer for dangerous missions."

"Going into battle like you did at Badajoz fits any definition of 'dangerous mission' for me," said Bonita, "especially when you end up in a prison camp."

Jose cherished Bonita's comment as well as the discovery of meaning in an occurrence filled with anguish. "When I was captured and stuck in a cell, I doubted the value of my experience. To be sure, it could have been a disaster, and it was for many, but I've come to realize the lessons I learned will leave a mark on me for the rest of my life, maybe more so than the years I spent at university."

"You had to go outside the scholar's life to find the social equality we were talking about," noted Bonita. "If anything, university education emphasizes the differences between human beings just as the rank-conscious military does."

No Greater Love

"The lowly recruit in the typical military finds out that rank has privileges he doesn't have and never will have if he doesn't rise in those ranks. Remember how a person flunking final tests at university was given first-hand knowledge of failure. Not only would he finish without a degree, but he had better leave hidden in a cart to avoid the garbage thrown by his classmates."

"I'm glad neither of us had to endure that disgusting custom. The school is supposed to be getting rid of it."

"I never participated in throwing food at anyone, but failure in the 'final exam' of the military means far worse: death or capture, imprisonment, torture."

"Just don't excuse the failure of armed humans to reconcile their differences with others, Jose."

"I'm not. I'm only being realistic, pointing out certain facts of life that I've learned since getting out of school."

They stopped their talking. Jose and Bonita brooded independently on whether the harsh and often degrading state of human existence in which they were now entangled would harden into a permanent stain on their relationship. How could university life have prepared them for what they were now facing? They could not keep the world out of their sights nor out of their minds. If current realities continued, what chance would there be of a normal, decent life?

Casting aside these thoughts, Jose broke the silence. "The only time I saw an officer in my militia pull rank, he never did it again. He was new and ordered a battle-hardened anarchist to shine his boots or face punishment."

"Tell me what happened," insisted Bonita.

Jose hesitated before answering. "The new officer was told to go and do something anatomically impossible with himself."

They laughed and then looked up at a sky that told them evening hours were approaching. Jose wondered if they should try to find a hostel for the night.

"We'd better not risk it," Bonita replied. "We'd be asked to give our names and addresses. They'd know we're Spanish as soon as we opened our mouths. They would want escudos, not pesetas, and to know if we're married."

"We are," proclaimed Jose. "Well, at least, in our hearts, we are. Do you think the ring you have would pass for a wedding ring?"

Bonita held up the fingers of her left hand. "What do you think?" she asked.

Jose held her hand and exclaimed in mock seriousness, "That's one of the finest wedding rings I've ever seen! The *hombre* who gave it to you must have spent a fortune on it. Where would have he found it? Must be from Corcubion's finest jewelry shop. Is it an amethyst?"

"Jose, you don't know jewelry. This is an opal. My grandmother gave it to me before she died. She would have liked you. We'll call it our wedding ring."

Jose examined the milky white gem. "It's beautiful. I never looked at it as closely as I am now."

"*Abuela* told me it's a form of polished silica."

"Silica. I'm glad your ring holds a stone, Bonita. The only silica I know is dust from the mines that caused my father's death. Isn't it peculiar how the same substance can become an object of great beauty or something that kills you?"

"If the ring brings unpleasant memories to you, Jose, I'll not wear it."

"No, no, I didn't mean for you to do that. I want you to wear it. Besides, it will pass for a wedding ring. You just hold it up to the hotel clerk and say '*marido*' and point to me. The Portuguese say the same word as we do for husband."

"*Si*, I know. And I am your *esposa*. I feel like we're already married. In spirit, we are. But, Jose, should we risk going to a hostel?"

"We're tired. We could use a good night's sleep. It's worth the risk. We can use fake names."

"Let's see. I've always liked the name Estrella. Call me that."

"*Si*, my star, and, I'll take my friend's name in Coimbra: Manuel. What shall we use for a last name? How about Garcia, my mother's maiden name?"

"We don't want to use anything that could be traced to you. We've got to be careful. How about Gonzalez? How many Gonzalez's are there in Spain? The more of them, the better; there must be a quarter of a million."

"Okay, Gonzalez it is. Senhor Clerk, meet Estrella and Manuel Gonzalez, the happy elderly couple from Spain. I trust your arthritis has improved with today's walk, my dear."

"And your lumbago, my husband? I trust it hasn't crippled you for tomorrow's journey. If I'm to help you, I'll have to walk alongside of you."

They both laughed at Bonita's implied protest about walking behind, but Jose insisted they maintain the appearance of tradition a little while longer.

Just before nightfall, the 'old couple' arrived in Monforte and found a hostel on the main road through town. "Senhor and senhora Gonzalez" were checked into a room by a young clerk who, if he suspected false identities from the Spanish accent and the use of pesetas, he didn't show it.

As soon as they closed the door to their room behind them, Jose and Bonita looked at each other for a long moment and then fell into each other's arms. The warmth that rushed into their bodies as they kissed one another made them feel alive again after the strenuous night and day they had experienced.

"Most of the past month I could only dream of a moment like this and wonder if it would ever happen again," whispered Jose into Bonita's ear. "I would often think of how much I love you, and I would ache all over, longing for you."

"I was going crazy not knowing what was happening to you," replied Bonita. "That's why I wrote to your sister when school ended last spring, offering to come and help with Mama's care. I had to get close to where you were."

"And, now, we are the closest we can be. I'll never be separated from you again; I know that now. I could never ask for any more devotion than that you've shown me. I love you with all my heart. We are married in spirit, like we said back on the road. We may not be married under the law, but in the eyes of God, I believe we are."

With all the loving tenderness Jose and Bonita could summon by their caresses and kisses, their bodies expressed the fervent desire they had for each other. When their lovemaking ended, Jose and Bonita lay in each other's arms. They fell asleep that way, sleeping deeply that night and not waking until the next morning was well under way.

Still glowing from their intimate love of the night before and refreshed by a long night's sleep and a bath, clean clothes, and food in the morning, 'Manuel' accompanied by 'Estrella' proceeded along a number of secondary roads heading north and west toward Coimbra. They ate more of the food provided by Marisa. Each time a car went by them, they girded themselves for possible capture.

Complete relaxation was inconceivable. Bonita could not get out of her mind the thought about the PVDE, the Portuguese internal security police, shipping hundreds of escaping Spaniards back home to trial and imprisonment or execution. The only governmental car they had seen so far turned out to be driven by a local citizen. The PVDE would most likely travel in unmarked cars, Jose reckoned, and for this reason the sight of every car became the occasion for an anxious moment.

The day was blessedly uneventful. As evening approached on the way toward Ponte de Sor, they found themselves stopping where a man was repairing a gate that allowed entrance to a prosperous-looking farm. Jose decided on the spur of the moment to take a chance, explaining to the farmer that he, Senhor Manuel Gonzalez, and his wife, Senhora Estrella Gonzalez, would simply like to rest in his shed for the night in case there would be rain. The senhor and senhora would be willing to work for an hour next morning to pay for their lodging. The request was granted with no work required and no questions asked. Jose could hardly believe their good luck.

To reassure the farmer, Bonita held up her ring, smiled, and said *"esposa"* pointing to herself and *"marido"* pointing to Jose. The farmer smiled approvingly. He introduced himself as Senhor Marcelo Marques. Just before nightfall, the farmer's *esposa* appeared with blankets, thinking they would be needed with the coolness of the night air. After Jose's *"mucho gracias"* and Bonita's *"muito obrigada,"* the two settled in for the night on a makeshift bed of straw.

"The average person is quite decent when you ask for a favor," observed Jose as he hugged Bonita beneath the blanket.

"Let's hope he's not telephoning the PVDE," said Bonita in a matter-of-fact way. "You're very trusting when it comes to the intentions of people. I hope you are right about our farmer, though. I'm sure both Senhor and Senhora know we are Spanish. It was very nice of him to let us stay here."

"My approach is to trust a person until he proves himself unworthy of that trust."

"You grew up in a loving family, Jose. I did too, but I've seen a little too much of the world lately. After writing about strikes and riots and all you went through at Badajoz, I would think your first reactions to people would involve a little more suspicion."

"Don't worry. I'm on guard as much as you are. This shed has plenty of tools that could make good weapons if we needed them, like that pitchfork and sickle over there."

"Those wouldn't stand a chance against guns, though. They'd shoot first and ask questions later. And, there would be more than one coming to get us."

"Ah, you are my down-to-earth wife. Yes, I know what you say is true. Every day, every night is going to bring its share of risks. We can only take them on; we don't have a choice. Are you sure you want to go through all this, being hunted if not by our enemies at home, by their collaborators here? I could put you on a bus when we reach Coimbra and send you home."

"Jose, I faced that question long ago. I didn't travel all the way from Galicia just to tell you good-bye and go back home."

"I love you, I love you completely," was Jose's earnest reply. "I don't know what I did to earn such faithful love, Bonita."

"It was just you, being you," said Bonita. "It's all very simple. You either love a person or you don't. To me, it's not a mystery that I love you."

"You are my loved one – forever," whispered Jose in Bonita's ear.

He started to embrace her earnestly as the headlights of a motor vehicle unexpectedly lit the yard. A small truck had turned into the driveway and stopped by the house. Lights and motor were turned off. Two men emerged from the truck, slamming their doors. In the gathering darkness, Jose took Bonita by one hand and clasped the sickle in the other. They crept to the lone window at the front of the shed. The only way out of their small building would put them in direct view of the men. They were trapped inside.

The men went on to the porch and knocked on the door of the house. The farmer appeared and talked with them for a few minutes. The shape of their figures gradually became more visible as they shifted standing positions and occasionally moved into the light streaming from the house.

"They may be all right," whispered Jose. "They look like they're other farmers. I think they're wearing work clothes."

Suddenly, the three figures moved off the porch and started walking toward the shed, flashlights lighting their way. Jose tightened his grip on the sickle.

If they are all right, he thought, *Senhor Marques will wonder why I'm holding this sickle like a weapon.*

He lowered the implement quietly to the floor.

As the three men got closer to the shed, Marcelo Marques called out to Jose and Bonita in Spanish, "Don't be frightened. My neighbor and his son are only coming to borrow some tools. They speak Spanish, too."

Bonita replied in *Gallego*, "It's all right, come ahead."

The farmer continued, "I told them about your being here. I didn't want them to be surprised when they saw you. Excuse the interruption."

"If they are coming to take us," Jose whispered to Bonita, "this is a well rehearsed act."

The three men entered the shed and Senhor Marques presented his neighbors to Jose and Bonita, who couldn't completely avoid the look of apprehension on their faces. "Senor and Senora Gonzalez, I'd like to introduce Senhor Andre Vincente and his son, Henriques."

They shook hands with Jose and Bonita and set about looking for the tools they needed. Jose remained anxious, particularly when Henriques asked where the sickle was. Jose handed it to him with as genuine a smile as he could construct.

When the farmer's neighbors found the tools they came for, Bonita said, "I have to admit we were a bit startled, Senhor Marques. *Gracias* for telling us they were here only to borrow your farm implements. *Obrigada*."

Henriques looked at Jose and Bonita and said, "You aren't escaping from *Espana*, are you? There's been a lot of that since your civil war started."

"Oh no, senhor," answered Bonita. "We couldn't be escaping since we are on our way back to Galicia. We've been visiting my sister at Vila Vicosa, and we decided to spend more time in your country because of the war. We stayed too long. Our escudos are completely gone. Our pesetas are almost gone. We are ashamed to tell you this. We'll be walking and hitch-hiking most of the way."

"It wouldn't matter to me if you *were* escaping," declared Andre Vincente. "I don't agree with our country's policy of sending back Spaniards who seek asylum in Portugal."

Bonita and Jose both indicated their approval. "It's kind of you to say that," said Bonita. "I'm sure there are desperate people on all sides of the conflict that need sanctuary."

"Your country may be starting down the road my country began a decade ago," Senhor Vincente continued, referring to the collapse of the democratic republic and military takeover Portugal had experienced ten years earlier. "My country may be in better shape economically today, but I'm not sure we could say Portugal is a better place to live. Most people here are very tight-lipped and withdrawn from political affairs. You can't say anything critical of the government nowadays."

"Speak for yourself, father," stated Henriques. "I think our country has improved greatly since the republic was turned into a 'New State.' I wouldn't want our guests to think we're under the absolute rule of one man. As Antonio Salazar has accurately said, we are a dictatorship without a dictator."

Everyone was driven into abashed silence by the son's brash confrontation with his father.

Jose couldn't help but think: *Oh no, I believe I'm hearing the voice of my oldest brother all over again.*

"You can see I don't impose censorship in my family," said Senhor Vincente after a pause. "I regard Salazar as a sincere person. He is respectable, very religious, and leads a virtuous life. A few years ago, he was given absolute control over our nation's financial activities, but now he has been able to extend that authority over all political and cultural affairs as well. If he had limited himself to finance, I would think more positively of him."

Jose agreed with the father's opinions; however, he sought to help him avoid the distress of an open argument with his son. "Our civil war must sound terrible from the accounts we read in newspapers," he remarked.

"Thank God our political differences didn't lead to warfare among ourselves," said Senhor Marques. "At least we were able to stay away from the sort of violence Spain is going through."

"When the war started, we had already started our travels in Portugal," said Jose, adding to the contrived story Bonita had begun. "I don't know what we'll find when we get back to Galicia."

"I can take you part of your way tomorrow," Andre Vincente offered. "That's a long way to walk. I'm going to Nazare on the coast in the morning. My brother has a fishing supply store there. I'm taking some vegetables to his family."

"We don't want to burden you, senhor," responded Jose.

"It's no problem. You'd be welcome to go along with me as far as you want. The front seat of my truck will hold three people. I can stop here at Marcelo's farm and take you to Batalha. You could visit the monastery there. It's quite a sight. Or, maybe you'd like to see Alcobaca nearby. That's worth a stop. I could drop you off at Tomar; that's not quite so far west. Those places are not out of the way for me. There are several ways I can take to Nazare. You can see a lot of Portuguese history in that area."

"You are most kind, Senhor Vincente," spoke Jose. Turning to Bonita, he asked, "What do you say, Estrella?"

Bonita indicated approval. "Our feet could use a day of rest," she said, putting aside any fears of danger she had. *"Obrigada, senhor, mucho gracias."*

Jose repeated the thanks Bonita had given. *"Obrigado.* We appreciate your kindness, all of you," he said with feeling and shaking hands with all three men.

"We'll be going," Senhor Marques indicated. "Have a good rest tonight. We won't be disturbing you any more. *Adios."*

"I'll come for you at eight hours in the morning," said Senhor Vincente. *"Adios."*

"Adeus," replied Jose and Bonita, waving their hands.

When the farmer and his neighbors had left the shed, Jose breathed a huge sigh of relief. "I hope we're doing the right thing," he said. "Senhor Vincente appears to be genuine in his offer to us. Batalha and Alcobaca are a little further to the west than I'd like to go. Tomar is right on our way to Coimbra."

"I'd love to visit Alcobaca," said Bonita. "That's where Pedro and Inez are buried. I've always wanted to go there. There's such a romantic story about those two."

"I take it these were friends of yours," grinned Jose.

Bonita laughed. "No, but I'll tell you the story their love has given to Portuguese history."

"Before you do let's decide where we're going tomorrow. Alcobaca is further west than I'd like to go, but it's much closer to Coimbra than we are now. We'll be traveling about a hundred kilometers in Senhor Vincente's truck."

"I know we're not on a sightseeing trip, Jose. If we can keep up the pretenses we've established here, I believe we'll be safe. I agree with you about Senhor Vincente; he seems to be sincere in wanting to help us."

"So, watch him deliver us to the nearest police station in the morning."

Bonita pretended to be shocked. "Here I'm the one who thought you were too trusting."

"All we can do is to rely on Andre Vincente tomorrow."

Jose smoothed out the blanket on the straw and held the top blanket for Bonita to crawl under. "Now, tell me your story about Pedro and Inez."

"When you hear it, you'll know why I'd like to visit Alcobaca," started Bonita. "Pedro was the son of a Portuguese king, Afonso IV. When Pedro was in his late teens, his father arranged a marriage for him with Constanca of Aragon. It was one of those political marriages; you know, kings were doing that all the time back in the 1300's. When he met Constanca, Pedro happened to glance at one of her ladies-in-waiting, the beautiful Inez de Castro from – guess where?"

"I couldn't imagine," said Jose, smiling. "You'll have to tell me."

"Where else but Galicia!" exclaimed Bonita. "Now you know why I like this story. For Pedro, it was love at first sight. Inez vowed to be loyal to Constanca, but soon she fell in love with Pedro. They married in secret. He set her up in Coimbra at a palace later called *Quinta das Lagrimas*. When we get to Coimbra, we'll have to go there, Jose."

"Somehow, I knew that was coming," laughed Jose.

"When King Afonso heard about the marriage – well, he was not amused. He ordered Inez to leave Portugal. Afonso hated improper romances; he was tormented by the memories of all the illegitimate children forced upon his own family. So, Inez went just across the border to live with her aunt.

Meanwhile, Constanca died giving birth to Pedro's son named Fernando. Pedro went through a proper period of mourning. After that, he brought Inez back to Coimbra. Afonso may have even given Pedro permission to do so, and, if he did, he soon regretted it. Spanish nobles in Castile were rebelling against their king. Afonso saw Inez as a connection between Pedro and the Castilian schemers. To get military help, the Castilians offered their crown to Pedro. Afonso thought of Inez as nothing more than a Spanish spy and he didn't want any Spaniards wielding influence over his son; after all, he would be King of Portugal someday."

"Ah, politics again," muttered Jose. "Somehow, we always get back to politics and power."

"Quite true. Inez lived comfortably at *Quinta das Lagrimas*. She and Pedro had four children; naturally, this was disturbing to Afonso. Here was Pedro's legitimate son and heir, Fernando, away in a home of his own while Pedro's illegitimate children got all the attention from their loving parents. More bad memories for Afonso! Not only was Afonso unhappy, but the public began to disapprove of Inez. She was blamed for all sorts of disasters: an earthquake in Lisbon, a plague that devastated the country, and a drought that ruined the crops. Her love for Pedro was seen as the cause of every bad thing that happened."

"We aren't the only ones who love in the midst of evil times," said Jose as he craned his neck to look at the yard and farmhouse and make sure no flashlights were winding their way toward them. "I'm afraid I know what's going to happen."

"Yes, King Afonso's advisors plotted the assassination of Inez. Afonso went to *Quintas das Lagrimas* to confront Pedro and Inez about the situation. He took with him three knights who were among those conspiring to get rid of Inez. Afonzo found Inez at home, but Pedro was away, hunting. Afonzo was enchanted with her beauty. He admired the innocence and courtesy of her children. He wasn't able to make a decision about Inez. As they prepared to leave, the three knights argued that she must be done away with. Afonso washed his hands of the matter, saying 'do as you like.' "

"Pontius Pilate did the same thing at the trial of Jesus," recalled Jose. "Or, like Henry II of England and Thomas a Becket, Afonso was saying in effect, 'Will no one rid me of this meddlesome woman?' "

"Exactly. When Pedro returned, he found screaming children, frantic servants, and a dead wife – her body slashed with dagger wounds, her neck sliced open, and her blood soaking the ground. The servants told Pedro that they recognized the assassins as the King's men. Pedro searched for them.

Of course, they had left the country. Inez was buried in Coimbra at the old convent of Santa Clara. Pedro went mad with thoughts of revenge. A year or two later, Afonso died and Pedro became king. Pedro declared to all that he was married to Inez. He began to have two tombs constructed, one for Inez and one for himself. Despite his passion for retribution, he was a good king. He ruled in a time of peace. Pedro paid out of his own pocket for public feasts. He gave generously to the poor."

"Did they ever find the killers?"

"Yes. Two of the three assassins were found in Castile, and brought back to face Pedro's vengeance. As Pedro looked on while eating his lunch, they were tortured and their hearts were ripped out."

"Nice guy, this Pedro, and quite a story, Bonita. Gruesome in the end, but a rough sort of justice was served."

"Historians sometimes call Pedro 'the Cruel' and sometimes 'the Just.' That's not all, however. The story gets stranger."

"It does? Continue." Jose started to laugh.

"Jose! How can you laugh?"

"How can it get worse? Isn't this enough?"

"No. You see, Pedro figured he'd had his revenge. Now it's time for Inez to have her revenge. She had been in the ground four years. Her decomposing body was secretly taken from her grave and dressed in royal robes. King Pedro summoned the court to a coronation ceremony. He believed many courtiers were implicated in the murder of Inez, but he didn't know which ones were guilty. When the crowd came, they thought the king had chosen a new wife to be queen because they saw two thrones in front of them. Pedro was seated on one throne, but on the other throne was an elegantly dressed royal cadaver. The court watched in fascinated horror as Pedro named the dead Inez as Queen of Portugal."

"The odor must have been terrible. You said she was four years dead?"

"Yes, but Pedro was not done with his courtiers. He demanded they must pay homage to the new queen."

Jose interrupted Bonita to say, "There was nothing they could do; the doors of Santa Clara had been bolted shut. One by one, they were required to press their lips to the rotting flesh of the corpse. The body of Inez was taken for burial in one of the two tombs Pedro had made at Alcobaca. When he died, Pedro was also buried at Alcobaca. And, that's why we're going there, tomorrow."

"Jose!" cried Bonita. "You knew the story all along. You were just leading me on. I wondered why you were smiling and laughing as I told it."

No Greater Love

"I read about Pedro and Inez sometime ago, somewhere," he admitted. "I didn't remember all the details, but no one forgets the last part. I wanted to hear you tell it, though. I'm sorry about the laughter; the story isn't humorous. You told it very well. You were so earnest about it."

"The story makes me sad. They had a pure love for each other, but look at what it came to. Why does love so freely given and so naturally expressed become so crushed and so mutilated by the world?"

"I suppose love can be extinguished because we are in a world that is a constant contest between good and evil and human nature is both virtuous and sinful. What we have been through and are going through now must not change the way we love each other. Broken and mutilated people can have their love destroyed. We mustn't let that happen to us."

He reached for Bonita and brought her close to him. "You *are* wonderful, my loved one," he said softly. "Such vital power you have in your mind and such energy you have in your body." He marveled at the spirit and the life force she possessed and shared with him.

Bonita pressed her lips on Jose's forehead. "If something happened to me like it did to Inez, I would not wish for you to seek vengeance on my behalf."

"Why?"

"I would think I had turned your love to hate, and that hate would destroy you. Revenge and hate ruin people who carry it within themselves."

"What would you rather I do? Let your murderers go free?"

"Maybe it's better to simply leave it and, in time, even forgive."

"Suppose I were the one to be done in by killers. What would you do then?"

"Now you're making it difficult for me, Jose. I'm too tired to work this out tonight. Let's solve it tomorrow."

"*Buenas noches*, Bonita. I love you. Isn't that where we started this evening?"

"Yes. *Buenas noches*, my love." After a moment's hesitation, Bonita said, "A thought just occurred to me. When Pedro had the two tombs constructed at Alcobaca, they were built to face each other. On the Day of Resurrection, Inez and Pedro will rise to see each other. Jose, when I wake in the morning, the first person I will see is you."

"And, the first sight I will have is of you, Bonita."

Jose and Bonita were soon fast asleep curled up next to each other.

Chapter 21
Marcelo and Andre

Jose and Bonita awoke next morning as Senhora Marques knocked politely on the shed door. "Pardon, senor, senora," she said. "I have prepared *pequeno almoco* for you. Come to the house before you start on your way with Senhor Vincente."

"Pardon us, senhora," answered Jose. "We should have risen before you came to wake us. We walked so much yesterday; it must have tired us more than we realized."

"I'm happy you had a good night's sleep. My husband is almost done with his morning rounds. He hopes you will eat with him at the breakfast table."

"*Obrigado*, senhora. We'll be there as soon as we can."

Jose and Bonita brushed their clothes free of straw and readied themselves for the day. They walked through the back door of the house, found the table, and sat down with Marcelo Marques. Breakfast consisted of *café, torrada, ovos, yogurte, and sumo de laranja* – coffee, toast, eggs, yogurt, and orange juice – more than the usual Portuguese *pequeno almoco*. The farmer expressed his regrets again for the interruption of the night before. Jose and Bonita assured him it was no problem and that they were grateful for the opportunity to get a good night's sleep.

"Looks like Andre Vincente and his son have a slight difference of opinion when they talk about political matters," observed Senhor Marques. "I hadn't particularly noticed that before."

"It's not unusual these days," replied Jose. "The Gonzalez family has had its share of political debates, although my *esposa* and I see eye-to-eye on most things. Senhor Vincente appears to be more liberal than his son. Younger people are usually more liberal than their parents."

"Yes, that seems to be true. Andre Vincente and I tend to be similar in our political beliefs. We are quite liberal when the subject involves the freedom to express opinions and conservative when it is a matter of family and religion. We share many of the same opinions toward Antonio Salazar."

"Your Prime Minister seems more conservative to us than, say, either of you," judged Jose.

"Yes, he is," agreed Marcelo Marques. "In many ways, he is a good man as my neighbor said last night. He lives quietly, takes his religion seriously, and hasn't enriched himself in political office. He is competent and highly educated. He doesn't run all over the world, showing off and getting involved in foreign intrigues. He seems to admire Mussolini, but considers Germany to be a pagan state under Hitler. Senhor Salazar keeps to himself, perhaps too much. He might be better off if he got out more and mixed with his own people."

"Wasn't Salazar from Coimbra?" asked Jose.

"Yes, Senor Gonzalez. Salazar gained recognition as a scholar and writer at the University of Coimbra. The military dictatorship gave him absolute control over national finance. Portugal had a huge debt at that time. Salazar straightened out the nation's financial mess by cutting spending on public programs and balancing the budget; unfortunately, the burden fell heavily on the rural poor and the working class. Because of his success, Salazar was appointed Prime Minister. Today, economic groups can function according to their interests, but only within a framework the government considers best for the state. He created the National Union; now, it's the only legal political party in Portugal."

"Some of my Portuguese acquaintances think he oversteps his authority, trying to impose his own values on the whole country," said Bonita. "Is this true?"

"They have a point, Senora Gonzalez. Salazar came from a peasant family in a rural village near Coimbra. He once studied to become a priest. In some ways, he is the nation's priest. He has never married; one could say he is married to the state. He thinks a life of poverty is the most virtuous way people should live because Christ lived in poverty. Salazar thinks modern society is going in a wrong direction. Only religion, family, and country should prevail. His piety is sincere; that makes arguing against him difficult. As nations around us industrialize, some of us wonder if we're going to be mired in the past until Salazar leaves."

"How does Portugal keep modern ideas from getting into the country?" asked Bonita. "I would think trying to keep a cap on that would bring an explosion."

Marcelo Marques appeared a little hesitant to discuss the one characteristic of Portugal that bothered him most. "You bring me to a subject I wish I didn't have to say anything about."

Bonita politely apologized. Senhor Marques waved it off, saying, "It's all right, senora. I don't mind talking about it with you. We have internal security police that enforce a rigid censorship on all of us. If your rebellious militarists are victorious, you will be facing the same thing in Spain. The government says it is protecting us against subversives, communists, and anarchists; actually, it's out to crush all opposition to the regime. I can talk about this to you alone, but if I were to make these comments publicly, I would be in real danger. No serious resistance challenges our government. People are afraid to criticize openly; they've heard too many stories of rough treatment by the police. I don't want to be involved in a rebellion and I'm not about to join an underground party. I'm only a farmer and admit I'm rather well off compared to others, but I wish we could talk out our differences openly and honestly."

"That's a hope of people everywhere," said Bonita plainly.

The sound of Andre Vincente's truck was heard in the driveway. "Your neighbor must not be doing too badly; he owns a truck," commented Jose.

"He's generous with his tools and equipment," replied Marcelo Marques. "That's why I didn't want to turn him down last night, even though I knew you two were in the shed. We're good friends. We help each other."

While Jose and Marcelo walked outside to greet Senhor Vincente, Bonita went into the kitchen to help Senhora Marques wash dishes and put away food.

"*Gracias* – I mean, *obrigada, muito obrigada* – for everything, senhora. My *marido* and I are grateful for all you have done for us."

"I couldn't help but hear Marcelo discussing politics with you. I hope he didn't bore you with all his talk. He does get carried away."

"Oh, no," said Bonita. "His comments were fascinating. He seems like a knowledgeable person. I like talking with a person who tries to understand things that are happening in the world."

The two finished with the dishes and then went outside to join the others. They greeted Andre Vincente. Jose and Bonita exchanged embraces with their good-byes to Senhor and Senhora Marques.

"You've been wonderful to us," said Jose, warmly. "You've taken care of us as if we were your children. Whenever we get home, we will write to you."

Bonita tried to conceal her warning glance at Jose. "Yes," she said, "if you don't hear from us, it won't be for lack of trying. I understand the mail service in Spain is chaotic or nonexistent these days."

"Senhor Marques gave me your address," explained Jose as he said farewell to Senhora Marques. "I couldn't do the same because I don't know exactly where in Galicia we'll be."

Jose and Bonita climbed into the front cab of Senhor Vincente's truck setting their rucksacks on the floor in front of them. As they rode out of the driveway, they waved to the couple who waved back.

"What kind, generous people," said Jose to Andre Vincente. "I didn't know what kind of a reception we'd get yesterday when I asked if we could spend a night in his shed."

"You were very fortunate," remarked Senhor Vincente. "There would be plenty of people around here that would bluntly tell you 'no' or turn you over to the police. There's a lot of suspicion and resentment of anyone Spanish now. An article in the newspaper appeared the other day saying the government was urging people to notify authorities when they saw a Spaniard. If they don't do that, according to the government, we can expect an invasion of the country by a 'Spanish horde' – their words, not mine."

Bonita gave Jose an unexpressed acknowledgement: *It was a good thing Jose had us disguise ourselves while we were walking.*

"Well," stated Jose, "we don't plan to stay. We hope to cross the border into Galicia as soon as we can."

"Did you decide where you wanted to be let off?" asked Andre Vincente.

"I talked him into visiting Alcobaca," said Bonita. "Both of us know the story of Inez and Pedro and we would like to visit their tombs there. Then we plan to stop at a friend of Manuel's in Coimbra before going on to Galicia."

"Good choice, Alcobaca. I just have one stop along the way. Among all those vegetables in the back of my truck, I have a basket to drop off to a friend of mine. He's stationed about ten kilometers up ahead in Ponte de Sor and the delivery will take only a minute. My brother and his family can't eat everything that's riding in this truck."

They drove on for several minutes. Then Andre Vincente said, "When I stop, don't get out of the truck. My friend works at the local police station. There's no reason for you to talk with anyone, and you shouldn't. Don't be concerned. With the vegetables in a basket, I can be quick about it."

Jose and Bonita looked apprehensive enough for Senhor Vincente to reassure them.

"I can imagine what you're thinking. Don't worry. It will be all right. As long as you don't start a conversation with any one, no one will know you are Spanish."

The truck stopped. Andre Vincente climbed out, grabbed a basket of vegetables from the bed of his truck, and went inside the police station.

"Are you as nervous as I am?" asked Bonita of Jose.

"Yes," he answered, "especially when I see that little sign over there."

On a door to one side of the station were the letters 'PVDE.'

"Oh no!" exclaimed Bonita. "I thought he was our friend."

Chapter 22
Caught in a Lie

The minutes seemed like hours as Jose and Bonita waited in the truck for Andre Vincente to reappear. Jose kept his eyes on the PVDE door. No one came out or went in.

"I'm surprised the PVDE advertise their whereabouts, especially in a small town like this," commented Jose. "I wonder if they're really located here and not at some other place."

Another minute went by until Bonita said, "Here he comes."

A man in a police uniform walked behind their driver. The policeman started to move toward the truck. Both Jose and Bonita were tense as they prepared for some kind of action. The two men came to a stop. Senhor Vincente was explaining something to his policeman friend. Jose and Bonita tried to determine the content of the conversation, but they could not hear the exact words with the window closed tight. Finally, the policeman turned and went back to his building. Andre Vincente came over to the truck and got in.

"He wanted to talk with each of you," Senhor Vincente explained as he pulled the truck out into the road. "I had to convince my friend that you were long-time *amigos* going with me to my brother's place at Nazare. I'm sorry it took longer than I had expected."

"That's no problem," said Jose with relief.

"Apparently, the police know you have escaped from a Nationalist prison, *Jose*, and that you are accompanying him, *Bonita*."

Jose and Bonita were stunned and speechless upon hearing their real names spoken. Their bodies stiffened from the discovery of their true identity.

"Senhor Vincente," stammered Jose, trying to sound as normal as he could. "What is this all about?"

"That's the question I should ask of you. I have to assume from the expressions on your faces that the information I just heard from my policeman *amigo* is true."

Jose quickly concluded there was nothing to be gained from continuing to use the false names they had invented.

"I am Jose Martinez," he said openly. "And, yes, this is Bonita Sanchez. She helped me escape from Nationalist custody. We hope to be married whenever our civil war will permit."

"Senhor," Bonita began. "We did not wish to deceive you, but it is so hard to know who we can trust. We hope you won't hold this against us."

"My police *amigo* also told me something else you should know," replied Senhor Vincente sharply. "The report the police have is that both of you are implicated in a cold-blooded murder in Trujillo."

"Murder? What murder?" cried Jose. "I swear to you by everything that is holy, Senhor Vincente, we know nothing about a murder!"

"Believe me, Senhor," added Bonita. "I truly don't know how they're coming up with murder. I helped Jose escape from the Nationalists at his mother's funeral in Trujillo. We certainly didn't kill anyone to get away."

"There's one other matter involving only you, Jose," said Andre Vincente, with an edge remaining in his voice. "The police in this part of Portugal also know this from their contacts in Spain: you have been charged for being part of a firing squad that executed up to a hundred people when the Republican militias controlled Badajoz."

"Executed up to a hundred people," repeated Jose bitterly. "How lies grow! First it was a dozen, now it is a hundred. The Nationalists are saying this to cover up their own crimes. Again, I swear to you . . ."

"Should I trust you?" interjected Vincente caustically. "I didn't say anything to the policeman before hearing your side of the story, but false names, escape from jail, murder, firing squad – what's next?"

"Senhor Vincente, please do not be angry with us," urged Jose. "Yes, listen to our account because, while it's true about our made-up names and my escape from Nationalist detention, the murder and firing squad stories are absolutely false. And, ask yourself: What would you have done had you been in our situation?"

"The information your police are getting is biased," asserted Bonita. "It's all being filtered through Nationalist sources."

"I simply don't like to be misled," said Andre Vincente. "Surely, you can appreciate that."

"Yes, we can," said Jose. "We didn't know whether you would help us or turn us over to the police."

"Those are serious charges against you."

"The charge about murder has no basis in fact," insisted Jose. "As for the firing squad, I was never a part of one. I came to Badajoz in a Republican militia unit on the very day of the battle. The only firing squads that day belonged to the Nationalists who slaughtered hundreds of Republican prisoners in the town's bullring. I can verify that as truth because I was held in a prison cell with a window after I was captured. I heard the machine-gun fire. I saw bodies fall and stacked in trucks. I smelled the decaying corpses."

"Yes, we read about that massacre at Badajoz," said Andre Vincente. "It was reported by foreign correspondents and spread throughout the world. That bloodbath was so outrageous that it caused quite a sensation here. The newspapers in Portugal reported events like that quite openly in the early days of the civil war."

"Before the rebellion I was a part-time news writer for *El Sol*," said Jose.

"Yes, I've heard of *El Sol*," responded Andre. "It's supposed to be one of the better newspapers in Spain."

"Some day I'd like to go back to my journalism career and continue from where I left off. I welcomed the Republic and hoped for its success, but I was always fair in reporting its failures as well as its accomplishments. My editors insisted on truthfulness. Today, I think your news is slanted more toward the Nationalists since the Salazar government leans heavily in favor of its victory."

"That's true," confirmed Andre. "Nowadays, we're getting no news about Nationalist atrocities and hearing a lot more about Nationalist victories. It's no secret that Salazar is on good terms with Nationalist leaders."

"Senhor Vincente, please understand how desperate we've been," pleaded Jose, looking directly at him. "Using my mother's funeral to escape was painful. Getting to Portugal and being on the run has been frightening to say the least. We've had to conceal who we are. We haven't known who to rely on. Everything we do involves such a risk. I've never been in a situation like this."

"Nor have I," responded Senhor Vincente. "I can only imagine what it's been like. Being without knowledge of current events must be difficult for you, a newspaperman."

"Has anything important happened recently?" asked Jose, hoping Senhor Vincente was persuaded by his pleas of innocence. "We've been so busy avoiding capture that we really don't know what's going on."

"Only this morning, I'm sorry to tell you, the radio brought news about a Nationalist rout at Talavera de la Reina. The Republican army is in complete disarray trying to get back to Madrid."

"The war that was once so immediate and significant now seems lost and so far away even though here we're being hunted," spoke Jose in a forlorn manner.

Senhor Vincente drove on, lost in his thoughts for a minute.

"Look," he said. "I'm going to take your word that the information you've given me about yourselves is true. Yes, I can understand why you would want to conceal your identities, even from those who would help you. And Jose, I'll accept your explanation about the firing squad accusation and being blameless of murder in Trujillo."

"*Gracias*, senhor. *Muito obrigado*," replied Jose with renewed spirit.

"Jose is speaking the truth," confirmed Bonita. "*Obrigada,* senhor."

"It's hard to know what the truth actually is" said Andre Vincente. "Any civil war is going to split a country apart, but this one is especially intense and violent. We get wildly different reports, depending upon which side issues them. It's difficult to know who to believe anymore, but at this point I'm willing to give you the benefit of the doubt. You seem like decent young people."

"We are indebted to you for your help, especially for not turning us over to the police back there," said Jose. "How will we ever be able to repay you?"

"We're supposed to lend a helping hand to those in need," replied Andre. "Our religion teaches us to behave toward our neighbor as we would want to be treated, and when the time comes to do it, we are to practice what we preach. I said last night I don't agree with my country's practice of turning Spaniards over to our police or back to Spain where they face imprisonment or death."

"I thank God we ran into you," said Bonita earnestly.

Senhor Vincente was not done.

"Now, I don't think you should go to Alcobaca," he said. "You could run into security guards there. I'd better take you to your friend in Coimbra."

"Oh, senhor, Coimbra is too far out of your way," they both protested.

"I can't just drop you along the side of the road," responded Andre. "Let me give you a piece of advice. I recommend you lay low in Coimbra for a while before attempting to reach Galicia. Maybe the urgency of the search for you will blow over."

"Sort of blend into the university community," suggested Jose.

No Greater Love

"That's right. Don't go out into the streets for a couple of weeks. There are police in Coimbra. Let your friend get your food and any supplies you need. Maybe he can work out a way for you to get into Galicia, if that's still where you intend to go."

"He spent a two-week stay with me at Salamanca a few years back," said Jose. "Manuel owes me a favor."

"And, I can cook meals for the three of us," Bonita offered. "Oh, Senhor Vincente, you've given us hope. We are grateful for everything you've done."

Andre Vincente smiled and drove on toward Coimbra.

Chapter 23
Ramon's Mission

"Here are your marching orders, Ramon," said Antonio as he opened a map of Portugal, the country only a few kilometers away from their base in Badajoz.

"Aye, captain," replied Ramon. "This chase should be exciting. I'm looking forward to it. I'm glad you were able to arrange my transfer so I could do it."

Spreading the map on a table, Antonio asked Ramon, "If you were to head north to Galicia near Bonita's home, what route would you take?"

"I'd take the road to Lisbon and hop on a boat going to Porto and then probably another boat going from Porto into Galicia, maybe to Vigo or Pontevedra," answered Ramon.

"Remember, they're on foot. Would you want to walk all the way from Badajoz to Lisbon?"

"They could hitch a ride," suggested Ramon. "That's a major route, so there would be cars going by. Sooner or later, one of them would be bound to stop and pick them up."

"One problem they would have: police cars are also on that road. I think they'll keep away from a main thoroughfare; they're smart enough to know those kind of roads are too risky. As for the boat, they'd have to get a ticket. Their language accent would give them away. The same thing would happen trying to get on a bus or a train. And, if they do get on any kind of public transportation, there's no place to go if any police are on it. Any other ideas?"

"Maybe they've holed up in an abandoned cabin just across the border from here."

"Why would they do that?"

"They'd want to be as close as possible for talking with Republican officials. I'm thinking of your theory that Jose is a major figure in Republican circles. Their leaders would want to contact him without having to travel all over Portugal to do it."

"That's a possibility, Ramon. Keep going. You haven't hit upon the trail I think they're most likely to take."

"If they're walking, Antonio, they'll be on some back roads through the Alentejo. Eventually, Jose and Bonita would get to Porto."

"That's the route, Ramon. I think you've found the most likely one. Do you know why?"

"No. Why?"

"Porto is a center of liberal opposition to Salazar. Jose could have some friends there. And, it's a gateway to the north and Galicia."

"He would most likely go through Coimbra to get there," said Ramon, pointing to the map.

"Yes, the university at Coimbra might attract both Jose and Bonita. Our little brother was always quite the scholar. He likes the university atmosphere. He might have friends there in school, Bonita too."

"Do you know who these people might be, Antonio?"

"No. I never was well acquainted with Jose's *amigos*. I was thinking you might know who some of them were and where they'd be."

"I never paid close attention to Jose and his friends as they grew up. Of course, now I wish I had."

"Well, do the best you can. Keep in mind we've got the Portuguese government on our side. We've notified the internal security police about the escape by Jose and Bonita and their likelihood of committing murder. There's an alert to apprehend them and send them back here."

"Would I be interfering with the Portuguese police in any way, Antonio?"

"Your official papers I made out for you explain everything. Portuguese security is cooperating with us in any way they can. Your job is to locate Jose, keep him under surveillance, find out who is contacting him, and discover where he is going. If the secret police get to Jose first, let them do with Bonita whatever they want. Ask them to release Jose into your custody. Let Jose escape from you, which he will try to do, I guarantee it. Get help and keep him in your sight. Don't relent in your surveillance. I can almost promise you he'll lead you to bigger fish in the Republican pond."

"Of course."

"Stay in touch with me. I'm going to give you several telephone numbers to reach me. Here are dates and places where I expect to be. Telephone me between twenty-one and twenty-two hours each night. We can coordinate activities as we go along. As long as I'm not able to be with you, I'm relying on you, Ramon."

"Absolutely! You're really into this."

"Yes, I am. I think you'll be surprised how important to the anti-Nationalist underground our little brother really is. If my assumptions are correct, we'll be in a position to catch some very big people in the web we'll prepare for them. If you ever wanted to be a hero, Ramon, this is your chance."

I can't tell if Antonio is deluding himself about Jose's status, Ramon thought. *Maybe he's right. After all, he's in a position to know information I wouldn't have.*

"I'll certainly try to do my best to follow your instructions," Ramon said to Antonio. "I'm ready to do my bit for the cause."

"I have a suggestion about clothes. Wear the Nationalist uniform when you're in the car I've requisitioned for you and when you're dealing with the police or the PVDE. Wear your civilian clothes when you need to be inconspicuous and blend in with other people. Use your best judgment."

"Right."

"I'm depending on you, Ramon. I wish I could go with you, but I can't until I'm released to do so by my commanding officer. I'll catch up with you as soon as I can. You have the authority to act in my name."

"I won't abuse that authority," promised Ramon.

"One more thing, Ramon: I know your impulses. Please, no bordellos. You leave yourself wide open there. This is serious business. You've got to control yourself."

"I give you my word of honor, Antonio. I won't stray from the job and the opportunity you've given me. I'm duty-bound to do everything I can to make this mission a success."

"Good," said Antonio. "I think we've covered everything. Let's have a glass of wine to start this mission, as you so aptly have called it."

"By all means, my brother, but the best thing we can do is start with a prayer for our mission."

"You're right on the mark, Ramon. That's a marvelous idea." As he poured the wine, Antonio could scarcely believe Ramon had initiated a prayer.

CHAPTER 24
SANCTUARY

As promised, Andre Vincente delivered Jose and Bonita to the university town of Coimbra. Nearing the Santa Clara bridge over the Mondego River, Bonita directed Jose's attention to the right.

"Over there is *Quinta das Lagrimas*, the House of Tears, where Inez de Castro and Dom Pedro lived with their children and the agents of Afonzo killed Inez. And, ahead of it is the old Santa Clara Convent where Inez was buried."

Andre stopped the truck and parked along the side of the road. "Queen Isabella was buried there, also," he said. "She is the patron saint of Coimbra. You must know Portuguese history, Bonita."

"I was telling the Inez story to Jose last night. Turns out he knew the story, too. I've read about Isabella, the sainted queen. If you know that story, Jose, please tell me. I don't want to be repeating something you already know."

"I promise I won't play that trick on you again," Jose pledged. "However, I have to admit I don't know about 'the sainted queen.' Sometime, you'll have to tell me about her."

Andre glanced across the front seat of the truck at them. "Apparently, both of you have studied at university. You seem to know many things about Portugal."

"We met at Oviedo, senhor, then transferred to Salamanca and graduated there," said Jose, "but we certainly don't know everything about Portuguese history. We want to give you credit, too. We were saying last night that you and Senhor Marques are intelligent people and you keep up with the political events of the world."

"Marcelo and I did spend some time at university; however, we didn't graduate. Our fathers died within a month of each other, and being the only sons in our families, we had to come home and tend to the farms they left behind."

"What occupations were you planning to enter?" asked Bonita.

"I didn't know; neither did he. That made it easier to come back to farming. Now, I would suggest we head across the bridge and go up to the university. I need to leave as quickly as I can."

"Of course," said Bonita. "We've delayed you long enough. Those vegetables you're carrying won't stay fresh forever."

Crossing the bridge, the truck lumbered up the hills that characterize the town of Coimbra. When they had gone part way, Jose said, "We can get off anywhere now. My friend Manuel has an apartment close to the university. The streets there are very steep and narrow and they'll be hard on your truck. I've been here before. I have his address. We can find his place now."

Pulling to a stop, Andre said, "I guess this is the end of the line. I'll say *adios*, my *amigos*."

"Senhor Andre," said Jose. "We are so grateful to you for all your kindness to us. We thank you for bringing us here. That would have been a long walk."

Bonita gave her thanks, and added, "We are sorry about using those false names. It's just – we didn't know what to do – we . . ."

"You don't need to explain. I was taken aback at first, but while we were traveling, I asked myself the same question you asked me before: What would I have done? I would have done exactly as you did. I recommend you keep up that practice."

"With Manuel, it won't be necessary," said Jose. "With everyone else, we'll follow your suggestion."

"Good. *Adios*, again. *Vaya con Dios*." Andre hesitated, and then repeated, "Go with God. I'm happy to help you. Actually, I feel very good about it."

Taking their rucksacks from the front seat of the truck, Jose and Bonita said *"Adeus"* and waved good-bye to Andre Vincente.

They watched him drive away, motioning farewell by waving their hands. When the truck disappeared, Jose said, "Let's find Manuel."

Bonita didn't move. "Jose, before we go on, answer me this question. Do you think we can trust Senor Vincente? The way he let us off the hook, he was almost too good to be true."

"Why do you think I asked him to let us off before we got to Manuel's apartment?"

"That was clever of you, but he would still know we're in the student section of Coimbra and could report that to the PVDE."

"I'm ninety-nine and nine-tenths percent sure he was genuine in his desire to help us. I wouldn't worry about Vincente. After all, think how easily he could have turned us over to his policeman friend at the beginning of today's trip."

"Okay, Jose, I guess you're right. Now, we need to find your *amigo*."

The university buildings loomed higher up the hill. Jose pressed on in front of Bonita, eagerly looking ahead toward a meeting with an old friend.

As Bonita fell behind, she remembered her first day of walking in Portugal. She asked, "Jose, do you want me to walk those absurd six paces behind you again? Do I need to keep limping like an old woman?"

Jose walked back to her and put his arm around Bonita's shoulder. "We're students once more," he said. "This is the way we walk now."

In ten minutes Jose and Bonita were standing in front of Manuel's address. "This is it," announced Jose. "He lives on the second floor in Apartment 2C. Let's hope he's in."

After they climbed the stairs, they arrived at a hall. Jose knocked on the door to the room marked 2C.

Silence. No one answered. In the street below, they heard the sounds of the *fado*, sung by a young man serenading someone in the building.

"I wonder if he's singing a love song, or maybe it's a protest verse about the heavy hand of Salazar."

"Sh-h-h," warned Bonita putting her hand to Jose's lips. "You don't know who could be listening. Remember, Salazar was on the faculty here, only a few years ago."

A door opened on the other side of the hallway. A young woman, presumably a student, peered out.

"We're looking for Manuel Silva," Jose explained. "He is a friend of ours."

"Yes, you came to the right place," said the woman. "However, you're out of luck; he's not here. He told me he was going to Salamanca, not too far over the border from here."

"Ah, our old university," said Jose. "He visited me while I was a student there. Do you know when he is coming back?"

The woman shook her head indicating 'no.'

"*Obrigado.*" To Bonita, he said, "Nothing is ever simple."

"There's a vacant room upstairs on the third floor," the woman said. "I'm the manager here. If you want to, you could rent the room until he gets back."

"If you can take Spanish pesetas and it doesn't cost too much, we'll take the room," bargained Jose. "Could we see it?"

"*Si*." Luck was with them. The woman was not curious about who they were. They had found sanctuary again.

Looking around the two-room apartment, Jose said, "Not too bad. It's a typical student set of rooms."

"How do we get food, Jose?" Bonita asked.

"We'll have to risk it. I don't intend to starve here."

"There's still some food in my rucksack, enough to get by for a couple of days. We've eaten better than I expected so far, considering what we've been through."

"I've got some food, too, Bonita. What you suggest is fine, but we'll go crazy restricting ourselves to these two rooms."

"Three rooms, Jose," Bonita smiled. "There's the bathroom down the hall. Manuel may show up soon. Meanwhile, you'll have to put up with me."

"I have no problem with that. I plan to do that for a lifetime."

When she heard those words, Bonita embraced Jose and kissed him.

"I've been waiting to hear you say that all summer. 'I love you' are nice words, but what you just said takes commitment." She stroked his dark hair and gazed lovingly into his soft hazel eyes.

Jose kissed Bonita. "You are my love forever," he proclaimed ardently. They sat on the room's only couch. Jose wanted to kiss her again and again, but she unexpectedly became preoccupied in thought.

"What's going to happen to us?" asked Bonita. "Until this morning, we were escaping your Nationalist brothers and you were to be brought back to face the charge of shooting innocent people as a member of a firing squad. Now, according to the information Senhor Vincente got from his policeman friend, we're made out to be murderers. This latest accusation may put us in a different light, distorted as it may be. We've got to think about where we go and what we do after we leave here."

"First, we pray for a quick Republican victory," responded Jose. "I know, I know – that is unrealistic. Unless the Republic gets help from the Western democracies, the liberal Republic is doomed. We have to face the harsh truth that you and I, my sister Marisa and Jorge, and people like Andre Vincente and Marcelo Marques, are not in the mainstream at the present time. The tide is running against us. The world is going fascist. I don't have any good answers."

No Greater Love

"Jose, you know we were fantastically fortunate to run into Andre and Marcelo. Our guardian angel was watching over us. We should offer a prayer of thanks."

"Yes, I know. I have already."

"One thing I do know. We can't go to Galicia. I only said 'Galicia' when Henriques Vincente asked if we were escaping from Spain. I thought my story would be more believable to him with my *Gallego* accent."

"Do you think Senhor Vincente will tell his son he was right to suspect us?" asked Jose.

"I doubt if Andre will give Henriques that satisfaction."

"Bonita, you could still go home. You've got a job there. School will be starting very soon, if it hasn't started already. If you are questioned about the murder, tell them the truth. We had nothing to do with it. If they don't believe you, tell them I did it."

"Why?"

"I'm the one that got you into this mess."

"Jose, don't feel guilty about it. I don't want to be separated from you. We're in this together. We – you and I – are not going to Galicia. If the Republic survives, fine, we'll go back. But, as things stand now, the Nationalists control Galicia, and too many people there know my political beliefs. So, we're back to my original question: What happens now, after Coimbra?"

"There's another question. Can we stay in Portugal? If we do, it's possible we'll be hunted by the internal security police here almost as much as by the Nationalists in Spain."

"Back to our old disguise as old man and old lady?" posed Bonita with mischievous humor. "Am I forever condemned to live six paces behind you?"

"Never," said Jose, shaking his head. "We won't live that way. I suppose Antonio was right about one thing."

"What was that?"

"Whatever possessed me to join a Republican militia. He thought I was out of my head. Antonio questioned whether I belonged in any army, much less the Republican militia. Maybe he was right. I could have done more for the Republic's cause by remaining a newspaper reporter."

"You acted according to the principles you thought were right. After all, a lot of pressure was brought on young men like you to fight Fascism and defend the Republic. You went into armed combat. You put your life on the line. You went beyond words and into action. You stood up for the values you believe in. I'm proud of you."

Jose reached over to Bonita and squeezed her hand. He felt ineffective by recent experience and trapped by present events, and she offered the supportive anchor any man would want. After the battle at Badajoz and all the risks of the escape, he counted himself lucky to be alive. But, more fortunate than any of this was the unconditional devotion freely given to him by Bonita.

"I am blessed beyond all measure to have your love," he said, looking into her eyes. "Whatever happens, I'll always believe that." His words trailed off as he drew her to him.

I've got to find a way to protect her, he thought as he held her. *I value Bonita's love more than anything I can think of. How can I make her secure when we're hiding or running away from people?*

Jose went back to the 'life after Coimbra' question Bonita had posed. "Maybe, we should leave Spain and Portugal and emigrate to Mexico, or somewhere in Spanish America, or even *los Estados Unidos*. Let's not limit our thinking. I want to take care of you, and I can't do a very good job of that here."

"I'll follow you wherever you go," was Bonita's response. "We'd have to work and save money to get across the ocean. The adjustments we'd have to make would be enormous."

"Thousands have done it before, including those who had less going for them than we have. Think of what people have done in the past just to have a normal life."

"Isn't it something, Jose? Sometimes our families have probably thought we're so radical and foolhardy, and yet, we simply want to get married, have children, enjoy our work, and live a decent life. How traditional can you get?"

Chapter 25
Manuel

In the morning two days later, Jose heard noises in the apartment below. "I'll bet Manuel has returned," he said to Bonita who was getting the last of their food ready to eat. "I'll check downstairs."

He was gone for a moment. Returning, Jose announced, "Yes, we're in luck; my friend Manuel is back. Come and meet him."

Going into Manuel's apartment, Jose introduced Bonita to Manuel Silva.

"So you're the gorgeous Galician girl Jose has told me about," said Manuel. "I am pleased to meet you. I can see why Jose didn't want me to meet you while I visited him at Salamanca."

Bonita blushed. "I'm pleased to meet you, Manuel." She smiled modestly.

Manuel went on. "Welcome to Portugal. Welcome to Coimbra. Welcome to the university and welcome to my apartment. I'm sorry I wasn't here when you arrived. I could have saved you the bother of paying for another room. There's enough space here."

"The room upstairs doesn't cost much, and the manager was willing to take our pesetas, so there was no problem," explained Bonita. "I was about ready to shop for some food."

"She doesn't want me to go out," protested Jose. "Bonita says it isn't safe for me. I'll need to explain why."

"I blend in better than Jose would, Manuel. Since I am from Galicia, I'm half Portuguese, anyway."

"Let me take that burden off both of your shoulders," offered Manuel. "I know the best places to buy food around here. Now, tell me why it's dangerous for you to leave your apartment, Jose."

Manuel listened while Jose and Bonita went through the details of their existence over the past weeks. When they finished, Manuel exclaimed, "You two have been through enough to last you for a lifetime. Being Portuguese and stretching the truth about my political inclinations, I was able to enter Spain, visit my friends, and come back with no interference. My trip was an interesting and sometimes frightening experience."

"Tell us about it," prompted Jose. "We're eager for any news from the home country. We heard you went to Salamanca."

"I was trapped there when the Nationalists took over the city," Bonita informed Manuel.

"Salamanca is a wonderful place when it isn't filled with fascists," said Manuel. "I was there as an official representative of the University of Coimbra at the Festival of the Spanish Race in the ceremonial hall at the University of Salamanca. A big crowd of Nationalists and Falangists attended the ceremony."

"How did you stand it?" asked Jose.

"Inwardly, I cringed, but to all outward appearances I was an enthusiastic Franco supporter. On the stage sat a whole bunch of high-ranking big shots in the National Front, along with Franco's wife and the bishop of Salamanca. This is the same bishop who only a few days before had described the territory held by the Republic as an earthly city laden with sin, hate, communism, and anarchy while the Nationalist zone was the City of God filled with love and peace."

Jose and Bonita groaned.

"I've been on that stage," reflected Jose. "I was given an award there for my work on the student newspaper."

"I was in that hall," said Bonita, "watching you and falling in love with you."

"So that's when it was," Jose smiled as he winked his eye. Then he turned serious again. "Is it true Franco intends to make Salamanca his headquarters? I know Salamanca has been conservative, but I hate to think of it becoming so thoroughly Nationalist territory."

"I don't like to be the one telling you, but it has happened," declared Manuel. "At the festival after two brash harangues, a professor gave a particularly obnoxious speech. He declared that half of all Spanish people are criminals and traitors. He attacked the Basques and Catalans as cancers on the body of Spain. He claimed only surgery could exterminate the cancer that would save the nation. Spain must have a health-giving operation which is Fascism."

"Where have I heard that before," cut in Jose. "Surgery performed by an 'iron surgeon' – Franco. The fascists are forever using that metaphor."

"The word 'surgery' must have been a signal. General Millan Astray and the Falangists started shouting *'!Viva la Muerte!'* – Long live death! People became fanatic with Falange slogans. They thrust their right arms forward and gave fascist salutes toward a huge picture of Franco hanging above his wife."

"What a disgusting sight that must have been," declared Bonita.

"Was our rector there?" asked Jose. "At first, I think he mistakenly gave support to the military uprising, hoping it would return honor to the Republic."

"Yes, he was there," answered Manuel. "*Miguel de Unamuno* rose to speak when the noise died down. He told the audience he was not able to remain silent; if he did, it would be a lie appearing to be in agreement with the words of the professor. He would dismiss the insults toward Basques and Catalans, reminding everyone there that he was a Basque philosopher born in Bilbao, and that the bishop was a Catalan from Barcelona whether he liked it or not."

"That must have quieted the crowd," commented Bonita.

"They were frozen, momentarily. No one speaks like that in Nationalist Spain anymore."

"Especially if you value your life," added Jose.

"Your words are more prophetic than you know, Jose. *Unamuno* went on to say when he heard the insane cry, 'long live death,' it was especially repulsive to him since he had shaped paradoxes all his life. He called Millan Astray a cripple, and that Spain was full of cripples now. If God did not help the Spanish, there would be many more cripples. He said *Cervantes* was crippled in battle too, but a cripple that didn't have the greatness of a *Cervantes* would cripple the entire country of Spain. The one-armed general couldn't restrain himself any longer. Millan Astray could only scream *'!Muera la inteligencia. Viva la Muerte!'*"

"Death to intellectuals, long live death," repeated Jose with bitter irony. "What a wonderful inspiration for those who value learning. I'll bet not only Millan Astray but all the Nationalists in the crowd were furious with Unamuno."

"Were they ever! Falangists took up his slogan. Army officers brandished pistols, but even this show of intimidation did not stop the rector. He finished with words I committed to memory and wrote down later.

"'This is the temple of the intellect,' he said, 'and I am its high priest. It is you who profane its sacred precincts. You will win because you have more than enough brute force. But you will not convince. For you to convince, you need to persuade. And in order to persuade you would need what you lack: reason and right in your struggle.' "

"I wish I had been there to lend him support," proclaimed Jose.

"Jose, you would have needed his world reputation to save you. Some Falangists started to move toward the stage. Millan Astray's bodyguard aimed a machine-gun at him. They gave every indication they wanted to kill the great Unamuno on the spot, and they might have done so had not Senora Franco – I'll give her credit – taken his arm and walked off the stage with him. That, and his international standing as a philosopher, probably saved him."

"World reputation didn't save *Garcia Lorca*," said Bonita.

Jose reached for a piece of paper and asked if he could copy Manuel's notes of Unamuno's speech. "I'd like to have his words in case I ever get an opportunity to use them in a newspaper report or a magazine article sometime," he pointed out.

"Always the reporter isn't he," Manuel said to Bonita.

"It's in his blood, Manuel. A story like that, though, deserves to be told to people everywhere, especially students. I hope Jose has a chance to use it."

"Your story was worth waiting for," said Jose. "I still wish I had been there to witness it and to give my old rector whatever assistance I could."

"He'll need help, I'm sure of that," replied Manuel. "Later that day, a Nationalist general said in referring to Unamuno that Spain had been stabbed treasonously by a liberal Masonic pseudo-intellectual. When I left yesterday, the word was that he was about to be removed as rector and put under house arrest."

"That's bad," said Jose. "I fear for his safety."

"Despicable as they are," interjected Bonita, "I have to admit some of the Nationalist generals are quite colorful in their speeches and radio talks."

"You've been listening to Nationalist generals!" exclaimed Jose in mock horror. "And your mind hasn't been warped by them?"

Bonita ignored Jose's outburst. "While I was stuck in Salamanca, Jose, I heard General *Mola* in a speech on Radio Burgos. Spaniards!" she mimicked in a high-pitched voice. "Our Government, the wretched bastard of liberal and socialist concubines, is dead – killed by our valiant army. The true Spain has laid the dragon low, and now it lies, writhing on its belly and biting the dust."

"Mola, once a protector of the Republic but now its attacker, always did have a quick, cunning way of expressing himself," said Jose.

"Over Radio Castile, you should have heard what he said about Manuel *Azana*."

"Our beleaguered President and former Prime Minister of the Republic," responded Jose. He had once been critical of Azana for his indecision at the beginning of the Nationalist revolt, but eventually came to realize the impossible situation he was in. "I can imagine the abusive tongue-lashing Mola gave him."

"Your words are mild, Jose," said Bonita. "He referred to Azana as a monster who couldn't have been conceived from the love of a woman and a man. Instead, he was invented by an insane Frankenstein."

"Oh no."

"Oh yes. Mola said Azana should be put in a cage so brain specialists can study perhaps the most interesting case of mental degeneration in history."

"The President's mental state is fine," pronounced Jose. "At least it was until this war started."

"Monsters and dragons," said Manuel in a comic tone of voice. "Mental degenerates, too. No wonder the Spanish Republic is in trouble! We can make light of long-winded prattling, but I've heard of the threatened savagery that's promised to people identified with the Republic, especially women conquered by Franco's Army of Africa."

"I can't imagine anything more horrible," exclaimed Bonita.

Manuel continued. "Some Nationalist generals seem to put a mighty emphasis on the sexual prowess of the Army of Africa. Before our newspapers were muzzled, they carried reports of one *Queipo de Llano*, who promised the women of Madrid to those troops when they took the city. And, as Nationalist forces went through southern Spain, they scrawled graffiti on village walls: 'Your women will give birth to Fascists.' A Nationalist commanding officer bragged to a journalist that two young girls would not last more than four hours when they were turned over to his men."

"You were reading about some of Quiepo's 'bedtime stories' as they were called on Radio Seville," explained Bonita. "Marisa told me about them, how they were laced with all sorts of sexual imagery."

"I've heard a lot of criticism of the Republic's liberalized attitudes toward sex, and it usually came from people backing the Nationalists," recalled Jose. "I suppose now they can't admit to themselves the possibility that Nationalist forces could commit rape and murder since the Army of Africa is essential to their winning the war."

"They probably don't recognize their hypocrisy," declared Bonita. "The Nationalists are so self-righteous it's sickening. Quiepo promised for every right-wing person in Republican prisons, he would kill at least ten in his prisons."

Changing the subject from the civil strife that engulfed them, Jose exclaimed, "Enough of this! Bonita and I were preparing some food a few minutes ago. We'd better get back to our apartment upstairs. Would you like to join us for *pequeno almoco*, Manuel?"

"*Si*, I'd love to."

"We've about exhausted our supply of food," said Bonita. "I'm planning to go shopping. Can you recommend a good market that's close to us, Manuel?"

"Remember, I'm going to be managing your food," said Manuel. "Neither of you should go outside, at least for a while. I'll do the food shopping for all of us."

"You're sure we must stay inside," complained Jose.

"Yes," ordered Manuel.

"What a way to live! Come to think of it, we have something in common with Unamuno."

Bonita and Manuel couldn't imagine what Jose was talking about until they heard him say, "He's not the only one under house arrest."

Chapter 26
Happiness

For the next two weeks, Jose and Bonita occupied their apartment in the third floor flat near the University of Coimbra. Their friend Manuel Silva supplied them with food and other necessities of life. He exchanged most of their Spanish pesetas for Portuguese escudos. They were restless, but these days and nights were counted as among the happiest times they had ever spent with each other. The days dissolved one into another as they contemplated their future, explored ideas about where they would live, gave and received love with genuine and unequivocal affection, read books and newspapers furnished by Manuel, put together meals, and talked about anything that came into their heads.

One diversion was to go downstairs and talk with Manuel when he came back to his apartment after classes in the late afternoon or from shopping for food in the early evening. Those were the best times for visits; Manual preferred to relax with a glass of wine, avoiding the plunge into a pile of assigned readings immediately after his arrival. They would take turns preparing food and cleaning up afterwards. The three would often be together at the dinner table when light was fading from the sky. Jose and Bonita did not want to bother Manuel when he needed to study for his following day's classes, so they urged him to tell them when it was time for them to go.

"I'm a late-night student," he would explain. "Many of my classmates in humanities are. I deliberately schedule my classes for late mornings or afternoons whenever I can. Don't worry about me; if I need time to study, I'll let you know."

One evening after Manuel provided a fish dinner, Jose began a political discussion with "Here's a question I've asked myself many times. How does a democratic republic preserve its own principles when it is threatened by an insubordinate military which has all the armaments needed to overthrow its government by force?"

"I assume you have your own republic in mind," speculated Manuel.

Jose motioned 'yes' and went on. "Modern progressives support free speech, constitutional rule, and all the trappings of democracy, but often they are too weak to withstand a military juggernaut that has overwhelming strength in lethal weapons and manpower. In this situation, the dilemma of a liberal democracy is that the only alternative available is to break faith with its own reasons for being – in order to survive."

"Oh, Jose, that's too pessimistic," objected Bonita. "There must be democratic ways for people to resist a takeover by a military dictatorship."

"What are they? The only ones I can think of involve violence and counter-force which by their nature are anti-democratic."

"A democratic government that's been attacked has the right to defend itself," asserted Manuel.

"I agree, but the real question is: How?"

"Realistically, the only way you can defeat a rebellious military is to organize a superior military force against it," replied Manuel. "Your republic will resort to conscription if it hasn't already and must enlist the help of allies beyond its own country."

"And, the people must become active with demonstrations and protest rallies," added Bonita. "If the military *coup d'etat* is successful, they can resort to acts of civil disobedience, go on a general strike, or refuse to pay tax."

"I've considered all the methods of resistance, forceful and passive," responded Jose. "A brutal military dictatorship would have no qualms about crushing opposition – jail, concentration camps, terror against the population, interrogation, torture – the whole works. They would possess the ammunition to control the population: tanks, aircraft, bombs, machine guns, flamethrowers – you name it, they'd have it. The people couldn't stop them."

"Then, some kind of moral force is the only answer that would bring any benefit," asserted Bonita. "Overcome evil with good, even love our enemies; that was the difficult teaching of Jesus. Revenge only increases the evil."

"Jose's question deals with the real world of power," said Manuel. "Jesus was talking about getting into heaven – quite a difference in those two places."

"Speaking of that real world," said Jose, "I worry about my sister Marisa and my brother-in-law Jorge, who was like a father to me when I was young. They have their home in Nationalist-held territory. Here, at least in this apartment, we have the luxury of talking about coping with a dictatorship;

they have to face it daily. The Nationalists will settle only for total control and eliminate any group or anyone that gets in their way. That's what we ran from, Bonita."

"Don't feel guilty about running away," advised Bonita, looking at Jose. "We had to. And, as I told you while we were running, Marisa and Jorge are very adept at camouflaging their true intentions."

"Your words are helpful to me personally," said Jose. "But my own concerns are only a small part of the larger issue I proposed."

"Defeating a power-mad military by a democratic republic still comes down to whoever has the most military firepower," repeated Manuel, "and that includes planning, logistics, organization, and some intangible things like *esprit de corps*, a sense of common mission and purpose."

"There's where I'm afraid the Nationalists have an advantage," said Jose. "The factions that belong to the National Front are authoritarian; they will obey orders and commands more willingly than the groups in the Popular Front. I'm amazed liberal republicans, socialists, anarchists, and communists have been able to unite as much as they have, but I'm also afraid that if the war goes on for any length of time, it's more likely the Republican coalition will split apart."

"The Republic may have to resort to some temporarily anti-democratic measures to stay alive, just so it doesn't become a habit," suggested Manuel.

"That's the danger," replied Jose. "I've told Bonita how my anarchist militia operated; it was very democratic in that everyone, including officers, was equal. It was a revolution in military organization that reflected the social revolution the anarchists have advocated for years."

Manuel weighed his reaction carefully. "With all due respect for the courage shown by you and your comrades, how successful were the anarchist militias against the Army of Africa and the Spanish Foreign Legion?"

"Not very successful," admitted Jose, "but our militias were thrown together with inadequate equipment on the spur of the moment and were fighting against battle-hardened troops with years of experience. I imagine as time goes on the Republican military will become more disciplined by rank and organization which may be necessary to be victorious on the field of battle."

"Thus, for military success, authoritarian elitism prevails over equalitarian democracy," summarized Manuel. Turning to Bonita, he said, "But, here's where people and moral force come in. If the citizens create and maintain a cultural tradition where military leadership respects civilian leadership, a democratic republic can withstand some minor, temporary departure from the normal procedures of democracy, allow the military to function in its way, and come back to constitutional rule once the emergency is over."

"I notice you used the words 'if the citizens,' Manuel," said Bonita. "I'm not sure the people of Spain have created the political culture you describe. If the Nationalists are victorious, one-third of the people will rejoice. A third will leave the country or land in prison, or go into hiding. The other third will join the winning side however reluctantly."

"Unfortunately for the Republic, the violence in Spanish politics paralyzed the moderate center," declared Jose. "Fascism led the right-wing astray and, to counter that development, the left has become more extreme. Paradoxically, the only hope for our Republic may be a wider war in Europe."

"Why do you say that?" asked Manuel. "That's the last thing we need."

"We have to concede that Fascism is spreading. Hitler and Mussolini are arming their countries for war. France and England will not send arms to our Republic; they signed a non-intervention agreement with other European nations, even though everyone knows Nazi Germany and Fascist Italy are helping the Nationalists. Now, let's say the Nazis invade Czechoslovakia or Poland; England and France would likely be drawn into war against Germany and Italy. The Spanish civil war would become a part of a general European war. To fight Fascism, the armies of England and France would have to aid the Republic."

"Your theoretical projections are making my head swim, Jose. But, the fascists will keep their aggressions somewhere below the threshold of triggering a wider war. And, England currently relies on conciliation and appeasement."

"Well, you're right; all this is hypothetical. Right now, only the Soviet Union seems willing to help the Republic and that prospect has worried plenty of moderate people on the Left."

"Really? The Soviets have a bigger army than Germany or Italy, plus Russia could enlist many other Communists throughout the world."

"Moderate liberals worry the Communists will gradually come to control the Republican leadership," objected Jose. "Few Spaniards are Communists, but the PCE has the strongest organization of any party supporting the Republic. The Socialists have divisions among themselves. The Anarchists by their very nature don't believe in organization. Liberal Republicans were not effective at the start of the Nationalist insurrection. So, if this war goes on and on, the Communists are likely to start dictating to the other parties of the Popular Front. When they take over, Communists have historically gone after liberals, even eliminating other Marxists who don't agree with the party line."

"I thought the Communists were trying to tamp down the revolutionary demands of the more radical elements of the Popular Front," said Manuel.

"They have opposed social revolution, like the one begun by anarchists in Catalonia, hoping it would bring support from France, Britain, and America. Right now, they want an alliance with all anti-fascists. They believe capitalist dominance is necessary to provoke the start of their own proletarian revolution."

"You suspect the Communists will ultimately undermine your liberal Republic," suggested Manuel.

"It's possible, yes," replied Jose. "Mr. Stalin has bigger fish to fry and won't let a bunch of Spaniards get in his way."

"Speaking of fish," said Bonita, "maybe we'd better clear the table and clean the dishes. Politics can wait, but the smell of uneaten fish won't."

Another time when his classes had ended, Manuel brought home a newspaper with an article about Toledo having fallen to the Nationalists, ending the Republican siege that had gone on for two months.

"The Nationalist defenders in the Alcazar were rescued by several columns of the Army of Africa that had been diverted from an expected assault upon Madrid," he reported from his newspaper.

Then he read the following opinion: "The usual bloodletting that follows a Nationalist victory appears to have taken place."

"That's an unusual anti-Nationalist statement to be made in a Portuguese newspaper these days," observed Jose.

"Yes, it is," agreed Manuel. "Some of our reporters and a few newspapers have remained independent of the government, although I have to say that there are those, like Salazar, that have favored the Nationalists from the beginning of the war. I suppose the newspaper I'm holding will be shut down before long."

"The old axiom," remarked Bonita, "truth is the first casualty of war."

Manuel turned back to the newspaper and continued reading aloud. "When the Nationalists entered Toledo, they found two mutilated Nationalist soldiers. In reprisal, no Republican prisoners were taken alive, despite assurances that those who surrendered would be safe."

After those sentences, Manuel read selections from the article depicting the aftermath of battle – beheaded corpses littering the ground, blood flowing ankle-deep down the steep slender streets of the city, grenades thrown among incapacitated men in a hospital.

Manuel finished reading the article.

"Justifying the bloodshed, a Nationalist officer explained, 'We are fighting an idea among men and, to kill the idea, we must kill the men.'"

"Obviously, this reporter was considerably offended by the behavior of Franco's troops," said Jose. "I admire his courage in telling the story the way it happened. I had an encounter with those same troops. There's a consistency between my experience at Badajoz and the fall of Toledo written and recorded by the reporter."

"Here's an editorial that will be of interest to you," said Manuel. "Franco is about to be appointed Chief of State of Nationalist Spain in the next few days. Presuming the Nationalists will win the war, the writer predicts Franco will be Head of State as long as he lives. He doesn't indicate whether this development is good or bad."

"Already hedging his bets," remarked Jose. "I guess I can't blame him too much. Any editor wants to stay in business."

"If this prediction becomes reality," said Manuel, "you'll be dealing with General Franco for a long, long time. Franco made an astounding statement not long ago: 'I do not make war on Spain; I am bringing Spain's liberation.' How twisted words can become. Somehow, I've never been able to associate Franco's words with freedom."

"He seems to have a great capacity for self-delusion," noted Jose. "You are free under Franco only if you say yes to everything he does. He believes he's not driven by a thirst for power; instead, power has been thrust upon him by others."

"If the Nationalist rebellion wasn't a grab for power," remarked Manuel, "I'd like to know what it was."

"Oh, the Francoists say they are on a God-given mission to eradicate atheism, communism, materialism, freemasonry, separatism, and just about every other ism," responded Jose. "I think we'd better add democracy to that list."

"There are more delusions of Franco's," added Bonita. "He claims to draw strength from peasants who in his 'Real Spain' would actually suffer the most. He believes the rural areas are for the Nationalists while the Reds and liberals control urban areas like Madrid, Barcelona, and Valencia. He says he wants to enjoy life as an ordinary Spaniard, but he cannot ignore the heavy burden of responsibility and must serve his country every hour he lives."

"What about his poor wife and children?" asked Manuel. "Doesn't he have any time for them?"

"I don't know how he schedules his day," replied Bonita. "Your question concerning his current family brings up some interesting notions about the family he grew up in. He makes his mother into a Madonna-like figure. Dr. Freud would have a field day with him. Some analysts have speculated about Franco's Oedipal complex."

"Oedipal which?" questioned Jose, wrinkling his nose at an unfamiliar term. "I've read *Oedipus the King*, but I didn't think it was too complex." That misconstruction brought laughter from the other two.

"The Oedipus complex, as Freud explains it, comes from the unanswered desire of the little boy to have sex with his mother," clarified Bonita. "His father stands in the way and becomes a rival to the boy, who would eliminate dear old Dad but isn't strong enough to do it. Freud's idea comes from the ancient Greek play of Sophocles you referred to, Jose, where Oedipus unknowingly kills his father and marries his mother."

"Did you know Franco had this complex?" Jose asked Manuel who had indicated with his head that he agreed with Bonita's explanation. "Something in my education is missing, although I can understand why this guy would go *loco* after murdering his father and committing incest with his mother. What a monstrous act! No wonder families get messed up."

"He's not a monster, Jose. Oedipus is a tragic hero. Read the play again, now that you're older."

"I was never aware of any sexual feelings toward my mother."

"Well, of course not," Bonita explained. "Those feelings are unconscious, says Freud. I'm not saying the Oedipus complex is as universal as Freud implies, but it's an interesting theory that could apply to some people. Getting back to Franco, little Francisco was his mother's favorite child, but she couldn't – or wouldn't – protect him and his two brothers from an abusive father. They had plenty of reasons to dislike their father and love their mother."

"Sometimes, I've compared the family I grew up in with what I know about Franco's family," said Jose. "There are some strong similarities."

"Oh, Jose!" exclaimed Bonita. "Please, don't torment yourself with thoughts like that."

"Think about it," he insisted. "In my family, there were four children – three sons and one daughter. In Franco's family, there were three sons and a daughter. Another daughter died at an early age. My mother was very religious; so was Franco's mother. My father was not mean like Franco's, but he and Mama didn't always see eye to eye on things, particularly religion and politics. I don't think my father lost his belief in Christianity, but he stopped going to Mass. He would say to me: the Catholic lay people serve only to pray, pay, and obey."

"My father described the Church with those same words," remarked Bonita. "Well, why not, Jose, both of our fathers own the same first name."

"Had he been living," Jose went on, "I'm sure my father would have been involved in the Asturian miner's strike, much to the dislike of my mother even though she would have remained silent about it. I'll always wonder if he would have tried to stop Antonio and Ramon from joining the Nationalist army."

"What both of you have said about Franco's family seems to resemble Spain on a larger scale today," noticed Manuel, curious to learn more about the person who could become Spain's future leader.

"In some ways, it does," allowed Bonita. "As Jose mentioned, Francisco's mother was very religious, pious, traditional, and moralistic – all the things her husband was not. Nicolas Franco scandalized the family as well as the local population with his womanizing, drinking, and gambling. Francisco could never gain his admiration as a child. Even now, he hasn't succeeded in getting Papa's respect – as far as I know. Nicolas has been described as intelligent and strong-willed, yet relaxed with those outside his family. He may have displayed an easy-going mask to the world, but at home with his children he was a severe disciplinarian and little Francisco bore the brunt of it."

"And now, Spain will bear the brunt of all those misfortunes Francisco suffered as a child," Manuel suggested.

"Well, the authoritarian personality is like that," interjected Jose. "People who are beaten as a child usually take out their frustrations on those who aren't in a position to defend themselves – and now, it's Spain that is getting clobbered."

"Speaking of being clobbered," said Manuel, "I read only yesterday in our same brave newspaper that a number of political executions ordered by Franco are being performed by the garrote."

"How awful!" cried Bonita. "Isn't that where an iron collar is fitted around a condemned person's neck and then tightened?"

"Yes," said Jose. "It's a deliberate form of torture before death. As a large screw is turned, the iron collar gets smaller and the victim is slowly strangled by suffocation. Another type of garrote shatters the spinal column at the base of the brain. The length of the agony depends upon the desires of the executioner."

"Civilized nations have outlawed the garrote for some time now," commented Manuel.

"Franco is not the head of a civilized movement," said Jose. "His clearest command is to execute as many prisoners as possible. I'm sure to him it makes perfect sense. The nationalists believe they are wasting food if they feed captives. Mass executions free prison guards to join regular soldiers at the front lines. I know I would have been executed if my brother hadn't stepped in."

"I understand Franco's father is opposed to the Nationalists," revealed Bonita. "Though he was brutal to Francisco, he now scorns his son's repressive ways. Nicolas became a Freemason and didn't go to Francisco's wedding, probably out of spite. His son has never forgiven him for snubs like those."

"You know a lot about the would-be *Caudillo*, Bonita," remarked Manuel.

"I know some things, Manuel. His family has a rather long history in Galicia. Franco grew up in El Ferrol, not far from my home. I once learned that the mother of Franco's great-grandfather had the same last name as mine, Sanchez. I pray I'm not related!"

"Even if that's the case, I'm sure it's a very distant relationship," said Jose.

"I appreciate your kind words," responded Bonita. "I'm not about to pursue my family history."

Jose picked up an old week-old newspaper Manuel had left in his apartment.

"Look here," he said, pointing to a photograph. "It's a picture of Franco leaning over a map of Spain. And, see this caption: Franco, the surgeon, operating on the body of Spain. And below the picture, the writer is suggesting Franco's tragedy is that he must operate on Spain like he would on his beloved wife while his tears fall upon her body."

"Ugh!" Bonita uttered in disgust. "More delusions! How obscene Nationalist propaganda becomes when it indulges in absurd metaphors."

Chapter 27
Sunday

Church bells rang one bright autumn morning. "Must be Sunday," said Jose to Bonita as they rose. They had considered the idea of going to Mass to give thanks for their escape from Spain and their safe arrival in Coimbra, but then decided to wait for another Sunday.

"Too dangerous even to go to church!" he reproached himself aloud. "What kind of courage is this?"

Bonita overheard his words and sensed the mental argument Jose was having with himself. "We can thank God for His blessings right here in this apartment," she declared.

"I think you're more spiritual than you let on," he suggested.

"What makes you say that?"

"Oh, just little things I've noticed, like thanking God after we could have come to grief."

"When you think of the things we've come through," said Bonita, "it has occurred to me that we've had some kind of extra help from somewhere."

"At times I've had the same thought," admitted Jose. "I've always accepted God's existence; still, I've wondered if there's some other kind of transformation happening to me."

"Maybe the same thing is happening to me," Bonita disclosed.

"We probably *have* changed and haven't noticed," said Jose. "For me, it's not physical as on a mountaintop with Moses, Elijah, and Jesus appearing before me. I'm sure it comes from the experiences I've had over the last month and a half. Why wasn't I killed at Badajoz? Most of my comrades were. Why did Antonio intervene? He didn't have to. How did I escape captivity with your help? The odds were against it."

"We could come up with completely rational reasons for answers to those questions, Jose, but the truth is we'll never know with any certainty."

"Maybe God has been with me, keeping me alive, to perform some kind of mission, perhaps one as small as carrying out my mother's wish."

"That's possible, only I hope you'll do it when it's safe."

Jose smiled. "Yes, I know," he said, "but I know I won't rest until I've made that pilgrimage for her."

"And, I'll be only too happy to help you – when the time is right. Jose, you mentioned transformation a moment ago. I've never told you this, but I believe you had a lot to do with changing me."

Jose said nothing, but looked at Bonita questioningly.

"When I was much younger, growing up at home in Corcubion, I was skinny, rather short, kind of a tomboy, and had lots of freckles. I believed I wasn't pretty."

"No, you never told me that. I'd say you filled out very nicely," he said appreciatively.

Bonita's face reddened slightly before she went on. "I wanted to forget those days. When I left home to attend university, I think the thing that motivated me most of all was that I wanted to leave my old self in Corcubion and acquire a new self at Oviedo and then at Salamanca."

"I think a lot of us hoped to do that."

"When I met you, Jose, you made me feel differently about myself. You valued me in a way no other man has ever done. I'll always love you for that. It's the greatest gift you could have given me."

Jose looked into Bonita's eyes and simply said, "Thank you for telling me." His eyes moistened with tears and he closed them.

"I love you so much," he said earnestly.

In the midst of a divine moment, there was a loud knock on the door. Jose and Bonita froze.

"Maybe our fortune has run out," whispered Jose. He went to open the door.

Manuel stood outside, juggling a bottle of wine and three glasses in his hand. *"Buenos dias* and *bom dia,"* he said. "I heard you two talking up here and I was feeling lonely downstairs. I hope I didn't startle you."

"It's a little early to partake of alcoholic drink, isn't it?" inquired Jose facetiously, motioning Manuel to come in. "We were just talking about the place of religion in our lives, and how much more faith and belief has meant to us in this unexpected journey we've had together."

"Oh, I'm not surprised at all, given the narrow escapes you've been through," responded Manuel, filling the glasses about half full. "Here, mix a little wine with your religion. You can wax more philosophical in your spiritual revelations that way."

"I had a lot of time to think about religion while I was in prison," said Jose. "All of those thoughts were reinforced when my mother made her request the night before she died. I can't get it out of my head that I should make that pilgrimage for her."

Like Bonita, Manuel had been urging Jose to steer clear of Santiago de Compostela and his mother's pilgrimage for the time being. "As I've pointed out, it's too dangerous now," he said. Then Manuel posed a question.

"Suppose someone came to you and said this: 'To carry out a mission you thoroughly believe in, one that gives you a purpose for living, or one in which you could achieve another person's great hope, you will undergo great suffering and death.' Would you do it?"

Jose paused for a moment and said, "Isn't this the same thing God asked of his Son?"

"Well, yes, I suppose so," said Manuel, "although, I didn't expect that for an answer from you."

"Of course, I'm not the same as Jesus, but I can't help but be intrigued – no, inspired – by his example," Jose explained. "Could I do anything less, especially when I run a smaller risk of suffering and death happening to me?"

"It's still too dangerous. Bonita loves you too much and I care about you too much as a friend to let you do such a fool thing as that. I'm not saying you should never do it. All in good time, my friend, but not until the Nationalists leave Galicia."

"That could be forever," muttered Jose, looking off into the distance. "Even if the Nationalists win the war and Franco is dictator until he dies, at some point it will be safe for me to enter Spain."

"You wouldn't be the first person who allowed their religious faith to destroy them," replied Manuel bluntly. "At Badajoz, you saw what Nationalist soldiers are doing to supporters of the Republic, and I saw the same kind of fanaticism at Salamanca." He looked at Jose and Bonita, smiled, and said lightly, "As Portuguese, I said to myself, how Spanish!"

They both laughed. "Jose can speak for himself, but I plead neutrality on that," said Bonita. "I'm Galician."

Manuel pressed on. "Jose, I respect your religious beliefs even though I don't fully share them. I'm a student of humanities. If I had stronger spiritual beliefs, I would have entered the School of Theology. Don't get me wrong, I find religion very interesting and also very dangerous. In your case, I don't want to see you become another Christian martyr when it serves no good purpose."

"I'm not seeking martyrdom, but I don't agree with your idea that it serves no good purpose," said Jose. "Now, I can just hear you say again: 'How Spanish!'"

This time Manuel laughed. *'Touche!'* he acknowledged, clinking his glass of wine with Jose's. "But you can't deny that you Spanish have always had an absorbing fascination with martyrs. I'll always remember the story of Saint Eulalia who marched into Merida and told the Roman conquerors their gods and emperor amounted to nothing. The Romans bound her and ripped her body apart with hot pincers. Did her martyrdom change anything? I don't recall the Roman Empire collapsing in Spain because of it."

"Her spirit became the form of a dove which flew out of her and up into heaven," remembered Bonita. "I know that's unbelievable, but then maybe her sacrifice, however small, had something to do with Spain becoming Christian."

"Even the Romans conceded she must have some great, hidden power they didn't possess," added Jose.

Manuel was disturbed that Jose and Bonita could so easily accept the idea that martyrdom would be beneficial to the person undergoing its agonies and be a positive worth to society as well.

Bonita noticed his discomfort and said, "I know, Manuel, you must think Spanish culture is totally consumed with the idea of glorious pain and misery."

"Well, we must admit that it is," conceded Jose as he helped himself to more of Manuel's wine. "We've always been absorbed, even entranced, by the theme of suffering. How many of our saints in the past have contrived to become martyrs? Even today, to suffer as Christ did on the cross is considered by some to be helpful, even essential, in one's spiritual journey."

"Essential?" asked Manuel. "That's really quite a stretch."

"Yes, it probably is." replied Jose. "Yet, how often Spanish artists picture that kind of witness as an ideal to be admired. I remember a painting in Leon's cathedral where you can see Saint Erasmo's intestines being cranked out of his body and on to a wheel before he dies for his faith. Another painting shows Saint Lorenzo grilled over flames. Saint Sebastian is always portrayed pierced with arrows. Once, I visited the Museum of Navarre in Pamplona where the artist puts a smile on Saint Agatha's face as her breasts are about to be hacked off. Saint Lucia had her eyes torn out and bled to death. The artist paints her holding her eyeballs on a plate; furthermore, she looks happy about it."

"Does God require that kind of pain and suffering from his people before they can be admitted to his kingdom?" Manuel asked.

"I don't know; I hope not," responded Jose.

"You know, Jose, maybe, just maybe, the desire for recognition and prestige has as much to do with making your own crown of thorns as genuine religious devotion," speculated Manuel. "Saint Eulalia had to practically beg the Roman authorities to make her into a martyr. Human ego could be involved in martyrdom, just as it is in seeking power over others."

"I think the artists were trying to communicate the idea that suffering, something we naturally avoid, can bring rewards in heaven – nothing more, nothing less," reasoned Jose. "I would guess some martyrs had motives you've ascribed to them, but I'm also persuaded that many who died for their faith did so because they were ordered to deny those beliefs or suffer the consequences. I think the Church thoroughly investigated a person's intentions before they conferred sainthood on any individual."

"Speaking of the Church," said Manuel, "Christ's own Church forgot its origins under tyranny and persecuted its own so-called heretics in his name, consigning them to the flames during Spain's so-called Golden Age. You could be suspected of practicing forbidden acts. It didn't take much to be called a betrayer of the faith. Once you were taken into the courts of the Inquisition, you had no chance."

"If you confessed, you had to supply the names and actions of many other dissenters to prove your honesty," contributed Jose. "If you didn't admit guilt, you were strapped on a rack and stretched by turns of the winch until your bones crackled and muscles split. You confessed to stop the pain."

"And, whether you were burned at the stake or not," Manuel declared with a certain amount of indignation, "the Inquisition took your property to finance itself and the war chest of the Catholic Monarchs to complete the Reconquest. The Church multiplied the number of martyrs by indulging in conduct they condemned when Christianity was an oppressed religion."

"Oh Manuel!" protested Jose. "How well we know this part of the *leyenda negra,* the Black Legend! You've heard it, we've heard it. Spaniards were the intolerant, backward, lunatics of the world, as if these traits applied to no one else. Weren't so-called witches being burned at this time throughout Europe? Did no other nation ever impose its rule on others? No other monarchs executed rivals to keep power? Every country has had its own forms of cruel retribution. Spaniards themselves have condemned the Inquisition in words far stronger than I've ever used. I'm sure we agree on one thing: the Spanish Nationalists will take us back to something resembling those repressive days."

He turned to Bonita and explained, "We had a lot of discussions like this over wine when Manuel was with me at Salamanca."

"Religion, philosophy, politics, history, money, love, sex, family – always great subjects for a good discussion," she commented. "However, I've noticed religion can cause the sharpest disagreements."

"Oh, that's quite true, Bonita," agreed Manuel. "You no doubt have figured out that I am more of a secular humanist than Jose and probably yourself, too. I can argue that God exists on one day and then on the next day argue he doesn't exist. I think it's safer to say I don't know – I can't really prove either position with natural, observable evidence."

"You're always calling for scientific proof in a domain that requires faith, Manuel," said Jose. "Faith goes beyond human logic and rationality."

"And into superstition, magic, and the occult," concluded Manuel.

"Yes, it can do that," granted Jose. "Some religious people fall into that pit. I believe that religion requires reason; God gave human beings a brain to work with. We should remember, though, reason will take us only so far. Beyond human intellect, we can rely only on faith. 'There are more things in heaven and earth . . . than are dreamt of in your philosophy,' Manuel. Unfortunately for rationalists, God did not mean for us to know everything."

"Well, we keep trying to know. Look at the great strides science is making in understanding our world, using that knowledge to cure diseases and eliminate suffering."

"And that's marvelous. We are progressing, but we need to remember for every answer we find, a dozen new questions spring up because of that discovery. God designed a very complex, mysterious universe – from the tiniest atom to planets and solar systems. I can't believe the creation of the universe happened by accident; if it did, nothing makes sense."

"But, look around you, my friend. The world seems to be going mad. How does an all-powerful God allow it? Does anything make sense?"

"I believe without God, a supreme intelligence, nothing does. When the world goes mad, well, that's man's doing, not God's."

"Yes, that's true," declared Manuel, "and we have to rely on the secular state to avoid or get us out of the mess we're in."

"I'm not about to abandon the principle of separation of church and state, but the secular state hasn't done too well in the twentieth century – world war, economic depression, totalitarianism, brutal ideologies."

R. D. Lock

"The theocratic state didn't do any better. Again, consider sixteenth century Spain, its 'golden age' – absolute monarchy, enforcing a single religion, the barbaric Inquisition, expulsion of Jews, book-burning, racial purity, enslavement of New World natives, plundering of colonies."

"Quite a list, Manuel. And, I could add the ruinous effects of all that wealth which poured into Spain: idleness replacing hard work, luxury instead of moderation, arrogant pride sweeping away a sense of justice. If only Spain could have learned from the downfall of Rome."

"I won't defend the Romans on everything they did," interrupted Manuel, "but they were smart on one thing: they offered citizenship to non-Romans. What did Ferdinand and Isabella do? With monumental intolerance, they kicked out Jews and Muslims, probably their most productive citizens."

"I agree; that was a historic mistake. The Catholic Monarchs should have learned a thing or two about justice from the Hebrew prophets. Think of Nathan confronting King David who arranged Uriah's death in battle so he could marry Uriah's wife, Bathsheba. Nathan, speaking for God, says to David: 'I will rise up evil against you out of your own house.' As king, David could have had Nathan killed on the spot and no one would have blinked an eye. No, David's response was: 'I have sinned against the Lord.' "

"Jose, you could become God's prophet to Spain in the twentieth century," was Manuel's frivolous reply. "There's your ticket back into the home country. Franco wouldn't dare touch you."

"I can just see Franco like King David falling on his knees in front of me, begging to be forgiven!" exclaimed Jose putting all the irony he could into his voice and smiling at his friend's absurd statement.

"I'm relieved you've given up martyrdom," remarked Manuel.

"Spain is not as hopeless as you probably believe," countered Jose. "The conquistadors were greedy, uneducated, and ruthless, as you might say, but they sprang from the common class and were courageous and heroic. Many priests ran from a corrupt Church hierarchy to carry out the idea of mission and unselfish devotion to the natives of America. Saint Teresa of Avila and John of the Cross bore witness to such an intense mysticism . . ."

He stopped and suddenly hit himself on the head in a masquerade show of horror. "I suddenly realize I've been sounding exactly like my brother Antonio! Nonetheless, the Golden Age brought forth a flowering of Spanish culture – think of *Miguel Cervantes*, his *Don Quixote*, the greatest novel of the Western world. In the fine arts, we have Velazquez, later on, Goya . . ."

"Enough, enough," interjected Manuel. "I've heard the litany." He turned to Bonita with a gesture of hopelessness. "You see what I've had to put up with."

"I'm glad you two can have such spirited conversations and still be friends," she said. "I take it both of you got accustomed to discussing controversial topics starting back at Salamanca."

Manuel began to give a mischievous smile. "I'll never forget the 'mind before matter' argument we had there. We called it 'MAM' – *mente ante materia*. You can imagine who was for mind and who was for matter."

Jose looked at Bonita and simply rolled his eyes.

Manuel continued. "Jose offered this fantastic illustration to prove his point – or attempt to, I should say. Since then, I've referred to our discussion as MAM."

"MAM?" inquired Bonita. "Would you care to spell this out, Jose?"

"MAM simply means Mind-above-Matter," explained Jose. "The origin of our debate was with how our *madre* raised us; Manuel's was secular and you know mine was religious. I used an earthy illustration to demonstrate the power of MAM – mind above matter. Babies have no control over filling their diapers, but around the age of two, humans begin to become toilet-trained. If we didn't handle that situation with our minds, think of the embarrassing moments we'd have every day in public. The important point is we exercise our minds over matter."

"However," Manuel playfully rebutted, "MAM can mean Matter-above-Mind. In Jose's illustration, matter will ultimately have its way. You can't hold it back forever. Those who do – make a real mess of it in the end." Jose held his nose at Manuel as they dissolved into laughter.

"Oh, no!" cried Bonita, feigning disgust. "I'm leaving. No, on further thought, why don't you boys take your discussion into the bathroom."

"I always appreciated the times we could have such frank conversations and spike them with good humor," replied Jose. "They were particularly useful when we would disagree and challenge each other. Like a good counselor, Manuel would help me make clear to myself what I really believed."

"During those days Jose was quite taken with the issue of certain regions within Spain becoming self-governing," said Manuel to Bonita, switching the subject abruptly and pouring more wine into his empty glass. "I take it, being Galician, you would agree with his desire for regional independence?"

"I don't know," she answered. "We haven't talked much about it. I know he's been sympathetic toward Catalans and Basques, though not the violent ones."

"I'm not for Spain breaking up into three or four countries," said Jose.

"I am for regional self-rule where it's wanted by the majority in those areas but not total separation from Spain. We were speaking of Spain's 'Golden Age.' I'll say this for the Catholic Monarchs. Ferdinand and Isabella had a reasonable goal: to unify Spain. Granted, they often used terrible methods to accomplish their objectives. I'm not excusing them. Their purpose was Spanish nationalism at a time that, as Karl Marx would say, put them in the mainstream of history."

"Wouldn't your brother Antonio be shocked to discover he was at one with even a part of Marx's doctrine?" suggested Manuel. Jose and Bonita smiled, picturing Antonio's irritated reaction.

The thought of Antonio once more cloaked Jose's mind. "My brother has had military training, not university education, but that doesn't mean he can't reason intelligently. Antonio was always quite taken with Ferdinand and Isabella in the way they forged Castilian dominance over all of Spain. Ferdinand, that 'clever fox of Aragon' as he's been called, knew Castile was necessary to build a nation. His marriage to Isabella united his kingdom with Castile which developed into a greater Spain, creating the ability needed to master much of the New World and make Spain the dominant power in Europe and the Americas."

"Yes, and to subdue Portugal at the same time," said Manuel with a sour note to his expression.

"Our ancestors paid a terrible price for the way they seized territory and subjugated people at that time and I definitely don't favor Spanish nationalism as it is being expressed now. And, since 1580," said Jose, referring to Spain's sixty-year occupation of Portugal and bowing to Manuel, "Spain overextended itself militarily and financially, losing battles and lands over three hundred years. The defeat of the Armada, inept kings, famine and plague, state bankruptcies, guerrilla wars, civil wars – our history has been one disaster after another. We've fallen to where we're now called *'invertebrate,'* no backbone; we've lost our strength."

Manuel wiped his eyes with a handkerchief in mock sympathy. "A sad tale, Jose – keep in mind I'm from Portugal. I find it difficult to shed tears for Spain."

Jose ignored Manuel's contrived act. "Our current misfortunes could be comprehended in the context of a nation trying to find its identity. It makes me think of a controversy in the 1620s over which patron saint could rescue Spain from its sense of decline. Should Saint James be chosen, having saved Spain from the Moors, or should it be Teresa of Avila, who was both a favorite Spanish saint and a woman? Spain was divided: should it keep Saint James as its traditional defender or could Saint Teresa be a better mediator for us in heaven?"

"Who won?" asked a half-serious Manuel.

Jose took a long swallow of wine before answering.

"It's too early to tell," he finally said.

"I vote for Teresa," disclosed Bonita.

"But, I still say," insisted Jose, "Spain's achievement is remarkable when you consider where it came from after the Muslim subjugation, centralizing power at home and establishing a world-wide empire. Looking at events with the eyes of Ferdinand and Isabella, their forceful, often cruel, methods had purpose."

"Don't tell me you've adopted the 'ends justify the means' strategy, Jose," challenged Manuel, now completely serious. "If you have, I'm disappointed. Portugal has conquered and exploited as other nations have done, so I'm not letting any imperialist country off easy. Remember, the Nationalists draw inspiration from the ideas of conquest you've just expressed."

"Forgive me, Manuel. The wine befuddled my thinking."

"It wasn't my wine. You've been listening to your oldest brother too much."

"Maybe so," acknowledged Jose. "Antonio can be persuasive, particularly when he has the power of life and death over you."

"Your wine certainly did loosen his tongue," said Bonita to Manuel.

"It never fails, Bonita."

Chapter 28
A Complication

A few days later, Jose asked Manuel if it was all right to go shopping with him.

"I can see you're about ready to go insane cooped up in your small room," responded Manuel. "How did you ever survive while you were in prison?"

"Not very well, but I resigned myself to confinement because I had no choice. Here, I have a choice. I would think our trail, if anyone was on it, would be getting cold by now."

"If you go outside, Bonita will want to have the same privilege. How can you deny her? You're liberal; you do believe in equal treatment, don't you?"

"Of course. She's an adult woman and can decide for herself," Jose answered. "We could use some kind of disguise."

"Not the 'old man and old woman' routine you were telling me about?"

"No, you could buy me a fake mustache and I could shave my head. I could wear a big nose and call myself Cyrano de Bergerac; you know, act like I'm not all right in my brain."

"Come on, Jose, get serious."

"No, I have a better idea. Get me a lance and a sword, and I'll dress up as Don Quixote. I'll grow a beard on my chin and powder it white. I'll call you Sancho Panza and Bonita will be Dulcinea. Cervantes would be proud of me. I'm mentally deranged from too much study at university. I thought I saw a flock of sheep on the way into town. Could they be the Nationalist army?"

"Jose, Jose! Calm down," beseeched Manuel. "I don't think you're always aware of the kind of trouble you're in."

"I'm not allowed to shock people?"

"You can do that when times are different in this country or in Spain. You and Bonita have talked about going to Spanish America. Did you ever think about France? That's the most promising escape route for you. Quite a few Spaniards have already fled to France."

"Yes, I read about that. I don't want Bonita or me to live in a refugee camp."

"Maybe Belgium, Netherlands, or England?"

"I've got to earn money to do traveling of any length, Manuel. To get a job, I'll have to go outside the apartment."

"Now, you're talking common sense. I've been looking for any possibilities of employment for you. So far, I haven't found anything, but I'll keep looking."

"What sort of employment would there be around here. I can't work for a newspaper; that's too public and the PVDE would be on me in a minute."

"Ever do farm work?"

"Yes, while I was growing up near Trujillo."

Manuel thought for a moment. "I could check with several growers that come into town to sell their wares on market day."

"Would you? I'd be willing to give it a try. Maybe Bonita could work – if not outside in the fields, maybe some kind of housework. I'll talk it over with her. Field labor and house cleaning is not the kind of work we had envisioned for ourselves at university, but it's better than sitting in the apartment all day."

"Now we're starting to be creative, Jose, and it's not madness."

Bonita came through the door.

"I thought I heard you two discussing my future," she said. "I agree with the idea of getting work to do. Quite a bit of the money I brought with me has been spent, including the money Marisa and Jorge gave us. I'm sure they gave as much as they could afford; after all, how much did they have to spare?"

"I hope to repay my sister and her husband," said Jose. "I've kept a small bank account in Trujillo, which I don't dare touch at the present time. I had hoped my newspaper work would add to my savings; then I could have taken care of school loans from the university."

"Last I knew you were working for *El Sol*," said Manuel.

"I was working as a part-time reporter for them, hoping to turn that position into a full-time job, but *El Sol* has lost circulation and come upon hard times. Now, there is war. Other more thriving newspapers support the Republic, but I'd rather not join any of them unless I'm completely desperate. Most of them are attached to a party and I want to be an independent journalist. They probably wouldn't hire me anyway; I won't be a slave to anyone's party line."

"You may have to swallow some of that independence to make a living," cautioned Manuel.

"I'm aware of that, Manuel. I've thought of trying to reach Barcelona and work for *Vanguardia*, if they would have me. Maybe I could shock Antonio and work for the socialist paper, *Solidariad Obrero*. *ABC* is too conservative for me. I couldn't stand working for any Francoist publication; I'd be selling my soul if I did that. If the Nationalists are victorious, let's face it, their censorship will ruin or close down any independent paper that doesn't follow the official line. With government control, I think I know what will happen. Most Spaniards will simply quit reading newspapers."

"You paint a bleak picture for your profession."

"The Republic had its faults, but widespread censorship was used only under the worst circumstances. I can accept some of my oldest brother's criticism of the Republic, but I fear what's coming if his side wins this war."

"Sometimes I believe Jose makes too many requirements of the kind of organization he would work for," said Bonita, "but then if I were in his line of work, I'd be saying the same thing."

"Ideals are great," concluded Manuel, "and they usually make life more difficult for us."

Remembering Jose's desire to get outside and shop, Manuel abruptly offered, "Let me do one more shopping trip for you by myself. The next one, both of you can come along. I'll take the names of the items on your list, Bonita. Soon, you'll be on your own."

Before any protest could be made, Manuel was out the door. He quickly disappeared into the street, leaving Jose and Bonita standing in his apartment.

"It doesn't take Manuel long to make up his mind and act," observed Jose. "Well, no matter, he's been doing us a great favor. He's being a good friend; he wants to take care of us."

"Jose," said Bonita with a sort of forced calmness. "Now that we're alone, I've got something I should tell you."

"What is it?"

"I don't know how to say this." She looked at Jose with a touch of apprehension appearing on her face.

"What is it?" repeated Jose, a tone of anxious concern coming into his voice.

"I'll tell you plainly. I think I'm pregnant. If this is true, Jose, I'm carrying your child."

Jose's mouth fell open, his eyes widened, he stood looking at Bonita as if he had been struck by a thunderbolt. He didn't know what to say.

Finally, he spoke hesitantly and softly, "It's wonderful, Bonita. The baby will truly be our love child. I know I shouldn't be surprised, but I didn't expect it. I can hardly believe it." His heart began to pound. He couldn't begin to comprehend the conflicting emotions that assailed him.

"I can scarcely believe it," were the words he brought forth again.

Bonita began to cry. "I know it will complicate things."

Jose came to her and wrapped his arms around her.

"This is the most wonderful news you could have brought me," he declared. "We're married in spirit, remember? I will have to take good care of you – that is, both of you. Having children is what we've dreamed of."

"I know. You're pleased, Jose?"

"I'm thrilled." He kissed Bonita tenderly. "You've made me feel very proud and humble at the same time. If it's true, I'm going to be a father. In prison only a short time ago, I would have said something like this was impossible."

They moved outside Manuel's apartment, locking the door behind them and started climbing to their third-floor room.

"There's nothing like caring for a baby and a wife to make you start thinking about *manana*," he said halfway up the stairs. "It's fantastic, Bonita. Our next steps are to earn some money first and then move to a place where we'll be safe. We've even got more to live for now."

Reaching the top of the stairs, Bonita turned to face Jose and whispered, "Let's not say anything to Manuel for a while. We can, when I'm absolutely sure. I'm so excited; I don't know if I can keep it a secret." She thought momentarily and then murmured, "Oh, Jose, I wish we lived in normal times."

"I suppose a cynic would say we *are* living in normal times. There are more war years in human history than peaceful ones, sad to say."

"The war is bad enough," said Bonita bluntly, "and being hunted the way we are makes everything a hundred times more difficult."

"I would think the hunt for us would have cooled off now. The longer we're out of sight means it's easier to forget about us. I'm sure Antonio was deeply offended when we first escaped, but he must have other things to think about now."

"And Ramon?"

"Ramon doesn't really care if we're in prison or not. The Nationalist cause means nothing to him, except being a soldier is a way to make some money and look good in front of the girls."

"So you think Antonio is the one we have to worry about?"

"I did two weeks ago," replied Jose. "He's probably forgotten us by now. I suspect Antonio is fully absorbed by military matters. He's probably intimately involved in the battle for Madrid. If he does think of us, it's like a bad dream he had last month."

"Maybe your brother simply went through the motions of trying to locate us and actually wanted us to get away."

"I doubt that, Bonita. I'm sure we were an embarrassment to him when he had to explain to the camp commandant why his little brother wasn't his prisoner any more."

"Meanwhile Jose, we've got our baby to get ready for. We need to try to prepare a secure place for it."

"We could find a cave in southern Spain where no respectable Nationalist agent would ever think of looking for us. I've seen people coming out of caves so well-dressed, you'd think they were going to a wedding. I recall a man wearing spotless clothes and polished shoes telling me the cave he lived in was cleaner than many houses he'd seen, and he wouldn't live anywhere else in the summer."

"We're not going back to Spain," said Bonita firmly, "not after the way we got out of there. And, Jose, I'm not raising a child hidden in a cave."

"Okay, I understand. I'm not being serious about living under the ground. Maybe Portugal would be the safest place for now. We're here in a country that's not at war. I'll keep my nose out of political affairs. I could work as a farm laborer for a while as Manuel has suggested. I would save enough money, buy some land north of here – say, around Mesao Frio – and develop my own vineyard. Drinking wine will never go out of fashion."

"Jose, you don't know a thing about growing grapes."

"I could learn. I was willing to apprentice myself in journalism; I could do the same thing to manage a vineyard."

"You know how to write about current events and politics. I want you doing the work you love."

"Remember, I've got two people to support, plus myself."

"I know and appreciate that, but I don't want you to deny yourself either."

"When I think of playing with my son or caring for my daughter, I don't see how I could be denying myself." Jose made a cradle with his arms, pretending there was a small boy or a petite little girl being rocked in them.

No Greater Love

On and on they talked about their prospects of being a family until Manuel came up with the food he had purchased for the next several days.

As much as she was grateful that Jose thought about his responsibilities as a parent and a husband, Bonita wondered at times if he was being truthful with himself about their future.

And, as much as Jose wanted to reassure Bonita concerning a chance for their safety and well-being, the person he needed most to convince was himself.

That night as he lay in bed next to a sleeping Bonita, Jose inwardly posed questions that without warning entered his mind.

Now that I am to be a father, have I simply rationalized our intimacy? With the pressures of being hunted, have we like so many others in times of stress and war succumbed to our desires?

The emotion of their impassioned love was wonderful, no denying that. Yet, another voice brought forth more questions.

What was God's judgment? Was this child that could now be on the way a blessing or a punishment in the midst of trying circumstances?

Jose privately confessed: *Forgive us, Lord, if we have gone against your word. Be merciful to us. We are lost in this tumultuous world. We have only each other.*

Jose stopped himself and started again: *No, I have that last part wrong. We have God with us, even as sinners.*

He reached for Bonita and pulled her closer to him, thankful that somehow in this chaotic world, he had found her and could love her so completely.

CHAPTER 29
A SAINTED QUEEN

Next day after spending hours planning and preparing their minds to be a family, Jose made a request of Bonita.

"Tell me about the sainted queen," he said. "You promised to tell me the story when we first rode into Coimbra. We've talked enough about the future for a while; let's discuss something about the past. At least the past is more certain than the future."

"I don't know about that," remarked Bonita. "We've studied history. People are endlessly arguing about events that happened long ago. Was there ever a conflict that wasn't a grievance about something in the past?"

"I can't think of any. But, why was this queen sainted?"

"Her name was Isabella, a daughter of the King of Aragon. As a princess, her beauty attracted King Diniz of Portugal. The proposed alliance with Aragon found favor with the people of Portugal, as did Isabella. Diniz and Isabella were married with a great celebration. Soon after the wedding, Queen Isabella invited the poor in the surrounding countryside to be her guests. She humbled herself by washing their feet and feeding them a meal with her own hands. Everyone, including King Diniz, was impressed with her generous, kind nature."

"Oh, oh," interrupted Jose. "I think I see a problem coming."

"I'm sure you can guess. Are you sure you haven't heard this story before?"

"Yes. I'm not deceiving you this time."

"Well, throngs of beggars began appearing at her door. She received them all, but Diniz had to pay the bills. He had expected a wife; instead, he got a saint, one who loved all human beings."

"Did Isabella and Diniz have children of their own?"

"Of course. She couldn't turn anyone down, much less her own husband. She gave him two children, one of them being the kind every king desires, a healthy heir to the throne. After their birth, Isabella became completely absorbed by her good works – so much so that King and Queen grew further apart. Diniz sought other feminine friends."

"Didn't the sainted queen become jealous?"

"No, apparently not. Isabella made no effort to bring Diniz back closer to her. She even welcomed his illegitimate children into her home. She was entirely devoted to her works of charity and spent enormous sums of money on them. King Diniz finally had to stop her raids on his treasury."

"Probably had a war he wanted to finance."

"Don't be such a cynic, Jose. Anyway, legends of Isabella's generosity grew around her. She would hide bread for the poor under her clothes. When the king tried to find out what she was carrying, the bread she was concealing turned into roses."

"Divine protection of a saint!" proclaimed Jose with dramatic humor. "This wouldn't be much of a story if we didn't have a few miracles."

"I'm ignoring your attempt to be flippant. Isabella directed the building of her Santa Clara convent. We passed it on the way into town. Of course, by now she had no way to pay for the convent's construction, so she gave roses to the workers."

"The least she could have done was save the bread and give it to the people."

"Jose, just listen to the story! Naturally, the workers grumbled, but they accepted the flowers. When they did, each rose turned into a bag of gold."

"Hey, I'll bet that got the king's attention."

"Actually, Diniz was considered to be a wise king. He sponsored projects that improved farming, industry, and education. He founded the university at Lisbon, later moved here to Coimbra. When he died, his Queen retired to her Santa Clara convent to pray and prepare for her own death. Many years after Isabella died, Santa Clara was flooded by the Mondego River and her coffin was moved to a new Santa Clara. By that time, Rome had officially declared her to be a saint."

"Bonita, you've told quite a story. I love the way you really get into it. I'm really serious when I say that. You remind me of my mother. I didn't know you were such a good storyteller."

"Thank you," said Bonita modestly. "It helps when you are teaching small children." However, she immediately dropped her humble countenance.

"You'd better say something complimentary after all your interruptions. I still haven't forgotten the trick you played on me when I told the story of

Inez and Pedro. I was about ready to throw you out the window if you had made one more wisecrack."

Jose couldn't resist making one more prankish remark. Putting a hand in front of him to form a make-believe microphone, he posed as a reporter asking a question in a deep voice.

"Senor Martinez, to what do you attribute the endurance of your long-standing love affair with Bonita Sanchez?"

In a weak, frail voice, he squeaked an answer. "Terror, sir, sheer terror."

Bonita laughed, ran over to him, kissed him, and pointed a finger at him. "At last," she said, "a proper attitude. Let's keep it that way."

Two days later, Jose answered a knock on the door of the apartment. He saw an excited Manuel standing before him.

"Good news. I believe I have a lead on a farm job for you, Jose. I know the farm owner. He's reliable and needs help. His farm is about three kilometers outside Coimbra. It sounds perfect, Jose. You will need to meet him at his place and see for yourself."

"You are really looking out for me, my friend, and I thank you many times over. Yes, I agree. I want to meet him and ask what he would want me to do and how much he's willing to pay me."

Bonita came out to greet Manuel and ask, "Could you find out if this farmer needed a person like me to do housework?"

"We didn't get that far in our discussion," Manuel answered. "Let's determine whether this is the right spot for Jose. If he does get a job there, then we can ask the farmer's wife about housework. It's also possible there is a place in town where you could work. While you would rather be together, you two don't have to be at the same location."

Bonita agreed it was more important for Jose to begin working and start acquiring some money for their future. She reminded the two young men that she intended to contribute.

"When do we go?" queried Jose. "I'm ready anytime."

"Tomorrow, *amigo*. The farmer is too busy at market today. We'll meet him at his home at seventeen hours; that's the time and place we established."

"I hope this works out, Manuel. You're right; I'm about ready to jump out the window. If it wasn't for my lovely young wife here, I'd think I was back in solitary confinement."

"Wife?" Manuel grinned as he asked. "When did this happen?"

Bonita almost gave away her 'secret' right then and there. "Jose and I are married in spirit – that's what he meant," she simply said.

"Senor and Senora Martinez," spoke Manuel with a touch of comedy, "I never thought it would happen so quickly."

"We haven't had an official ceremony yet," explained Bonita. "When we do, and we hope it's very soon, you're invited to stand with us as our best man."

"I'll be most happy to, Senorita," said Manuel, bowing to her.

"And, as for you, Manuel, you've already gone into counseling job-seekers," observed Jose, "and now you can take up marriage counseling. We have been and will be your first clients. You see, we've considered your future prospects, too."

"That is most kind of you. Now, I must be going. Until tomorrow, Jose, *adios*. We'll leave here a little after fifteen hours, plenty of time for the walk."

"If you two are going off for Jose's employment interview tomorrow afternoon," announced Bonita, "I think I'll celebrate my first day of freedom by visiting the *Quinta das Lagrimas* on the other side of the river. I want to commune with Inez de Castro and discover if she has any secrets about love and marriage she can pass along to me."

"Be sure to write them down," requested Manuel. "If I'm going to become a marriage counselor, I'll need all the help I can get."

Chapter 30
The Manor House

Next afternoon as Jose was preparing to go with his devoted friend for the employment interview, Bonita handed Manuel a letter to mail. He looked at the envelope.

"Are you sure this is a good idea?" he asked. The Nationalists are in control of Galicia, you know. Posting the letter in Portugal may be all right, but once it gets into Spain, it's likely to fall into Nationalist hands and they won't hesitate to open it. I imagine you've written to your parents assuring them you're safe and that you're with Jose?"

"Yes. I didn't want them to worry any more than I'm sure they have already."

"I see you haven't put any return address on the envelope. That's being careful, but is there any information you have in the letter that could reveal where you are? Also, the envelope will have a Coimbra postmark. An alert postal worker who is cooperating with the Nationalists would be able to give them your location."

Bonita dropped her head, chagrined. "I didn't think of the postmark," she said. "You're right, Manuel. As much as I would like to relieve their anxieties, I'd better leave the letter here and wait for an opportunity to mail it from another place."

She turned to Jose and said, "I wrote to my parents from Trujillo after I arrived at your sister's house, but before you came with Antonio. Of course, I had wanted to find you there. I didn't know where you were. I knew nothing about you being a prisoner at that time. I only wrote I had finally arrived safely and you weren't at home in Trujillo, but I hoped to see you soon. Marisa mailed the letter the day before Antonio hijacked you back to prison. I never

No Greater Love

thought of it then, but now I wish I had sent a letter to them from Monforte or somewhere near there."

"We were a little busy staying out of the sight of the PVDE that day," recalled Jose. "Besides, what would you have written? 'Dear Madre and Padre: I'm having a wonderful time. Helped Jose bust out of prison. It was a wild night fleeing the police. Other than that, it's been barrels of fun. Have a pleasant day!' "

When Bonita and Manuel stopped chuckling at Jose's ridiculous improvisation, he added, "They would not have been reassured at all about your safety or the state of mind of their future son-in-law."

"There will be a time when you can contact them," insisted Manuel. "Right now, we just don't know when that will be."

Looking at his watch, he said to Jose, "We'd better get going."

Jose kissed Bonita good-bye. He said to her, "Be careful and have a good time visiting the university and the manor house."

"I hope your interview goes well," she responded, waving at the two as they departed.

"We'll be back before nightfall," he called back to her. "You do the same." She nodded her head in agreement.

Jose and Manuel proceeded on foot down the street. Jose turned around just before they were to go around a building and on to another street. Bonita saw him and blew a kiss from her lips and outstretched hand. Jose returned the kiss and looked briefly at the radiantly beautiful figure standing in the doorway. Then he turned, caught up with Manuel, and disappeared out of sight.

Bonita scurried upstairs, impatient to get started. She quickly made a sandwich for her lunch and put it in a pocket of the light jacket she planned to carry in case the weather changed. Locking the apartment door, she deposited the key in a small pocket of the jacket, buttoning it shut for safety. She moved outside into the street and headed for the University of Coimbra.

White clouds billowed in the sky as the sun shone brightly on a pleasant autumn day. She walked among the university buildings and visited the King John Library with three hundred thousand volumes in bookshelves completely covering the walls. Bonita shivered slightly as she strolled inside the imposing Private Examination Hall, imagining herself as a student facing questions from a multitude of professors. Next, she stepped into the Grand Hall, where the Rector opened the academic year and presided over scholastic ceremonies. She approved of the seating structure; the Rector's chair was no higher than the professors' benches which lined the walls around the whole room. Outside, Bonita looked up at the Iron Gate, which could be seen from anywhere in the city. She walked over to Saint Michael's Chapel. There, she walked through the portals covered with stone leaves and branches that twisted and turned upward in the *Manueline* style unique to the country. Inside, she viewed the *azulejos*, the brightly colored glazed tiles that decorate the surfaces of Portuguese buildings.

Bonita realized she was spending far too much time at the university and needed to begin her trek down the hills into the lower commercial district of Coimbra. She wanted to look into some of the store windows if only to get an idea of the merchandise the city had to offer. Then, she would move on to the Santa Clara bridge over the Mondego river, the only way she could reach the *Quinta das Lagrimas*, the "House of Tears." Now a manor house, this was where the lovers, Inez de Castro and Dom Pedro, had lived with their children. This was where, in 1355, agents of Dom Pedro's father stabbed Inez to death. Their tragic love gave rise to the legend she had told Jose. Where Inez was killed, a spring had turned into a fountain, the *Fonte dos Amores*, the Fountain of the Lovers. It was a romantic place, celebrated in story and poem, and Bonita wanted to see it for herself. She couldn't help but compare the love of Inez and Pedro to the love she and Jose had for each other. She cherished the words Jose had spoken to her last night as they embraced and kissed before falling asleep.

No greater love have I ever received than the love you have given me.

On the way to the bridge, Bonita stopped at the Church of Saint Bartholomew. Manuel had suggested that she visit a statue of Jesus located to the right as one entered the sanctuary. An elderly woman was kneeling at the statue when Bonita first came into the church. The woman prayed and then reached to touch the robe Jesus was wearing and knelt to kiss his feet. At first, this behavior struck Bonita as something close to idolatry, examining human activity as she often did with a critical mind. Tears dropped from the woman's face and she took her hair to wipe the statue clean. Backing away, the woman nearly bumped into Bonita.

The woman excused herself, saying *"Desculpe."*

Bonita touched the woman on her shoulder, and responded in *Gallego* and as best as she could in Portuguese, "That was a beautiful thing you did there a moment ago."

The woman smiled and kissed Bonita on one cheek and then the other. In an instant, the woman left the church and was outside, disappearing into the throng of people in the street.

Bonita was surprised by her own reaction. Normally, she would have found fault with the woman's blind adoration of a piece of painted metal, albeit representing Jesus. Now, confronted face-to-face with a simple expression of veneration, she was touched by the obvious sincerity implicit in the woman's devotion. A man came to the statue and repeated the same reverent observance, this time without tears. Whatever the spiritual idea was that the Church wanted to have represented in the minds of its people, Bonita couldn't get around the straightforward love and emotional attachment human beings brought to the sculpture. Bonita had wrestled with religious dilemmas and uncertainties in her young life, but here she encountered directly the woman's pure, unadorned belief that faith in Jesus as her savior was sufficient for her eternal future and by touching the metal garment, her prayer would be answered.

Bonita moved closer to the statue. Maybe her analytical self could detect the mysterious force that drew the woman and the man, making visible the reverence they felt within. Could this magnetic power have come from the statue? Bonita gazed at the feet; then, her eyes slowly rose until they came upon the face of Jesus. She beheld the kindest, most compassionate expression in a face she had ever seen in an artistic and spiritual portrayal of sacrificial love. She was amazed by her reaction once again. Bonita turned, unable to look into that face any longer, but she knew she would never forget it. Her eye caught for an instant the painting over the altar; it was Saint Bartholomew being martyred for his faith in Christ. The apostle was depicted being flayed alive, a gruesome sight, certainly, but one that displayed the pains a disciple would endure to be in the company of God.

Manuel, she thought, *Spaniards aren't the only ones to venerate martyrdom as pictured by artists.*

Bonita hurried out into the street. She was astonished by her sudden *sympatico* with the woman kneeling at Jesus' feet, the man's unquestioning faith, and the impact of the sculptor's rendition of Jesus' face. She was also surprised at her own unexpected suspension of reasoned analysis in favor of uncritical approval of all that she witnessed.

Maybe the Church has something I haven't considered before. This idea shocked and surprised her: The symbols and sights accompanying the rites of religious reverence contained a meaning for others that had escaped her thus far.

Reaching the Portagem, the gate that welcomed the visitor to the city, Bonita walked on to the bridge, the *Ponte de Santa Clara*. The waters of the Mondego rushed below her as she moved quickly over the expanse of the bridge and came upon the old convent of Santa Clara. She found a bench on which to rest, reached into the jacket she was carrying, and pulled out her sandwich.

As she sat eating her food, Bonita contemplated the story of Isabella, the 'Sainted Queen' of Portugal, hopelessly naïve for this world yet perfectly gifted for God's heaven. When she finished her sandwich, Bonita continued her journey, going past the new Santa Clara convent built in the seventeenth century. Isabella's story persisted in Bonita's mind.

She wondered: *Could I ever be as virtuous as Queen Isabella?* As quickly as the thought occurred to her, she pushed it from her mind.

Another fifteen minutes of walking brought her to *Quinta das Lagrimas*, the eighteenth century manor house built in the park where the love drama of Pedro and Inez had transpired. The house and grounds were now quite deserted with overgrown vegetation. Bonita imagined the intensity of the desperate love Inez and Pedro had for each other, the horror Pedro must have felt when finding Inez dead, and the fury of his revenge as he sought and punished her killers. A dense growth of bushes and trees surrounded her. Splashes of fading sunlight came through the branches. On the paths tree roots spread above ground like arms and fingers reaching into the soil of the earth.

Bonita shivered with delight as she found the spring that had become *the Fonte de Amores*, the Fountain of the Lovers. Here was the water, created by the tears of Inez as legend claimed. Here were the marks on the stones, stained by the blood of Inez.

"Oh, I'm glad I came," Bonita whispered. Several minutes went by.

Inner words spoke to her. *The story of Inez is so beautiful, yet so tragic. I was compelled to come here. I wouldn't have missed this for the world.*

The shadows on the ground lengthened as daylight slowly ebbed away. Bonita was so absorbed in her venture that she hadn't noticed the passage of time. She was about ready to leave when she heard a footstep and a branch of a tree snap behind her.

"*Hola*, Bonita," a voice said.

Bonita turned. She saw no one.

"I'm so glad I found you," the voice spoke again.

Thinking she recognized the voice of Jose or Manuel, Bonita smiled and said in a coquettish call, "Well, you might have the decency to show yourself!"

From behind a tree stepped Ramon Francisco Martinez Garcia. He was not wearing his Nationalist uniform; instead, he was clothed in a simple short coat that covered a plain shirt and black pants.

"Ramon!" Bonita cried, startled by the sight of him. "What are you doing here? You should be back in Spain."

"I'm here just to see you, Bonita. I wouldn't miss being with you for anything else on earth."

"You're not wearing your Nationalist uniform, Ramon. What happened? Did you get sick of army life?"

"There are things more important than winning military battles. One of them is seeing you. I'm on extended leave. I'll have to report back soon enough."

"What brought you to Portugal, to Coimbra? Did you decide to desert? I can imagine there are a lot of desertions in Nationalist ranks."

"I haven't deserted. Like I said, Bonita, I came to see you."

"Ramon, I don't believe a word you're saying. What are you up to?" she demanded.

"What am I up to?" he smirked. "I keep saying I'd walk to the ends of the earth to see you. I didn't know you were here until I saw you starting to walk across the bridge. How fortunate we are together again."

Thinking she could protect Jose's whereabouts by referring only to herself, she framed another question. "How did you know I was here?"

He merely smiled, saying nothing.

Bonita was becoming more unnerved than annoyed by Ramon's unforeseen appearance. How could she get back to the apartment without endangering Jose? Better confront Ramon immediately to get at the truth.

"You're on an assignment to find us, aren't you," she said flatly. "That's why you're here." Her voice sharpened. "Don't play me for a fool!"

"Oh, Bonita, when you get worked up, did anyone ever tell you how utterly beautiful you become. It's one of the most wonderful things about you."

His mocking voice was maddening. Bonita couldn't get the truth from him, no matter how hard she tried. She started to move away. Ramon quickly blocked her path. She started the other way. He immediately moved in front of her.

"Once again, Bonita, Jose is not here. Once again, I've come a long way to make love to you. Once again, you resist me. You need a man in your life. Jose is never around. It's quite possible he doesn't deserve you."

"I have a man in my life, Ramon. That man is Jose, not you."

"You don't know what love is like. I can show you. All you need to do is give me a chance."

"Please, Ramon. I've wanted to have the love of friendship with you, not sex. Don't you understand?"

"I only know the power of your beauty, your spirit, your attractiveness, your body, your – everything! I'm intoxicated with you, Bonita. I can't get you out of my mind."

"There are many women that deserve your attention, Ramon. Just look around. There's not just me."

"But, it *is* you, *only* you, Bonita. When you turn me down, that makes you all the more desirable. Just this once, that's all I want. If I can make love to you now, I won't ask you again. You'll find I'm good. Plenty of ladies have told me how good I am. A girl as good-looking as you must have had many suitors. A woman as seductive as you must have lured many a man into her bed."

Ramon's words did nothing to help his cause. Bonita felt utterly disgusted with him. Moreover, she had been ignorantly insulted by him. He may have thought he was giving her compliments, but she was deeply offended by his insinuation that she was a promiscuous woman.

"No, Ramon. A thousand times no. You and I are simply not cut out for the kind of relationship you're suggesting."

"Please, Bonita. Just this once," he repeated.

"No, no, no," she cried with defiance in her voice. "You should hear yourself begging me. It's terrible! It does nothing for you. A real lover doesn't do that."

A flash of anger spun across Ramon's face. "I will take you then. I command you! You can't get away from me this time. I've tried to be reasonable, but you're pushing me to my limits. You don't have Marisa's house to run into."

Bonita turned and started to walk away, her lustrous black hair swaying in the breeze.

Stay cool, she thought, gripping her jacket. Ramon ran to stop her, grabbed her by an arm, and spun her around. She spit in his face, struggled and shook herself free from him, and continued on her way. A wave of blind fury bore through Ramon.

"You can't do this to me," he roared. "You won't get away this time!"

From a holster hidden by his coat, he pulled out a revolver and disengaged the safety. Holding the gun with both hands, he pulled the trigger. The bullet hit Bonita in the middle of her back; its force knocked her down headfirst on to the ground. Ramon was upon her in a split second, tearing the jacket from her grasp.

"Galician whore," he cursed as he had at Marisa's house. "I ask you, who is pathetic now?" He turned her over to stare at her face. Her eyes flickered and closed. Stunned and losing blood, she began to lose consciousness.

"It didn't have to be this way, Bonita. You're making me do this. Women submit to me; it's not the other way around. You were doing it all wrong."

Ramon pulled a knife from inside his coat. Bonita started to say something. In a fleeting instant, her mind pictured the memory of Inez, struggling to get away from her assailants. Tearing open her blouse, Ramon swiftly drew the sharp-edged blade across her throat and severed the carotid arteries. The words she was trying to say were lost in a flowing gurgle of blood.

"Don Juan is not denied, Bonita. He is not pathetic, far from it. He is forceful, he never gives up. You didn't want to know that. I tried to be pleasant about it, but you wouldn't let me. Now, you will pay for your stupidity."

She was completely under his control. Ramon felt a rush of power and exhilaration surge through his body. A lifetime of suppressed resentment against the real and assumed slights of his family enraged him. The pent-up wrath from Bonita's rejections and Antonio's scorn came pouring out in an act of savage vengeance.

This will be the most exciting moment of my life, he thought as he entered the mute body of Bonita. "I will have you," he panted as he thrust his way toward sexual climax. "Don Juan is never denied." He spit in her face and slapped it.

"Galician bitch! You're the pathetic one. I will have you," he bellowed in spasmodic bursts again and again.

There was nothing Bonita could do. Spurting blood profusely, she was losing strength. Her last thought was an image of Jose's figure mixed with the statue of Christ she had seen in the Church of Saint Bartholomew. Their faces were monumental contrasts to the sight Bonita saw as she weakly opened her eyes. Her last look on earth was one of carnal lust painted on Ramon's features.

The last sounds she heard were Ramon's repeated words 'I will have you' punctuated by his animal cries and convulsive breaths. As he finished, life went out of her body. In the darkness that was falling, Ramon pulled himself from her. He staggered to stand upright. Whatever sorrow he might have felt for the stricken form below him was quickly replaced with a feeling of triumph and vindication.

"I've done it," he proclaimed. "Galician whore!" he uttered under his breath. "She had it coming."

Then, reality set in.

What to do with the body? Ramon asked himself. He looked around for a way to bury the evidence of his merciless deed. Any feeling of remorse would come later. The only emotion he felt now was the fear of being caught. Society would never see it his way. He saw a shed in the fading light. He opened its door and groped among several tools until he came upon a shovel. He went back to the site of the killing and dug a deep hole into which went the mixture of blood and dirt that lay on the ground. After completing that task, he began digging a pit nearby for a grave in which to place Bonita's body.

Jose must be around, he thought. *He'll never find her. He'll think she left him.*

A moment after he started digging, he looked up and cursed. A light bobbed up and down in the distance. It came steadily toward him.

Ramon pulled the body from where it lay in the open and dragged it several yards into the bushes and away from what he figured was a path. He came back for the shovel and the jacket. Scooping dirt with the shovel, he quickly covered up the blood that had drained on to the soil from Bonita's body. He hid behind a tree. Minutes later, a slow-moving old man carrying a flashlight went past him and moved on toward the manor house.

It's only a night watchman, Ramon reassured himself.

He stayed motionless for several minutes. When he believed he was alone again, Ramon started digging once more with the shovel. He stopped almost immediately and looked at Bonita's lifeless body.

If you had only given me a chance, it could have been so good, Bonita.

Without warning, a dog howled an unearthly cry as the wind whistled through the trees. An eerie sensation gripped him. Voices seemed to resonate out of nowhere. He could have sworn he had seen and heard something.

Could those sounds be coming from Jose and his friends looking for Bonita?

Ramon decided the best move for him was to get away from the place as fast as he could. No one had seen anything. There were still a few scattered drops of Bonita's blood left uncovered, but no one could tie him to its cause. Ramon tripped over Bonita's jacket; he picked it up, threw it around his neck, and began walking quietly holding the shovel in front of him. Getting further away from the scene, he walked faster casting the shovel from his grasp. A moment later, Bonita's jacket fell to the ground.

Terrified, Ramon ran. He did not stop running until he reached the Santa Clara bridge. He crossed the river and disappeared into the streets of Coimbra.

Chapter 31
Darkness

"If Spain's Nationalists are victorious," Manuel said to Jose, "they are likely to resemble the kind of political arrangements we already have here in Portugal."

Before returning to their apartments, Manuel had suggested they stop briefly for a dish of *gelado* in a nearly empty café. They had walked a considerable distance that day, and the prospect of eating ice cream had been too enticing to turn down. Jose's interview with the farm owner had gone well, but no commitments had been made. Manuel was disappointed an employment offer had not been forthcoming, although he could appreciate the farmer's hesitation. Hiring a Spaniard nowadays involved a certain amount of risk for a Portuguese citizen. After Jose and Manuel discussed the fine points of the interview, they now concentrated their attention on how the recent political history of Portugal might apply to Spain.

"Portugal ended its monarchy in 1910," Manuel went on. "A new constitution established the first Republican government a year later. Workers gained the right to strike, women were given the right to vote, civil service positions were awarded according to merit, the church was no longer supported by the state, and religious instruction was taken out of the schools."

"Was that a good thing?" asked Jose. "I mean, did taking religious teaching out of public education create a better society?"

"Always the theist, aren't you? I thought you were for separation of church and state. How would you like to be a Christian in a Muslim country and have Mohammed shoved down your throat all the time?"

"I don't disagree with you. The problem I have with some of my friends on the Left is they push their anticlerical beliefs too far. They want public education to be completely devoid of religion, even in a historical or literary sense. They want it to go away, like it doesn't exist. They're just as absolute as those who think only their own 'true' religion should be taught. Given that human beings are naturally religious – maybe including you, my friend – suppression of religion will create conflict at some point."

"That is what happened in Portugal," said Manuel, "although I don't necessarily go along with your assumption about humans. When the government attacked the church, many people found it impossible to support the Republic though they would have otherwise been on its side."

"That's not surprising," said Jose. "The same thing occurred in Spain."

"But, it wasn't religious conflict alone that paralyzed democracy here. The two major Republican parties – one radical, the other moderate – lost the ability to compromise with each other; this led to a splintered political system with no stable governing majority. The government lost support when the economy ground to a halt. Politics became violent. A limited civil war was started by monarchists. The military imitated Mussolini's march on Rome with their own march on Lisbon; its *coup d'etat* succeeded when the government couldn't enlist anyone in its defense. Everyone thought we'd have a monarchy again. It didn't happen; too many military officers favored a republic. General Carmona finally emerged as President because he was both a Republican *and* a devout Catholic."

Jose indicated he understood, then added, "I have the impression your military in general was more supportive of a liberal Republic than ours." He was familiar with some aspects of modern Portuguese political history. Yet, he wanted to hear the account Manuel would give and discover whether some of it would match his own version and the one Marcelo Marques gave. Having acquired the habits of the news reporter, he was constantly double-checking his sources of information.

"Carmona appointed Antonio Salazar as Minister of Finance. Salazar balanced the budget and even achieved a surplus in his first year. Military executives came and went, but Salazar soon consolidated power into his own hands. His appointment as Prime Minister became inevitable, making him clearly the most dominant person in the government."

"As Franco is doing right now in my country," commented Jose.

Manuel dropped his voice, speaking in hushed tones so he wouldn't be overheard by anyone who might have a connection with the police. "Salazar set about writing a new constitution that would develop into an authoritarian political system with all the trappings of repression. So you see, Jose, you can have a Republican political structure *and* a military dictatorship, all at the same time.

"The 'New State,' as Salazar named it, shifted authority from our Congress to an executive branch that stands above any review by the courts. And we have a cabinet that is totally controlled by Salazar. The New State, indeed; it's more like a return to the wonders of feudalism."

"Total control, return to a make-believe glorious past," reflected Jose. "I think those words define the aspirations of fascists everywhere."

"Salazar wouldn't call his system Fascism; he claims he has organized Portuguese society according to corporatist ideas. Under the Republic, individuals were free to organize groups and parties. Today, the government organizes them. Political parties are banned. You vote for only one party, Salazar's National Union. Labor unions and strikes are illegal. All independent associations have been disbanded. Capitalists as well as workers don't have the self-governing organizations they once had; instead, both make up a corporation that represents a section within the economy. Government-appointed bureaucrats, employers, and workers make up the corporation, but the decisions they make must agree with state-dictated policy and those decisions are binding on everyone. Corporatism doesn't necessarily require autocratic rule, but that's what we have now in Portugal."

"It's discouraging to see so many people in so many countries throughout Europe ready to overthrow democracy as a failed experiment," said Jose. Taking his cues from his companion, he spoke in a lowered voice. "Italy approves of Mussolini, Germany votes in Hitler, France has *Action Francaise*, even in England there are those who admire dictatorship. Any time a liberal democracy develops a crisis, the reaction brings on some kind of Fascism or strongman rule. Almost every European country has a fascist party. Maybe half of the people in my country have embraced the Nationalist rebellion. Why do you think the Republic failed here in Portugal, Manuel? I wonder if it's the very openness of liberal democracy that creates the political instability which brings about its downfall."

"Well, I would hope not, but you've probably answered your question," said Manuel as he finished his ice cream. "I think dictatorship creates more instability of every kind, but you don't hear about it because grievances are squashed and pushed underground. Our Republic once allowed complete freedom for people to form labor unions, religious groups, business organizations, and political parties that served as go-betweens, linking the people and the state. It was a way people gave the state the legitimate authority to act. The Republic exercised its power through its parliament, and the judiciary regulated that power. Now, we have a republic in name only; one man wields all political power, is responsible to no one, and no one dares speak out publicly. If you criticize, that borders on treason – and we know what happens to traitors."

"We had the same freedom with a progressive Republic in Spain," said Jose. "People like my brother Antonio say the liberals failed miserably, but they overlook how the lives of many workers and peasants became better. Unions could organize, church and state were separated, women won greater protections, and schools were improved – just to mention a few benefits. Thousands of new teachers were trained; Bonita was one of them. The Republic came to power without violence. The peseta was stabilized. The economy moved toward a democratic capitalist system. Now, these gains are threatened. If we lose them, we'll be worse off. If people express their grievances as they could under the Republic, they'll find their lives in danger. With silence, the Nationalists will say life is better because no complaints are heard."

"With all of its accomplishments, why wasn't the liberal Republic supported by an overwhelming majority of the people?"

"It's still a mystery to me. Maybe we expected too much. We needed more time and education to establish democratic traditions. When the Republic arrived, it tried to do everything at once. The government couldn't succeed in all of its aims, but people could express their dissatisfactions. Many conservatives, monarchists, big landholders, Church hierarchy, and military officers hated the Republic because of the achievements it *did* make. The Left believed the Republic hadn't done all it should have. Given enough time, I believe even more progress could have been made, particularly in land reform and worker rights. Looking back on all the turmoil of the Second Republic, I ask myself: 'Did democracy really have a chance of succeeding in my country?' "

"Yes, we've had our share of those discontents, too," reflected Manuel.

Jose continued. "After the Popular Front coalition won the elections earlier this year, Azana was unable to govern as his supporters hoped he would. The Prime Minister's cabinet was composed mainly of Left Republicans; they weren't wild-eyed extremists. When Falangist paramilitary squads attacked left-wing parades and marched on prisons causing a riot, the Republic banned further demonstrations. Socialists and moderate liberals condemned church burning in the most clear-cut terms. Right-wingers blamed the Republic for not stopping lawlessness in the cities and countryside, forgetting the greater violence when conservatives were in power. Reactionary provocateurs renewed old hatreds and then paid the real criminals who drove through working-class neighborhoods shooting so-called 'Reds' at random. After two years of censorship, the press had the freedom to report everything, and I think this made the turmoil seem worse to people than it actually was . . ."

Jose was ready to launch into further commentary when four people occupied a table, close by. Manuel interrupted him.

"We'd better move," he said. "We can continue talking in our apartment. I'm sure Bonita will want to join in."

"That's the great thing about Bonita," said Jose when they got outside. "She gets her Celtic blood worked up by political conversations as much as you and I do."

After ten minutes of walking, Jose and Manuel bounded up the steps to their building. As they entered the third-story apartment, Jose called out. "Bonita, we're back. Bonita?"

"Doesn't look like she's here," said Manuel.

"I told her she must get back here before nightfall."

"Look, here's a note, Jose." Manuel picked up the paper and gave it to Jose. In the note, Bonita had written her itinerary for the day.

"She planned to end her day at *Quinta das Lagrimas*, the old manor house of Pedro and Inez across the river. I wish she hadn't planned to go there without me, but I didn't say anything about it. It's nearly dark now. It's not safe for a young woman to be outside at night."

"She'll probably be back any time," assured Manuel.

"If she's not back in fifteen minutes, will you go with me to the manor house?"

"Of course, Jose. You could get lost going there by yourself in the darkness."

Five minutes went by. Bonita hadn't arrived. Jose announced that it was time to go; he couldn't wait any longer. Manuel nodded agreement, and said he had a couple of flashlights to use if they got all the way to the manor house. Jose scribbled a note telling where they were in case she returned before they got back.

After gathering the flashlights from his apartment, Manuel joined him saying, "We'll probably meet her coming up the street in the next few minutes."

But the streets did not yield any sign of Bonita. When they arrived at the Santa Clara bridge over the Mondego River, Manuel became worried.

Jose had all but arrived at the conclusion that something dreadful had happened and said flatly, "This is not good, Manuel. This is not like her. We must get to *Quinta das Lagrimas* as quickly as we can."

They rushed over the bridge and on to the deserted street that would take them to the manor house. Flashlights were turned on to illuminate the path ahead. They broke into a run as they neared their destination. Jose was filled with a foreboding sense of impending disaster.

He kept asking himself: *Why did I let her go alone?*

When they came to the grounds of the manor house, Jose immediately spotted Bonita's jacket.

"She's been here; that's her jacket," he confirmed, shining the beam of his flashlight on the garment. "Could she still be here?"

They moved on further. Manuel called to his friend, "I'm going off to the right and around the manor house; you go to the left and we'll meet on the other side."

Manuel moved to the back of the house. Coming to the other side, he did not see Jose. He kept moving until he came to the place where he had moved away from Jose. In the darkness came the sounds of absolute despair. Manuel moved in its direction. In the next instance, he heard a sobbing voice pleading, "No, no, no. Oh God, no."

In the illumination of his flashlight, Manuel saw his friend holding the fallen body of Bonita next to the bushes where she had lain. Jose looked at him with a face torn in anguish.

"She's not breathing, Manuel," he struggled to say in a voice wracked with pain. "Bonita – my Bonita is dead. Someone put a knife to her throat." After those words, Jose fell into a series of low, mournful cries. "Why – Why – Why," he beseeched the darkness again and again.

Manuel stood, his body frozen, his spotlight upon the two figures with Jose swaying his lifeless loved one back and forth in his arms. Sightless eyes stared back at him. Manuel could see for himself that Bonita had been viciously attacked. Her face was smudged with dirt. Blood saturated her blouse. The knife wound on the neck was deeply cut from one side to the other. As Jose pulled the body of Bonita close to him, Manuel noticed where a bullet had penetrated her back. He lowered his eyes to where her undergarments had been torn from her body. Manuel concluded her killer had raped her as she died; the telltale semen was damp on her dress and drying on her thigh.

Oh, God, this is awful. I've never seen anything as horrible as this, he lamented to himself. Never in his life had he felt so helpless. There was nothing he could do for Bonita, but he must somehow help Jose who wouldn't let go of Bonita and kept repeating 'Oh God, no, no, why?' Manuel knelt and put his arm around Jose.

"Why?" Jose asked again, tears streaming from his eyes. "I never should have let her come here alone. I'll never forgive myself, Manuel. Never, never. I never dreamed anything like this could happen to her. If we hadn't talked so much about stupid politics at the café, we could have gotten here in time."

"Jose – my friend – you must not blame yourself. You didn't cause or intend it. There was no way you or I could have known a deadly attack was happening to Bonita."

"Who could do such a thing as this?" Jose implored his friend.

"Whoever it was is a sub-human monster with absolutely no feelings for anyone but his own miserable self."

"We were so happy, Manuel. These past two weeks here have been the happiest days of our lives. We said this so many times to each other. And now – this."

"I know. I could tell you both had found your paradise in each other."

"And, Manuel, I must tell you," cried Jose, clasping the shoulder of his friend. "There was more than one murder." As soon as he had spoken those words, Jose buried his face into Manuel's chest. Manuel could not tell whether Jose was referring to himself or another person was involved.

Jose choked over his words. "Now, every hope for the future is gone."

Manuel gripped his friend's shoulder. "Jose, I do believe there is a Creator of us all, but there are times, like right now, God seems absent. I wonder how an all-powerful Being could let this happen. Oh, I know God is not responsible for this murder. A man did it. If I ever can find out who is guilty, I will tear that person from limb to limb. And, I will tell you, so you can do the same."

Revenge had not yet occurred to Jose; that time would come later. He instinctively knew his whole life had changed forever in the one blinding moment he had found Bonita lying on the ground in the blackness of the night – his beloved Bonita – bludgeoned, violated, dead.

"Vengeance," he said deliberately. "I know why it exists all too clearly now, but it won't bring Bonita back to me."

Manuel shook himself from his numbed state. "Jose, I'm going to look around here for a few minutes. Bonita was murdered only a short time ago. Her killer could be here, even watching us. It's been said they often come back to the scene of the crime. You stay alert. You've got to do that. I won't be gone long. I want to satisfy myself that no one is here. I'll call out your name as I come back."

Jose indicated approval. "I'll be watchful," he said in a choking, steely tone. "If I see her killer, I'll kill him even if it means my death."

Manuel quickly went into the darkness, beaming his flashlight ahead. Jose pulled Bonita closer to him. He kissed her forehead. "I have loved you so," he whispered to her. "There will never be anyone other than you. We would have had such a wonderful family together. God would have blessed us. If we could have lived in a better time, it would have been so beautiful."

He paused, wishing he would wake up from this nightmare but knowing this was not a dream. "I promise, Bonita, I'll never leave you. I will be with you forever. Your spirit will always hold me. We had so much to give each other; we still do. I'll always love you, as I know you would have always loved me."

The crushing realization of loss pierced him as sharply as the knife that had penetrated her body; it conquered him completely and he began crying uncontrollably.

Wind rustled the branches of the trees around them. He stopped his sobbing almost as quickly as he had started it. Jose held Bonita as he looked around the grounds, remembering Manuel had suggested the killer might return. The moonlight made shadows on the ground and the breeze made those shadows from the trees move in a ghostly, ominous manner. Jose laid Bonita's body in front of him; he might need to be ready for action.

So many conflicting emotions seized him, one after another. He felt the warm embracing love for Bonita, an impossible longing for her return to life, and the outright hatred toward her unknown killer. He was crushed once more by a despondent helplessness, stemming from his inability to make things right again. There was a desire to join her in death. He had an overwhelming feeling of guilt that he hadn't been with her. All this was too much to deal with now.

After several minutes, Jose began to straighten Bonita's clothes. He saw the hole in the back of her blouse, caused by the bullet that had stopped her. Her back was still bleeding; he took his handkerchief to staunch the flow of blood seeping from the wounds. His tears had washed some of the bloodstains from her lacerated neck; he would need to get some water to help her look presentable. He reached into his pocket for a comb to brush her hair. His hand touched the opal ring they had used to convince others they were married. He slipped the ring from her finger; he wanted to keep something of hers for the sake of remembrance and perhaps he could return it to her mother. He slid the ring into his shirt pocket and buttoned it to make sure he wouldn't lose the keepsake. He held her in his arms until Manuel's voice and flashlight signaled he was returning.

"No one's here. I couldn't detect a sign of anyone."

"Who can we contact to give Bonita a decent burial?" he asked Manuel. "We can't leave her like this."

"No, we can't," agreed Manuel. "That is our first order of business, Jose. You and I, we've got to bury her, right now, on these grounds, tonight."

"Shouldn't the burial be done by a priest?"

"Think, Jose. He will be required to register the burial with the appropriate government authorities. They'll know Bonita was Spanish and that you are, too. Bonita's family would have to be notified. The police would soon know who you are and why you're here."

"Does any of that matter now?"

"Yes, it does. I know you want to do the right thing and give Bonita a proper burial. That's what we'll do tonight. If Bonita were here, she would be telling us to bury her here and for you not to give up. While I was searching the grounds, I located a shed with some tools in it; we can use them to dig a grave for Bonita."

"What can we use to put her body in?"

"I saw some wooden boards by the back of the manor house. I think we'll be able to construct a casket for her body. It will be a bit crude, but it's the best we can do."

"Maybe burying her here will be all right, Manuel. She was so taken with the Inez and Pedro story, and this was the place where Inez was murdered. I just can't believe . . ."

"Let's get the job done. We'll need to work steadily and silently. The ground is rather hard on top. We may need most of the night to dig as deep as we should go. We've got to be done by morning."

"I can't believe any of this is really happening," said Jose. "Tell me what to do, Manuel. I can't think. Where's the best place to bury her?"

"Over by the Fountain of the Lovers is too obvious, despite it being the most suitable place to bury her. Too many people come to that spot. We've got to find an inconspicuous place close by and mark it with a sign known only to us."

Jose and Manuel found a site at the edge of the manor house grounds. On their way to the shed to find tools, Jose spied a shovel lying on the ground. "Look, Manuel," he said. "Someone threw away a shovel here. It's just what we need. Let's take it back."

Accompanied by Manuel, he carried the shovel to the burial site, neither of them noticing in the darkness specks of drying blood mixed in with the dirt on the shovel. They went to the shed to find more tools for digging. At the back of the house they found the boards to make the coffin.

"I hope whoever was using these boards won't miss them," said Manuel. "I see a hammer and a saw. Here are some nails they were using. We'll just borrow a few."

R. D. Lock

"And I'll borrow this canvas to wrap up her body," announced Jose. He looked at Manuel. "Tell me this isn't happening, please. It's all a dream, isn't it?"

"It's real, Jose. I wish with all my heart it wasn't real. Come on, now. We've got work to do."

Through the night they dug the grave, making as little noise as possible. Manuel started by loosening the topsoil using a pick-ax he had found in the shed and Jose used the shovel he had retrieved. During intervals of digging, they built the coffin. They worried about hammering the nails, even though Jose used his shirt to muffle the sounds. At times, Jose broke into a crying spell, unable to keep his emotions of tragic loss silent. Manuel would periodically stop what he was doing and put his arm around his friend.

"Keep digging, Jose," he would say. "Keep working. You're doing this for Bonita. You've got to keep going."

And, Jose would say, "I know. I will. Thank you, my friend, for all the help you are giving me. How can I ever repay you? We'll finish this job quickly so you can get some sleep."

"Think nothing of it," Manuel would respond. "I only wish we didn't have to do this, but we must."

The two got through the top crust of earth and then the shoveling came easier. A mound of soil slowly rose around the excavation site. Jose and Manuel were soon dripping with sweat. When the hole in the earth reached about two meters deep, they pronounced their work done. Jose drew a bucket of water from a well next to the manor house and washed Bonita's face. He cleansed her neck with his handkerchief; by now, the bleeding had thickened and stopped. He put the jacket around her, covering the blood that stained her clothes. He washed the drying, encrusted semen from her dress. Manuel fashioned a cross from two sticks of wood and gave it to Jose who laid it in her cold hands across her body. Jose kissed Bonita on her forehead and her lips and then on both cheeks.

"I'll leave you alone with Bonita for a moment," whispered Manuel.

Jose held the lifeless body of Bonita, never wanting to let her go, but knowing the time was drawing near when he must. These were the last moments he would have to gaze upon her. The only time he would be near her again was through his own death. All he had now was his abiding love for her and his sorrow; these would be his companions for the rest of his life.

Jose began his internal words of lamentation: *How does life go on without you? How I wish I could go with you and never have to open my eyes on this world again.*

He looked at her eyes; they seemed to be staring at him again, intently. He ran his fingers through her hair and kissed her tenderly on her pale red lips, not seeing the mutilation below.

"Dear God," he prayed quietly with a voice barely audible. "Receive the body and soul of my beloved Bonita into your kingdom. Forgive her sins, knowing that she loved you and her friends with all her heart. If it was to be, take the little body and soul of the life that was to come. In Jesus' name, Amen."

He took one last lingering look at her. He wrapped Bonita's body in the canvas and lowered it into the coffin.

"Good-bye, my love, my soul mate forever," he said simply, with tears running down his face.

Manuel came to him and signaled it was time to close and seal the makeshift box made for Bonita's body. Then, Manuel and Jose held each end of the coffin and slowly lowered it into the ground. The box caught on a piece of earth about half way down. Jose took the shovel to clear away the obstruction, and the coffin settled at the bottom of the pit.

Just as Jose was about to start shoveling sawdust and dirt on to the coffin, Manuel grabbed him by the arm and stopped him. "Listen," he whispered into Jose's ear. "I heard something, like a twig or branch being snapped." They turned off the flashlight that had been illuminating the ground on which they had been working and stood still.

The wind picked up again, rattling the branches of the trees. A dog barked in the distance. All was silent.

"I could have sworn I heard someone over there," Manuel said softly. "It must have been my imagination. What I heard could have been an animal. I didn't see any thing move other than those branches in the trees."

They remained silent for another five minutes. Nothing stirred. "I guess we had better finish our job," Manuel finally said. "The dawn can't be far off and we need to be out of here by then. We'll keep our flashlights off; there's enough moonlight to see."

Quietly and methodically, the two young men piled the earth over the coffin. Jose smoothed the soil and scattered grass, weeds, and leaves over the surface. They returned the tools to the shed. Coming back for one last look at the gravesite, Jose spotted several rocks and stones that could be used to give the area a more natural look. He used some of the rocks to form the letter 'B' and to mark the edges of the grave in a rough sort of way that would not be apparent to others unless they were looking for it. In his mind's eye, Jose etched the outline of the site. He would remember it forever.

CHAPTER 32
COMPULSION

The sun was beginning to come through the clouds when Jose and Manuel returned to the building in which they were living. Not wanting to leave his friend alone, Manuel insisted on Jose staying with him in his apartment. Jose readily accepted the offer, not wanting to face the emptiness of the apartment he and Bonita had shared. At first, being so overwrought with sadness and shock, Jose could not think of sleep. Manuel prepared some food to eat and the two talked for a while about their memories of Bonita. Then, inevitably, they turned again to the fateful questions: who could have committed such a hideously cruel act and why was it done? As before, the main conclusion was that the perpetrator was a monstrous madman and Bonita had been in the wrong place at the wrong time.

Soon from sheer exhaustion, drowsiness overcame both of them. As Jose drifted into slumber while sitting on a couch, Manuel closed the curtains, removed his friend's shoes, lowered his head on to a pillow, and covered him with a light blanket from the bedroom. Then, Manuel sought rest in his own bed.

Jose slept fitfully, but did not become wide-awake until evening. He could not believe his depressed state of mind had allowed him to get as much sleep as it did. As he woke, he was unable to accept the tragic experiences of the last twenty-four hours. He listened for sounds of Bonita in the apartment upstairs. No, it was all too true; she was gone, a victim of an unspeakable, hellish act. A rush of heartbreaking grief swept over him.

In the gathering darkness, he felt utterly alone. Not only was Bonita his one true love, she was his best friend, a person to whom he could speak his deepest thoughts. Manuel was kind, merciful, and full of compassion, but he could not replace Bonita. Returning home to Trujillo was out of the question;

even if Jose could get back there, he would put his sister and her family at unacceptable risk. Both of his parents were dead. His mother's recent death had been unsatisfactorily surrounded with his own pressing needs; the chance for escape was inexorably connected to her funeral.

Images of the three women who meant the most to him came to him. Jose dwelt on how much he owed them. His mother had given unconditional love to him. Marisa had exposed herself to danger in arranging for his escape. Bonita had given her life to be with him. He also thought of his generous friend Manuel who had guided him through the most unbearably painful night of his life.

I've been so fortunate to have their love and their concern, were the words now coming into his mind. *In the desperate circumstances I've been in, I haven't had any time to think of how blessed I've been to have them with me.*

His following thoughts were of what to do next. He couldn't stay with Manuel much longer. Bonita had talked of moving on only a couple of days ago. As he was thinking, Manuel came into the room. Seeing Jose move at his entrance, he turned on a light.

"I hope you haven't been awake long," he inquired. "After all the things you've been through, you need all the sleep you can get."

"I woke up a few minutes ago. When I first lay down here this morning, I didn't think I could sleep at all. I must have slept for nine or ten hours."

"I'll fix something for us to eat."

"Manuel, you've done everything and more that a friend could do. We can eat out and let me pay for the food. It's the least I can do for all you've done for me."

Manuel started to protest, but Jose held up his hand saying, "I insist. I want to talk over some ideas and plans of mine with you and see what you think of them."

Hearing this, Manuel said emphatically, "If you want me to listen, you'll have to talk about your plans here. It's too dangerous for you to venture out."

The two gathered food from Manuel's kitchen and were eating in silence when Jose asked, "Tell me what you know about Braga, and while you're at it – Lamego."

Manuel seemed startled. "What about Braga and Lamego?"

"These are places of pilgrimage. People who have been disabled or wounded and need healing go there."

"That's right, but what's that got to do with you?"

"I'm disabled and wounded – inside myself," said Jose. Thinking of Manuel's skeptical views of religion, he added, "Maybe you'll think this is stupid, but it would help me heal if I went there and climbed the staircase on my knees for Bonita. It's one way I can remember her and ask God to accept her. It would mean I was close to her. She would be with me in spirit."

"Braga is directly on your way to Galicia, if that's what you are thinking. The church you're looking for is *Bom Jesus do Monte*, a few kilometers east of Braga. A lot of pilgrims come to *Bom Jesus*. There could be some police and security people there – same for Lamego, which is further to the east and more out of your way. Are you sure you want to take that risk?"

Jose paused for a moment. "I haven't shaved today and I'll let my beard grow. That will disguise me somewhat. I'm determined to do this, Manuel."

"I can only advise you to be vigilant and take care of yourself."

"That doesn't matter anymore."

"Yes, it does," said Manuel sharply. "You've got your life to live."

"My life without Bonita isn't worth living," said Jose fiercely.

"I know you think this way about life now. I don't blame you for that thought. One thing I hope for is that somehow out of all that's happened you'll find meaning and purpose for your life."

"What meaning or purpose was there in Bonita's brutal murder?"

"None. It was completely senseless," granted Manuel. "However, now you have a job to do."

"What is that?"

"To live your life in a way that gives Bonita's life meaning. That is one thing you can do for her."

"How do I give her life meaning?" Jose asked.

"I don't know. That's your job – to find that meaning and then do it."

"I know you're trying to help me. So much has taken place, and I'm so confused. One thing I can do, though, is go to a place such as the sanctuary at Braga and carry out an act of penance for Bonita. That's something she can't do now, but I can do it for her."

"That's noble of you, but keep in mind that you are being hunted."

"If it's true I'm still being hunted, I believe my hunters wouldn't expect me to go there."

Manuel could sense Jose's resolute intention. All he said was, "We'll talk about this at another time. Any other plans?"

"From there, I'm thinking I'd better go to Corcubion in Galicia and tell Bonita's parents about everything that has happened. I'll take the letter she wrote to them the day before she died. I haven't read the letter; maybe I should to be sure it would bring some comfort to them."

"I think looking at her letter is a good idea. I'm sorry I can't say the same for going back into Spain."

"Because her death was a murder, it will be a dreadful thing to reveal to them. I've got to do it, though. I'm not looking forward to it. It will be the most difficult message I've ever delivered in my life."

"I understand, Jose. I know I'd want to get something that burdensome off my mind."

"After talking with Bonita's parents, I must go to Santiago de Compostela. I promised my mother the night before she died that I would make the pilgrimage for her since she was unable to do it herself."

"As I've mentioned many times before, couldn't the pilgrimage wait until a more favorable time?"

"Santiago is about eighty kilometers from Corcubion," Jose pointed out. "I can walk that distance in three days. I haven't had time to give much thought to Mama's pilgrimage, but I'd like to fulfill her wishes while I'm able to. I don't know when I could get back in Galicia to do it."

Manuel began to struggle against Jose's plans more earnestly. "Jose, wake up, get real. The police are looking for you. Nationalist agents are trying to find you. Suppose Bonita's murderer was one of them. Now, they know you're here."

"I haven't a clue who took Bonita's life, but it seems to me her killer couldn't have been the Portuguese police or a Nationalist agent. Either of them would have kept Bonita alive as a captive and waited for me to join her."

"I see your logic, but don't you see how dangerous your situation is? We were too indifferent to the threat that still existed, thinking the danger had subsided and gone away, and I include myself particularly in that judgment. I think the best for you to do is stay in my apartment for a time – a month, six weeks – and then venture out."

"I'll go insane if I do that, Manuel. Please, don't misunderstand; I appreciate your generosity more than you know, but I know myself. I've got to do this. All I can know is that her murder was the work of a hideous rapist, a madman possessed by the devil. I believe I'm compelled to carry out these responsibilities – the pilgrimages, telling Bonita's parents the awful truth."

Jose was unable to say he was under a compulsion from within. His companion would not understand. Not that he would make light of this kind of obligation; he would be too considerate to say anything.

Manuel looked at his friend and silently realized Jose had already made his decision to go. There was little or nothing Manuel could say or do to restrain him.

"You've got important responsibilities to carry out," acknowledged Manuel. "Maybe it's just as well that you go to Braga – only you've got to be careful and look out for yourself. I'd go with you, if I could."

"Oh, I don't expect you to come with me. Don't think I wouldn't welcome your company, Manuel. You have your classes. It's better that I go alone."

"When do you think you would start? You're welcome to stay in my apartment for as long as you want."

"I'd like to begin, say, the day after tomorrow. Thanks for the offer of your apartment, but I think it's better for me if I get moving as soon as I can. If a Nationalist agent was responsible for Bonita's death, he'll figure I'm somewhere in Coimbra."

"Yes, that much is true. But, are you well enough to go off on your own so soon? It seems awfully sudden after such a shock."

"I'm going to be numb for a long time, maybe forever. I think it will be healthier for me if I can accomplish the things I can do for her right away. When I'm done at Corcubion and Santiago, I'll come back here."

Manuel looked at Jose critically, but didn't argue with him, saying only, "I'll be waiting for you, my friend. I wish I could do more for you."

"You've done plenty, Manuel. I couldn't have gotten through last night without you."

As soon as Jose had spoken these words, the remembrance of the events of the previous night came rushing into his consciousness. He turned his head to the wall, tears coming to his eyes. Manuel rose and came over to Jose, pulled up a chair, and put his arms around his bereaved comrade. They sat there for several minutes.

Then, Jose turned to Manuel and asked, "Do you know the story of Job?"

Manuel looked puzzled. "Yes, I've heard the story of Job. It's one of the great stories of the Bible," he stated.

"Two responses of Job came to me before I fell asleep last night. You remember how Job, a good and righteous man, lost his children and everything he owned. He suffered the most loathsome sores and sicknesses. He was told by his wife to curse God and die. Three friends came and told Job he must have done something terrible and God must be punishing him. Tell me, is God punishing me for something I did or didn't do?"

"No, Jose. God is not punishing you by having Bonita killed. Her murder is man's doing."

"I am like Job, Manuel, and I know this: you are a better friend than those three companions of his."

"I am pleased to hear you say that."

"The answers that come to me for dealing with Bonita's horrible death are these two. The first one is the words of Job as he patiently bore all his sorrows and torment: 'The Lord gave, and the Lord has taken away; blessed be the name of the Lord.' Does that make any sense to you?"

"I can't say that it does. Is it a reason for Bonita's death?"

"No. There's no way for you or me to comprehend that."

"What's the second answer?"

Jose thought a moment and then said, "Simply, trust God. In Job's words, 'Though he slay me, yet will I trust in him.' I know death is the final end on this planet for us, but I believe there is life beyond our time on earth and whenever and wherever it is, I will be with Bonita again. What else can I do but trust God?"

Manuel looked squarely at his anguished friend. "Jose, I must say I admire the strength of the faith you have. I know people who would have been destroyed by the ordeal and misery you've gone through. After experiencing the worst possible loss that could happen to a human being, you seem to get stronger as you face it."

Jose listened carefully to the genuine regard that accompanied Manuel's words. For a moment, he was unable to speak and could only move his head in agreement. Among the multitude of emotions he had experienced, power and stamina had accompanied the despair and grief. In the days that followed, Jose slowly came to believe the words Manuel had spoken as well as the message delivered to him from within.

You didn't want Bonita to die, but you must accept it. You have suffered and you will suffer because of her death, but you will be given the strength to endure it.

In a moment, Jose said, "Thank you for sticking with me and being so understanding. All I can rely on now is a steady faith."

"That faith of yours, I have to say, is truly extraordinary. I don't know whether it will cure you or kill you."

Jose looked up, smiled, and said, "I don't know, either. Maybe, it will do both."

CHAPTER 33
EDUARDO

Jose waved good-bye to Manuel, peering through a bus window. Now alone again as he had once been in the Nationalist detention camp, he placed the two rucksacks – his and Bonita's – underneath his seat. The bus was bound for Porto, the second largest city in Portugal, a destination straight north from Coimbra. Using his own name, Manuel had purchased the ticket for Jose and given him a letter of introduction to Eduardo Salgado, a friend who lived in Porto.

Manuel had given up trying to dissuade the distraught Jose from his pilgrimages, and sent him on his way with the unexpressed hope he could be convinced by Eduardo to lay low in Portugal for a longer period of time. Porto was a large enough city where one could disappear into the anonymity of city life. If Jose remained hidden in Porto until the end of the school semester, Manuel could come north to visit Eduardo and invite Jose back to Coimbra. The political and military situation in Spain might have improved by then. Jose had gratefully accepted Manuel's bus ticket, keeping to himself that he would be 120 kilometers closer to his main objective of reaching Braga and Galicia.

Porto was the most important city of the industrializing northern area of Portugal. It had been the site of a heroic defense against the attacking French army during the 19th century Peninsular War, a small group of soldiers and volunteers holding the bridge to the city against impossible odds. When they were finally overwhelmed, the invaders set Porto's buildings on fire and took their revenge on the residents. Regaining its freedom with the help of the English, Porto became known as the *Cidade Invicta*, the Unvanquished City, because of its fierce opposition to Napoleon's imperial army. Two decades later, the troops of an absolutist Portuguese King had laid siege to the city, and resistance by the people gained the attention of England whose troops and ships contributed to Porto's liberation. The city then went on to establish a reputation of being in the vanguard of Portugal's progressive tradition, becoming well-known for its spirit of enterprise and respect for honest labor.

Even though the bus trip was thankfully uneventful, Jose couldn't help but be apprehensive. He scrutinized nearly every person riding with him, worrying that they could be a PVDE agent tracking him to discover where he would go and whom he would meet. Every new passenger coming on the bus was a cause for uneasiness. Jose thought of putting both rucksacks on his lap in case a person made moves to take him prisoner.

That's a stupid idea, he thought. *How far would I get carrying these backpacks? Better to look normal than nervous. One thing good about being in Portugal, the buses are running here and probably not yet in Spain.*

On the letter of introduction, Jose looked at the name of the person Manuel had advised to seek out. Eduardo Salgado was a former student friend of Manuel's at Coimbra. He had graduated in Finance a year ago and secured a job at the Porto Stock Exchange housed in the *Palacio da Bolsa*. Jose was instructed to meet Eduardo there at the end of the business day.

Jose arrived at the Porto bus station in the middle of the afternoon, asked for directions to the palace stock exchange, and began walking the steep inclines of the streets rising from the river banks of the Douro. Upon reaching the neo-classical *Palacio da Bolsa*, he inquired at the entrance desk if it was possible to meet Senhor Salgado. Appraised he was in a meeting expected to last up to another hour, Jose seated himself in an overstuffed chair provided for visitors.

Was it a good idea to be contacting an employee of a stock exchange?

Jose began to wonder. He had thought Manuel would send him to a representative of the working class, a carpenter or a waiter on the river bank or a dock hand perhaps, not an aspiring member of the bourgeoisie. Jose had to trust the judgment of his friend. Maybe Eduardo would be far more progressive than the stereotyped image of the avaricious capitalist Jose sometimes had in mind.

Best not to have a prejudiced opinion, he reasoned. *Had not Manuel and Eduardo remained comrades in Coimbra?*

Still, doubts about the wisdom of involving and becoming dependent upon another person assailed his thinking. He could trust Manuel; he knew nothing about Eduardo. Thoughts like these hounded Jose for another twenty minutes.

If I simply leave now, Manuel's university friend will never know the identity of the person waiting for him. He'd assume the person gave up and left.

Jose had just about convinced himself he should go when a young man in a business suit approached him. "I'm Eduardo Salgado. You must be the man who is waiting for me."

Jose struggled to explain his being there. "I'm Jose Martinez," he began, inwardly speculating that Eduardo must be asking himself how many people on the Iberian Peninsula had the same name. "We have a mutual friend in Coimbra, Manuel Silva."

"Oh, yes – Manuel. He and I met in a history class and became close *amigos* at the university there."

Jose gave the letter of introduction to Eduardo. It was in a sealed envelope, giving an impression Jose had no idea of the letter's content. The message explained Jose's circumstances without mentioning Bonita's death.

Eduardo quickly read the letter.

"Of course, you are welcome to stay with me for a few days," he said, looking up. "Now I remember Manuel saying some good things about you. Any *amigo* of his is certainly a friend of mine."

"*Obrigado, muito obrigado*," said Jose with relief. "I would not ask you for more than a night. I am on two journeys, a pilgrimage for my intended wife and my mother. I'll give you more details about it later."

"You can plan on staying with me tonight and again tomorrow night if you wish, Jose. My girl friend is on a trip to Lisbon. I'd appreciate some company. I can take some time off during the day tomorrow and show you a few places around Porto. Now, if you'll wait here for another ten minutes, I have one telephone call to make from my office and then we'll walk to my apartment, about a kilometer from here."

Eduardo dashed upstairs and disappeared around a corner.

Well, thought Jose, *if he's calling the PVDE after reading Manuel's letter, it's the end of me. Wait a minute; that doesn't make any sense. If he's doing it, why would he tell me he's calling anyone?*

In Eduardo's three-room apartment, the two relaxed with some wine in the living room before going out to Eduardo's favorite restaurant in Porto's Ribeira section. "That's the market area, Jose," Eduardo explained. "You'll want to see it, although it's more colorful in the morning."

Jose felt awkward being so dependent on a person he had known for less than two hours. There was nothing he could do about it, so he comforted himself with the thought that if the roles were reversed, he would do the same thing for the friend of a friend.

"Manuel wrote that you were being hunted by the Nationalist authorities in Spain. I'm sure he told you if the police in Portugal were to discover your whereabouts here and capture you, they'd send you back to Nationalist Spain."

"Yes, I'm aware of all that," said Jose. In as few words as possible, he went on to give Eduardo his version of being pursued by the Nationalists.

"As long as you don't become politically active here, I think the chances of being caught are rather slight. Maybe the best thing to do, though, is get you on a boat to France or England, or possibly around Gibraltar and over to Valencia or Barcelona. Now, tell me about the two pilgrimages you mentioned back at the Palacio da Bolsa."

"Yes. These are things I must do first. Then, I can think about the destinations you suggest." Eduardo inquired about those 'things' and Jose started with the pilgrimage to Braga.

"This pilgrimage is for your intended wife?" Jose was asked. "She should be with you for such a thing."

Jose had feared he would need to reveal why Bonita wasn't there if he got into a discussion about himself. Yet as long as he was asking for help, he owed Eduardo an account of the tragic story. He consoled himself with the thought that, with Eduardo, he could practice the dreadful explanation he must later give to Bonita's parents. While struggling with his emotions, Jose was able to keep his composure with Eduardo, but he wasn't confident he could do the same with Bonita's mother and father.

"How horrible," was Eduardo's reaction upon hearing the story. "I'd want revenge, Jose. I've got contacts both here and in Coimbra who could try to hunt down the murderer." That comment took Jose by surprise.

Did a reputable employee of the stock exchange have connections with hired killers?

"Under other circumstances, I might welcome your idea. Actually, I would have stayed in Coimbra and notified the police, but these are not normal times, Eduardo. I cannot reveal who I am or where I'm from, except to people like you and Manuel."

"Sadly, you are right. You said something about a journey for your mother. What is that about?"

When Jose told about the plan of going to Santiago de Compostela and Corcubion, both in Galicia, Eduardo exclaimed, "Those places put you back in Spain. You shouldn't do that; it's too dangerous."

"I've got to, Eduardo. I can't adequately explain my motivations and maybe I don't understand them myself, but I believe I'm compelled to complete those missions."

"I don't want to sound blunt or hard-hearted, Jose, but Bonita and your mother are both dead. You are alive and owe it to yourself to stay that way."

"Bonita's parents are alive, too, and deserve to know of their daughter's death. I owe that to them. I can't depend on the mail; letters are being opened by Nationalist authorities. I would put them at risk sending them a letter. And, as long as I am in Corcubion, I'm close to Santiago. I can carry out my mother's pilgrimage and get out of Spain again. All of this should take no more than a week, if that long."

"You are a devoted fiancé and a faithful son," pronounced Eduardo. Then he continued his attempt to dissuade Jose from the missions into Spain, but like Manuel, he could not convince Jose to do otherwise.

Finally he said, "Come on, let's go to the restaurant. I want you to try their *linguado grelhado*, the grilled sole, or *bife de atum*, the tuna steak, and of course, the Port wine." Jose promised he would do so; this was a suggestion he would cheerfully follow.

At the restaurant, Eduardo telephoned the bus service and discovered there was a bus going from Porto to Braga next day in the early afternoon. Jose thanked Eduardo for obtaining that information and said he should be on the bus tomorrow to achieve his objective as quickly as possible.

"I can obtain a bus ticket to Braga for you," said Eduardo, "and after you've completed your pilgrimage there, you can reconsider your plans, come back here, and spend a second night with me. I'd like you to meet Maria, my girl friend. We may be engaged by the time you return."

Jose expressed appreciation for the suggestion of another night's lodging, saying he would like to meet Maria. He thanked Eduardo for his help in securing a bus ticket. "If I'm stopped trying to cross the border, I'll take you up on your offer of a second visit."

That comment didn't completely reassure Eduardo. His new companion seemed determined to disregard danger, but it did blend into another topic: his job at the stock exchange. Eduardo revealed he was a clerk in the administrative offices at the Palacio da Bolsa, a job won mainly through recommendations of faculty members at the University of Coimbra.

"At university, I kept most of my political opinions to myself," he said. "Maybe I should have challenged my professors more than I did, but then I would have been on the outside looking in. Remember, this was the same department of the university that at one time had a member no less than Antonio Salazar himself."

"I was in a similar situation at Salamanca," responded Jose. "Manuel tells me Franco's headquarters is now close to the university. When I was there as a student, we had professors from all sides of the political spectrum."

Eduardo winced before he made his next statement. "My parents are the ones with whom I have the most conflict. They're unhappy Maria and I live together, although they like her personally. They don't like my liberal opinions, which I believe are quite moderate. They think Salazar is the greatest thing since the invention of money. I could partially agree with them if we were talking economics, but it's in politics where we get into trouble. Why do so many capitalists get into bed with so many dictators, especially when they don't need to? That's what we've got here in Portugal, a dictatorship that borders on Fascism. The result will be tempting people into *Marxism* or some type of extreme socialism, but those in power here are sure that will never happen."

Jose started to respond, but Eduardo looked around the restaurant and suggested they finish their dinner and continue their talk after they departed. Jose agreed and offered to pay for the meal with his remaining escudos, but Eduardo wouldn't hear of it.

Back at the apartment, Jose and Eduardo carried on the discussion. A sudden revelation came to Jose: here he was, lapsing into a typical political exchange with a new friend just after the devastating loss of the woman he loved.

How is this possible? he chastised himself. *Only three days ago, I was going through the worst night of my life. Maybe people need to reach for something familiar when they're wracked with grief.*

As if Eduardo had discerned his new friend's thoughts, he encouraged Jose to go on with the subject they had been talking about in the restaurant.

"Jose", he said, "you began to say something when I thought we should move our political comments to a safer place, my apartment."

"Marxism was brought up, Eduardo. We may have some disagreements about *Marx*, but I think we could agree on one thing: he got it right when he praised the productive capabilities of capitalism. It's all there in the *Communist Manifesto*."

Eduardo wasn't about to dispute that statement. "Capitalism isn't perfect by any means," he said, "but it is the most dynamic economic system ever devised by man."

Seeing an opening for a critical comment, Jose jumped in. "I believe Marx was also correct about certain social effects of capitalism such as the problems of inequality and a disturbing neglect of the social injustices the competition of a capitalist economy can create. However, he was wrong about the need for violent overthrow of governments and entrusting society to a dictatorship of the working class. The proletariat is no better or no worse than any other class, but allowing them to construct dictatorial rule means they'll behave like any other dictatorship, a bad government no matter what it's called."

"I can see why Manuel sent you to me, Jose. We had many political talks with each other on subjects never covered in my finance courses." Eduardo asked Jose about his home, education, work, and fight against the Nationalists. Jose gave some details as quickly as he could and then returned the focus again to his host. "You have a respectable job at the stock exchange, Eduardo. What's life been like for you under the Salazar regime?"

"I grew up adopting the political, social, and religious attitudes of my parents, particularly those of my father, an accountant," answered Eduardo. "They were middle class people, and like so many of them, they became disgusted with the unstable politics of the First Republic. In sixteen years, we had forty-five governments. There were insurrections, *pronunciamentos*, assassinations, and dictatorships. We tried coalitions, single-party governments, presidential executives, charismatic leadership, and all kinds of formulas. Nothing worked except force. I think people gave up on democracy here, much like they did in Germany's Weimar Republic later. The generals abolished the Republic, sent the politicians home, and set up a dictatorship welcomed by a majority."

"As I remember, your military wasn't as cruel as our Nationalist military under Franco has proven to be," offered Jose. He went on to tell Eduardo about the aftermath of the Asturias uprising plus his own experiences at Badajoz and then encouraged Eduardo to continue his summary of Portugal's recent history.

"Our military couldn't do any better than our politicians; they had come from different parties and were paralyzed as much as the Republic was. National bankruptcy loomed, requiring the *junta* to appoint Antonio Salazar as Finance minister. He accepted the position on the condition he could cancel any spending he chose. The military leadership was in over its head on economic affairs, so they consented. Salazar balanced the budget with drastic cuts. Middle class people like my parents backed him. Salazar was asked to form a government when he became Prime Minister."

Eduardo gave a sardonic laugh before he launched his next comment. "I was at university acquiring a set of different political viewpoints from my parents, who must have thought I would be safe and not go astray in the

Department of Economics and Finance. I guess father never thought I would meet liberal or even socialist professors, or students like our mutual friend, Manuel."

Jose had a question. "Salazar got the country back on a solid financial footing. Wouldn't people at the stock exchange approve of him?"

"Some do," acknowledged Eduardo. "But, they forget capitalism requires free competition and trade, something the corporate state can suppress at any time. Salazar puts the economic life of the country under strict governmental control; the system he has established resembles a kind of *mercantilism* far more than it does liberal capitalism. He exploits colonies like Angola as sources of cheap raw materials. Wages at home are kept low; hours of labor remain long. He doesn't encourage the industrialization that could bring wealth to the country; he's content with keeping people poor. Capitalism means the freedom for each person to follow their economic interests with no interference from the state as long as one's business is done within the law."

Eduardo lowered his voice slightly, a habit acquired from living in an autocratic state. "As I'm sure you're aware, Salazar has come to secure his political power through intimidation. He now runs a government with a secret police, censorship, and absolute power. Political opposition is not tolerated; it's been squashed and rivals are now either in exile or in prison. The PVDE takes its cues from the *Gestapo*, maybe even the *Cheka*. Rumors of torture are nurtured by the regime. Sometimes, screams are heard from a police station. Word gets around and the fear it creates is very effective."

"That's quite an indictment from the standpoints of morality, politics, and economics," remarked Jose. "Salazar's rule is not likely to end anytime soon. Do you consider him to be a Fascist?"

"Let me answer by saying he's a political genius even though he made his mark in finance. He brought together three separate elements in Portuguese politics – Corporatists, Catholics, and Fascists – blending the programs of the first two. As for Fascism, he would reject that label, claiming Nazism to be barbarian. The Fascists say they are all for progress in science and technology, and I don't see where Salazar wants either. So, I'd say he's technically not a Fascist, although his henchmen certainly adopt a good deal of their methods."

The conversation kept going until two o'clock in the morning. At that point, Eduardo asked Jose if he was getting tired after being under so much stress in recent days. Jose couldn't believe he and Eduardo had talked for so long, nor could he believe Bonita had left him only three days ago. So much had happened. There was so much he had to do. They agreed to call it 'a night,' and he would be on his way tomorrow. Before sleep overtook him, Jose gave thanks for God's blessings in leading him to another supportive person.

Next morning, Eduardo proposed going to the *Museu Nacional de Soares dos Reis* before Jose's bus trip to Braga.

"The museum is in the same general direction as the Palacio da Bolsa and your bus station," Eduardo told Jose. "There is a sculpture of San Jose there; you should take a look at your namesake."

On the way to the museum, Eduardo made one last try to convince Jose that he should make haste to England.

"We have boats constantly going back and forth from Porto to London and I have contacts that could get you on one of those ships. You could go across the Eiffel bridge to Vila Nova de Gaia, visit the wine cellars where the Port wine is aged, and sail to England. Return to Spain when it's safe."

"Your offer is tempting, Eduardo, but no thank you. I know you're thinking of my best interests. I certainly appreciate your concern, but I simply can't rest until I have accomplished what I have set out to do."

The museum was decorated in the *Manueline* style, characterized by the lavish use of tropical vegetation and seafaring themes of ship's cables, granite anchors, and knotted ropes all twisted around doorways, windows, and spires – reminding Portuguese citizens of their time of naval greatness and discovery. Adorning the walls were the *azulejos*, or Portuguese tiles, depicting religious scenes and floral designs in colors of blue, white, and yellow, not the geometric shapes of triangles and squares of its Moorish originators.

"The sculptures by Antonio Soares dos Reis here are truly outstanding," said Eduardo. "We are justly proud of his work."

Jose walked through the gallery admiring the marble carvings Eduardo had brought him to see. As he walked into a room off to one side, Jose caught the sight of a man who appeared to be weeping. The man noticed Jose and quickly left the room. Jose walked in, curious to discover what had moved the man to tears. He came to a bronze statue. The title marked on a card told Jose that this was the sculpture Eduardo had referred to: San Jose holding a child. Jose Martinez beheld the baby Jesus and then looked up at the kindest and most tender face he had ever seen represented in a work of art.

With all his heart and soul, San Jose was devoted to the child he is holding, thought Jose Martinez. *The artist was certainly successful in conveying that impression. It's amazing. Here is God, a baby, vulnerable, being cared for by a human being.*

The simple nobility of the figure evoked an everlasting image for Jose.

I can understand why Eduardo wanted me to see this sculpture, he noted. *Now I know why the man I saw here was moved to tears.*

He instantly thought of Bonita and the child she believed she was carrying.

I might have held a child like that, he said to himself, not intending a comparison with the Holy Family. *It would have been the greatest moment of my life, the miracle of birth, the privilege of all my years, being at one with God and nature.*

Tears welled up inside and rushed to Jose's eyes. As he wiped the wet drops from his face, the man Jose had seen reappeared and came to him.

The man said, "I saw how intensely you were inspired by this sculpture. I was strongly affected, too, and wanted to share the moment with a person who had the same emotion as I did."

The man paused for an instant and then excused himself with these words, "*Desculpe* – if I broke into a private moment."

"Maybe we share something that's so deep within us, we can't express it," responded Jose. "I've never seen a sculpture with such love and compassion."

The man nodded and smiled. Softly patting Jose on the shoulder, he quickly left the room and disappeared into a group of people descending a flight of stairs. Jose stood rooted to the spot for a moment longer and lifted his eyes to San Jose's benevolent face. He found it difficult to gaze for any longer than a second and immediately moved away.

Twenty minutes later in the bus station, Jose and Eduardo said their good-byes. As he pressed a rider's ticket into Jose's hand, Eduardo urged him to reassess the chances of success in carrying out his intentions, knowing it was useless to argue with a person so dedicated to completing an assignment he had given himself. He wished all kinds of good luck for Jose and hoped to see him again with a happy story of accomplishment.

"Don't forget, Jose, you've got a reservation for a second night at my place."

"If you see Manuel before I do," said Jose, with a sparkle in his eye, "tell him we'll get together soon and start a revolution for mankind, the three of us."

CHAPTER 34
BRAGA

Jose surveyed the six hundred steps leading up to the pilgrimage church of *Bom Jesus do Monte* six kilometers outside of Braga. The archbishop of Braga had designed the Baroque stairway in 1723; the structure was finished in 1811. After the first steps, the stairs on the steep forested slope did not travel a straight line; instead, they turned to one side and then sharply toward the other. At each turn were chapels that symbolized the fourteen Stations of the Cross. Each chapel had life-size terra-cotta figures from Christ's last journey.

Braga was of central importance to the Church in Portugal, reflected in the saying: 'Lisbon is having fun and Porto is working while Braga is praying.'

Jose had arrived late in the afternoon. The walk from Braga to the pilgrimage site had taken more time than he expected. The distance to the top of the hill was more formidable than he had imagined. The dense woods around the massive stairway and stations at each landing gave the whole location an atmosphere of mystery. Jose needed time to prepare himself mentally. He was making this penitential journey for himself as well as for Bonita, and he wanted to be in the right frame of mind to make the slow struggle up to the church at the summit. Next day, he learned, groups of pilgrims were expected. Jose could blend in more easily with them, whereas if he went up on his own he would be more noticeable. He found a nearby hostel in which to stay overnight. He would need all the energy he possessed to ascend those stairs on his knees.

Sitting at a table outside the hostel, Jose finished the food Manuel had given him. He went into his simple, unadorned room and sat on the bed. Jose glanced at Bonita's rucksack he had brought with him in addition to his own.

This is the first night I've been alone with you, Bonita, he said to her silently, as if she was sitting next to him. *Tomorrow, I will fulfill an act of atonement for both you and me. Do not be concerned, my beloved. God will take care of me.* He thought of the words of the psalmist: '*Though I walk through the valley of the shadow of death, I will fear no evil, for thou art with me.*'

"And I am with you, always" was the message plainly spoken to him.

Jose turned around, looking for Bonita. He could have sworn she was in the room with him. There was no doubt in his mind the voice he heard belonged to Bonita. The sense of her presence was so authentic in that dimly lit room, he had to stand up and study the surface of every wall. He looked under the bed and in the closet, finding nothing. He opened the door and stared down the hall; no one was there either. Jose came back and sat on the bed again. He was too much of a realist to think Bonita was physically present in the room, yet her spirit was somehow with him.

If God can create the universe, he told himself, *God is then capable of anything. Bonita is here, somehow. Our existence is more than our five senses tell us, as I said to Manuel.*

For the first time since Bonita's grotesque death, Jose experienced a quiet awareness of peace and calm coming over him. The belief that by some miracle she was with him in this room brought unbounded joy and serene comfort. He knew he could never explain this moment to anyone. No rational interpretation could be given; he was simply convinced by unequivocal faith that Bonita had spoken to him. After marveling at the mysterious occurrence with astonishment for several minutes, Jose lay down on the bed and pulled a blanket over him, inspired and determined to perform the obligations that stretched out before him. The rest and slumber he received that night would also serve him well next day in his strenuous journey up the steps of the stairway of *Bom Jesus do Monte*.

The morning dawned clear and bright in the autumn sky. Jose ate his *pequeno almoco* hurriedly, gathered the rucksacks, and paid for his room. He walked to the foot of the vast staircase. He stood there for a few minutes, peering through the portico. A number of women, most of them older and dressed in black, ascended the steps ahead of him. Several pilgrims moved by him. Most of them continued walking while a few fell to their knees and started slowly up the stairway. Jose went to the first step, lowered himself, and placed the rucksacks on his back. He carefully made his way past the first two chapels, the Chapel of the Last Supper and the Chapel of Christ's Agony in the Garden.

Jose had anticipated the hard contact with the granite steps and stopped momentarily to tie pieces of cloth around his knees at the Chapel of the Kiss of Judas. From this point on, the route zigzagged upward to the top of the hill. He moved past the Chapel of Darkness. When he came to the Chapel of the Flagellation, Jose looked to his left and noticed a funicular making its climb to a terrace at the summit. For a moment, he envied the tourists riding in the funicular. Then he thanked God for giving him the strength to make the trip on his knees.

Moving to the right, he came upon the Chapel of the Crown of Thorns. Next, the steps went left to the Chapel of the Road to Calvary and the Chapel of Jesus before Pilate. As he started toward the Chapel of Simon the Cyrenian, Jose began placing Bonita's rucksack in front of him to soften the impact of his knees hitting the concrete below. The steps continued straight to the Chapel of the Crucifixion. It was here the fabric on Jose's knees gave way to the constant pounding and scraping. The skin, now exposed and not accustomed to this rough treatment, became scuffed and began to show a patchwork of blood.

He rested before the Chapel of the Crucifixion, thinking: *My pain is small compared to the misery Jesus must have suffered from the studded whips tearing into his flesh, the crown of thorns pressing down on his forehead, and the sharp spikes piercing his hands and feet.*

Jose reflected again on the inclination of some human beings to inflict torment and humiliation on other human beings who had the courage to patiently endure oppression without striking back in anger.

That thought was followed by a revelation. The cross – an instrument of suffering and death – became transformed by Christ into a symbol of redemption and life. God's reasoning throws man's thinking upside down. Despair is recast into hope. The beaten down are lifted up. The stricken are strengthened. We, the dying, are reborn into new life.

Is not the same experience happening to me? Why should I carry out the mission requested by my mother? How would this pilgrimage help Bonita?

I don't know, Jose admitted to himself. *However, there is some power working inside of me prescribing this journey of danger. My efforts will make no sense to a logical mind, but here I am carrying out my promise to Mama and my prayers for Bonita in spite of my own misgivings and the warnings of my friends. And, it may be that this mission is as much for me as it is for these women I love.*

Jose moved toward the Fountain of the Five Wounds of Christ. A man in worker's clothes approached, taking Jose's preoccupied mind away from his contemplations. The man produced a wet cloth and wiped the blood from Jose's knee.

"Obrigado, senhor," Jose offered, thanking him warmly. He reached into his pocket for some escudos.

A woman walked by, but not before casting a frown upon the man helping Jose.

"I wonder what that was all about?" asked Jose of the man after she was out of sight.

"Oh, she caught the heel of her shoe in her dress a couple of stations below," explained the man. "She was trying to free her shoe and asked me to lift her dress. I said, 'Madam, I can't lift your dress because that is exactly the reason I am doing penance today!' She didn't appreciate my excuse."

Jose laughed, wondering if the man told the same story every time he came to these steps and received disapproving looks from local people when he was given coins for rendering a service to someone in need. The man walked on ahead and was quickly gone. Jose wrapped his bruised knee with a handkerchief and started up the Staircase of the Five Senses with its whitewashed walls and its fountains representing sight, sound, smell, taste, and touch.

Reaching the top of this staircase, Jose decided to rest. He was getting much closer to his final destination when a man in a security uniform came running in his direction. Jose drew back and crouched, hiding his face and fearing the worst. The security man ran by Jose and moved to a platform below where a group of people had gathered.

Must be an accident, Jose thought to himself. *"Keep going,"* he believed he heard Bonita saying to him, remembering the same words said to each other on the night of their escape into Portugal.

He turned and continued toward the Staircase of the Three Virtues; these were allegorical figures symbolizing Faith, Hope, and Charity. Drops of sweat were running down Jose's face and moistening his shirt as the heat of the day bore down. The cloth over the bloodied knee turned red once more as Jose reached the summit of the hill. He went over to the Chapel of the Descent from the Cross, where terra-cotta figures depicted the lowering of Jesus' body. Here, he knelt and said a prayer for the soul of Bonita and gave thanks once again for the endurance and stamina to complete his climb to the top of the hill. Getting up, he spotted the Pelican Fountain, the legend being that the pelican takes blood from its own breast to feed its young thereby symbolizing Christ's sacrifice for mankind. Ahead was the *Church of Bom Jesus.* Jose went inside for rest and meditation.

As he sat on one of the benches in the church, Jose considered again his own intentions for making religious journeys to Braga and Santiago de Compostela.

My mother planted the idea of pilgrimage in me. I sincerely want to carry out her dying wish. Yes, I can admit I was flattered by her request. I was the chosen one, not Antonio or Ramon. The truth is, though, the compliment of being selected has burdens to go along with it – so my actions are not unworthy. But how do I keep my own ego out of this mission?

Then he knelt and prayed, asking God to keep his motives pure.

While he could not know whether Bonita would have asked him to perform a pilgrimage for her, Jose thought it would help her in some way he could not put into adequate words.

I believe it is important that I perform something spiritual for her. Her death is a blunt reality and the manner in which she had died is the most loathsome way I can imagine. The stark truth is I will never see her again while I am physically on this earth. My only contact with her will be spiritual, through God. When I die, we will be reunited.

With this belief mixed in with actual fact, Jose went a step beyond his last conversation with Manuel.

'Trust in God, trust also in me,' Jesus said to his disciples. 'In my father's house are many rooms . . . I go there to prepare a place for you . . . that you also may be where I am.'

Jose quietly whispered an addition, "And that is where, Bonita, I will find you again."

For one more time, Jose asked God to accept Bonita's soul, the vital part of her being.

I don't know what else I can do for her. I wish I could do more than climb pilgrimage stairs, but I don't know what it would be.

Leaving the church and staircase, Jose observed other motives for establishing a pilgrimage site. Noticing the inevitable stands selling religious medals, post cards, booklets, and trinkets, he saw how a pilgrimage site could bring money to a town. Some people seemed to be using the site as a way of getting together with friends. Others were taking photographs around *Bom Jesus do Monte*. People had other interests than spiritual ones; also evident were economic, social, and artistic reasons.

How does God ever sort out the myriad purposes humans carry in their minds? That's a job for God, acknowledged Jose. *Jesus told us to be discerning but not to judge others – that's probably the hardest idea for me or anyone else to follow.*

234

CHAPTER 35
THE NEW MISSION

"Great news, Ramon!" exclaimed Antonio. "We've had a fantastic Nationalist victory here at Toledo. I can't wait to tell you and everyone about it."

Reluctantly, Ramon had returned to Spain. His orders were to report directly to Antonio's company near Toledo. Antonio had given Ramon explicit directions to communicate with him every night, but ten days had gone by without any message. Antonio became impatient, suspecting Ramon had grown weary of the hunt for Jose or the search had degenerated into one for the comfort of brothels. While Antonio was jubilant over the military success, Ramon was afraid at some point his brother would explode in fury for his failing to follow orders and keep him informed day by day.

"After our victory at Talavera," Antonio exulted, "I prepared myself for the push on to Madrid. However, the *caudillo* had other plans. Franco was criticized in some quarters for not staying with the original plan to take Madrid, but perhaps only the mind of a genius could anticipate the tremendous propaganda value in coming to the aid of the surrounded garrison at Toledo. Let me tell you the story."

"Please do," said Ramon, hoping Antonio would become so involved in his tale that he would forget the reason Ramon had been called back.

"Toledo was taken by Nationalist troops when the rising began," Antonio started, "but the victory was only temporary. With vastly superior numbers, the Republican militia rallied, overpowered our forces, and drove them into this fortress, the *Alcazar*. This place was well chosen by Colonel Moscardo, our commanding officer here. The *Alcazar* is a natural place to defend, being on high ground and overlooking the Tagus River. A weapons factory was near by, so our men were well supplied with ammunition. Food, however, was in short supply and the Republican militia had overwhelming manpower. The

Republicans decided to carry out a siege. They blocked all avenues of escape and shut off all routes over which food could be delivered."

"Sounds like the situation was hopeless for us," ventured Ramon.

"Well, here's where leadership becomes so important, as I keep telling people," exclaimed Antonio. "Colonel Moscardo led his soldiers brilliantly under the most difficult circumstances, considering his men were outnumbered and hundreds of women and children were trapped inside. Republican leaders telephoned the Colonel, trying to convince him that his position was impossible to hold and he should surrender for the sake of the women and children. All of this was steadfastly refused."

"No surrender," said Ramon, "the only way for a true warrior."

Antonio rushed to tell the next part of the story. "A Republican militia leader telephoned Moscardo, telling him if he didn't surrender, his captured son, Luis, would be shot. If you don't believe me, our commander was told, I will put your son on the line so you know it's true. Luis Moscardo spoke next, saying only 'Papa.' 'What is happening, my boy?' asked the colonel. The son answered: 'Nothing. They say they will shoot me if the Alcazar does not surrender.' Colonel Moscardo replied: 'If it be true, commend your soul to God, shout *Viva Espana* and die like a hero. Goodbye, my son, a last kiss.' Luis answered: 'Goodbye father, a very big kiss.' The Republican leader came back on the phone and before he hung up, heard Colonel Moscardo say that the Alcazar would never surrender. Later, his son was executed."

"Somehow, I knew the bastards would do that," Ramon remarked. "Keep going, though; this is the stuff legends are made of."

"You are definitely right about that," said Antonio. "Rifle fire went on between the two sides for over a month. Our men were such good shots that the Republican militia never tried an assault to end the siege. The Republicans sent agents to propose surrender by the *Alcazar* defenders. Naturally, Moscardo refused this appeal. They even sent a priest who had escaped execution by the militia because he was considered a liberal. The priest gave general absolution and delivered a sermon about the honor that awaited the defenders in the next world, like he was giving extreme unction to the dying.

"The priest left and the siege continued. The Republicans tried to tunnel under the walls and they planted land mines under the towers facing the city. Civilians were told to leave because of the danger posed by the explosions of these mines. The press was invited to watch the fall of the *Alcazar*. One tower was blown up. The militia poured in; they were met by fire from the defenders and thrown back. Next, the walls of the Alcazar were sprayed by petrol. Grenades were thrown to set fires going, and that attack was repulsed."

No Greater Love

"When did Franco come in?" asked Ramon.

"Your question is timely because the *caudillo* acted at that very moment," answered Antonio. "Our men lived in the cellars of the fortress. Water was almost gone. Mules and horses had to be slaughtered for food. Bread rations were reduced. Hearing all this, General Franco decided to relieve the garrison. He was told he should keep moving toward Madrid before a defense of the capital could be organized. The *caudillo* believed coming to the aid of such gallant men was more important and the value of a victory at Toledo would be the greatest morale boost our forces could possibly obtain.

"Meanwhile, Republican Assault Guards were rushed to Toledo, and the Government began announcing the fall of the *Alcazar*. Our troops under my commander, General Varela, left the camp at Talavera and started for Toledo. We cut the Republican road communication with Madrid and came within sight of our surrounded garrison. Those brave men saw us coming, and they knew their defense had not been in vain."

"What was it like, coming into the city?" Ramon inquired, trying to keep Antonio talking about the Nationalist victory as long as he could.

"We came upon mutilated bodies of our troops on the way in. There was the evidence that indiscriminate killing had gone on. We saw sights beyond description. We resolved right then and there that no Republican militia was going to leave Toledo alive. Some Republicans escaped, but no prisoners were taken. Wiping out these diseased types is the only way the evil nurtured by the liberal Republic will be stamped out.

"A few of our men went into the hospitals and took lives there, and I'm sure the Republican press will call it an atrocity. What they won't report is that able-bodied militia, not wounded, went into the hospital for their own safety, and that is where our men found them. Some of the Republican militia committed suicide; no doubt, Republican reporters will call it murder."

"Any lie for a story," commented Ramon. "What happened next?"

"The next day was glorious. Colonel Moscardo, as he paraded his men before General Varela, told him there was 'nothing to report.' *'Sin novedad,'* you may remember, was the very password that started this noble crusade to liberate Spain in the first place. The defenders breathed free air for the first time in two months. Afterwards, we offered our prayers to the Subterranean Virgin, Our Lady of the *Alcazar*."

"No wonder you're excited and proud to be a part of this, Antonio."

"I'll remember it forever, Ramon. We've got the Republicans on the run. People are beginning to see we have right, as well as might, on our side. When we saw the lacerated bodies of our fallen soldiers on the way into Toledo, our determination became so fierce that no one could have stopped us. It is a monstrous evil we are fighting, Ramon. Never forget that. And, never forget, our little brother Jose is a part of that evil."

"It's still hard for me to think of Jose as an evil person."

"He didn't start out to be an evil person, Ramon, but he became one through his association with communists, anarchists, socialists, liberals, atheists – all the criminals who have tried to turn Spain away from its true destiny. His relationships with those people have turned him into an immoral creature. Jose fell under the guidance of those people when he went to university; it continued when he became a newspaperman. You and I chose a military career, and we were spared the subtle influence some intellectuals can weave over a person. Never underestimate them; they are very appealing and well-informed. It's easy to fall for their sweet talk."

"Poor Jose," commented Ramon. "He didn't have a chance or a choice."

"Oh yes, he did. I beg to differ with you on that. Jose had an abundance of chances and choices. There is any number of true sons of Spain in our universities. Jose had many chances, but he made the wrong choices. He chose liberalism, socialism, and God only knows what else. I once supported the Republic, but it made a whole string of wrong choices – choices guided by foreign anarchists, atheists, and communists. These people say they're advocates of liberal democracy; that's only a catch phrase to disguise their real agenda, the subjugation of the authentic Spain to serve their own narrow purposes."

"What is the authentic Spain, Antonio?" asked Ramon, hoping to keep his brother away from the subject he dreaded would be addressed all too soon.

"The Spain of true religion and nationhood, above all," responded Antonio. "When the people reclaimed their country for Christianity and drove out the infidels, the real Spain became a genuine nation. Think of this: that half-wit *Azana* decrees Spain is no longer Catholic. For that alone, he deserves to be shot! He proclaims church and state are separate, steals Church property, and turns over the Catholic schools to godless educators. For that, he deserves to be shot a second time."

Ramon aimed an imaginary rifle at the wall and said, "Give me the order to fire and I'll do it. Now, there must be more to tell about the real Spain."

"Yes, there is. We once had the nation of empire, the Spain of power and conquest. When was our country at its greatest? It was at the glorious time when the Spanish Empire was built by its courageous conquistadors, its mighty army and navy, its forward-looking monarchs, its devout priests bringing salvation to a whole new continent. There's your answer, Ramon. And when has Spain been at its weakest in the last hundred years? It's been nothing less than when the liberals of the First and Second Republics were in power."

"But, haven't there been weak monarchs and incompetent generals?"

"Certainly. Not all monarchs and generals are fit for leadership. But, look at what's happening now. Which nations are surging ahead? Those that have strong leadership: Germany, Italy, and Portugal and I'll even include Russia in that group. Bismarck gave Germany its first taste of military victories seventy years ago; he scoffed at parliamentary government and said the great questions of the day will not be settled by resolutions and majority votes, but by blood and iron. There are things about Hitler I dislike, but he took over a disillusioned country three years ago and lifted Germany out of its depression and is turning it into a powerful nation. *Il Duce* has made Italy a new Rome again. Salazar has restored strength and integrity to Portugal. Stalin, though I hate his ideology, is driving Russia into the modern world by the force of his leadership."

Ramon played the part of the interested listener. Antonio kept going.

"Who are the nations that are floundering, not knowing how to remain powerful? I suggest France and England for starters; they glorify appeasement. Liberal democracies are on the run these days. They don't have to be losing, but they are. Why? They don't have strong leadership, first and foremost. Their politicians have become feeble and weak, swayed by selfish private interests that cause their countries to lose the military and economic strength they once had."

"But, haven't Germany and Italy become dictatorships that bludgeon people into submission?" suggested Ramon.

"Some people need to be bludgeoned into submission by great leaders, Ramon. I know that's blunt, but it's the truth. We could take a lesson from the Moors who conquered us at one time. What's their message to their followers? Submit. To whom? In their case, submit to an idea of one God and to a great religious prophet. All great spiritual leaders ask submission of their followers. And, when we submitted to revered men of religion and their cherished ideals, we overthrew our Moorish conquerors and chased them out of Spain."

"This is all heady stuff for me, Antonio." This neutral comment was Ramon's undoing, his first mistake in talking to his brother. There was nothing of substance to which Antonio could respond. In the twinkling of an eye, the contours of his face produced an appearance of anger as he reminded himself of the reason Ramon had been summoned.

"Ramon, where in hell were you keeping yourself while you were in Portugal?" The words of that question came like a bolt of lightening shooting out of the sky, hitting Ramon's ego and mentally sending him reeling.

"I told you to telephone me every night," barked Antonio. "You knew I needed to tell you where I would be next day. Everything went fine for a while. Then, I didn't hear a single word from you for nearly two weeks. You don't know how embarrassing it was for me to ask the Portuguese police to find you."

"Nothing was happening, and I didn't want to just keep on saying that," said Ramon, excusing himself and trying to back away from a showdown with his brother. "It seemed like a waste of time to say, 'Nothing to report.' "

" 'Nothing to report,' " reflected Antonio, "the very words that started our liberation of Spain. Every night, how I hoped I'd hear those words, followed by this message: 'I've found Jose and Bonita and I'm keeping them under surveillance.' "

"I never saw them. I suppose I was afraid you would think I wasn't trying hard enough. I imagined you'd get angry with me when there were no results."

"You're in the military," snapped Antonio jabbing his brother on the shoulder with his finger. "You don't 'suppose' or 'imagine' anything. You follow orders. It doesn't matter how stupid you think they may sound, you follow them because you've been told to do so. That's your job."

Ramon recoiled at each shove and every stinging sentence. He could do nothing but express regrets which did not help. As the reprimands got to be more intense, he grew increasingly resentful of Antonio's obsessive badgering.

Ramon became silent absorbing Antonio's verbal blows. He drew back into himself, barely hearing Antonio shout, "If you fail to report again, I'll kick your rump so hard my boot will be lost in it forever!"

Ramon was tiring of trying to find Jose. He vowed Antonio would never discover the truth of Bonita's demise.

Only I know about what happened to Bonita, he told himself stubbornly, *and that is what will stay in me forever.*

Finally, a chagrined Ramon had had enough. "How many apologies do you want?" he demanded. "I tried to find Jose. I thought he should be brought to justice. I still do. What do you want me to do? Sit here and feel bad."

"No. I want you to go back and keep going with the search. I had to confront you, look at you, and try to drive through your head the seriousness

No Greater Love

of your mission. Jose must be dealt with at all costs. Bonita, too, if need be. He's part of a conspiracy against our country, Ramon. Don't you see that?"

"I suppose I don't see it as well as you do," replied Ramon, thinking maybe he could get Antonio off his personal attack and move him back to the 'mission' as he called it. "What is this conspiracy?"

"A lot has been discovered while you've been gone. The elections that brought the Popular Front to power earlier this year have been revealed to be fraudulent. The right-wing coalition had over a half-million more votes than the Popular Front, but got over a hundred fewer deputies in the Cortes."

"How could this happen?" asked a relieved Ramon, apparently not on the spot any longer.

"Election returns from entire provinces were rejected, according to a report to the nation by the Catholic bishops. Our country's parliament is now and has been illegitimate."

"So, the Republic was taken over by a leftist conspiracy, and now we must take our country back," said Ramon.

"Exactly," declared Antonio, enthusiastic over Ramon's acceptance of his message. "And, that's not all. The destruction of churches has been deliberately planned, not entirely by Spaniards, but also by professional agitators from Russia. Over three hundred thousand people have been killed in Republican-held territory – exterminated for their religious and political beliefs – eyes gouged out, limbs hacked off, tongues cut off, throats slit. They've been burned alive or killed by hatchet blows. Centuries of civilization have perished: paintings torn apart, sculptures smashed, archives burned, libraries sacked, and more. All this ruin under the cry: 'Long live libertarian anarchism! Long live free love! Long live Russia' – and God knows what else!"

"The Republic has lowered itself to the level of lawlessness," pronounced Ramon. "I never thought I'd live to see anarchists rule in my lifetime. What do you think will come next in this sinister atmosphere, Antonio?"

Keep going with your bitter diatribe, master brother, he beseeched privately.

Antonio accommodated him. "Already, we can see the broad outline of the evil to come if we fail. Our highest court calls cinema a school for criminals. The Communists are masters at using theater to promote sensuality and protest. Press and radio are sources of decadence, dishonesty, and revolutionary propaganda. It doesn't have to be this way. The media can be used for good purposes, but immoral and obscene theater is still immoral and obscene however artistically it may be portrayed."

"I didn't know things could get this bad," said Ramon. "Is there more? I need to know every detail."

"Do you know what the anarchists are doing in Catalonia?"

"I don't know," Ramon confessed.

He wondered: *How long can I keep Antonio going in his harangue?*

"This conspiracy consists mostly of Red anarchists bringing foreign ideas and customs into our country. The landowners and their families have their land taken from them and are shot – the same thing the Reds did in Russia after their revolution. The anarchists build a big bonfire. They take any document having anything to do with ownership of rural property and burn them. Private property is abolished. Payment of debts is cancelled. Money itself is declared illegal. Stores, banks, and factories are taken over and run by former workers. Everything is being collectivized, Soviet-style. In the countryside, harvested wheat is stored in churches. If a church doesn't serve an economic need, it is burned. Have you heard what's going on in Madrid and other cities under Republican rule?"

Again, Ramon had to shake his head, "No."

"La Pasionaria makes violent speeches, telling women to fight with knives and boiling oil. She goads them, saying it is better to die on your feet than to live on your knees. If we ripped the dress off her, I think we'd find she was a man!

"People have unbridled sex in Popular Front cities. They don't seem to know there's a civil war going on. Holy matrimony has been profaned. A woman is regarded as married to a man if she has lived him with for ten months – less than that if she is with child. And, it's shamefully easy to get a divorce."

Ramon inwardly confessed: *Information like this could make me consider switching sides or becoming a civilian in republican Madrid.*

Wisely, he kept those opinions to himself in the company of Antonio.

"Do you know how many Nationalist soldiers and supporters have been executed and murdered in the last two months alone?"

Once more, Ramon indicated that he did not.

"Seventy-five thousand is the estimate, and that may be short of the actual number. The Republicans have their imitation of the Soviet *Cheka* in Madrid. They scan lists of right-wing party members, track them down, and torture them before they are killed. Killers are freed to hunt the judges who sentenced them and they get their revenge, often in front of their victims' families. These murderers enjoy their killing and often get a sexual pleasure from it."

Without knowing it, Antonio was getting too close to the feelings Ramon had experienced on the grounds of the *Quinta das Lagrimas* in Coimbra. Antonio's comments were a reminder of the ghastly scene that had ended Bonita's life.

Ramon started to sweat under the stress of painful memories. Often, the vision of a resolute Bonita bleeding to death under him disturbed his sleep in the middle of the night. In the darkness, he thought he heard voices of condemnation – were they were coming from within? He cast his eyes away from his older brother, afraid his reaction would suggest to Antonio that something was not quite right with him.

Antonio looked at his brother. "Are you all right, Ramon?" he asked. "You seem upset about something."

"I'm upset because you are upset with me," said Ramon, trying to recover his poise. He cringed at the thought he had said the wrong thing and wanted to lead Antonio away from the reason for his return. "I just don't like to think of the misery and killing that goes with war. It unnerves me at times."

"This is why we must stop Jose on any objective he has for the Republic, Ramon. I've got orders to track him down and bring him to justice. Eventually, he should get the same treatment he gave to our driver and no doubt to others. You've got to help me with this. I can't do it all by myself."

"I understand."

"I want you to head back where you've come from. Keep going where you left off. If Jose can lead you to others, fine – find out who they are. If not, take him."

Ramon started to demur, but Antonio cut in to say, "Jose and Bonita may be slowly making their way to her home – Corcubion, wasn't it?"

"I think so."

"Her town is small. There shouldn't much problem in finding a Sanchez in such a tiny place."

"Probably not," agreed Ramon.

"Get up there. Jose is part of this evil conspiracy against the country we love. He must be prevented from his treason, whatever it takes. Do this for Spain, Ramon."

"I'll try, Antonio. I just can't guarantee success for you, much as I would like to."

"Ramon."

"Yes."

"You may need protection. You have a revolver?"

Ramon murmured that he did.

Antonio reached into a drawer and pulled out a German P08 Luger pistol. "Here, use this," he said. "It's just like mine. The Germans have used this model since 1908."

Antonio thought for a moment. "You don't have to get close to him, Ramon. Put a rifle in your car. I'll give you one. Keep it hidden. If it's discovered while you are wearing your uniform, tell the truth; you're a soldier. Tell them you're a hunter if you're in civilian clothes."

"Yes. A rifle?"

"No mercy for traitors."

"No mercy, even for Jose?"

Antonio looked at Ramon squarely in his eyes.

"No. Kill him, if you have to."

CHAPTER 36
RETURN TO SPAIN

Leaving Braga, Jose walked toward the Spanish border at the Minho River, some sixty kilometers away. He worried about being stopped by security officials of both Portugal and Spain. He would have to find a way over the river to set foot on Spanish soil. Swimming across the river was out; the rucksacks he was carrying precluded that possibility. Anticipation of going from one country into another reminded him of the frantic night he and Bonita had experienced in making their escape into Portugal. Once in Spain, he would make his way to Vigo, another thirty kilometers further north. In the harbor of that city, Jose hoped to find a boat that would take him to Bonita's hometown of Corcubion, or at least close to it. The fjord-like *rias*, cutting into the coastline of northwestern Spain meant there was no straight road up to Corcubion.

Jose thought of going first to Santiago, but decided he needed an unburdened mind to carry out his mother's pilgrimage. He was already bracing himself for the agonizing ordeal of telling Bonita's parents about her shocking death. The excruciating part of his account would come when he described how she died. It was a task that he dreaded but firmly believed he must do. Other than Manuel and Eduardo, his two Portuguese friends – and the unknown murderer – no one on earth knew Bonita was no longer among the living. In Jose's mind there was no question about it; her parents had a right to know the horrible truth.

Jose estimated he would be walking for the better part of two days before reaching the border. He spent the first night in a hostel. He placed Bonita's rucksack on a chair in his room; looking at it made him feel so desperately lonely without her. Jose picked up the backpack and held it closely to his chest.

Her image stirred and moved in front of him. He rose and began dancing, holding the knapsack as if Bonita had just become his partner.

If she's watching me now, he thought, *she must think I'm becoming unhinged.* A couple walking in the yard outside his room window looked in at the curious sight and smiled. Jose waved at them and smiled back.

As he lay in bed that evening, sleep would not come despite his tiredness. Like Manuel, he was perplexed at how the tragic experience of Bonita's death had strengthened a spiritual resolve within him.

I suppose people become religious when they can't explain catastrophic things happening to them, he reasoned, but misgivings kept assailing his thoughts.

Why did I feel driven to make the pilgrimage to Braga and climb those steps on my knees for Bonita? How did that transform anything in this world?

Nevertheless, he found value in his endeavors. *Despite my doubts, I must admit the change within me. After I deliver the dreadful news to her parents, the same compelling inner force requires me to fulfill my mother's request. It must be more than the desire to spit in the face of the enemy. My mind could say it doesn't matter; the world will go on its way even if I don't keep my pledge to her. Only days ago, before Bonita's death, all I could think about was escape. Now, I must go to Santiago and carry out Mama's pilgrimage. No one knows why I have no choice except, perhaps, the two women who are no longer with me.*

Jose pondered his religious upbringing. He didn't think of himself as an outwardly religious person. He would describe himself as a believer no doubt heavily influenced by his mother.

Did I go through the motions of spirituality merely to please her?

From Maria, he learned and remembered many great episodes in biblical history. One such significant event occurred to him now.

The flash of light and the voice of Jesus heard on the road to Damascus changed Saul into Paul and made him an apostle forever. A conversion must be happening within me, although in a slower and different way.

Another transformation Jose went on to contemplate was the change that had happened among Jesus' disciples after the crucifixion. The world might think they had become drunk on wine at Pentecost with their report of fiery tongues and speaking in languages other than their own; however, a miraculous change transpired. From a frightened group of followers fleeing the trial and crucifixion of Jesus, they had turned into a fearless band of believers, boldly proclaiming the Messiah even at the cost of their own martyrdom and death.

Jose wondered: *Am I receiving an irresistible commission in the same manner as the disciples? If so, could I do no less than they?*

Sleep finally overcame his thoughts and questions. He woke the next morning more intently resolved to carry out his objectives: the painful disclosure to Bonita's parents and the pilgrimage for his mother, Maria.

Jose arrived in the border town of Valenca in the late afternoon. On the other side of the *Minho* river was Tui, Spain. The easiest way into Spain was by walking across the bridge spanning the river, but he was fearful of running into antagonistic border patrols, particularly on the Spanish side. He headed east along the river for nearly an hour until he caught sight of a small boat that could transport him across the river during the night. About the time he walked over to the boat, a man who seemed no more than four and a half feet tall came up to him. Seeing no one else, Jose assumed he was the owner of the boat.

"*Ola*," called Jose as the man nodded his head. "I'm Spanish and I need to cross the river."

"There's a bridge in Valenca, about four kilometers from here," the little man responded.

"I'm on a pilgrimage to Santiago," said Jose. "I need to make a stop before going there. It's a shorter distance for me if I can cross here than if I use the bridge and have to double back. I'm willing to pay. It would take less than an hour to row over there and back."

"Who are you hiding from?" the boat owner asked.

"The Nationalist police," answered Jose who reckoned he might as well be truthful with this man and hope for the best. "I promised my mother before she died I'd make the pilgrimage for her. The Nationalist military told me to join their army, but I ran away from them. I thought traveling through Portugal would be safer, but now I've got to go through Spain to reach Santiago."

"Galicia is in Nationalist hands now. A lot of people have gone over to them, thinking they're the winning side."

"That's a risk I'll have to take. I'm determined to go there for my mother."

The man carefully regarded Jose for a moment. "I'll do it," his voice rang out. "I'll help you because I like the way you've been honest with me. Others like you have told me some ridiculous story. One even tried to steal the boat. At least your story sounds genuine."

"*Muchas gracias, amigo. Muito obrigado.* How much do I owe you?"

"It's risky. Spanish rifles fire real bullets and I suggest, no, I insist, we cross at night. How much have you got?"

"I'll give you all the escudos I have – which is about five hundred."

The man grumbled a little but agreed to the amount. "Pay me two fifty now and the rest of it when we cross the river."

"Fair enough," said Jose, counting the Portuguese escudos.

After darkness had descended, Jose and the man carried the boat to the shore. "*Adeus* Portugal, *hola* Spain," Jose said, reversing the words he had spoken to Bonita when they had left Spain and entered Portugal. The two got into the boat and the man started rowing, dipping his oars into the water without making a sound. Halfway across, the name of the river changed from the *Minho* in the Portuguese language to the *Mino* in Spanish.

Clouds started to gather in the western sky. "Looks like a rainstorm is coming this way," said the little man softly as he quietly pulled up a canvas cover he used to protect himself from rain and the sun.

"If the weather didn't look like rain, I wouldn't think I was headed for Galicia," Jose commented, referring to the region's wet climate.

"I'd say you were lucky to have rain; it's more likely soldiers and police will stay inside."

"And the clouds will block the moonlight," said Jose in agreement. Lightning flickered in the sky. Thunder rumbled from the heavens. The electric atmosphere matched the sense of excitement growing within Jose.

As the minutes went by, lights went out one by one on the approaching bank of the river. Jose considered that to be a good sign; people were retiring for the evening.

"I'm aiming for a road that comes down to the shore," the little man explained, cupping his hands to speak softly into Jose's ear. "It will be easier for you if you don't have to make your way through private property."

"*Obridago, senhor.*"

The boat touched land. Jose picked up the rucksacks, paid the remainder of his escudos, and shook the man's hand. "*Gracias, amigo, obrigado,*" he said.

"*Vaya con Dios!*" whispered the man. Jose scurried off the boat and briefly watched the vessel disappear silently into the darkness. He moved swiftly up the road.

After several minutes, Jose turned once more to see where the boat was. Lightning illuminated the river he had crossed. He saw nothing.

"God keep you safe," he prayed for the oarsman in the boat. "Go with God."

At the first crossroads, Jose headed west to find the road that would take him to Vigo. He was in Spain again. The wind picked up. Rain began to fall. In the distance he saw a *horreo*, the granite drying shed raised off the ground on legs to keep rodents away from the wheat, barley, or corn inside. The structure would give him protection. He crawled under the *horreo*, the rain now pelting his back with soaking drops of water.

"Move over, fellow occupants," he whispered, thinking he might find a rodent or two seeking refuge from the storm. Jose felt a sudden kinship with mice and squirrels and any other hunted creatures that, like him, experienced the same kind of terror in trying to avoid a disastrous fate.

While he was uncomfortable from the moisture, Jose couldn't help but think of the good fortune he had encountered in Portugal.

I've been helped by Manuel and briefly made a new friend in Eduardo. The little man who ferried me across the Mino River turned out to be as sympathetic as Andre Vincente and Marcelo Marques. God is surely with me. One wrong person could have easily turned me over to police who would have sent me straight into the hands of the Nationalists.

He became contrite as he realized he had been thinking only of himself and his own set of circumstances.

Bonita met one wrong person and paid for it with her life.

"Forgive me," he murmured quietly, choking back tears. Inwardly, he continued: *My prideful self made me think I was being singled out for divine protection and forgetting what happened to Bonita. I could have been the one to have run into an inhuman wretch, instead of her. She didn't deserve to die in the awful way she did. No one as pure as she merits the violation she suffered. Certainly the main reason I must fulfill these pilgrimages is to honor the sacrifices Bonita and my mother made for me.*

The rain stopped as quickly as it began. Jose decided to resume walking, as the ground under the *horreo* had become too wet for sleeping.

"Adios, amigos," he called to any small animals nearby. An hour later, he found the road that would take him to Vigo.

Chapter 37
Two Nationalists

Jose reached Vigo in the morning. The city's port was home to one of the largest fishing fleets in Spain. Jose walked to the docks. He was able to locate an excursion boat that would travel to Ribeira, with stops at the Cies islands and two coastal towns. Jose considered himself to be fortunate; possibly, only fishing boats would be operating with the tourist season disrupted by the war. He picked up a discarded newspaper. One article gave a report about Jose Calvo Sotelo, the martyred conservative leader whose murder had been the spark igniting the civil war; he was to be honored later in the year at a memorial in his hometown of Vigo. Another article revealed that all Republican resistance in Galicia had been crushed and the region was now completely in Nationalist hands.

With that depressing news was another anxiety. A Nationalist soldier or civil guardsman could be on board to check on the identities of the passengers; however, no official appeared to be performing this kind of duty. The captain of the boat seemed interested only in collecting fares. Jose searched through his rucksack for the pesetas he hadn't used for weeks. He was desperately hungry; there had not been enough time to obtain food for the trip. He couldn't afford to pay for an expensive meal abroad the boat and would have to content himself with the thought of all the kilometers saved by taking this trip on water. A straight road along the coast did not exist. Most of the population clung to the land along the finger-like indentations made by the waters of the Atlantic. Traveling by boat had its dangers, but Jose figured the distance and time spared from walking was worth the risk. He would be sheltered at Corcubion by Bonita's parents, after which he could walk to Santiago and complete his mother's pilgrimage.

Beyond those tasks lying immediately ahead, Jose considered his options.

I could return to Coimbra and stay with Manuel until I could figure out what to do. If getting back to Portugal becomes impossible, I might try searching for Republican forces holding out in Asturias. Rather than resort to violence, though, wouldn't it be better to join a group working toward a sort of healing process, binding the wounds of my war-torn country? Or is the military option the only one currently powerful enough paradoxically to achieve a peaceful solution?

The motion of the boat helped Jose to unwind from the exertions of his days and nights on the road. He wanted to relax and enjoy the beauty of the scenery that surrounded him. The magnificent panoramas and pleasing vistas of the undulating coastline created a peaceful atmosphere, as if the war had never touched the area. The tensions of recent days and the thoughts of an unknown future pulled away from his mind and body. Jose placed the cap over his eyes. Sleep soon caught up with him and overtook his exhausted body.

Within the hour, he was jolted awake when several noisy tourists sat next to him. They had been drinking wine and liquor in search of a good time. One member of the group became sick to his stomach and vomited over the railing, much to the amusement of his companions. With the clatter and commotion, Jose could not get back to sleep despite his tiredness. This clamoring crowd complained of the war and how it could threaten their leisure plans. They didn't seem to care which side prevailed or how many were killed in the conflict; they simply wanted the war to go out of their awareness. When asked for his opinions, Jose played the part of an uninterested traveler as best as he could.

Later, a distinguished looking gentleman who had been listening said confidentially to Jose, "I couldn't help but overhear your talk with one of your fellow travelers a few minutes ago. Some people live in a fool's paradise. If the Nationalists hadn't taken matters into their own hands, this whole territory would be in the hands of the Reds by next year."

"Really, do you think so?" Jose responded as noncommittally as he could.

"Those buffoons, Azana and his government, would have delivered the nation to the communists if they hadn't been stopped. Thank God we have men like Franco and Mola."

"I don't know much about General Franco, but I've heard he was a brave soldier," said Jose, trying to think of a way to get out of the discussion.

"If I were a young man like you, nothing would please me more than to serve under men like him. A war like this would be the thrill of a lifetime."

"I'll have to give it some thought when I get home."

How do I stop this? Jose thought to himself.

"Do that, young man. You won't regret it." The older man looked at his wristwatch. "I'm going to get something to eat in the bar downstairs," he said. "Care to join me?"

"I'd like to, but I can't afford it."

"I'll be happy to pay for your lunch. You look like you could use something to eat."

Jose did not want to accept, but his stomach overruled his mind. Fortunately, the topic of the civil war didn't come up again. They exchanged impressions of Galicia's green appearance and how the land and its culture and people resembled that of Brittany, Ireland, and Wales. They made observations about the shoreline of Galicia, its fishing and shipbuilding industries, the *ria* waters piercing the land, and how its citizens gathered near the sea, leaving the interior with less population. Jose pointed to the numerous *bateas*, floating rafts they saw in the *rias*, used for growing mussels on the underside of their platforms. He remarked how profitable the mussel industry was for the owners and that it was a good thing each *batea* could be passed along from father to son.

How much Bonita would have loved this conversation, except for the politics, he thought. Her father had owned one of the floating platforms.

The only time Jose felt a little apprehensive was when the man asked whether he had been to Santiago de Compostela.

"I'm going there in a few days to complete a pilgrimage," Jose answered. "I'm not taking the route most people take, but I don't think I'll walk eight hundred kilometers to Roncesvalles just to walk back."

The man smiled. "Good for you," he said. "When you become as old as I am, you'll comprehend even more the importance of religion."

As they finished their meal, the man rose from the table and shook hands with Jose, saying, "I don't know when I've enjoyed talking with a young person as much as I've enjoyed talking with you. *Vaya con Dios*, my son."

Jose thanked him for the meal and said, "I was hungrier than I realized. *Mucho gracias*, senor." Looking out at a harbor, he added, "Looks like we're coming to our destination."

The sun shone overhead as Jose waved a final farewell to the man with obvious Nationalist sympathies. Picking up the rucksacks, he walked ashore. He reflected briefly on the pleasant, benevolent nature of the man with whom he would disagree on politics. The experience inspired a hope that some day there would be some kind of reconciliation, even with his militarist brothers. Now, he was on his own again, and Jose had to concentrate on where he was going. There was enough time to walk the fifteen kilometers to Porto do Son and find a room.

Porto do Son was straight north and a little east of Ribeira. The only traffic on the road was an ox-cart making its way back into town. The only sounds were the waves as they struck the shore when the road wound its way close to the sea. Jose became aware of how tired he was after he had walked about a half-hour. Camping near the ocean with the rhythmic sound of the waves lulling him to sleep was an idea becoming too powerful to resist. Jose was ready to seek a sheltered place when a military truck spun past him on the road, then skidded to a stop and abruptly backed up with the dust swirling around it.

I wonder what this is all about, Jose said to himself, as he dodged the tail end of the truck. A uniformed young man wearing a blue shirt turned off the engine, got out of the vehicle, and came up to Jose.

"Get in the truck," the young man ordered. The words were a command, not an offer of help.

"Why?" asked Jose apprehensively.

"We're rounding up young men like you for the military."

"I don't have any intention of serving in your military."

"Intention doesn't have anything to do with it. We're going for a little ride."

"Who says I must."

"Says this," the military man answered, brandishing a pistol. "This is all the persuasion we need."

He circled around in back of Jose, stripping him of the rucksacks.

"Your army must be in bad shape, using force to recruit," shouted Jose, turning to face the young man.

"Shut up! Don't open your mouth." The pistol wavered menacingly in one hand. "Turn around. I don't want to see your face."

Jose made a motion to pick up one of the rucksacks.

"Don't touch that backpack!" screamed the young man. A rope was firmly tied around Jose, pinning his arms next to his body. The pistol jabbed him in the back.

"Move. It doesn't take much to set this thing off." A hand pushed Jose ahead. "Get in the truck," he was ordered.

Jose was trapped. He got in the truck. "What now?" he muttered aloud.

The young man locked the passenger door from the outside. Keeping his gun pointed at Jose, he came around in front of the truck to the driver's side.

He got in and put the gun in a holster under his shirt, clicking on the safety. The engine started and they moved down the road.

"My rucksacks" protested Jose. "You're forgetting the bags I was carrying. Everything I own is in them."

"You won't need them any more," was the harsh reply.

Jose thought to himself: *What do I say to this jerk? He's got to be some kind of Nationalist renegade; this is not the way they recruit people – or is it?*

Then an idea impulsively entered his head. "You don't want *my kind* in your military," he said to the driver.

"What do you mean – my kind?"

Jose merely smiled at him, shrugging his shoulders and hating himself for the pretense he was making.

"Civilian clothes. O Gawd, I should have known," the young man exploded. "Only girls, old men, and homosexuals wear civilian clothes these days!" He launched into a string of venomous invectives of which 'queer', 'pervert', and 'faggot' were only the mildest.

Belligerently, he asked Jose, "Are you a man, I mean a *real* man?"

"Yes, a hundred times more than you." Jose glared at him.

A fist came out of nowhere and smashed into Jose's face. "What are you going to do about that, you dirty little faggot?" Another blow sent Jose's head upward into the metal roof of the cab. Blood streamed from his nose. Jose struck back with a kick of both feet into his assailant's ribs. The truck screeched to a stop.

"Get out!" thundered the driver. "Get your pansy ass out of my sight!"

"I can't," yelled Jose. "Your door is locked. My hands are tied."

"My hands are tied," mimicked the driver in a high-pitched voice as he bent over from his seat to unlock the door. The door gave way as Jose pushed hard against it. He took a violent shove from behind and tumbled out of the cab.

The driver sprang out of the truck, reached back under a seat, and pulled out a tire iron. He advanced on Jose who picked himself up off the ground. To run could invite the use of the gun.

"You are about to get the thrashing of your life," Jose was told. "It will be a lesson you'll barely survive to tell all your castrated little fairies."

The tire iron was aimed swiftly at Jose's head. It missed. "Don't worry, I can swing until I connect," assured the young man in the blue shirt.

Jose didn't wait; he flung his bound body into his adversary with a savage kick, turning himself over trying to avoid the tire iron as it slammed flat into his back. Jose fell, unable to brace himself as he hit the ground, and took a vicious kick to a shoulder. He tried to get up, but collapsed under another blow.

He heard: "You won't be chasing any pansy butts tonight."

The young man held his foot on Jose's chest as he prepared to deliver more punishment.

"No one will recognize your fairy face when I'm done with you," he told his fallen victim.

Jose was defenseless. He tried to loosen his arms from the rope that bound him, but it was tied too firmly. He had no way of defending himself. The sense of helplessness enraged him.

"You are the worst yellow-belly coward I've ever seen," Jose screamed at the brute, yelling with all the strength he could summon.

"I should shoot you," threatened the savage beast, "but we'll just give you a pistol-whipping instead." He retrieved the weapon from his holster, holding the gun ready to strike. Then, he hesitated.

Jose waited, dreading the damage to be done.

"First, we'll baptize you; I've got a little 'holy water' to sprinkle over you."

Unbuttoning his pants, he made ready to urinate on his victim's face when a car approached them over a rise in the road. The young man hurried to his truck and started the engine. He spun the wheels in his haste to race away, raising a cloud of dust and dirt behind him. Jose, gasping for breath, could not get up in time to hail the oncoming car. He cried out when the car went past, but the driver kept his eyes straight ahead.

Jose groaned as he lay in the weeds by the side of the road. He swallowed blood and mucus from his nose. His shirt was drenched with red blots and sweat. He wondered whether any bones had been broken. His shoulder and back were pounding with pain. Slowly, he was able to free himself of the rope that had tightly bound him. The nosebleed finally stopped and Jose gently wiped as much blood as he could from his face. He gingerly reached over the unbeaten shoulder and cautiously rubbed his back. The skin had broken in several places. Miraculously, he determined, the force of the tire iron hadn't broken any bones.

Slowly, he got to his feet and hobbled a short way down the road to recover the rucksacks. Jose reached into his bag and brought out a clean shirt.

Discarding the bloodied shirt after removing Bonita's ring from the pocket, he said, "Good-bye, old friend, it is better that you stay here. I don't want you to shock Senor and Senora Sanchez."

Jose looked around. How crazy his words would sound if anyone were listening to him. He decided to carry the unblemished shirt until he came to a stream he noticed a short distance away. There, he could wash the dirt and drying blood from his body. While his legs were sore, at least they had not been injured. After cleansing himself as best as he could, he steadied himself and began to slowly move again toward Porto do Son, gingerly carrying a backpack in each hand.

In the Galician fields, he glimpsed a sight of the granite crosses designed to thwart demons and monsters.

"You didn't help me this time," he called, shaking a fist at them.

He heard the engine of a vehicle approaching him beyond a curve in the road. Ignoring his pain, Jose scurried off the road to hide in a field behind some bushes. He feared the young barbarian in the military truck had decided to come back along the road and hunt for his wounded victim. A car roared past and Jose was alone again. He waited for the dust to settle. Shaken, he elected to walk in the fields and in back of trees, keeping the road in sight.

After two hours of labored walking alternating with pauses to rest, Jose spotted a sign with the word "dolmen" painted on it. An arrow was also painted on the sign, pointing the direction of the dolmen to the traveler. He had read about these structures which were made of two columns of vertical stones supporting a large horizontal stone several feet from the ground. They were thought by archeologists to be ancient burial places.

There could be water at this place, Jose thought to himself. *Maybe the person who was buried there won't mind if I occupy his space for one night. I can't go into Porto do Son looking like this and ask for a place to stay.*

About a kilometer along a path that led from the road, Jose found the dolmen. A few picnic tables and a water pump were set around a grove of eucalyptus trees.

All the comforts of home, he thought, as he arranged the rucksacks as comfortably as he could make them. Jose washed himself with the cold spring water. Cupping his hands for water, he swallowed two aspirin tablets from a small bottle in the rucksack Marisa had thoughtfully provided and settled in under the stones as night began to cover the sky.

During fitful bouts of sleep, Jose dreamed of being lashed by whips from Nationalist soldiers as elderly men in ecclesiastical robes stood by.

Chapter 38
A Death Revealed

Jose slept into the morning as soft rain fell on the trees and the massive stone above him. Clouds had kept the air relatively warm for an early autumn night. He moved his arms and legs very carefully. He had slept on one side, keeping the weight off his bruised back and shoulder. His neck was still pulsating with pain. He rose to his feet in a methodical fashion. He longed for a *desayuno completo*: *café con leche doble* (double milk), *zumo de naranja* (orange juice), and *churros* (fried batter rings). Two more aspirin disappeared down Jose's throat; the act of swallowing anything made him wince. He was content to rest under the dolmen until the rain stopped.

Once the sun began to peer through the clouds, Jose was walking again. At first he moved like a tortoise, giving the aching muscles in his body a chance to adjust painstakingly to motion. After resting against a tree or a boulder at several points to conserve energy, Jose arrived at Porto do Son. Before his encounter with the military truck driver, he had considered taking a short path to the *Mirador de la Curota* for the panoramic view that would enable him to see the four inlets of the entire Rias Bajas. On a clear day, Cape Finisterre could be visible to the north and one could see as far as the harbor at Vigo to the south. His body was sore and the day was cloudy. He needed no urging to give up on that idea.

In Porto do Son, Jose came upon a band of musicians marching on the main street through town during the noon hour. Young people wearing red shirts, black vests, and white pants played their various instruments, including drums, tambourines, and bagpipes. A man asked Jose if he had been to the town's Octopus Festival in August.

"We have the best *pulpos* in Galicia," he claimed.

Jose hoped to catch a fishing boat going from Porto do Son to Muros across the *Ria de Muros y Noia*. He was told 'too late in the day,' requiring a walk on the winding road around that body of water, extending the length of his travel on foot. Maybe his luck was running out; fate seemed to be turning against him.

Would he encounter the Nationalist brute again on the road? Every vehicle that passed Jose brought a quiver of alarm.

Keep going for I am with you, a voice from within him kept saying. He comforted himself with the impression that the encouragement was coming from Bonita.

I said I'd never leave you, he thought. *Now, you seem to be saying the same words to me.*

By early evening, a labored fifteen kilometers walk brought Jose to Noia, the town at the innermost reach of the *ria*.

Should I stop and tell Bonita's schoolmaster what happened to her? he asked himself. Almost immediately he rejected the notion; he might not be able to find the right school official and, if Nationalist forces were still looking for him, it was better not to let people know he was in the region. Bonita's parents could write an explanation – as soon as they knew the awful truth.

Jose bought an *empanada gallega* and paused at the 14th century Church of Saint Martin. He found lodging, quietly thanking Marisa and Jorge for enough pesetas to buy a room.

Exhausted, a deep sleep carried him into the morning. He continued his way along the winding coastal road toward Muros. A mid-day meal renewed his strength. He was walking more easily now. With darkness descending as he came into Carnota, Jose located a cabin to stay in for the night. He needed a place to gather his thoughts and a comfortable bed to rest his tired, sore body. Corcubion was about fifteen kilometers away and he wanted to be in the best possible condition to give the terrible news about Bonita to her parents.

In the late afternoon of the next day, Jose reached Corcubion, an old harbor town on the east side of a spit of land surrounding the *Bahia de Cabo Finisterre*, the Bay of Cape Finisterre. He walked by houses with glassed-in balconies, which afforded protection from Galicia's abundant rain. The Sanchez home was just off the main road that ran through Corcubion. Jose paused in front of the house, bracing himself for the ordeal that was to come.

"Jose!" spoke a feminine voice. "I thought that was you."

"*Hola*, Senora Sanchez!" called Jose as he caught the sight of Bonita's mother coming around the side of the house.

"Oh, it is good to see you!" remarked Senora Sanchez. They kissed each other on both cheeks. Remembering Bonita had left home to help Jose's sister with Maria, she said, "I hope your mother is doing well, Jose."

"I have much to tell you," parried Jose, sidestepping the inquiry until both parents were together.

"Have you seen Bonita?"

"Yes."

"Is she with you?"

"No. I will explain. Is Papa here?"

"*Si*. He's inside. I was in back hanging out some wash. Let's go in." She started up the porch steps. "Pablo!" she called to her husband.

"I'm coming, Mariana." Senor Sanchez appeared at the door and opened it. "I thought I heard a familiar voice," he said, shaking Jose's outstretched hand and exchanging kisses.

The three moved into the front room and seated themselves with Jose setting the rucksacks on the floor and then facing the parents of his beloved. The tension within Jose was unbearable. His anguished features lay bare the struggle to find the right words to say.

"I wish I didn't have to – I've got to tell you about something terrible that has happened," he began. No sooner than he said those words, he lost his composure and broke into uncontrollable crying.

"Oh, no," they said together taking each other's hand, startled at the sight of Jose's unsuppressed sobbing.

"This is about Bonita," whispered Senora Sanchez with a mother's intuition.

The apprehension in her husband's face was obvious.

Jose gathered himself together, and said, "I hate to tell you this, but I must. The reason Bonita – isn't with me is – that – she died about a week ago." Once this agonizing message had been released, Jose regained some slight sense of self-control, although his face continued to reveal his complete and utter misery.

"This is the most awful thing I've ever had to tell anyone," he said through his tears. They sat still, as though the message hadn't penetrated yet.

Looking at the distraught, shattered person in front of her, Bonita's mother muttered under her breath, "Oh, you poor boy, bearing this knowledge inside of you for so long." Jose could not tell whether they had misinterpreted the horrible news brought to them or had understood but were already in a state of denial.

"I would give anything in the world *not* to say what I *have* to say," Jose declared. "I haven't told you the worst part of it. She died at the hands of a person – who killed her." He barely got those words out before he began crying again.

Bonita's parents were stunned at this totally unexpected revelation.

"You're saying she was – murdered?" interpreted Pablo Sanchez, restating the last three words he had heard.

Jose moved his head to indicate 'yes' and murmured in a voice scarcely above a whisper, "She was killed by a depraved madman. I do not know who it could be."

Mariana Sanchez buried her face in her hands. Shock registered in the face of Pablo Sanchez. "This is too much," he burst forth.

Striving to maintain as much poise as he could, Jose began his explanation. "I must give you some detail. I was in a Republican militia at the battle of Badajoz and was captured there. My brother Antonio, who is a Nationalist officer, saved me from execution, explaining my dying mother in Trujillo had asked to see me. When we got to our home, I met Bonita – who was there, as you know. My mother made a request that I go on a pilgrimage for her to Santiago since she was physically unable to do so. The next morning, Mama died from a stroke."

"Oh, Jose!" exclaimed Mariana. "My daughter – and your mother, too."

Pablo looked down, shaking his head.

"What happened next, I can go over later," continued Jose. "Bonita and I were able to escape at my mother's funeral. We reached Portugal and made our way to Coimbra where we stayed in an apartment above a friend of mine who lives there. Manuel was very helpful. He took care of us for over two weeks, until all of us thought it safe for Bonita and me to go outside. I went with him to interview for a job because we were running out of money. Bonita wanted to look at the university. Then, she planned to visit *Quinta das Lagrimas*, a manor house across the river from Coimbra."

He stopped, overcome by emotion and tears. "Oh! I never should have let her go there alone," he reproached himself. "I should have insisted she stay in our apartment. I've condemned myself over and over."

"Her killer was at this place!" cried out Senor Sanchez.

"I don't know where else it would have happened. She was fascinated by the romance of Inez and Pedro; their story involves *Quinta das Lagrimas*. When Manuel and I came back that evening, we did not find her at home as we had expected. We went to the grounds of the manor house. It was deserted. After we looked around and called her name, I found her body. Manuel and I, we know of no one who would have killed her or what the reason could have been. If robbery was the motive, she didn't have much money with her. She must have been there alone – in the wrong place at the wrong time. It was the worst night of my life."

Jose looked down. "I thought of joining her in death."

Bonita's parents were numb and silent, not knowing how to respond.

Finally, Senor Sanchez asked, "Did you report her death to the police?"

"My first thought was to take Bonita's body to a priest for burial. Manuel was thinking more clearly than I was at the time. He said because this was a case of murder, the priest would be required to notify the Coimbra police, and they would next contact the internal security police. The current regime in Portugal supports the Nationalists. They would have sent me, an escaped Republican soldier, back to nationalist Spain for imprisonment and execution. As Manuel said, that's the last thing Bonita would have wanted."

Both parents agreed, "No, she wouldn't have wanted that."

"Manuel located some wooden boards next to the manor house and we constructed her coffin. We found shovels and we dug her grave."

Stumbling over his words, he described the gravesite: the rocks, trees, and bushes around her burial ground and how he marked it with the letter 'B' to indicate where they had laid the coffin.

"I tried to give Bonita as proper a burial as I could," finished Jose, peering beseechingly into her parents' eyes. "I went up the steps at the Braga shrine on my knees in her memory and to ask God to receive her into his kingdom. Then, I came here as quickly as I could – to tell you this terrible news."

Bonita's father stared into space. Tears flooded into his eyes as he cried, "Bonita, my little girl – dead." Then he looked hard at Jose. "You have no idea who killed her."

"None. I wish I did. I would hunt him down to my dying day."

"Are you sure the murderer was a man?"

"I'm not completely sure, but Manuel and I thought her death had all the signs that it was done by a man." Jose stopped short of going into the details of how her death occurred, a topic he never wanted to describe to anyone, especially Senora Sanchez.

"Oh God! Oh God!" bewailed Bonita's mother. Her face went back into her hands. "I can't bear this," she pleaded.

Her husband took her into his arms. "She is beyond all suffering now," he said, trying to comfort her.

"Bonita is in heaven and in God's care," added Jose.

He went over to them and knelt, putting his arms around them. They sank to the floor and drew Jose in. The three of them remained together for several minutes – crying, wiping tears from their faces, blowing their noses, and crying again.

"I – and my friend Manuel – we worked, digging all night, so she could be buried properly," Jose repeated. "We dug down almost two meters deep. Again, at that time, I prayed for God to receive her body and soul."

Mariana replied through her grief, "Thank you for doing that, Jose."

"I love her so much," he said, choking back his tears. "I love her more than I can say to you. Losing her has been unbearable."

Mariana acknowledged Jose had lost as much as she and her husband had lost. Pablo reassuringly touched his shoulder, not aware of Jose's slight shudder. Staggered by the sudden knowledge brought to them about their daughter, they slowly lifted themselves from the floor and fell back into their chairs.

They were silent again until Pablo Sanchez said, "Jose, as hard as it is for us to hear all this, I don't blame you for doing anything you've told us. You did the only thing you could do, giving her a decent burial. Nonetheless, I intend to find her body and bring it back here, and I want you to come with me. You can stay in the background; I'll refer to you as my son. Well, come to think of it, I've known you for so long, I do think of you as my son!"

"With both my parents gone, you are my father and mother now," responded Jose gratefully. "I'll do whatever you ask of me." He rose to his feet and sat facing them again. He remembered Bonita's parents did not own a car. "How will we get to Coimbra?" he asked.

"That shouldn't be difficult," answered Senor Sanchez. "I can borrow a truck from a good friend of mine. He owes me a favor."

"I may have problems at the border," said Jose. "They'll want official papers, identification – something like that. I don't know how closely they're checking."

"Yes, I've heard they're inspecting everyone. I didn't think of that. I haven't had time to reason things out. You had better stay here."

"I could give you Manuel's address in Coimbra," offered Jose. "He'll take you to the site and help with the digging. I'll write a letter of introduction so he'll know what you are asking for is genuine."

"How many days will it take to bring back her body?" asked Mariana Sanchez, wiping her face of the teardrops flowing from her eyes.

Her husband thought for a moment, then said, "I would guess three days, possibly four; one day traveling to Coimbra, one day or two days to locate Jose's friend and retrieve our daughter's body, and one day to return. Let me think. The return might take a little longer; I'll have to find a way to camouflage the coffin to get back into Spain. Maybe I'd better say five days. The more I think about this, the more complicated it becomes."

"Getting the coffin out of the ground may take a certain amount of planning," counseled Jose. "Manuel may suggest going to the manor house at night. We discovered her body after darkness had come. The place was deserted when we dug Bonita's grave. I don't know if there are people around the manor house during the day; I wasn't there. You could run into delays."

"In other words, I'd better make my estimate five to seven days. I don't want Mariana worrying her head off."

"You could say five to seven weeks," she replied. "I'd still worry."

"During those days, I could be making my mother's pilgrimage to Santiago," Jose reminded them. Turning to Pablo, he said, "I'd be back here in time for your arrival." As he spoke, he began slumping to the floor. The energy he had gathered to deliver his heart-rending message now without warning seemed to leave him.

"Jose! Are you all right?" they both inquired instantly.

"I'll just put my head on the floor," he suggested. "All of a sudden, I'm a little weak."

After a moment he recovered enough to continue. He mentioned again his pilgrimage for Bonita and gave an account of his journey across the Mino River. He told them about the episode with the vicious truck driver.

"If it hadn't been for that monster, I would have been here a day earlier."

"No wonder you look so tired and exhausted," remarked Mariana. "And, you've had the strain of telling us about Bonita and your dear mother." She made him take off his shirt to inspect his neck and back for wounds.

"I think if any bones were broken," he said, "I'd know by now. I was able to clean myself last night. I hope I don't look too bad."

"You're starting to heal," Mariana told him. "Jose, you've been through so much."

"I've put both of you through so much, too," he apologized.

Jose noticed the rucksacks he had placed on the floor. "This backpack belongs to Bonita," he said. Reaching into the bag, he pulled out the letter to her parents she had written in Coimbra. "This is a letter Bonita wrote to you the day before she went to the manor house."

He handed the letter to Senora Sanchez. She recognized her daughter's handwriting immediately. Mariana spoke Bonita's words describing the events that happened after arriving in Trujillo to help Marisa care for mother Maria and hopefully see Jose. Bonita had concluded her letter in a final paragraph.

"Don't worry about Jose and me," Mariana read. "God will take care of us. I have never been as happy with Jose as I am now. He is brave and honorable. We want to be married as soon as we can, have children, and settle down to a normal life. I don't know when or where we can do this, but I do have faith that somehow everything will work itself out for the best. I am writing because I care for you and miss you deeply. If you haven't already done so, please write a letter or send word to Senor Alvarez, the principal at my school in Noia. Explain why I was not able to start teaching this semester. Please express my wish that he won't hold it against me. I hope to be with you soon. With all my love, Bonita."

Mariana folded the letter and kissing it, held it in her hands. "We never did get the letter I'm sure Bonita wrote from Trujillo," she said. She looked at Bonita's backpack, picked it up and smoothed some wrinkles in it, and began crying again. She looked intently at Jose through her tears, saying, "I appreciate your bringing her things to us."

Jose reached his hand into his shirt pocket and brought out Bonita's opal ring. "I removed this ring from her finger. I want you to have it," he said, offering the ring to Mariana. She took the ring and held it in front of her, showing it to her husband.

"This ring was given to Bonita by my mother before she died," explained Mariana. "Jose, I want you to keep it as a remembrance. Bonita would want you to have it."

She handed the ring back to Jose.

"I will keep Bonita's ring forever," he said. *"Gracias."* He tried putting it on several fingers before he found that it fit best on the fourth finger of his left hand.

Jose and Bonita's parents were lost in their own thoughts for a long time. Finally, Mariana reached for something that she could do and had done for most of her life: prepare a meal for her family.

She remarked, "You must be famished, Jose. You've had such a long journey with so much walking. I have a bowl of *paella* I can heat quickly. Pablo, you can help me."

"I'll help, too," said Jose and three burdened people went into the kitchen.

Chapter 39
Pablo Sanchez

That evening after dinner and the clean up of dishes, Pablo Sanchez said to his wife, "Jose and I are going for a little walk. We'll be back in a short while."

"You go on ahead. I'm going over to the church," she announced. "I must pray for Bonita and for all of us."

Senor Sanchez guided Jose out of the house. They walked to a small park overlooking the bay and sat on a bench.

"Jose," Pablo began slowly. "Can you tell me how Bonita died? I didn't want to bring up the subject with Mariana around."

"Papa, are you sure you want to hear this?"

"That bad?"

"Yes."

"Go ahead. Tell me. I must know."

Jose braced himself once again. "As far as Manuel and I could determine, Bonita was shot in the back. The bullet probably stopped her from getting away. She must have fallen."

"She could have survived if the bullet missed her heart. People do live after taking a bullet wound."

"It's possible," Jose agreed.

"I'm assuming more happened. Were there any other wounds?"

"The killer used a knife on her. After shooting her in the back, he must have drawn his knife across her neck. Her arteries were cut on each side."

Senor Sanchez put his head in his hands. After a minute he said, "This thing gets worse and worse. It will be only a matter of time before my wife asks how she died."

"It's horrible – horrible," said Jose despondently. "There's no other word for it. I can only imagine the suffering Bonita went through. That night will haunt me forever. Adding to this whole pathetic tragedy was the reality that I was trapped and couldn't do anything except bury her."

Pablo Sanchez was quiet for several minutes. Then he turned to Jose and prepared to ask a question for which he already feared the answer.

"When we were talking in the house, you said Bonita's death had the signs of being done by a man. I sensed there was more, but you didn't want to go on, especially in front of my wife. Jose, was my daughter raped?"

Jose looked straight at Senor Sanchez. He didn't know how he could cushion the truth.

"Yes," he said plainly. "She was violated, raped. It was a crime of passion. Why he had to kill her, I'll never know. She must have put up quite a struggle."

"Bonita would not go down easily. She was always a scrapper. She wouldn't back down for anyone. Do you know if there was more than one man?"

"I really don't know."

The two sat in frozen silence on the park bench for several more minutes. Then Pablo turned to Jose and said, "Thank you for telling me. *Gracias*. Thank you for coming straight to us. I know this hasn't been easy for you."

"There isn't anything more to tell you. I know I said that before, but I dreaded going into the details of how Bonita died, especially in front of Mama."

"Leave that to me. I'll tell her before I go tomorrow so you won't have to tell her. Speaking of Mariana, she will probably be done with her church prayers now. She likes to get home before dark. I suppose we'd better get back."

Together again at the Sanchez home, Jose, Mariana and Pablo spent the evening exchanging memories of Bonita. About an hour before midnight, a worn-out Mariana excused herself and went upstairs. Jose and Senor Sanchez found themselves unable to unwind and face the empty darkness of the night. They sat in the kitchen and continued talking about Bonita and her death until they could think of nothing more to say.

To change the focus of their talk, Jose asked him, "How has the war gone here, in Galicia?" Jose knew Pablo Sanchez liked discussing politics and current events as much as he did.

"The Nationalist rebellion triumphed only after much street fighting. I suppose the peasants thought they're so poor that they had nothing to lose except their lives. They fought in many Galician towns until they died, either in battle, but mostly by execution. I think there was more murder here than killing in combat."

Pablo last words were spoken so bitterly that Jose was almost sorry he had shifted the conversation away from Bonita's death.

"Did Pedro and Julian enlist when the nationalist rebellion started?" inquired Jose, referring to Pablo and Mariana's two sons.

"They joined a Republican militia about three days after the rising started. At first, it wasn't clear whether the rebellion would succeed or go on for a day and come to nothing like it has so often before. At Vigo where you were, Jose, the soldiers who went over to the Nationalists struck down a people armed only with clubs, shovels, and sickles. At the El Ferrol naval base, some officers who wanted to join the rebellion were killed by their crew, but then the same thing happened to seamen trying to stay loyal to the Republic when the rebels took over.

"In Corunna, the civil governor was arrested and shot after military officers had pledged not to rebel. The governor's pregnant wife was in prison; she miscarried when hearing of her husband's murder. She was released; I heard she was raped and later killed by Falangist thugs. Government leaders here refused to give arms to the workers; all that meant was the defenders here were crushed by armed blue-shirts of the Falange."

"Same thing happened in Madrid at the start of the uprising," said Jose. "However, there the workers finally got enough rifles to beat back the rebellion. The Republic might have stopped the revolt dead in its tracks if the government had taken more decisive action throughout the country."

"The miners and *dinamiteros* coming from Asturias to aid the Galician workers arrived too late. The last we heard from both of our boys was two months ago; they had joined the guerrillas in Asturias. Just as with Bonita, we haven't learned about anything that's happened to them." Pablo looked wistfully into space, thinking he might hear he had lost his sons as he had Bonita.

"She mentioned writing a letter to you from my sister's house near Trujillo," remembered Jose. "Apparently, the letter never got through. She couldn't telephone; there isn't one where my sister lives."

"My daughter wouldn't have called from anywhere else," said Pablo. "We don't have a telephone either, nor do our neighbors."

"Maybe Pedro and Julian wrote and their letters got lost, just like Bonita's."

"Maybe," allowed Pablo. "The last thing I heard about the miners was that they were resorting to guerrilla warfare and heading back to the hills of

Asturias. I've thought about going there to look for my boys, but how would I find them? I've even considered offering my services to the Republican army, but how can I leave my wife here?"

"You can't. Let me go in your place. After Santiago, I've thought of joining the Republicans in Asturias. That's my old home region."

"Well, before you do, come back from Santiago and think about it. Don't rush into anything right now. You've been through enough. We'll take you in."

"*Gracias*, Papa," said Jose with feeling. "I'll return and be with you. I told Manuel I'd come back to Coimbra and try to figure things out, but I think that's for a later time."

The two were quiet for several minutes. Then Pablo broke the silence. "Galicia gave the Popular Front a majority of its vote in the February elections. That's all changed. Now it seems all you hear is that it's so wonderful Franco is from Galicia. Do you think Franco will allow Galicia to keep the statute of autonomy it negotiated with the Republic? Seventy-five percent of those qualified voted in June, and over ninety-nine percent approved it. Now that the Nationalists control Galicia, our hopes of self-government are gone."

They looked longingly at each other. "One day we'll have more pleasant conversations," Jose offered hopefully. "God grant it."

"God will need help from people other than many of his priests," Senor Sanchez commented bitterly. "My wife tells me there are good ones around, but I haven't seen any lately." Jose was familiar with his criticisms of the church from previous discussions. Bonita's progressive opinions clearly came from him, although she had not adopted his strong anticlerical prejudices.

"The cardinals, archbishops, bishops, and the rest of the hierarchy have, for the most part, lined up behind the Nationalists," stated Jose. "They told us voting for a liberal or socialist candidate would be sinful and against God's will. I think they want a Nationalist victory mainly to hang on to their own power and add to their wealth."

"It angers me when priests and church authorities enrich themselves, just the opposite from Christ's example and his teachings on poverty and self-sacrifice." Pablo warmed up to his favorite complaint. "Think how bad it must have been in those days before their church lands were taken away from them. They owned half the country!"

"I hope we're not going back to the way things were a century ago. It's not completely hopeless; there still are the *curas obrero,* the 'worker priests' who care about the poor in working class centers and peasant villages." Jose told

Pablo about Father Augustin in Trujillo, keeping Antonio occupied while he and Bonita made their escape at his mother's funeral.

"You wouldn't have gotten help like that from our priest here. He's the fattest beggar in town. He thinks of Franco as our savior."

"You've heard him say that? It sounds blasphemous to me."

"It is. I'd find something else to do if Mariana ever wanted to bring him in the house for a meal. I'd sooner see him starve. A shortage of food wouldn't hurt him in the least. One reason his belly has grown so big is he rides around in his new car instead of walking. I have a bike to ride, and you, Jose, must walk. Nothing seems to be too good for him, a so-called man of God."

Jose knew the topic of religion or politics would probably provoke Pablo into a subject other than Bonita's death. He listened to him vent his anti-Church sentiments. He had heard the complaints before; this was only an updated version.

"How does Mama put up with your priest? Can't she find another parish?"

"She won't try. I went to one Mass with her to see what he was like. He muttered through his sermon. You might as well sleep through it. No one knew what he was saying. The only part I caught was his tirade against the Freemasons – how they were agents of Satan threatening Catholicism. He raced through the Mass. The only thing he gave plenty of time for was the collection."

"First things first," was Jose's sardonic remark.

Pablo was not finished. "People tell me he was good with young people, but I haven't seen it. The only reason the young men go to church is to whistle at the girls. If any girl pays attention to them, she gets a scolding from her mother. My friends tell me when he blesses the fishing fleet, he doesn't know one boat from another. Ah, well, Jose, you've heard all this before. We should try to get some sleep." He yawned. "I need to get an early start for Coïmbra in the morning."

They rose from their chairs. Each started to say 'good night' to the other when Pablo's eyes moistened.

"Never in my wildest dreams did I ever think I would be going into another country to dig my daughter's body out of the ground," he growled. "If it was one of my sons – well, of course I wouldn't like it – but, somehow, I guess I could take it better."

Jose looked at Senor Sanchez squarely and said in a quiet tone, "How many times I've wished it could be Bonita telling you about my death than me telling you about hers. How many times I've thought it would have been better had I been herded into that Badajoz bullring to my death. If my brother Antonio hadn't been there to rescue me, how different everything would have been."

"How?" Pablo wanted to know.

"Bonita would still be alive. She would be back here, home with you now."

"You couldn't have predicted the events that followed, Jose. Don't scold yourself over things you can't control. You didn't intend anything that happened."

"No, I didn't," said Jose. "But, thank you, Papa, for those words. It's just that I feel guilty that I'm alive and she's not. I'll never get over it."

"It will take me a long, long time," Pablo responded, "before I can concede to myself that she died at the hands of a murderer and a rapist. How do you ever reconcile yourself to that? I guess war is different now. Civilians get killed along with soldiers; women become casualties as much as men."

"Bonita and I thought we could overcome the deadly power of this war with our love for each other," recalled Jose, his eyes now glistening with tears. "We talked about insulating ourselves against the passions of battle. I guess we were wrong. Like everyone else, we were entangled in the time and place we found ourselves. The poison of politics and power – it was too much for us."

"Do you think my daughter's death was a political murder?" asked Senor Sanchez.

"I simply don't know," replied Jose. "I can't give you an answer. All I know is that if there hadn't been a civil war in the Spain of 1936, we wouldn't have been hunted as we were and her murder would not have happened. To that extent, I guess you could call her death a political murder."

"We'll never really know," reflected Pablo. "Sooner or later, politics – even religion – gets transformed into war."

"I urged Bonita on several occasions to leave me, come back here to teach, and wait for me to rejoin her whenever that would be possible," said Jose.

"Son, there was no way for her or you to know this, but Bonita could not have continued with her teaching here."

"Why?" asked a startled Jose.

"Nationalist bosses are conducting massive purges all the time now, especially with teachers, doctors, intellectuals. Anyone with a brain was for the Republic, although you won't hear that said openly these days. Teachers are being removed from their schools if they have ever expressed anything favorable about the Republic, and Bonita was quite outspoken about her

No Greater Love

beliefs. At least, she'll never know she wouldn't have gotten her job back. She would have been forced into some other kind of work."

"There it is; the essence of totalitarian rule – just one opinion is allowed, that of the masters in power." It was Jose's turn to speak bitterly. "At least we know what Nationalist domination will be like: getting your face stomped on with an iron boot. I've had enough of that already!"

"You got a taste of jackboot rule when that butcher tried to recruit you into the Nationalist army."

"My bruises are minor compared to the damage Franco and his friends are doing to the country," declared Jose. "When Bonita and I were reunited, we suspected a Nationalist victory would mean the loss of our occupations – teaching and news writing." The tone of his voice changed and became softer. "Whatever happens in the war and even without our jobs, we both believed that the most important thing was we would be together."

"Yes," Pablo Sanchez remarked, "that's what I call true love."

"The night we escaped," Jose recalled, "I said to Bonita we must get her back here soon because school would be in session again. She said, 'Don't be silly, Jose, you and I are in this together. Wherever you go, I will go.' There could have been no greater love from anyone. You and Mama can be proud of Bonita; she must have learned this selfless capacity for devotion from you."

Pablo Sanchez rested his hand lightly on Jose's uninjured shoulder. "Thank you, Jose for giving me those words. I will tell Mariana what you just said. I want to reassure you again, we do not blame you for our daughter's death. You must not torment yourself with guilt feelings over things that might have been done or not done. Your love for our daughter was with all your heart, and that's good enough for us."

The two men embraced each other. Jose flinched from his wounds as he felt the hug on his back. Pablo apologetically withdrew his hands and suggested they go to bed.

"We have long days ahead, both of us. We could talk on until dawn or into tomorrow evening, and it wouldn't change a thing."

They said their good-nights to each other and went upstairs.

Chapter 40
To 'The End of the Earth'

When Jose woke the next morning, he realized instantly he had overslept. Bonita's mother heard him moving in the upstairs bedroom and called up to him, "Jose, I let you sleep. There was no reason to wake you. You needed all the sleep you could get."

"I didn't mean to stay in bed so late," he replied, "but I appreciate it anyway. I guess I was exhausted."

"Pablo started out for Coimbra in Juan's truck three hours ago."

"I wish I could have seen him off."

"He said not to bother you. He has your letter of introduction for your friend. He knows the area; we've been there before."

"Good. I'll be down after I shave and get into some clean clothes."

Ten minutes later, he came downstairs and into the kitchen where Bonita's mother was preparing a combination of *desayuno* and *almuerzo* for him. Jose looked at Mariana. Her face was drawn as if life had been drained from her. She had had less than twenty-four hours to take in the information of her daughter's death. Her eyes were red from hours of crying. Her whole appearance revealed the lack of sleep. He went over to Mariana and held her hands.

"I know," he whispered. "Like you, I have lain awake unable to sleep and shed thousands of tears. On my way here, I went over and over in my mind how to tell you. I thought and thought about what I should say. I tried to think how I could soften the blow. There was no way around it; I had to give you the painful truth."

Mariana put her hand on Jose's unhurt shoulder and gazed at him. Then she closed her eyes as tears streaked down her face. A minute went by before she opened them.

"You were trying to be as kind as possible," she said. "It must have been horrible when you found Bonita, and then you had to relive it all as you told us." They cried in each other's arms.

A moment later she told him, "Come and eat. The food will be getting cold."

He noticed the clock on the wall. It read twelve hours, noon.

"Good heavens. I didn't realize it was *mediodia*!"

"You must have slept eleven or twelve hours, Jose. I don't think you knew how tired you were."

"I was thinking of beginning my walk to Santiago," he said, "but it's a little too late in the day to get going. I could get a better start early tomorrow morning."

"You need to rest, Jose. Don't try to do everything at once."

"Maybe I can walk out to Finisterre this afternoon, like Bonita and I used to do. It would be good for me. I'll be back in time for *cena*."

"Young people these days are in such a hurry," she commented automatically, echoing the eternal complaint of the older generation.

They continued talking for an hour, sharing some fond memories of Bonita. Mariana did most of the reminiscing. Jose was relieved she did not ask him for any more details about the way Bonita died. When he looked at the clock again, he said, "I'd better get going" and started for the door.

Mariana followed him outside. "Be careful," she urged him.

He turned and waved, saying "*Adios*."

"Jose," she called, coming up to him with a concerned expression appearing on her face. "Be sure to come back."

He noticed her worried look. Kissing her on the forehead, he said, "Don't worry, Mama. I won't leave you. You'll have company tonight."

Minutes later, Jose walked out of Corcubion along the road to Cape Finisterre, his gait now growing more sturdy and steady. The pains his body had suffered from the beating were diminishing. To the north was the *Costa da Morte*, the "Coast of Death," so named over the centuries because of the ships that had become lost in storms and smashed against the treacherous rocks that dotted the coastline. As he approached the cape, Jose fell to thinking about how people must have thought before the voyages of discovery. Little did they know in that remote time the ocean waters would reach the beaches of a New World, thousands of kilometers away. The misty atmosphere, the clouds in the sky, and the limitless horizon lent themselves to believing Cape

Finisterre was literally "the end of the earth." Bonita and he would imagine they were about to take one of the ships of Christopher Columbus and sail into the unknown beyond the horizon. Jose could see her in his mind's eye, chattering and laughing as she skipped along the edge of the road.

As he walked, Jose was unaware of a nondescript car slowly moving a short distance behind him. The car would stop occasionally, allowing more space between it and the walker ahead. On another road only two days ago, the same car had passed Jose, not closely observed by him.

When Jose came to the little town of Fisterra, the Galician name for the Castilian word, Finisterre, he started immediately for the lighthouse on the cape. The wind began to blow. Jose gave no thought to the fierce blast that typically lashed this particular projection of land. Billowing clouds darkened the sky. Cape Finisterre always appeared to be menaced by a gathering storm.

The car following Jose came to Fisterra. The driver swung his automobile to the side of the road and found a place to park where the car would be less noticeable. He opened the car door and reached into the back seat. He put his hands on a rifle hidden by a blanket. Ramon Ignacio Martinez Garcia took the rifle and wrapped it in the blanket. He walked uphill and away from the road until he found a path that headed in the direction of the lighthouse perched on the finger of land that extended into the ocean.

Jose reached the unoccupied lighthouse and moved cautiously among the rocks and blowing grass toward the pounding sea below. A group of pilgrims from Santiago de Compostela were fighting a futile battle with the wind as they tried to burn a shoe or an article of clothing they had worn on their journey – a medieval tradition they were struggling to maintain. Jose recognized them as pilgrims because some of them wore the familiar scallop shell and felt hat and held the long walking staff. He joined them, adding resistance to the wind. Matches were struck to light a fire; the gale swiftly blew them out. An undershirt briefly caught fire, but the wind shifted and extinguished the flame. After several minutes, the group gave up. They scurried up the rocks toward the lighthouse and disappeared from view. Jose was quite alone. He thought the whistling wind and the crashing waves were his only companions. He put his foot against an outcropping of rock, bracing himself from the bursts of wind.

Ramon came to the edge of the lighthouse and spied the solitary figure below him. *Perfect*, he thought. *No one is in the lighthouse.* He looked around, and determined no one was down on the rocks with Jose.

Nobody is behind me, he reassured himself. *No one will ever know about the little incident that is about to happen here.*

Crouching low like a leopard waiting to leap on its prey, he raised the rifle to his shoulder and put Jose in its sights. One move of his trigger finger would send a bullet spiraling through the grooves and out the end of the barrel toward its target. He waited for the wind to die down; the gusts were strong enough to make his stance insecure.

When the wind subsided, Ramon stood and took aim again. But this time he could not move his trigger finger. The thought to send a rifle shot toward Jose had come to him only moments ago while he was wavering in the wind, but now he was frozen solid, unable to move. Angered at first, he became aware of a strange, unseen obstruction holding him back.

Uninvited words reverberated in his head.

That man down there is my brother, he reminded himself. *My older brother wants me to kill my younger brother. Shooting Bonita was one thing, but the person standing there is my own flesh and blood.*

Alternately enraged and confused by his self-doubts, Ramon set the rifle down at his side. The words became "Words," an inner monologue that seemed to have a life of its own. Once the Words started in his mind, they couldn't be beaten back. Ramon tried to argue with the Words to no avail.

Antonio says Jose represents evil, does evil, is evil; so, he is to be killed. Evil must be rooted out, whether it's an idea or a person – or my brother.

Ramon lifted the rifle to his shoulder again. Once more, the Words came, only louder and more incessantly.

How does Antonio know Jose is evil? Who told him that? How do I know Jose is evil? Maybe it's Antonio who is evil. Why should I follow his wishes? He makes me do what he won't do; Antonio can't take Jose because he has 'other responsibilities.' No! This is his mission, not mine! Jose may have been a brat at times, but he's my brother. I'm not even sure he's on the wrong side in this war!

These Words gripping Ramon had been festering and lingering in his mind ever since he had taken leave of Antonio in Toledo. Remaining in that city for a couple of days, Ramon had avoided Antonio like his older brother had a permanent case of bad breath. Ramon could no longer stand Antonio's harangues on the righteous nature of the Nationalist cause and the revolting atrocities of the Republic's defenders.

Are the liberal ideas of the Republicans honestly all that terrible? he questioned himself. *The Nationalists have their share of big shots and pompous asses. With all of its richly-furnished buildings and mystical mumbo-jumbo, the Church forever tells me what to do and not to do. The monarchists parade hither and yon, trying* to put some feeble-minded idiot on the throne. The conservatives have their share of caciques, political bosses that rob the people blind. The Republicans might be wretched, as Antonio claims, but the people supporting the Nationalists can be just as bad.

Ramon watched Jose move closer to the shoreline below. A new line of reasoning became framed by the Words.

What would my padre be saying to me right now? These words were delivered from a fresh dispute within himself. He shook when confronted by a hazy image, a mental picture. His dead father spoke clearly to him.

"Ramon, are you out of your mind? Jose is your brother, for heaven's sake. Don't let your big brother bully you into doing something that you'll hate yourself for all your life."

"Yes!" Ramon revealed to the sky in an anguished whisper. "That's what Antonio is – a brow-beating bully, trying to push me into something I don't want to do."

Ramon sat down on the steps of the lighthouse, keeping his eyes riveted on Jose.

Yeah, Jose, he thought. *I've done enough to you. I took your bewitching Bonita from you. God Almighty, she was a beauty! Why was she so faithful to you? I would have given her love too.*

He moved behind the lighthouse in case Jose should look his way. His impulse to protect himself reminded him of the night he killed Bonita. A sudden rush of emotion pressed down on him and he began to weep. Crying episodes had come upon him while he was alone; they upset his composure several times at night after leaving Antonio. At first, he had defended himself when he thought about the way he had taken Bonita's life at Coimbra. As time went on, however, he was unable to erase the image of her mute, motionless figure beneath him. That memory was terribly unlike her; she was resolute and spunky, and so full of life, and he had taken that sparkling vitality from her.

Ramon began to blame his very nature, the portrait of Don Juan he had nurtured. From Don Juan – the bold, seductive and irresistible – to Don Juan – an immature destroyer; no, a murderer of women.

Now, Don Juan is destroying me; hadn't Antonio warned me of this.

He couldn't restrain his self-loathing. As an adult, he had become more selfish, deceitful, corrupt, decadent, and contemptible.

Does that kind of person even deserve to live? Bonita was not a bad person in spite of her rejection of me. She deserved to live. Now she is dead, and I can do nothing to bring her back.

Ramon tore himself away from the spot where he had been. He ran away, out of Jose's sight, to another hill overlooking the swirling water smashing into the rocks below. Crossing his mind were images of Judas Iscariot, throwing thirty pieces of silver and hanging on a tree. He took one quick look at his rifle. With a mighty heave, he flung the weapon toward the ocean, hoping it would reach the water and sink into the murky depths. He knew the rifle might be found.

Well, someone else can make better use of it. Antonio will rant and rave. He will thunder and roar. Let him. I don't care. Antonio could go hang himself. He'll never discover what has just happened anyway.

Ramon started to walk. He soon broke into a run. He kept walking and running, not knowing where he was going.

As Jose made his way back to Corcubion and Bonita's mother, Ramon disappeared into the misty fog of the Galician night.

CHAPTER 41
PILGRIMAGE

In the early morning of the next day, Jose quickly packed his rucksack with fresh clothing, cleaned by Bonita's mother while he was at Finisterre. She gave him provisions for three days travel to Santiago. Mariana pressed several peseta bills into his hand and said, "Buy some food in Santiago for your trip back to Corcubion."

"Thank you, but no, Mama," said Jose. "You've provided for me, and you will again. I'll use the remainder of the pesetas my sister packed in our rucksacks when we escaped from Trujillo." He paused. "That night seems like it was twenty years ago."

"You've been through so much, I'd like to make it easier for you," she responded. Mariana offered Pablo's bike for transportation. "You could ride on the coastal road you came on and head for Santiago that way."

"I'm accustomed to walking," he explained, pointing to his well-worn shoes. "When I was growing up, I hiked long distances in all kinds of weather through the *Cordillera Cantabrica* and the *Picos de Europa*. On some days, I'd walk the twenty or so kilometers to Oviedo, stay overnight with a friend and walk back next day. And, I don't want to risk anything bad happening to Pablo's bike like a theft; it's his only form of transportation. I'm going to have so much on my mind that I'd rather have only myself to take care of. Somehow, walking makes a pilgrimage feel, well, more like a pilgrimage. I think I should do it on foot."

He finished the early morning meal Mariana provided: *tortilla espanola*, *churros*, and *café con leche*. Jose conveyed his gratitude for the food she had prepared, the clothes she had washed, and her concern for his general well-being.

Mariana left the table for a moment, saying, "Wait, Jose, I've thought of something."

She came back with a map that outlined a walking route through the mountains to Santiago. "Pablo and I made this trip on foot before Bonita and the boys were born. As I remember, it took three or four days of steady walking. The route is a fairly straight line through the mountains. Plan to stop overnight at Olveiroa and Negreira; you should find a *refugio* at those villages. You could meet a pilgrim or two from Santiago extending the journey to Finisterre, although I haven't heard of anyone making a pilgrimage since the war began."

Mariana left the room a second time after saying, "I've thought of something else." While she was gone, Jose couldn't help but think of her earnest care for him that was so obvious.

No greater love, he thought, reflecting again on Antonio's words at their mother's funeral. *How often we fail to recognize the love given to us in ordinary ways each day. How can I ever repay my mother's faithfulness, bringing me into the world and nurturing me through childhood? Bonita stayed with me, making our escape together and demonstrating her love and devotion to me on a dangerous journey in the midst of war. Marisa risked her family and reputation in helping me when she could have remained uninvolved. Here again, I receive affectionate regard from Bonita's mother, who can't seem to do enough for me even though I've brought such devastating news to her.*

Mariana returned and gave him a scallop shell, the symbol worn by those making the pilgrimage to Santiago.

"For you," she said, simply. "Saint James will protect you, my son!"

"Oh Mama!" exclaimed Jose. "I will cherish this treasure each day and bring it back to you." He spotted two small holes on each side at the base of the shell and threaded string through each opening. Jose put the shell around his neck.

He hugged Mariana, saying, "*Mucho gracias,* Mama. My *madre* would be pleased."

A moment later, he was on his way.

Now that he was drawing closer to Santiago, the pilgrimage idea became much less a sense of obligation to his mother and more a quest Jose regarded with anticipation. He believed he was joining a great tradition. Ever since the ninth century, pilgrims had made their journey to Santiago de Compostela along the *Camino de Santiago,* or Road to Santiago, the Way of Saint James.

Throughout the Middle Ages and into the years of the modern era, a pilgrimage was no light undertaking. An estimated one-third of all pilgrims died on the way to and from Santiago. Another twenty percent never returned to their homes for reasons known only to them. Among the old, eighty percent were men, grandma remaining at home to help raise the children while their mothers worked in the fields.

A likeness of his mother Maria came to Jose's mind. Her image made him think of his last time in prison, nursing pain from the blows and kicks delivered by the vicious guard. Jose had used her tales of the Apostle James and of the pilgrimage to Santiago as a method to veil his awareness of the soreness from the bruises on his body. Now that he was actually on his way to Santiago, he thought again of the miraculous legends that grew around the pilgrimages. Jose did not fully believe them; they were too fantastic for anyone with an analytical mind. Nevertheless, they were wonderful stories. His favorite was the tale of the 'hanged innocent' of Santo Domingo de la Calzada.

The voice of his mother came to him once more from out of the past. "A German father, mother, and son made a pilgrimage to Santiago along the French pathway. They stopped for a night at a hostal in Santo Domingo. The innkeeper's daughter wanted the son to make love to her, but he spurned her. She got revenge by secretly putting some church silver in the young man's backpack and next day told the police the silver was missing. The pilgrims were arrested and searched. Naturally, the silver was found and the son was judged guilty of theft. He was sentenced to die by hanging. His body would rot on the gibbet, a medieval custom that served as a warning for others to mend their ways. The parents were stricken with anxiety, but there was nothing they could do to save their son. After he was hanged, they continued their pilgrimage to Santiago."

"Is that the end of the story?" Jose remembered himself saying to his mother, astonished that an injustice could so easily have happened.

"Oh no," Maria had answered. "On their return trip home, the parents came upon their son in perfect condition but still on the gallows! The son could even speak and he told them, 'Tell the judge that Saint James has supported me all this time!' The parents ran to the judge, who was about to eat a meal of prepared chicken. Unbelieving, he said scornfully, 'Your son is as alive as this roasted chicken.' Upon hearing those words, the bird immediately stood up on the plate and crowed, proclaiming the innocence of the young man! To this day, a rooster and a hen live in a coop over Santo Domingo's tomb in the cathedral."

A few days ago in Portugal, Jose had encountered a similar story near Barcelos on the Portuguese pilgrimage route.

No Greater Love

Other tales from Jose's mother involved the dead returning to life, healing for the deformed, singing relics, uncorrupted bodies found in their graves after hundreds of years, sight restored to the blind, forests grown from lances stuck into the ground, lost pilgrims saved by white doves, and so on. Jose couldn't accept the authenticity of the miracle stories that had become legends on the *Camino*; however, his new self was inclined not to be so skeptical about them either.

Who am I, anyway, to take away from the naïve faith of the simple-minded? Hadn't Jesus said, "Unless you change and become like little children, you will never enter the kingdom of heaven?"

Not all pilgrims made the journey moved by their religious faith. Some sought a cure for bodily ailments. Others provided services for the pilgrims, thereby gaining profit. There were people who wanted to test their physical endurance. Those convicted of a crime would make a pilgrimage in exchange for time in prison. Whatever the reasons – walking hundreds of kilometers as a testament of faith, atonement for one's sins, physical and mental healing, or mastering a challenge – the pilgrimage to Santiago de Compostela became a goal for millions of people.

Memories of his mother's stories and the family in which he was raised kept Jose's mind active as he walked the route mapped by Mariana. From Corcubion he walked northeast to Cee, and then ascended up mountainous paths in an easterly direction. His reveries were interrupted only as he would encounter oxen or a mule pulling a wagon carrying grain or several people, the ox-cart being a typical means of transport. His route took him along the mountainous trails toward Olveriroa where he spent his first night in a *refugio*, a haven for pilgrims. He was the only occupant. As Mariana had mentioned, pilgrimages were not a typical enterprise during a civil war.

Jose could not help but think about the isolation of the sparse population in this part of Spain. Famine in the middle of the nineteenth century had driven thousands of Galicians to emigrate. They had become the common laborers in many cities throughout Spain and beyond. Political allegiances went to extremes as the poor joined radical movements while the Galician upper classes moved politically into the most conservative parties.

Conserving his pesetas, Jose ate the food Mariana had sent with him. He looked at Mariana's map, noticing Noia below to the south of his current location. He thought of Bonita; in peaceful times but not now, she would be alive and teaching in her school at Noia.

"Somewhere, up there, you are with God," he murmured. "I'll be with you soon, in the twinkling of an eye, as God reckons time."

In the morning, Jose was on his feet again, continuing along the way to Compostela as he headed east. His journey took him past typical Celtic houses with their round shapes and thatched roofs, animals living on one side of the structure and people inhabiting the kitchen and sleeping areas of the other side. When Jose came close to Negreira, he knew he could arrive in the pilgrimage city tomorrow, perhaps early in the afternoon. With darkness beginning to descend, he found a hostal for the night.

Lying on the bed before going to sleep, his mind went back to the stories of pilgrimage. Many accounts strained credulity, to be sure, but there was a particular feature that impressed Jose.

No greater love can be expressed by humans than the devotion and sincere dedication that comes from the hearts of true pilgrims. False pilgrims profane the symbol of the scallop shell they wear when they seek only adventure, free rooms, and meals without cost. They have no interest in any spiritual renewal whatsoever. For myself, I'm amazed at how much I am caught up in the spirit of the pilgrimage. I wanted to carry out my mother's dying wish, but now this journey to Santiago is a pilgrimage for me and for Bonita as well.

Yet, not all of Jose's thinking was filled with hopeful optimism. Despite the anticipation of reaching his objective, disturbing thoughts about the Church would not leave him.

Yes, the Church is necessary; it's the guardian of the pilgrimage; however it has customs in its history that disturb me. Take indulgences. Thank heavens they're no longer practiced, although some people behave as if they still exist.

In an earlier time, each indulgence could reduce the number of days one's soul would spend in purgatory. One third of a person's sins were released if he or she made the odyssey to Santiago. If they had the good fortune to die on the way, all sins were forgiven. Hearing Mass on certain specified days meant fewer days in purgatory, and the higher the church official who said Mass the better.

It's troubled me the ways the Church made itself rich hoodwinking simple-minded poor people; taking money from them that they could not afford could not have been pleasing to God.

Once, he expressed that same idea to Ramon, who responded: "But when you consider the show they put on; it's worth it!"

Another concern bothered Jose, a current problem that affected him directly. His destination was now a Nationalist stronghold that had declared sympathy and support for the Nationalist cause. Church authorities in Santiago were not as blatant about their opinions as were the militant Nationalists. Nonetheless, Church officials made it clear who they favored in the civil war. They prayed for Nationalist victories. Church bells pealed when the Nationalists had gained control of Galicia.

Maybe I'm affected more than I realize from three days journey on foot, Jose said to himself, *but my thinking seems to be as much concentrated on the miserable practices of the past and the unknown fears of the present as it is with the hopes for the future. I can't get away from knowing I am going into the camp of the enemy no matter how much I want to fulfill the pilgrimage for the people I love.*

He was annoyed with himself because his reflections were plagued with uncertainties and reservations instead of being totally preoccupied with the boldness and determination necessary to carry out the pilgrimage.

Finally, before falling asleep, he set aside doubts and committed himself with resolve to honor his mother Maria and his soul-mate forever who were unable to complete the mission he had set out to do for them.

Whatever discouragement hounds me this day, tomorrow I will enter Santiago de Compostela in the midst of adversaries but fellow human beings nevertheless, and I will pray at the Cathedral for you, Mama, and for you, Bonita, as I have promised.

Chapter 42
Santiago de Compostela

The next morning dawned under a bank of clouds growing darker all the time. As Jose dressed, the wind picked up and blew mighty blasts against his window. He looked out at the approaching storm.

I may not get to Santiago at the time I hoped for, he thought.

The weather became more ominous in its appearance. Lightning flashed through the air with its electric spears and thunder rocked through the atmosphere with its earthshaking roar. Gusts of winds were followed by torrents of rain. An hour went by without any letup in the fury of the turbulence.

Any chance of arriving for the pilgrim's Mass at noon was gone. Jose wondered if he should take up any offers of transportation, but riding into Santiago was not his idea of a pilgrimage. He decided to wait out the storm, accepting an old adage Bonita had taught him: rain and Galicia go together.

The owner of the hostal commiserated with Jose over the frustrations of delay, saying the violent wind and the deluge of rain was one of the worst he had seen since last spring. As the two talked, Jose discovered that, indeed, Nationalist forces had begun to make military pilgrimages into Santiago.

"Republican officials and supporters have been cast into a new identity," the owner told him. "They've become the new Moors, the ancient Christian foe. I've heard that people identified with the Republic are now waiting trial in prison. Masses have already been attended by a number of Nationalist generals as well as their soldiers."

Maybe it's just as well I've missed noon Mass, thought Jose. He wondered where the hostal owner's political sympathies lay, but the man was noncommittal, as were most people who catered to the public.

"It's unfortunate either side would exploit the story of Saint James and religious pilgrimage for the purposes of political propaganda," ventured Jose.

The hostal owner agreed, stating the civil war had crippled his son as well as his business. Jose expressed his sorrow for the son's injury, but was unable to find out the nature of the wounds or which side the son had fought for.

As a clock pealed ten chimes, the wind died down and the rain slowed to a drizzle. Jose pulled a rain jacket and hat from his rucksack and started walking.

He arrived in Santiago in the late afternoon. The clouds had lifted and the sun began to brighten the skies. After being discouraged by the stormy delay, Jose was heartened by the sight of the lofty spires of the cathedral drawing him nearer to his objective.

My pilgrimage will be safer with Nationalist troops gone. And, nothing is written that I must complete the pilgrimage today. Maybe I can make a brief visit to the church of San Miguel dos Argos before leaving tomorrow morning.

There was a certain *simpatico* he had now with this church, having in mind it was once a place where condemned prisoners were brought to pray before their execution. After they had been killed, their bodies were brought back to San Miguel for burial.

As Jose neared the old section of the city, he believed the first thing he should do was go to the *Obradoiro Plaza* where the cathedral was located.

Perhaps I could spend the night in one of the alcoves of the Plaza where I can view the great façade of the cathedral – this would add meaning to my efforts. If there are any Nationalist soldiers wandering around, I can revise my plans.

If the cathedral stayed open all night, he could get into the Romansque interior, possibly meditate in front of the high altar, sleep on a bench using his rucksack as a headrest, and wait until morning.

Prudence dictated he not try to obtain the certificate, a *compostelana*, confirming that he, in fact, had made the pilgrimage on foot. Nor would he offer confession as tradition required. These rituals had the potential of giving away his identity.

Jose was familiar with the cathedral; he had visited it once before, though not on a pilgrimage. He recalled climbing the steps and proceeding through the inner doorway, the *Portico de la Gloria*, and acknowledging the masterpiece of sculpture by Maestro Mateo. He remembered the column depicting the Tree of Jesse which represented the ancestry of Christ with Mary at the top of the column where the twisting branches did not reach, signifying her purity.

And above, there was Santiago, himself, with his staff, greeting and receiving the pilgrims as their exhausting journey drew to a close.

As he pictured this majestic doorway, Jose knew he would say a prayer for his mother as he had promised her and place the fingers of his hand into the five hollows worn deep into the marble column by millions of pilgrim's hands for over a thousand years. To Jose, the central meaning of the pilgrimage was the effort of ordinary people, laboring step by step over hundreds of kilometers, humbling themselves, and risking so much to be in this reverent atmosphere of God's holy place.

I will pray for mother and Bonita, and also Marisa, me, and my brothers, and for all humans living, dead, and those yet to come. No one would be left out.

If time and safety allowed, he would look at the portal with its typical scenes of the Last Judgment and the saving grace of Christ and the Church.

If everything still seemed safe, he would go inside to see the main altar, chapels, capitals, and sculpted figures and to be swallowed up by the magnitude of the nave. He hoped to hear the organ playing and watch the motion of the *botafumeiro*. Attached to a rope suspended from the ceiling and guided by eight men, this giant incense burner would swing back and forth to such a height that it would nearly strike the highest point of the transepts. The purpose of the censer was to send forth a pleasing fragrance to God. But the *botafumeiro* had a practical human purpose as well. After walking for months over hundreds of miles without bathing, reeking of sweat, the stinking bodies of pilgrims pressed together in the packed church must have created a smell hard to imagine.

Jose wanted to catch a view of the Baroque façade of the cathedral in the light of the day. He walked hurriedly through the city's university. Several students passed by. He heard Galician accents that resembled the Portuguese language and made him think of Bonita. He had heard the university in Santiago was regarded as a bastion of conservative thought. Jose remembered Bonita had believed she would not be welcome there as a woman and a liberal. From an upstairs room came the strain of melancholy music; a student was playing *la gaita*, the Galician bagpipe.

Before long, Jose found himself on the *Rua das Hortas*. He was now by himself. He walked the length of the deserted street, coming upon the Church of San Fructuso.

"Only a few more steps and we'll be in the Obradoiro Plaza," whispered Jose to himself and the mental image he carried of Bonita and his mother. "Only a few more hours and our pilgrimage will be accomplished."

No sooner had he finished murmuring those words, Jose spotted two policemen coming quickly toward him, closing in from his right.

They must be after another person, he reassured himself, thinking of the security guards rushing by him on the steps leading to the cathedral at Braga. He stopped and looked around. No one was on the street behind him. No one was on the *Rue de Carretas* to his left.

"Halt! Stop!" voiced a command from one policeman.

"You!" called the other. "Come with us."

They surrounded Jose, making certain he would go no further. He lost hope that the summons was for someone else.

Jose gazed down the street from the place they had come. In his haste, he had not noticed the entrance to a clearly marked police station at the back of the *Palacio de Rajoy*. This massive building served several governmental units and anchored the west boundary of the *Obradoiro Plaza* opposite the great cathedral.

Four other policemen joined their two partners in their capture of Jose, as if they had come in response to a signal silently given. Escape was impossible.

"What have I done?" asked a stunned Jose, astounded by the suddenness of his seizure.

"We have some questions for you," was the only answer he got. The six policemen marched their reluctant prisoner into the station. Jose could not stifle the notion that these men were six pallbearers taking him to his grave. They took the rucksack from his back, removed his shoes, and emptied his pockets. Two men guided him to a room labeled *servicios*. He was told to relieve himself as he could be confined for hours. Unable to perform that duty upon command in the presence of others, he was moved down a flight of stairs and taken to an open cell door. Several hands thrust Jose inside a cave-like room. He wondered if he would become one of the disappeared, a person never to be heard from again.

"When will I be questioned?" he implored desperately as the door began to close. No voice, no person, no words acknowledged his request. The only sound was the clanging of the cell door, slamming shut. Jose was cast into complete darkness. He ran his hands blindly along a wall until he came to the door. He reached for the doorknob and tried to turn it. The door was securely locked. The room struck him as being soundproof. There was no impression of any noise coming from the outside. He was now very alone.

It's in a room like this where people are interrogated by ordeal, he thought. *No one hears your screams.*

The sensations of sight and sound were entirely gone. Taste and smell were nonexistent here. Only touch would be allowed – intense pain transmitted by instruments of torture.

He sat down on the floor. A wave of despondent emotions came over him. He had come so close to fulfilling his promise to his mother – to Bonita – to himself. Powerful, unseen forces had intruded again. Reckoning time was impossible. Questions without sure answers ran through his mind.

Who could have ordered my arrest? Antonio? My oldest brother is immersed in a war somewhere around Madrid, hundreds of kilometers from here. Ramon? Not likely, he's an ordinary soldier at the bottom rung in the Nationalist chain of command. A police captain? I'm not well known here; Galicia is a long way from Badajoz or Trujillo. Could it have been an ordinary citizen, recognizing a photograph of me on a poster? I haven't seen my face pictured on a wall.

He had been careful during the days of his escape. Perhaps the prospect of achieving the pilgrimage had made him less cautious than he should have been.

Do they leave you in utter darkness for so long that you welcome anyone, even someone who brings misery? Will I be fed or do they just let you starve to death?

Now a sudden urge to urinate became impossible to resist. Jose got up and slid his fingers along the walls until he thought he was in a back corner. There, he relieved himself, hoping the liquid would not spread around the room. He stood still, not daring to step ahead.

How does a person sleep? Is any rest possible on a cold, damp concrete surface? Do they require you to lie on the floor in your own filth?

The expectation of being beaten and suffering agonizing pain added to his gloom. The taunt of the vicious guard at Badajoz came back to him.

'You'll thank God you're alive each morning and by evening you'll wish you were dead.'

In this room, what was morning and evening?

After an interminable amount of time, he moved along the wall until he came to what he imagined would be the front of the room and then toward the door he had entered.

Whatever happened to the love of God the Nationalists claim to honor? Like most of mankind, they haven't gone past the eye-for-an-eye and a tooth-for-tooth mentality. Maybe they even haven't come that far! What ever happened to the second commandment – to love your neighbor as yourself? Didn't Jesus apply that rule to all people? The Nationalists apply it only to those who think and act like themselves.

But, shouldn't your love be greater than this? a voice somewhere within him

No Greater Love

was saying. *If your love is only for those who love you, what reward will you gain for that? Didn't you just say, even the Nationalists do that?*

Jose remembered this most difficult of Christ's teachings his mother had taught him: 'If you love your enemies, do good to them that hate you, and pray for those who persecute you, you become a child of God.'

Do not despair because you are alone in a soundless room with no light, the inner voice continued. *In the blinking of an eye, there will be much light.*

A small radiant beam appeared and became wider and wider. The cell door had opened. Jose shielded his eyes at first. Adjusting his vision to the increasing brightness, he recognized the policeman who had apprehended him.

"We must apologize to you, senor," the policeman said. "A thousand pardons for the inconvenience we caused you. This was a case of mistaken identity. You are free to go. We thought you were an anarchist saboteur."

Jose could not believe the words he was hearing.

These things don't happen in a Nationalist jail, he told himself. *Did I pray for my release?* He couldn't recollect having done so.

At the front desk of the station, he was handed the rucksack he had been carrying. His shoes and other possessions were returned to him. While tying his shoes, Jose noticed a clock on a wall.

Only an hour in that room, he observed silently. *I could have sworn it was a day.*

Emerging outside the station, Jose checked the belongings of his backpack in case the police planted something incriminating in there. He was surprised to look up and see fading sunlight amid a blanket of clouds that threatened to fill the sky. When the door had opened in the prison cell, he had calculated the time to be well into the night. With daylight slipping away, he quickly retraced his steps of a short time ago, coming to the corner where he had been taken into custody. He turned right, and directed his attention to the *Costa do Christo*, the short passage rising up to the *Plaza do Obradoiro*.

Jose realized he would be entering the Plaza from the west, the opposite direction of the usual route taken by pilgrims. A nagging notion gripped him; he was carrying out the essence of the Santiago pilgrimage, not necessarily wrong but different from the tradition. There wasn't time to walk around the city to arrive from the east and join the French Road, the path he would have taken if he had walked from his former home in Asturias. He hadn't been to *Monte de Gozo* (Mount Joy), the hill east of the city where he could experience the euphoric first sight of the Cathedral's towers. He had missed the Pilgrim's Mass and didn't dare ask for a *compostelana*. He questioned how visible he should be once inside the cathedral and whether he should chance an embrace of Saint James' statue behind the high altar. If the cathedral doors were closed, he could not get into the *Puerta de la Gloria* and be welcomed by Santiago. He felt like an outsider.

Stop this nonsense, he told himself. *A pilgrimage is a pilgrimage however a person chooses to define it. A pilgrimage is any way to a sacred place, as long as it's done with holy purpose and a pure heart. The direction a person comes from is not of primary importance. Conforming to all of the traditional rites and rituals is secondary. I have as much right to be here as anyone else.*

With determined steps, he began striding up the short span of *Costa do Christo*. Ahead, on the left side of his path, was the *Hostal de los Reyes Catholicos*, the Hostelry of the Catholic Monarchs. Under normal circumstances, he could have stayed in the hostal for up to three days free of charge. This hospice, on the north end of the Plaza, had been constructed upon the orders of Ferdinand and Isabella. The Catholic Monarchs had financed the building of the hospice to house pilgrims in Santiago and to serve as a hospital for those who had become sick on their long journey. The area in front of the hospice had once served as a place of refuge where one had the right of asylum. A person charged with a crime could find sanctuary here and not be taken by the police without prior permission of the hospital administrator.

Jose could hardly contain his excitement at the prospect of completing his pilgrimage. Perhaps it was this hopeful expectation and the unexpected release from jail that made him less wary. He never saw the shadowy figure emerging from the Rua de San Francisco behind him. He never heard the click of a trigger. As soon as Jose entered the wide expanse of the Plaza, the bullet that had been waiting for him found its mark. It pierced his back between the shoulder blades and came to rest inside. The force of the missile knocked him off balance. Jose staggered until he fell to the ground, shattering the scallop shell he had worn around his neck.

Jose was shaken with disbelief. He had heard no sound. He opened his eyes. He saw no one. Looking up, his vision took in the gray expanse of the sacred structure ahead of him. Thinking night had fallen, Jose was struck by a sudden ray of sunlight that shone in its brilliance upon the magnificent facade of the cathedral. Not a soul could be seen in the Plaza; evening walks had decreased greatly since the beginning of the civil war. No one was present to help him. He tried to get on his feet; he couldn't get up and collapsed again under the weight of his own body. He started to crawl on the pavement, inching his way toward the cathedral.

"Mama," he cried. "I will – make your – pilgrimage. I promised you."

Nightfall quickly gathered around him as the sun sunk below the horizon. A swirling wind brought a chill from the air. With great effort, he swung his head around to look back at the government building where the police were stationed in back. Apparently, no one had heard any unusual sound. He looked at the College of Saint Jerome on his right; it was completely dark and no help would be coming from any medical staff there. The student musical ensemble, the boisterous *tuna*, wouldn't present themselves for hours until near midnight. Even the dimly lit hostel on the north end of the square was empty of people. Jose reached a hand to his back. His fingers were spotted with blood.

"Mama," he groaned again. Once more he called, "Mama, don't give up on me – somehow – I will find a way."

In front of the cathedral, a man and a woman came into view, strolling several meters away from Jose in the gathering gloom. Hearing a noise from the man dragging his body, they turned away.

"Drunk!" muttered the man in a disgusted voice as he guided the woman from the wretched sight. Jose paid no attention to them and kept crawling slowly toward the cathedral.

"Mama," he uttered with effort one more time. "I will – do this – for you – even if – I die trying."

Jose stopped for an instant and glimpsed once more the imposing structure of the Cathedral of Santiago de Compostela. His heart sank; through the despairing darkness he could see the cathedral doors were closed. The wind became stronger and drops of rain began to fall. He became aware of losing strength, and with that knowledge, he started to lose hope.

It was then that a figure approached him. "Help me," he choked convulsively. "I've been shot!"

The person came over to the afflicted Jose. He wore a uniform; it was a resplendent uniform. The man in the officer's uniform peered down at the wounded creature below him.

Jose looked up into the face of his oldest brother.

"Antonio!" he gasped.

I must be dreaming, he thought. *Are we back in the Badajoz prison?*

The pain in his body brought him back to reality.

Jose cried spasmodically to his brother, "Thank God you're here! – I'm – I'm wounded – someone shot me in the back."

"My little brother, *I am here to save you.*" With those words, Antonio unfolded a blanket he had carried under his arm. Placing Jose's body on the blanket and wrapping him in it, he picked up his brother and carried him toward the north side of the massive building.

Jose started to protest. He sensed being taken away from his destination.

"Wait, Antonio," he pleaded with all the strained effort he could gather. "We're going – the wrong way! You're carrying me away – it's over there – the Portico of Glory." He feebly wrestled in his brother's clasp, fighting the blanket around him, frantic with the worry he wouldn't complete his mission and forgetting that the cathedral had closed its doors.

"I have a pilgrimage – to make – for madre. I beg you, take me – inside."

Antonio set Jose against the wall of the bishop's palace, the *Palacio de Gelmirez*, which joins the cathedral.

With military crispness in his voice, Antonio said, "Remember, Jose, I have always tried to save you, even from yourself."

Jose closed his eyes, not aware of the cold look in the eyes of his oldest brother.

Antonio quietly reached a hand inside his officer's uniform. He removed the German Luger pistol from his holster and unlocked the safety. He pressed the gun at the back of the head of his youngest brother and pulled the trigger. Jose slumped forward, his head swinging slightly as he lost consciousness and was carried into eternity. His body was limp and motionless when his brother wound a cloth around his bleeding head and carried him off to a waiting military car positioned at the darkened side of the *Hostal de los Catholicos*. The vehicle hastened to the church of *San Miguel dos Argos*. There, Antonio left Jose's body for burial. In this war as in so many wars, no one would ask questions.

Shortly before noon of the next day Antonio went to the Santiago cathedral. He climbed the steps winding their way to the *Portico de la Gloria* with its three doors that led to the interior. He paused momentarily at the top to take in Old Testament figures molded in the arches over the left door. He walked by the center entrance to the right door. There, he eyed the representations of God the Father and God the Son beholding the saved as they were carried to heaven and the damned as they were condemned to their fate. One of the fallen was seized by the tentacles of an octopus. A demon kept a glutton from swallowing food. An upside down drunkard could not drink from a wineskin. Antonio blanched when his sight reached the top of the arch where the neck of Judas was ringed with the rope by which he hanged himself.

Quickly returning to the central passageway, Antonio gazed upward at the tympanum where the resurrected Christ was surrounded by four ancient symbols of the gospel writers: the angel, eagle, ox, and lion representing Matthew, John, Luke, and Mark. Among more Old Testament and New Testament figures was Saint James himself, holding a scroll that told him to carry God's message to Spain. Moving forward, Antonio came to the Tree of Jesse depicting Jesus' genealogy. At the top was the Virgin Mary where the branches winding among the figures below did not reach her, indicating she alone was without sin. Above the column, the capital portrayed the temptations of the devil that Jesus resisted.

Antonio trembled for an instant, perhaps contemplating how difficult it was for him to withstand the lure of political and military power. The sculpture of Saint James here did not help; Santiago was presented as a pilgrim, not as a warrior triumphant over the fallen enemy and as not the soldier so admired by Antonio when he listened as a child to his mother's stories.

Reaching his hand for the central column, Antonio's fingers and thumb were placed in the five grooves worn into the marble by countless numbers of people in their travels to the cathedral.

Antonio entered the cathedral, walking down the nave until he found an empty bench. Bowing his head, he prayed for his mother, finishing with the words, "There, dear madre. Your pilgrimage is complete."

Following the celebration of the Eucharist, the organ played a stirring anthem, rich in bass tones. The giant censer swung high into the transepts of the church. Making the sign of the Cross, Antonio silently prayed for Jose, asking God to forgive his brother's sins.

"I have done my duty," he whispered emphatically as he glanced up toward a ceiling that seemed to reach to heaven. "Thanks be to God, I learned about mother's dying wish which led me here."

His next words were intended only for himself and his Father in heaven: *I am my brother's keeper. I have liberated him from the evil he carried within.*

Antonio hesitated for an instant and then added: *Forgive me, Father, if I have done wrong.*

He bowed his head, and wiped away the tears that quite without warning flowed from his eyes.

Epilogue

Jose and his beloved Bonita became casualties in the furious history of human conflict, yet there is the hope they were reunited in life's after-death voyage. Bonita's grief-stricken parents buried their daughter's body and worried that Jose had committed suicide. Marisa wondered but could never discover what had happened to her youngest brother. Antonio advanced in rank in his military career, the Nationalist army having won the civil war after many cruel battles and much bloodshed. Ramon was never heard from again. And, Manuel never quite gave up the hope that his good friend Jose would some day call upon him.

READER DISCUSSION QUESTIONS for NO GREATER LOVE

1. Do you detect any parallels in the present political and cultural conflicts of our times in the United States and the struggles that gripped Spain in the 1930s? Why or why not?

2. Do you believe the political divisions in the United States will be carried to dangerous extremes as they were in Spain of the 1930s? Why or why not?

3. Give reasons why you would have supported either Franco's Nationalists or the Republican government had you lived in Spain of the year 1936.

4. Think of the Prodigal Son story in the Bible. Jose speculates that Antonio would cast him as the prodigal brother. Is he right? Why? Jose considers Antonio as more like the elder brother in the Prodigal Son parable Jesus told. Is he right?

5. Is Jose too naïve to survive the deadly political conflict in which he is caught?

6. Should Jose have attempted his mother's pilgrimage to Santiago de Compostela or should he have quietly avoided it as others urged? Why?

7. In the earlier part of the story, how should Antonio have responded to "save" Jose? If you had been Antonio, would you have helped Jose escape instead of returning him to prison and what would have been the consequences for Antonio's career?

8. Did Jose and Bonita "betray" Antonio at Maria's funeral? Explain your thinking.

9. Knowing now what happened to Bonita in her relationship with Ramon,

what should she have done to have avoided the consequences that resulted?

10. Did Marisa doom Jose when she let Antonio discover the nature of their mother's pilgrimage request in trying to excuse Jose's behavior?

11. Would you have believed Jose and Bonita as Andre Vincente did when he found out they had used false names, escaped from prison, and were charged with murder? Why or why not?

12. Were Manuel and Jose right in burying Bonita's body at the site of her death? If not, what should they have done?

13. Discuss Bonita and Marisa, two strong-willed women for their times. Are they too "modern" for the Spain of the 1930s? Justify your opinion.

14. Do you believe Jose had hidden motives in carrying out his mother's pilgrimage or were they as "pure" as they seemed? Why?

15. Did it seem to you that Jose was being protected by a "higher power" right up to the last moment of his life? Explain your answer.

16. Should the Western governments of England, France, and the United States have intervened on the side of the Republic? (They didn't, but why or why not?)

17. Should religious leaders take strong positions in political and ideological disputes, as they did in the Spanish civil war or should they stay neutral?

18. Did this novel inspire you to learn more about the Spanish civil war or Spanish history in general? Why? (This civil war is one of the most heavily chronicled events of the 20th century, rivaling even that of World War II.)

Glossary

Anarchism: The doctrine that government is used by the propertied classes to exploit those without property; it must be done away with and replaced by voluntary cooperation among the people.

Asturias: A region in northern Spain featuring the Cantabrican mountain range and the Picos de Europa, the highest mountains in Spain. Asturias was loyal to the Republic when the insurgency started and treated harshly by the victorious Nationalist regime.

Auto-de-fe: The "Act of Faith," a public execution of heretics by burning at the stake after being condemned by the courts of the Spanish Inquisition.

Azana, Manuel (1880-1940): Left Republican intellectual; Prime Minister, 1931-1933, February to May 1936; and President of the Spanish Republic, 1936-1939.

Bolshevik: The Marxist majority of the Russian Social Democratic Labor Party which became the ruling Communist Party after the Czarist government collapsed in 1917. Under Lenin and Stalin, the Communists established a police state, industrialized the Soviet Union, collectivized agriculture, and joined the Allied coalition in World War II.

Bom Jesus do Monte (Good Jesus of the Mountain): A site outside of Braga, Portugal where pilgrims ascend the stairs to the Church of Bom Jesus at the top. Along the way they come to chapels representing events from the Passion of Christ as well as staircases dedicated to the senses of the physical world and the virtues of the spiritual domain.

Caballero: A gentleman mounted on a horse; a lady's escort.

Caciques: Local political bosses, usually the agents of wealthy, large landholders.

Campesinos (or Braceros): Landless farm workers hired to perform seasonal labor.

Carlists: Right-wing Catholic traditionalists; the name came from Don Carlos whose claim to the Spanish throne in the 19th century began an anti-liberal movement. The Carlist militia, called *requetes,* was an important component of the Nationalist army.

Castilla: A castle or fortress.

Caudillo: Leader or warrior king; title adopted by Franco as head of Nationalist Spain.

CEDA, Confederacion Espanola de Derechas Autonomous (Confederation of the Autonomous Right): Political alliance of right-wing Catholic parties that became a dominant coalition in the Cortes after the Spanish elections of 1933.

Cervantes, Miguel de (1541-1616): Spanish writer and author of *Don Quixote.*

Cheka: A Soviet police bureau organized to prevent counter-revolutionary activity.

Churros: A fritter or cruller of oblong shape.

Civil Guard: A rural police force organized in the mid-1800s to prevent banditry; later, its main function became guarding estates of the great landholders from the laborers who worked on them. The Civil Guard was usually hated and feared by the local people.

CNT, Confederacion Nacional de Trabajo (National Confederation of Labor): The anarcho-syndicalist trade union. The *anarchists* in Andalusia and Extremadura idealized the *pueblo* as a self-sufficient community. *Syndicalists* in Barcelona organized workers in factories as "syndicates" negotiating with other syndicates for food and lodging.

Communism: a social organization where all property and the means of production are held in common by the entire community or by the state acting as society's agent.

Conservatism: A doctrine emphasizing the preservation of wisdom, traditions, customs, and spiritual heritage of the past and of existing society. Conservatives value social order, authority, a governing elite, and prefer little or slow change to quick, abrupt change.

Cordillera Cantabrica: A chain of mountains extending across northern Spain.

Corrida: A bullfight, the corrida de toros.

Cortes: The Spanish parliament; the first Cortes was established in Aragon in 1162.

El Sol: The Sun, an independent liberal newspaper based in Madrid. Influential from its beginning in 1917, it declined in circulation in the 30s and ceased publication in 1939.

Empanada Gallega: Galician meat pie made of pastry filled with many varieties of food.

Extremadura: Bordered on the west by Portugal, this region has experienced widespread poverty for centuries. It is the birthplace of famous conquistadors: Hernan Cortes, Francisco Pizzarro, Vasco Nunez de Balboa, Francisco Orellana, and Henrnado de Soto.

Fado: Portuguese folk songs accompanied by a guitar; themes are usually about longing, nostalgia, happiness, love, and homesickness.

FAI, Federacion Anarquista Iberica (Iberian Anarchist Federation): Organized in 1927, these anarchists were "purists" many of whom increasingly resorted to violence.

Falange: The Spanish form of a fascist party founded and led by Jose Antonio Primo de Rivera, the lawyer son of the former dictator. The Falange combined with the Carlists in 1937 to become the sole political party in Nationalist Spain; headed by General Franco.

Franco y Bahamonde, General Francisco (1892-1975): Became leader of Nationalist Spain in September 1936; ruled Spain as dictator from 1939 until his death in 1975.

Fueros: Old laws of a region or locality; Basques see their *fueros* as constitutional rights.

Galicia: The region of Spain's northwest coastland, Galicia borders the Atlantic Ocean to the west, the Bay of Biscay to the north, Portugal to the south, and the regions of Asturias and Leon to the east. It has a mild climate, abundant rainfall, fishing, and shipbuilding.

Gallego: The Galician language, related to the Portuguese language; revived in the nineteenth century with the publication of Rosalia Castro's *Cantares Gallego*.

Garcia Lorca, Frederico (1898-1936): Spanish poet, dramatist, painter, composer, and pianist; executed by Falangist militia (shot because he was "a queer").

Gestapo: German state secret police during the Nazi regime, feared for its brutality and terror against selected victims such as Jews and opponents of Nazism.

Guerrilla(s), Guerrillero(s): Unofficial fighters who make surprise raids on a powerful, organized enemy.

Hola (Sp.), Ola (Port.): Hello. Other greetings in Spanish are *Buenas dias* (Good day or morning), *Buenas tardes* (Good afternoon or good evening), *Buenas noches* (Good night).

Horreo: Granite structures found along the coast of Galicia used as drying sheds for grain; they are elevated to keep rodents from destroying the grain inside.

Iglesia. A church.

Junta: A small group, usually military, which aspires to rule a country after a coup d'etat but before a legally established government has been installed; a deliberative council.

Latifundia: Large landed estates owned by wealthy, usually absentee, landholders.

Left Republicans (Izquierda Republicana): An important part of the Popular Front, this moderate liberal group drew support from the professions, small business owners, and urban artisans; its leaders aimed for a democracy but underestimated the ferocity of the insurrection that led to protracted civil war.

Legionairos: Members of the Spanish Foreign Legion which, despite its name, were mainly Spaniards; famous for violence and toughness. The Legion fought many battles in Morocco; together with Moorish *regulares*, these two units made up the Army of Africa.

Lenin, Vladimir Ilyich (1870-1924): Russian revolutionary leader; applied Marxism to a pre-capitalist society; advocated a small, dedicated elite to guide the Communist Party.

Liberalism: Rising in response to the absolute state, it seeks to change the political and social order to promote the well-being of the individual. Basic ideas include representative government, pluralism, equal opportunity, popular sovereignty, and majority rule.

Marx, Karl (1818-1883): German social scientist and revolutionary whose critical analysis of capitalism laid the foundation for the doctrine that bears his name.

Marxism: Explains history as a series of class struggles from which have come new social orders. It sees capitalism as an efficient productive system that creates internal contradictions bringing about its downfall through a successful revolution followed by a dictatorship of the proletariat and ultimately a classless, stateless society.

Mediodia (Sp.), melo dia (Port.): noon.

Misioneros: "Missionary" intellectuals, teachers, university students and artists who brought mobile lending libraries and museums, makeshift theaters, puppet shows, musical concerts, and slide shows to the rural peasantry in a Second Republic program known as the *Misiones Pedagogicas* (Teaching Missions).

Mola, General Emilio (1887-1937): Director of the military uprising in July 1936; military governor of Pamplona; killed in a plane crash in June 1937.

National Front: The coalition of conservative factions (Carlist, monarchist, Falange, and others) supporting the Nationalist uprising; these groups often had paramilitary units that added strength to the Nationalist army.

Ortega y Gasset, Jose (1883-1955): Philosopher and prolific writer; led republican opposition to the Primo de Rivera dictatorship, spent years in exile due to the civil war; wrote *Revolt of the Masses* depicting the twentieth century as dominated by the mediocre.

Patria chica: "Little fatherland"; usually refers to an area smaller than the national state.

PCE, Partido Communista de Espana (Spanish Communist Party): Became part of an alliance of liberal parties, dropping its revolutionary strategy of subversion and sabotage and combining its program with the Communist International to combat Fascism in the 1930s.

Picos de Europa: The "Peaks of Europe", a range of mountains in Asturias.

Plaza del Obradoiro: the "town square" of Santiago de Compostela surrounded by the Cathedral on the east, the Hostal de los Reyes Catolicos on the north, the Palacio de Rajoy on the west, and the Colegio de San Jeronimo on the south.

Popular Front: The coalition of liberal and radical political associations supporting Spain's Second Republic; most important groups: the Republican Union, Left Republican, Socialist, Communist, and Anarchist parties and the socialist and anarchist trade unions.

POUM, Partido Obrero de Unificacion Marxista (Worker's Party of Marxist Unification): Anti-Stalinist party of workers, peasants, and former Trotskyites (Leon Trotsky lost to Joseph Stalin in a Russian power struggle within the Communist Party); in 1937, the POUM was ruthlessly suppressed by Soviet Communists operating in Spain.

Pronunciamiento: A proclamation by military leaders announcing that they intend to change the regime currently in power by overthrow of the government.

PSOE, Partido Socialista Obrero de Espana (Spanish Socialist Worker's Party): Founded in 1879, the Spanish Socialist Party developed two wings: a left wing that was closer to Communist doctrine and a "right wing" that favored social democratic ideas.

PVDE, Policia de Vigilancia e Defensa do Estado (Police for Vigilance and Defense of the State): Special section of the Portuguese police for political and social surveillance; later became the PIDE, *Policia Internacional e Defensa do Estado*, routinely arrested suspects without warrants. Disappearance and torture methods were commonplace.

Pueblo: The people, or the 'common people' of a community, village, or town.

Quiepo de Llano, General Gonzalo (1875-1951): Seized Seville in the early days of the Spanish civil war and set up a reign of terror in Andalusia. Quiepo specialized in making threatening propaganda speeches over the radio for the Nationalist forces.

Quinta das Lagrimas: The "Estate of Tears" where Inez de Castro was murdered. The story of Pedro and Inez is remembered in the works of Luis Camones and Victor Hugo. The manor house is now a hotel.

Reds: The Communists; red was the color of the Communist movement.

Regulares: Moroccan troops serving in the Army of Africa.

Republicans: In the Spanish Civil War of 1936-39, those who were loyal to the Republic, the duly elected government. The term means a government which operates through elected representatives of the people.

Requetes: The paramilitary units of the Carlists absorbed into the Nationalist army.

Retablo: A decorative structure located behind an altar in a church.

Ria: An inlet of the sea at the lower end of a river or the mouth of a river; an estuary.

Salazar, Antonio de Oliverira (1889-1970): A professor at the University of Coimbra who became Portuguese Finance Minister in 1928 and then Premier of Portugal in 1930; ruled for 40 years. Three basic ideas dominated his thinking: Catholicism, anti-communism, and a distrust of popular government.

Sanjurjo, General Jose (1872-1936): One of the conspirators of the 1936 Nationalist uprising; killed in a plane crash as he was preparing to lead the rising against the Republic.

Tuna: A small musical group composed of Spanish university students. They perform folk music from the various regions of Spain and keep alive traditions that go back centuries.

Unamuno, Miguel de (1864-1936): Novelist, poet, essayist, playwright, and philosopher. Born in Bilbao, he served as rector of the University of Salamanca, 1900-1924 and 1930-1936. Removed as rector during the Primo de Rivera dictatorship, he resumed his old post six years later stating "As we were saying yesterday . . ." as though he had never been away. Supported the Nationalist revolt at first but later opposed Franco. He was removed as rector a second time in 1936 and placed under house arrest; died two months later.

UGT, Union General de Trabajadores (General Union of Labor): The trade union of the Socialists; its main strength was in Madrid, the Asturian mines, and Basque industries.

Union Republicana (Republican Union): A center-right party, part of the Popular Front supporting the government.

Yunteros: Owners of a mule or oxen team hired for plowing in preparation for planting.